Also by Sherry A. Burton

*Other books in the Orphan Train Saga**
Discovery (book one)
Shameless (book two)
Treachery (book three)

Tears of Betrayal
Love in the Bluegrass
Somewhere In My Dreams
The King of My Heart
Surviving the Storm
Seems Like Yesterday
"Whispers of the Past," a short story.

* *A note from the author regarding The Orphan Train Saga. While each book tells a different child's story, some of the children's lives intertwine. For that reason, I recommend reading the books in order so that you avoid spoilers.*

Guardian

Book 4 in The Orphan Train Saga

Written by Sherry A. Burton

ISBN: 978-1-951386-05-4

Published by Dorry Press
Edited and Formatted by BZHercules.com
Cover by Laura J. Prevost
www.laurajprevostbookcovers.myportfolio.com

To those who've suffered at the hands of others, may you find your way out of the darkness.

Table of Contents

Chapter One 2
Chapter Two 9
Chapter Three 17
Chapter Four 26
Chapter Five 34
Chapter Six 42
Chapter Seven 49
Chapter Eight 57
Chapter Nine 64
Chapter Ten 74
Chapter Eleven 84
Chapter Twelve 92
Chapter Thirteen 100
Chapter Fourteen 108
Chapter Fifteen 118
Chapter Sixteen 125
Chapter Seventeen 133
Chapter Eighteen 142
Chapter Nineteen 155
Chapter Twenty 163
Chapter Twenty-One 170
Chapter Twenty-Two 177
Chapter Twenty-Three 185
Chapter Twenty-Four 192
Chapter Twenty-Five 203
Chapter Twenty-Six 210

Chapter Twenty-Seven 218
Chapter Twenty-Eight 230
Chapter Twenty-Nine 238
Chapter Thirty 246
Chapter Thirty-One 254
Chapter Thirty-Two 265
Chapter Thirty-Three 273
Chapter Thirty-Four 282
Chapter Thirty-Five 291
Chapter Thirty-Six 300
Chapter Thirty-Seven 310
Chapter Thirty-Eight 318
Chapter Thirty-Nine 326
Chapter Forty 335
Chapter Forty-One 343
Chapter Forty-Two 350
Chapter Forty-Three 359
A Brief Note from the Author 371
About the Author 374

Chapter One

Cindy stood at the small buffet, loading her plate with all the breakfast delights and knowing she'd pay for her indulgence later. She looked to see if anyone was watching then added more bacon.

"Why so glum?" Linda asked when Cindy slid into the booth.

"Because it's impossible to practice self-control when I order off the breakfast bar," Cindy said, pointing to the pile of bacon on her plate.

"I'm surprised you didn't order off the menu like you normally do," Linda replied. "You only eat like this when you're upset. What's on your mind?"

Cindy shrugged. She'd never been successful at hiding anything from her mother. "Uncle Frank. I know the journals are supposed to be read in order, but this time, it's different. Uncle Frank is still alive."

"Frank's body is still alive. Frank's been gone for years," Linda corrected. "When was the last time he recognized you?"

"I don't remember the exact date, but you're right. It's been years, although he does have some lucid moments."

"If it would make you feel better, we can read the next one in line."

"I've thought about that, but someone took the time to number them, so there must have been a reason. I'd hate to miss something important."

"I agree," Linda said, swiping a piece of bacon from

Cindy's plate.

"That's stealing."

"No it's not," Linda said and shoved the entire strip into her mouth.

Cindy pulled her plate closer. "You didn't order the buffet. How is it not stealing?"

"I didn't tell you to put it on your plate. It's only stealing if you go back to get more."

"That sounds like some of the logic I hear from the students I teach," Cindy said, shaking her head. She looked around the room and smiled. "You know Uncle Frank loved coming here when he came into town. He'd always order the buffet, and so would I. I'd try to keep up with him but never could. He'd wink at me and say 'maybe next time, kiddo.'"

Linda chuckled. "Not many could keep up with Frank, although I never could figure out where he put it. He owned a bakery and yet was as thin as a rail. Heck, your father couldn't keep up, and that man could eat."

Cindy nodded to the front of the building, which she'd always referred to as the sunroom since it was mostly glass. "Uncle Frank always insisted on sitting in that section, and it had to be a table by the window. One time, we came in and the room was full. The tables were all together and I think they were having some kind of party. The waitress told him there weren't any seats available near the window, so we left. I remember being disappointed, but he made it up to me by bringing me back for lunch later that same day."

Linda's brows creased. "Huh, I guess I don't remember that story. There are plenty of booths. I wonder why he didn't just sit at one of them."

"He never said why he wanted to sit by the window, and I didn't bother asking. But it was like that wherever we went." She looked across the table to her mother. "Tell me, what do you know about your grandparents?"

"What do you mean, what do I know? They were my grandparents. They've been dead for years."

"Exactly; they were both already dead by the time I was born. All I know is what you've told me over the years, and that's not much. Do you realize how much history is lost just because we don't bother to take the time to ask? If we hadn't started reading these journals, I wouldn't know you'd been married before." Cindy didn't bother adding that that revelation was still a sore point. "It just makes me wonder if I would've learned even more if I'd bothered to ask more questions."

"Maybe, maybe not. Who's to say you would've asked the right questions?"

"You've got a point. Then again, I didn't even try with Uncle Frank. He was in World War II, and yet we never discussed it. The man had a wealth of firsthand information. Real history I could share with my students, and yet I have nothing but what is written in the history books. And the bakery. Why in Detroit and not here in town where he grew up? And what about Uncle Cornelius? Everyone knows he isn't my real uncle."

"He was Frank's partner," Linda said.

"Business partner," Cindy corrected.

Linda scrunched up her face. "Isn't that what I just said?"

"No, you said 'partner.' In this day and age, that means something totally different. Seriously, how did they become business partners?" Cindy said between bites.

"I think you're forgetting something," Linda said.

"What's that?"

"Your uncle's journals."

Cindy stopped chewing mid-bite. "You think he wrote about that?"

Linda laughed. "Have you seen the stack of papers I copied? And I may have seen something mentioned when I was standing at the printer."

"You snooped?"

"I had to make sure the papers were lined up on the printer correctly, didn't I?" Linda said, taking another piece of bacon from Cindy's plate.

Cindy thought to object to the thievery then reconsidered. The last thing she wanted was to waddle outside looking like the Big Boy statue on display at the front of the building. *At least he looks happy.*

***

Cindy sat on the couch, her mother by her side, and lifted the cover letter that accompanied the journals. Thus far, there'd been a cover letter that'd preceded each set of journals. She and her mother had taken to reading those together before diving into the main set of journals. She held the letter so Linda could see and began to read.

I started journaling soon after going to live with Mildred and Howard. I already knew how to read, and it was Howard who insisted I start keeping journals. He and Mildred had been keeping them for years and thought maybe I'd like to do the same, saying they would keep things fresh in my mind in case I wanted to look back on them someday. They were right, as I've picked them up a time or two over the years and never failed to read something I'd forgotten. Each time I re-read them, I was always surprised at where life has taken me. I thought to destroy them once. I mean, why would anyone else wish to read about my sorry soul? I even went so far as to light the burn barrel and drag the pile of journals outside. I burned the family trash first. Then, as I stood there watching the flames lift up the smoldering ash, carrying it off with the wind never to be seen or heard from again, I just couldn't bring myself to toss the journals inside. Maybe a part of me worried it would take the important parts of me with it.

I'm not sure who's reading this now, but whoever you are, I hope you enjoy reading about my life as much as I've enjoyed living it. Sure there are some dark spots, but what is life if not a compilation of light and dark mixed with humor, love, and regret? I don't think there is anyone in this world who doesn't have some regret about things they've done or haven't done. All I can say is I've lived my life the best I could and I'm happy with the choices I've made. Most of them anyhow. I'm not a saint. Then again, I've traveled the world and don't recall ever meeting one. Oh, to be certain, I've met a few who've professed to be, but you dig deep enough, and even the choicest apple has a few blemishes beneath the peel. My faults don't go all the way to the core, but I have some mushy spots here and there. I'll not be speaking of those, as they are between me and God. It is he who I'll have to answer to one day.

I do regret not searching for my Bella. Then again, I'm getting ahead of myself. If I tell you all my secrets upfront, then you'll have no reason to read my words. Since I took the time to place them onto the pages, I guess maybe someone should actually see what it is I had to say.

My name is Benjamin Franklin Castiglione and these are my words.

Cindy sat staring at the paper for a full moment before lowering it. She looked at her mom. "I'm sorry, were you finished reading?"

"Yep, finished a bit ago."

"He mentioned the mystery lady again. She has to have something to do with the bakery."

Linda cast a glance toward the double stack of journals sitting on the table in front of them. "I think we're about to find out."

"I doubt he's going to lead with that."

"We can always flip through until we see mention of the name."

Cindy shook her head. "As tempting as it sounds, I think we best read the journals in order."

Linda sighed. "I was afraid you were going to say that."

"It's his life story. He respected his words enough not to throw them into the fire, so I guess we should respect them enough to read them in order."

Linda stood, handed her a section, then pulled off an equal section from the matching pile before rejoining Cindy on the couch. "I hope you respect my journals as much as you do your Uncle Frank's."

Cindy blinked her surprise. "You've written journals?"

"I always called them diaries, but yes, I have some I've added to over the years. I guess I'm not as creative as Mildred and Howard, as my journals aren't hidden in the attic. But I suppose you'll read them someday. You best take care when you do, as I'm afraid there are some juicy parts in there. Your father…"

"MOM!" Cindy said, cutting her off. "I don't need to hear about that. Didn't you worry that someone else might read them someday?"

"Not while I was writing them. They were my diaries. I can remember the first time I got one. It was under the tree one Christmas. It was the big rage at the time and had an advertisement advising girls to write down their innermost thoughts."

"Smart advertising. Probably thought up by a frustrated parent who wanted to find a way to see what their child was doing or thinking."

"That wasn't a concern at the time because all the diaries came with locks. It didn't dawn on me that the keys were attached to the diary. Or that one key could open them all."

"Did your mom ever snoop?"

"Not that I'm aware of, not that she'd have read anything too juicy. Not in the early years anyway."

"Wait, you were in your thirties when you married Dad. Are you telling me you were still writing in your diary?"

"Not every night, but when something happened that I wanted to write about, yes."

"Did Dad ever snoop?"

"Your father was not the snooping sort."

"It's normal for a person to be curious."

"Maybe, but your father learned his lesson early on."

"What kind of lesson?" Cindy asked.

"When we were first married, your father found a stack of letters given to me by an old boyfriend. They were a bit randy, telling of some things we'd said or done. Well, your father was mighty jealous and we had a doozy of a fight. Later, we made up and spent the evening tossing the letters into the fireplace. After that, we made a pact never to discuss any of our previous dalliances."

"And yet, you've jotted them all down in your diaries for me to read."

"You may want to take one of my Xanax before you start reading. Where are you going?" Linda asked when Cindy shoved off from the couch.

"I need a glass of wine." *Or maybe a cheese grater to strip the unwanted images of you and Dad from my mind.*

"It's not even eleven. Should I be worried about you?"

"Only if I come back with a cheese grater," Cindy mumbled under her breath.

Chapter Two

Howard insisted I begin a journal, telling me to start with my first memory. I guess the first memory is when I was around four years old and still living in the asylum. I think the reason I can recall it so well is because that was the time me and some of my friends were moved to the four-year-old room. Birthdays in the asylum generally went without mention. That didn't bother me, as I, along with most of the children who lived in the asylum, didn't know they were a thing to be celebrated. Heck, many of the kids in the asylum didn't even know what day they were born. Don't go getting riled at those that ran the asylum; they did the best they could with what they had to work with. One day, a small group of us were told we were four years old and moved away from the younger children. That was the day a new world opened up for the lot of us. Until that day, most of us never even knew there was a world beyond the fourth floor.

***

Franky had just finished dressing when the door opened, and Mistress Florella stepped into the room. Another woman followed her in and stood beside her. Dressed in the same black dress and shoes, the woman would have been Mistress Florella's double if not for the fact that the new woman had lighter hair. Mistress Florella clapped her hands and the room grew quiet. "Listen up, children. I'm going to call some names, and when I do, I want you to come stand next to me."

To his surprise, Franky's name was the first called. He scrambled from the edge of his bed and hurried to Mistress

Florella's side. Before long, he was joined by a small group of boys and girls, each silently waiting to see why they were summoned.

Mistress Florella turned and addressed them. "Today is a big day, children. You will all be moving to the four-year-old room."

"Shall we bring our sheets, Mistress Florella?" one of the girls asked.

"No, Becca, you're all to leave everything behind as you'll get new bedding when you get to your new room."

The small group began to whisper amongst themselves, causing Mistress Florella to clap her hands once more. Instantly, the room became quiet.

"Remember, children are to be seen, not heard," Mistress Florella said, instantly silencing the whispers. "This is Mistress Vivian. She will take you to your new temporary room."

The new woman stepped forward and looked at each child in turn. "You children have each reached your fourth year. So you will be coming to my room for your transition. You're all to follow me, and remember, we must always be quiet when in the hallway."

Franky followed along with the others as Mistress Vivian walked to the door. She waited for them to get in line, then opened the door and led them down the long hallway and into a small dormitory.

Franky wasn't sure what he'd been expecting to find, but the temporary room was nothing more than a room similar to the one they'd just left, only smaller, with fewer beds, tables and chairs. The beds were divided into two sections on either side of the room. Double rows of tables lined the center opening, therefore creating a barrier between the rows of beds. Franky cast a glance at the others and saw he wasn't the only one disappointed.

"This room is only temporary. As long as there is no arguing, I will allow you each to choose your own bed." Mistress Vivian barely finished her sentence as the children scrambled, hoping to claim the best spot. She held up her hands. "Not so fast; we need to get you ready for the next transition. Boys will sleep on the far side of the room and the girls are to choose a bed nearest to where we are standing. Hurry along now, no dawdling. When you find your bed, you're to sit on the edge."

Once again, the children hurried to stake their claim. While most children preferred to be near the window, Franky didn't. His previous bed had been close to the window and he hadn't liked it. Sometimes rain would come in, dampening his bedding. The wintertime drafts chilled him to the bone. During thunderstorms, he worried the thin fingers of light would reach in through the windows and grab him. No, he didn't care for windows much at all. Franky claimed a bed near the center of the room and sat waiting to see what would happen next.

There was a clacking sound, and a moment later, the doors pushed open and six older children entered pushing rolling carts. Two girls who looked to be nearly as tall as Mistress Vivian and a boy, who was much shorter, rolled their cart to the boys' side of the room. The other three girls rolled a second cart to the girls' side. The boy stood in the center of the room with his hands at his side. One of the three girls stood in a similar pose in front of the girls' beds.

Mistress Vivian stepped up between the beds and clapped her hands twice.

"We'll be giving you each a new set of clothes. Boys will get a shirt, trousers, socks, and shoes, along with underclothes. The girls will receive a dress, stockings, apron, and undergarments." She pointed to the boy standing at the front of the room. "The clothes are to be worn like this with your shirt tucked inside your trousers. Put your socks on before your trousers as the socks are to be worn underneath. If anyone needs help buttoning your shirt, raise your hand, and one of us will help."

Mistress Vivian turned to the girl at the head of the room and repeated the dressing process to the girls. When she'd finished with the instructions, the older children began rolling the carts amongst the beds and handing out sets of clothing. As Franky dressed, he wondered how they knew what size clothes to give. It didn't occur to him that being the same age also meant most of the children were the same height and stature. Unlike the three-year-old room, where the clothes were heavily patched, these clothes were indeed brand new. When they'd finished dressing, Franky and the others were dressed identically to the older boy except for the fact that they were all standing in stocking feet. Franky looked to the girls' side of the room and smiled. He'd never in his life seen anything so delightful. The whole side of the room was filled with girls in pretty blue and white dresses with matching bows atop their heads. He'd seen a photo in a picture book once showing a bunch of flowers in a vase. For a moment, it was as if that photo had come to life right in that very room. He wondered briefly if the girls felt as pretty as they looked. From the smiles on their faces, he knew they must.

The door opened once more, and two additional girls came in pushing another set of carts. While they'd occasionally had older girls come into the room to help entertain the children, he'd never seen so many older children in one place. He scratched his head, wondering where they'd come from.

The girls who'd handed out clothes joined the others and rolled the cart to the end of the aisle. As they approached each bed, they instructed the child to stand on a piece of wood with numbers. One girl would call out a number and a second girl would hand over a pair of shiny black shoes. The rest of the girls moved through the room showing the children how to weave the laces back and forth, and how to catch the strings on the eye hooks before tying them into a bow. Though it was a small group, the process still took several hours to complete, but in the end, each child had a new pair of shoes and could tie them without any help. Though there were no mirrors in the room, the children could easily tell what they looked like, as they were each now dressed the same.

Mistress Vivian clapped her hands, dismissing the older children, who took the now empty carts and left without as much as a word. Mistress Vivian turned toward the children. This time, there was no need to clap her hands, as Franky and the others were sitting on the edge of their beds, silently waiting to see what happened next.

"You children are to have a seat at the tables. Girls on this side and boys over there," she said, pointing in turn.

The children jumped to their feet, each rushing to find a seat at the tables appointed to them. It was the first time they'd been segregated according to sex. Some of the children appeared upset by the fact that they were no longer sitting next to a particular friend or sibling. Franky had no qualms about the placement as long as he got fed. He was used to eating shortly after rising and his stomach was beginning to protest the wait. He was just beginning to doubt they would receive breakfast when the doors opened once more and the same group of girls came in pushing two large shelved carts. On each of the shelves were shiny metal trays with bowls and cups. The girls went to work placing the trays in front of the children, who followed the long-standing rule "wait to be told to eat."

The girls stepped to the front of the room, and Mistress Vivian clapped her hands, signaling time to commence eating.

Franky lifted his spoon and shoveled the plain mush into his mouth. It was mostly tasteless, not that he noticed; it was the only way he'd ever eaten it. The only children that ever complained of the taste were the new children who were brought in. Franky never knew where the children came from; every now and then, the door would open and a child would appear. Most of the time, they were accompanied by an older girl the children knew as Clara, who would introduce them to the mistress in charge and leave. Sometimes the new child would cry for a while, though Franky never knew why.

Mistress Vivian stepped to the front of the room and began speaking. "When the next meal arrives, you are to begin eating as soon as you receive your tray. There will be no speaking until you're finished eating and then you may speak in low whispers. You'll be given only one warning. After that, your tray will be removed. You must learn to eat the food placed in front of you in a timely manner. I know this is different than what you are used to, but it will help you with your transition. I assure you that you will soon see the necessity of it. As always, you are to remain seated until I dismiss you."

Franky didn't understand. He had no clue what a transition was, but from the quizzical looks on the faces around him, he knew he wasn't alone. He finished his mush and waited with the others to see what would happen next.

Several moments later, Mistress Vivian returned to the front of the room and clapped her hands. "Children, bring your trays to the front and place them onto the carts. No running or shoving. When you're finished, you are to form a line at the door."

Franky scrambled from his chair, placed his tray on the cart, and hurried to secure a place in line.

"Where are we going?" one of the children whispered.

"Maybe we are going back to our room," someone

answered.

Before anyone else could chime in, one of the older girls stepped up and held the door while Mistress Vivian led the group into the hallway. Only instead of turning the way they'd previously come, she led them toward another door. The girl came up beside Mistress Vivian and pulled open the door. Instantly, sunlight flooded into the small room and all the children began talking in excited whispers. Inside the brightly lit room were large windows and steps, lots of them. Some went up as far as the eye could see and others led downward. Most of the children, Franky included, had seen steps before. There was a small set of play steps in their old dormitory. Franky and the others would often march up the three steps, cross the flat plank, and hurry down the other side, only to repeat the process. But to have so many steps in a single room going in different directions was something new and the children couldn't contain themselves.

"Quiet, children. We must remember our manners in the hallway." She lifted a finger and pointed. "We are going upstairs."

As he followed Mistress Vivian up several flights of stairs, Franky craned his neck, trying to see beyond the concrete steps. They passed a door, turned, and continued to climb upwards.

Franky, along with the majority of children in the small group, had never ventured from the fourth floor, which had been his home for as long as he could remember. Until this moment, he hadn't even known there was a world beyond the fourth floor just waiting to be explored.

Mistress Vivian came to a stop in front of a door at the top of the stairs. She waited until the children caught up, then in one smooth motion, opened the door to reveal the most brilliant blue sky Franky had ever seen.

Not able to contain themselves, the children rushed from the enclosed space, each throwing their arms out and spinning in all directions. Franky turned around and around, looking for the walls, only to find none. He smiled as the cool spring breeze blew across his body like a whisper. Some of the children ran to the edge of the roof, peering out into the distance.

Franky followed, reached his arms to the top of the short brick wall, and was attempting to climb up for a better look when Mistress Vivian pulled him away from the ledge.

"I wanna see!" he complained.

"You can look with your feet firmly on the ground," she said, letting him go.

Franky waited until Mistress Vivian turned her attention to another child and then pulled himself up again. This time, he was rewarded with a view of the city. He dug his feet into the bricks and clambered onto the ledge in an effort to see more. As he perched on the edge, he cast a glance downward and gulped as his stomach lurched. A second later, strong hands plucked him from the bricks and pulled him back to the safety of the building's rooftop.

"Am I going to have trouble with you?" Mistress Vivian asked sternly.

Still too frightened to speak, Franky shook his head and waited for the scolding that was sure to follow.

"Good. Boys are expected to act foolishly now and again. You've seen all there is to see. Let that be the end of it." To Franky's surprise, her words were followed by the slightest of smiles.

Chapter Three

Cindy finished the page she was reading and looked over at Linda, who was firmly engrossed in the journal. She'd thought to ask her mother's opinion of the asylum allowing the children so close to the edge of the roof then decided against it, knowing her mother would merely say it was a different time. It was true, but that still didn't alleviate her worry. Were children really that expendable during that era, or was it truly a matter of letting them learn from their mistakes? If Mistress Vivian hadn't pulled him back, Uncle Franky would have fallen. If that were the case, he wouldn't have been there to watch over her grandmother or any of the other things he'd done in life that had made a difference. She'd heard the term butterfly effect, where one small deviation could radically change things. Surely this was one of those things that could have changed so many lives had it not been for one woman paying attention and saving a child from certain death. *Would I even be here had Uncle Frank died?*

The ramifications of the woman's actions boggled Cindy's mind. She glanced at her mother once more before picking up the next stack of papers.

***

A few weeks after being made aware of the world beyond the fourth floor, our group got a new surprise. We were led downstairs and introduced to a whole new world filled with children of all ages. The introduction was slow at first, allowing us downstairs for short periods then escorted back to the fourth floor. Then one day, we stopped at the second floor. The girls were taken to the girls' dorm and us boys went to our new sleeping quarters on the third floor. They assigned us a bed and said this was to be our new home. I stayed there until the day I left the asylum, but there I go, getting ahead of myself again.

I remember the day I met my birth mother. Of course, I didn't know it to be her at the time. Quite frankly, I didn't even know what a mother was. I was raised by the mistresses at the asylum, and truth be told, none were what one would call motherly. To be sure, they did the best they could with there being so many kids and all, but they did not coddle the children in their care. I don't recall ever getting a hug. Maybe I'm wrong, but you'd think a boy would be able to remember something like that.

Even at a young age, I knew my place. We all did, at least those of us who'd been raised in the asylum. Sometimes a new kid would show up and stir things up a bit. I learned to steer clear of those kids. They were constantly getting into trouble, and I didn't want to be caught up in any of that. It wasn't that the kids were bad; they just didn't know the how of things. If I liked the kid, I'd wait it out a bit. The mistresses were swift in their discipline and it didn't take long for the newcomers to learn the rules. There I go rambling again. I was supposed to tell you about the woman who gave birth to me.

***

Franky sat in the corner, watching some of the older boys play marbles. One of the boys missed his shot and said a word Franky hadn't heard before. He was just about to ask what the word meant when music drifted through the air. He rose from the floor and walked toward the sound. He recognized the girl playing the music as a girl that read stories that sent shivers up his spine. Just today, she'd read a tale of ducklings swimming in a pond. She'd made a sound like a duck, and for an instant, he'd thought there really were ducks in the room.

Franky walked to the edge of the piano, hesitated, then moved closer so he could watch the girl's fingers tap furiously at the keys. The music sped up, and for a moment, her fingers were a blur. He inched closer, she looked in his direction, he smiled, and her eyes grew wide. Her fingers hesitated, she returned his smile, and she started playing once again. He stared at her, wondering about the scar that ran the length of her face.

"Franky!"

Franky turned at the sound of his name and saw a dark-haired girl named Rose beckoning him to come. Rose had been in the asylum as long as Franky. Longer, as she'd been moved from the fourth floor with another group of children a year before. Franky gave a longing look toward the piano before joining Rose on the other side of the room.

"What were you doing?" Rose whispered fearfully.

"I wasn't doing nothing. Just hearing the music."

"You can hear it from over here. Stay away from Anastasia. She's mean."

Franky looked over his shoulder. To his surprise, Anastasia was staring in his direction as her fingers continued to drum at the keys. She smiled at him once more.

He shrugged. "She don't look mean."

Rose's blue eyes went wide. "Oh, she's mean alright. She steals food and everything. See that scar on her face?"

Of course I do. He nodded.

"She got it in a knife fight. The other girl didn't even do nothing—just looked at Anastasia the wrong way, and Anastasia pounded her real bad. I heard the girl picked up a knife and cut Anastasia. They say Anastasia was so mad, she grabbed the knife and cut the girl's ear off."

Franky's hand flew to his ear. "How does she hear if she don't got a ear?"

Rose laughed as if it was the daftest thing she'd ever

heard. "Why, with her other ear, I suppose. You just stay away from her before she cuts your ear off too."

Franky glanced at the girl playing the piano then lifted his hand to his ear before returning to where the boys sat playing marbles. While he enjoyed the sound that came when she played, he didn't think he'd be happy listening with only one ear.

***

Franky set his tray onto the cart and took his place in line behind the others. The doors opened, and the line moved forward. Today's routine was different. On occasion, Mrs. Gretchen pulled one of the children aside, and speaking in German, told them to form a new line against the wall. While the children were encouraged to speak English, the mistresses who cared for them didn't have to adhere to the rules. Most only spoke broken English and preferred to revert to their native language whenever the headmistress wasn't within earshot. The children in their care quickly learned what was expected of them, mostly from watching the children around them. Like many who'd lived in the asylum all their lives, Franky knew bits and pieces of many languages, German included.

Franky looked at the line, wondering what the children had done to be singled out. As he approached the door, the mistress pointed to him and motioned him to the newly formed line.

He walked toward the others, searching his memory for something he'd done to warrant a reprimand. To his knowledge, he'd done nothing. He remembered his conversation with Rose and wondered if Anastasia had told the mistress that he'd been staring at her. *Would that be enough for a reprimand?* At least it was better than getting his ear cut off.

As he passed the line of children, he could see they were as oblivious to the reason as he. He saw Gideon, the Italian boy who slept in the bed beside him, as he stepped into line. Gideon could bend his arms and legs in such a way he looked like a spider walking across the floor. The boy knew it was good for a laugh and had done so the previous day when one of the new kids was feeling low. Still, to Franky's knowledge, none of the mistresses had seen him act a fool.

Clara came into the room and whispered something in Mrs. Gretchen's ear. The mistress nodded and looked in his direction, then motioned for him to come.

Franky gulped, once again wondering what he'd done.

"Franky, there's been a mistake. You are to go to your dorm," Clara said, sending him off to find the others.

Instantly filled with relief, he hurried to catch up with the group of children who'd already been dismissed. He caught up just as they reached the stairs and silently followed them to the third floor. As soon as the large group of boys entered the dorm, they began speaking in excited whispers.

Several of the boys circled Franky.

"What'd you do?" one of the older boys asked.

Franky shrugged. "Didn't do nothin."

"Then why'd they make you get in line?" the same boy asked.

Franky shrugged again.

"You must've done something," another, taller boy remarked.

"Did not!" Franky said, narrowing his eyes.

"Leave the kid alone," another boy said, pushing the boys aside. Franky recognized the boy. His name was George, and from what Franky could tell, the boy didn't cause any trouble. He often sat in the corner reading books to his younger brother, Alfred. George had a calm voice and Franky often grabbed a book of his own and sat close whenever the boy read.

Franky couldn't read, but he'd look at the pictures in the

book he'd chosen and pretend George's words went with the pictures in the book he was holding. "The kid's here, isn't he? If he'd done something bad, he'd still be downstairs with the others."

This seemed to make sense to the others as they quickly moved away and began whispering amongst themselves once more.

Franky looked toward Gideon's bed and sighed. In his haste to join the others, he'd forgotten the boy was still amongst the others that hadn't returned. While he and Gideon weren't actually close friends, they spoke on occasion, and he was used to having the boy near.

"Ready yourselves for sleep, children," Mistress Lorna, the boys' dorm mistress, said as she closed the heavy door. A large-nosed woman with a heavy Irish accent, she looked in Franky's direction and a shiver raced up his spine. Though the woman had never given him reason to distrust her, there was something about her that gave him the chills. Something in the way she stared at him as if she knew all his secrets. Not that he had any, but he kept his distance from her all the same.

Franky looked toward Gideon's bed once more. His friend was not returning. At least not tonight.

***

Franky sat on the piano bench next to Anastasia and listened as her fingers made the music drift through the air. He glanced over at the wall and saw the long line of boys and girls who'd been called aside after the evening meal. He looked at each child in turn and realized they were all crying and pointing in his direction. Though their mouths moved, he couldn't hear their shouts. He looked at Anastasia, hoping to ask her if she could hear what they were screaming. That was when he saw the bloody ear clenched beneath her teeth. He scrambled off the bench, landing hard on the shiny floor. Within seconds, his clothes were covered in blood. He looked at his reflection on the floor and realized the bloody ear belonged to him.

"Boy, wake up."

He called out into the darkness and instantly felt a hand clamp over his mouth.

"Shh, quiet yourself. It was only a nightmare, child. Now settle yourself before you wake the others," Mistress Lorna said sternly. Removing her hand, she leaned in and whispered in his ear. "You must've been up to no good today. Nightmares are the heavens' way of purging evil from the souls of wicked little boys."

Franky blinked back his fear as Mistress Lorna rose from the bed and walked off into the shadows of the room without another word. Franky stared out into the dark long after she left his side, wondering what evil he had inside him and where it had gone, further afraid it would return and have him banished to wherever the others had gone.

***

It was just after the midday meal, and Franky's stomach hurt. He'd eaten everything on his plate, so he didn't think it was hurting because he was hungry. He was still troubled from the nightmare and worried over the empty seats within the dining hall. He'd noticed the same thing in both the meeting room and the common room. Though what really worried him in the common room was the way Anastasia kept looking in his direction as she read the morning story. Though she smiled on occasion, he kept picturing her as he'd seen her in his dream. *No, it was a nightmare because he had a wicked soul.*

The door opened, and Anastasia stepped inside the room, said something to one of the other girls, then glanced in his direction. A frown crossed her face and he shivered. *She's mad about something.* Unconsciously, his hands drifted toward his ears.

His fear deepened when he realized she was no longer wearing the blue dress most of the other girls wore. Instead, she wore a long black dress, which told him he was now supposed to call her Mistress Anastasia and was to obey her without question. He swallowed his fear as she began walking in his direction.

"You don't look very happy today, Franky," she said when she approached.

She knows my name.

"Sorry, Mistress Ana…Mistress Antas…Mistress," he said, leaving off her name.

"My name is pretty hard to say. Why don't you just call me Mistress Anna, okay?" she said and smiled. When she smiled, her face didn't look scary.

"Okay, Mistress Anna." He beamed with relief realizing he hadn't done anything to make her angry.

"There now, look at that smile. That's so much better. What's got you so sad today?" she asked when he frowned once more.

"My friends are gone. Some of the others too," he said, hoping she wouldn't guess his secret. It wouldn't do for her to know he was terrified of her.

She leaned in close, and his hands flew to his ears once more.

She took hold of his left hand, pulling it from his ear.

He held his breath.

"Can you keep a secret?" she whispered.

A secret? Sure he could. Now that Mistress Anna was wearing the black dress that made her a grown-up. He'd never been asked to keep something secret by a grown-up. He nodded his relief.

"Your friends are not missing; they're going on a big adventure."

"What's an adventure?"

"Well, in this case, they're going to be sent out on a train where they will each find a family to love and take care of them."

"A train like in the picture book?"

She smiled. "That's right. They are going out on a train just like in the picture book."

And to think he'd been happy about being pulled from the line and sent upstairs.

"Then why did they pull me from the line?" Franky instantly regretted his words as Mistress Anna stopped smiling. He was just about to apologize when her smile returned.

"Maybe you'll ride a train someday. But not today, Franky. Today, you're going to stay right here. I've got to go, but I'll check on you later. Would you like that?"

Franky nodded his head.

"Good," she said.

He wasn't sure why she wanted to check on him, but it seemed to make her happy, and if she was happy, he thought it unlikely she'd try to bite off his ear.

Chapter Four

September, 1926

Franky opened his eyes, wondering what had pulled him from sleep. He lay there for several moments and was just about to nod off once more when he heard whispers. He turned onto his side, blinking his eyes to focus in the darkness. It took several blinks before he was able to ascertain the direction of the sounds. Just to his left, standing near the open moonlight-filled window, stood Mistress Lorna and another woman speaking in soft tones. The second woman had her back to him, but something about her tall, thin silhouette looked familiar.

He scooched to the edge of the bed and strained to hear their conversation, catching every other word. He heard something that sounded like children and trains, and his heartbeat quickened. *They're planning to send more children out on the trains.*

They'd sent two groups since the time he'd almost gotten chosen, and each time, the children left without saying goodbye. They were simply plucked out of line, never to be seen or heard from again. He wouldn't have known if not for Mistress Anna, who seemed to like him enough to answer his questions when he'd asked where the children had gone. She'd told him it was their secret and that he never was to tell anyone she'd told him. He'd gone as far as to ask her one time why she'd told him. She'd smiled and told him he was her special friend. Maybe that was because all of the other children seemed to be afraid of her. He'd been afraid too, but the more he spoke to her, the less fearful he became, though he always held his breath when she got too close to his ear.

He lay there wondering what it would be like to ride a train and further wondered why he was never chosen to do so.

"We are still in need of a few more names," the tall woman whispered.

"Me!" Franky didn't realize he'd spoken aloud until both women turned in his direction. He gulped his regret as the tall woman turned, and he saw her face in the moonlight.

Headmistress!

She lifted her hand and waved for him to come. Trembling, he did as he was told, his bare feet slapping against the cool tile floor as he walked.

"Little boys are not supposed to listen in on private conversations," Headmistress said, keeping her voice low so as not to wake the others. "Why are you not sleeping?"

He lowered his gaze to his feet. Headmistress took his chin in her hand, tilting his head so he had no choice but to look her in the eyes. "What did you hear?"

He blinked, and she tightened her fingers. "Answer me, child."

"Franky, Headmistress asked you a question. You'll answer her at once," Mistress Lorna urged.

Headmistress tilted his head from side to side as if she were inspecting him to make sure he'd washed behind his ears. "Franky, is it?"

He tried to shake his head, but the headmistress' grip was too tight.

"Yes, that's the boy's name," Mistress Lorna replied.

"Correct me if I'm wrong, but I do believe we only have one by the name of Franky?"

"Yes, ma'am, this be the only one."

Headmistress released her hold on him and stood. "Why were you eavesdropping on our conversation?"

Franky didn't understand the question.

"Headmistress asked you a question, Franky. You'll do best to answer her."

"I can't."

"Well, why on earth not?" Mistress Lorna asked.

"Because I don't know what eavesdropping means," he said, voice trembling.

"Oh, for heaven's sake," Mistress Lorna said. "Tell the headmistress why you were listening to us talk."

"I guess because I didn't have anything better to do. I woke up, heard you both talking, and my ears…they just thought to listen to what you said." Franky wanted to add that their talking was what woke him in the first place but decided to leave that part out.

The headmistress blew out a sigh. "Off to bed with you, boy."

Franky turned to leave.

"Franky?"

"Yes, Headmistress?"

"You'll not tell anyone about anything you heard tonight. Understand?"

"Yes, Headmistress."

"Franky?"

"Yes, Headmistress."

"Not even any of the mistresses should they ask. Understood?"

"Yes, Mistress," he said and hurried off before she had the chance to stop him again.

***

Franky pushed his bowl aside and waited for his friend Jack to finish his morning meal. They'd only recently become friends after Franky's friend Lenny and several others had ditched him out of fear of Mistress Anastasia. Lenny had taken a roll from Franky's plate after Franky said he wasn't hungry. Mistress Anastasia had seen Lenny take the roll and had acted before Franky could stop her, slapping the boy firmly across the face. Franky had understood why she thought Lenny had stolen the roll; older kids took things from the younger kids all the time.

Not that anyone had ever tried to take Franky's from him. He wanted to think it was because the others were his friends, but in reality, it was because they were all aware that Mistress Anastasia had taken a liking to him and no one wanted to get on her bad side. The incident with Lenny reinforced that fear.

Jack looked up from his meal and dropped his spoon. Franky looked to see what had caused this and saw Mistress Anastasia headed directly toward him. He looked back toward Jack, who'd turned white with fear. Franky sighed, knowing Mistress Anastasia's attention had cost him another friend.

"Everything okay here, Franky?" she asked, approaching the table.

It was until you came. He nodded.

"Good," she said and glared at the boys sitting near him.

"Find another table tomorrow," Jack sneered after Mistress Anastasia was out of earshot.

"Yeah, maybe you should just sit with your girlfriend," one of the other boys agreed.

"She's not my girlfriend," Franky replied.

"Yeah, tell her that," Jack said with a laugh.

One of the other boys made a kissing sound, causing the boys nearby to burst into laughter.

"Franky loves Anastasia," Jack sang out, and the others joined in, chanting in low whispers.

Franky doubled his fist and was just about to use it when a shadow fell across the table. He looked up, and his fist went limp. *Headmistress.*

Headmistress looked at each boy in turn. "Is there a problem here?"

"No, Headmistress," the boys said at once.

"Good. Franky, grab your tray and come with me," she said and turned without waiting for a response.

Franky took his tray to the cart and hurried to catch up with Headmistress. She opened the door and led the way down the hall. Even without her saying, he knew she was taking him to her office. *She thinks I told.*

"Close the door behind you and have a seat," Headmistress said. She circled the large desk, pulled out the rolling chair, and sat facing him with nary a smile. "The boys at your table didn't seem too pleased with you."

"No, ma'am."

"What did you do to ruffle their feathers?"

"I didn't do nothin at all."

"Boys don't get that riled up about nothing. Now tell me on your own, or I will have to find another, more unpleasant way of finding out," she said, looking over his shoulder.

He turned, his eyes resting on a large wooden paddle with several holes. While he'd never done anything to warrant getting it used on him, he'd heard stories from others who weren't so lucky.

He turned his attention back to the headmistress, who surprised him with a smile.

"I see we understand each other," she said. "Now, from the beginning, why were the boys so riled up?"

"They think Mistress Anna is my girlfriend."

Headmistress tilted her head in question. "Well, is she?"

"Course not. She's too old to be my girlfriend."

"What would make them think so?"

He shrugged, and Headmistress looked toward the

paddle once more.

"She's nice to me is all."

"How nice?"

"I don't know, just nice. She talks to me sometimes. Tells me secrets." Franky covered his mouth with his hand.

Headmistress' face grew red and she leaned forward in her seat. "What kind of secrets, Franky?"

Franky wasn't sure what to do. If he told Headmistress what Mistress Anna had told him about the trains, Mistress Anna would be mad. But if he didn't tell her, Headmistress would be mad. He glanced over his shoulder once more, knowing all the headmistress had to do was use the paddle on him and he'd end up telling her anyway. Why not just tell her and save himself some pain. *What's a little spanking compared to Mistress Anna biting my ear off?*

Headmistress rose from her chair, sending it rolling backward. She came around to the front of her desk and sat on the edge. "I don't want to hurt you, Franky, but rules must be followed. I've asked you a question, and by law, you must answer me. I'm a grownup and you're the child. It is simply the way things are done."

Franky felt a tear trickle from his eye and angrily pushed it away. "Mistress Anna told me not to tell, and she's a grownup too."

A sly smile played at her lips. "Is that all that's troubling you? Well, then you've no reason to fear. When she told you not to tell, she meant you shouldn't tell any of the others. You see, I'm Mistress Anastasia's boss, which means it is okay to tell me anything she's told you. Truth be told, I probably already know."

That made sense.

"Now tell me what secrets Mistress Anastasia has told you."

"She told me about the trains," he said with a sniff.

"The trains? What about them?"

"She told me they take children out and find them new homes. She said I was lucky that I didn't go because that meant I get to stay here with her."

"And why was that?"

Franky stared blankly.

"Why did Mistress Anastasia tell you that you are lucky to get to stay here with her?"

"She said it is because she likes me."

The headmistress stood and looked toward the paddle once more. "Is that all she said?"

He wasn't sure what she wanted him to say. "Yes, that's all she said."

She must have believed him, as she rounded the desk and took her seat once more. "Do you think you are lucky staying here?"

Franky looked at his shoes.

"Head up, Franky," she said firmly.

Franky lifted his head and looked at her.

"Let me rephrase the question. If you had the chance to go out on the trains, would you go?"

"You mean go on a big adventure?" *Of course I would.*

"Oh, yes. It would be the biggest adventure of your life. Would you like that, Franky? Would you like to see the world?"

Up until now, the biggest adventure he'd had was learning there was a world beyond the fourth floor. Even still, the asylum was the only home he'd ever known.

"You seem hesitant. Are you afraid you'll miss your friends?"

"No, my friends have already gone off on the trains." He didn't want to tell her Mistress Anna had scared the rest away.

Headmistress softened her tone. “Franky, I’m the grownup. I can say the word and send you away, and there is nothing you or anyone else can do about it. But I’m asking you now, do you want to live in this place all of your life, or do you want to find a home with someone to love you? You’ll go to school, make lots of friends, and you might even get to have a dog.”

A dog? He’d never considered that. “Maybe.”

“Mistress Anastasia would be pleased if she found out you went to a home with a dog,” Headmistress added.

“I want to go.”

A strange smile crossed her face. “Good. The train leaves tomorrow. I will see to it they find a place for you on it. Now there is one more thing.”

“Yes, Headmistress?”

“You are not to tell anyone about our conversation.”

“Even Mistress Anna?”

Her smile widened. “Especially Mistress Anna.”

Franky frowned. He didn’t like all the secrets. “She’ll be sad if I don’t say goodbye.”

“Oh, no, Franky. Mistress Anastasia will be very happy for you, but you must remember I’m the boss. It is my job to give her the good news. She will be so happy, she will cry, but they will be happy tears. But if you tell her and she cries, the other children might think she is weak and they wouldn’t respect her. If they don’t respect her, they won’t listen to her, and that would make her sad. You wouldn’t want to make your friend sad, would you?”

Of course not. Franky shook his head. Then again, he wouldn’t want to make her mad either.

Chapter Five

Franky followed the children up the stairs after the evening meal. He heard a commotion further up the line and wondered what was amiss. He found the answer a moment later when plucked from the line and told to stand along the opposite wall as he reached the third-floor landing. Mistress Vivian stood next to Mistress Lorna, surprising, as he hadn't seen the woman since transitioning to the third floor. For a moment, he was afraid she'd come to collect children to return to the fourth floor, a thought he rejected when he scanned the line and realized most of the children were older than he.

When the last of the boys filed through the door to the third-floor hallway, Mistress Lorna followed, closing the door behind them.

Once she'd left, Mistress Vivian turned her attention to the remaining boys. "For those that do not know me, I'm Mistress Vivian. I'm going to take you boys into the dorm. When we get inside, you're to go to your bed and retrieve your bedding and any personal items you may have. You're to collect everything and return to the door where I'll be standing and form a line. Do not make eye contact with the other children, and if they question what you're doing, you're not to reply."

A low murmur grew among the children.

"Hush now; all will be explained to you in due time," Mistress Vivian said, silencing the boys. It was then Franky realized he was the only one in the group that knew about the trains. Something about the knowledge empowered him and he smiled. It wasn't often he knew more than the others.

Mistress Vivian opened the door and led them into the boys' dorm. Sure enough, as the boys gathered their belongings, the other boys bombarded them with eager whispers inquiring as to what was amiss.

Franky heard a sob and looked to see who'd produced it. He swallowed when he realized it had come from George's brother Alfred. While George was in the group of children chosen for the trains, Alfred was not. The younger boy grabbed his brother's arm, his face full of fear as he asked where his brother was going.

George turned and shook his head in response. It was then Franky saw the tears in the older boy's eyes.

Franky's stomach clenched. This time, he wasn't as pleased with the knowledge he carried. It was the first time he could remember being thankful he didn't have any family. It would make him sad if he thought he was leaving someone behind. He hurried and gathered his things, which included his bedding, a nightshirt, and a small kit he used when cleaning himself before bed. With a few exceptions, it was all most of them had.

Items in hand, he hurried to the door and stood in line staring forward to avoid questioning eyes. When the last boy stepped into line, Mistress Vivian opened the door, led the children from the room, and closed the door to silence the sobs of those left behind.

She led the group down the stairs, stopping at the second-floor landing. Motioning the boys to remain silent, she opened the door. Franky studied the hallway carefully, as it was the first time he'd been allowed onto the floor normally reserved for girls. Disappointment set in as he realized it was a carbon copy of each of the other floors, with stark white walls and white tiled floors. The only pops of color came from an occasional picture hanging in the hall and the large red crocks that were spaced evenly throughout the hallway.

To his surprise, other than Mistress Vivian, there wasn't a girl in sight. She led them past several doors before stopping and ushering them into a nearly empty room.

"You're to use your bedding to make yourself a sleeping pallet on the floor," Mistress Vivian said, closing the door. She walked further into the room and pointed. "Stay on this side of the room."

"Is this to be our new room?" a tall boy asked, looking around with disgust.

"It can't be; there aren't any beds," another said in return. He narrowed his eyes at Mistress Vivian. "If we are being punished, at least be so good as to tell us what we've done."

"You haven't done anything," Mistress Vivian said loud enough for all to hear. "Go on and do as you were told and be quick about it. Go on now. I assure you, this arrangement is only for tonight."

The boys did as told and soon had rows of bedding spread all over the left side of the room. They were sitting on the thin layers of blankets when the door opened once again and Mistress Scott lingered in the doorway. Just the sight of the woman sent a chill up Franky's spine. She was a floating mistress, going where she was needed. She once spent a week with the children when Mistress Lorna was ill. While he was afraid of Mistress Lorna, she seemed like the nicest woman in the world compared to Mistress Scott, who walked around with a perpetual scowl on her face.

Mistress Scott glared around the room before entering, bringing a small group of girls with her. She stopped, turned to the girls, and pointed to the empty space on the right side of the room. "You'll sleep here tonight. Place your bedding on the floor and be quick about it." As the girls scrambled to do as told,

Mistress Scott and Mistress Vivian set to work placing cots in the center, further cordoning off the boys and girls.

"This is in case any of you have any ideas about fraternizing during the night," Mistress Scott said, glaring at the boys.

Franky didn't know what "fraternizing" meant, but from the deep scowl on Mistress Scott's face, he didn't want any part of it.

There was a low rap on the door, and Headmistress came in, followed by Clara, the girl that often accompanied the woman or did errands at her bidding. Clara carried a large brown woven basket, its handle draped over the crook of her arm. At a nod from Headmistress, Clara moved through the rows of children. Franky watched as Clara stopped briefly in front of each child, handing them something that made their eyes grow wide. He waited in eager anticipation as Clara made her way toward him then stopped, handing him a warm biscuit.

Franky recognized the biscuit as the cheese biscuits reserved for special occasions he'd come to learn were days called Christmas and Thanksgiving. Franky's hands trembled with eager yearning as he gazed at the treat, hoping he'd get the chance to taste the delicacy while it was still warm.

Only when Clara handed the last child their biscuit did Headmistress give the signal to eat. Franky resisted the urge to shove the entire biscuit into his mouth. Instead, he took slow, deliberate bites, knowing he didn't have to worry about anyone stealing his treat as long as Headmistress stood watch. As he ate, he looked about the room. If the headmistress had hoped to soothe the children's fears, it didn't work. A treat such as this, given in such a way, would only prove to heighten the children's fears. Once again, Franky was glad he knew the answer to the question most assuredly on everyone's mind.

Headmistress looked about the room once more.

Satisfied the children had finished eating, she began speaking. When she spoke, her voice was low. Franky wasn't sure if it was so she couldn't be heard outside the room or if it was merely so the children had to be quiet in order to hear. If the latter was the case, it worked, as all eyes were now focused on the woman.

"I'm sure you're all wondering why you are here, so I'll tell you. A few years ago, our asylum was chosen to join with the Children's Aid Society and send children out to find new homes. Children from our asylum went out west and in turn were all able to find new homes with loving families to care for them. In the years since, we have been invited to participate again and again. This year is no different. I've personally chosen each and every one of you from your impeccable behavior and the way you carry yourself."

Mistress Scott coughed, and Headmistress shot her a look normally reserved for a child who'd broken a rule. A brilliant red crept up over Mistress Scott's neck and traveled to her face, and she quickly lowered her eyes. This action caught Franky by surprise. He didn't know adults could get in trouble too.

"Tomorrow morning, well before the others rise, the lot of you will be on your way to the train station, where you will board your own train and take a great journey west to find your forever home," Headmistress continued.

A low wail bubbled from behind him, and Franky turned to see George, whose brother was still in the main dorm, struggling to keep himself under control. Though the boy tried to wipe them away, tears continued to pour from his reddened eyes. Franky turned back in the direction of the Headmistress, wondering about her reaction. She must have been used to children's tears, as she didn't look at all bothered by them.

Franky raised his hand.

"What is it, Franky?" Headmistress didn't look pleased with the interruption.

"If it is the same to you, I'd rather stay."

Headmistress' eyes grew wide. "Why, Franky, just this afternoon, you agreed to go onto the trains."

Her comment caused a rash of excited whispers as the other children realized Franky had known all along. As his peers shot accusing glances in his direction, it was Franky's turn to blush.

"Hush now, children, before you wake the rest of the floor," Headmistress said, then turned her attention back to Franky. "What is the meaning of your request?"

Swallowing his fear, Franky pulled himself to his feet and spoke directly to the headmistress. "I haven't changed my mind. I'd welcome the grand adventure you spoke of, but I wouldn't be sad if I were to stay. This is the only home I've ever known and I like it just fine. It's just I thought if I were to stay, maybe George's brother may go."

Headmistress' eyebrows rose slightly then settled once more. "I admire your words, but I'm afraid the decision is well out of my hands. I sent over the list earlier today, and the arrangements have already been made."

"But what about his brother?" Franky implored.

The headmistress set her jaw. "I'll not have you or anyone else questioning my decision. One more word from you and I'll see to it you have to stand the whole trip."

Remembering the paddle on the wall, Franky nodded and returned to his pallet. Offering his spot to George's brother was one thing. Having blisters on his backside was another. He'd tried and there was no shame in that.

"Good. Clara and I will come for you in the morning. When we leave this room, I will expect you all to follow us down the stairs as quietly as possible. As I said, we will be leaving early and I would not wish to wake the others. We are to exit out the front door where we will walk two blocks before taking the trolley car to the train station. The trolley service has agreed to keep a car available for our travels and we are all to be on our best behavior. Once at the train station, you will be joining others from the Children's Aid Society, and there we will say our goodbyes. Our asylum was chosen because others before you behaved so well. I'll not have you spoiling future chances for children from our asylum. If you misbehave, you will be sent back." Headmistress intentionally made eye contact with the boy whose sobs could still be heard. "If you are sent back for any reason, you will answer to me."

Headmistress didn't have to tell the children what that meant. They'd all heard enough stories to keep them on their best behavior.

Franky had witnessed Headmistress' wrath shortly after coming down from the fourth-floor nursery. A nine-year-old boy they called Rat had been discovered sneaking into the kitchen late one night stealing food meant for the morning meal. After a firm scolding by the kitchen mistress, the boy had been allowed to return to his bed that night thinking all was forgiven. Upon his arrival in the dorm, he'd boasted about what he'd done and how he'd lied to the kitchen mistress, saying he'd gone so far as to squeeze out a few tears to make her feel sorry for him. The next day while eating his morning meal, Headmistress arrived, walked straight to the table, pulled Rat from his seat by his ear, and led him to the door, where a policeman was waiting to take him off to prison.

Stone-faced, Headmistress then stood in the front of the room and described in great detail what would happen to the boy once the murderers and rapists at the prison got hold of him, further saying she'd had no choice but to send him off, as when a person steals from the asylum, they are stealing from each child that lives inside. The whole ordeal had a lasting impact on Franky, who'd lived a sheltered life up until that point. It must have scared the others as well, as to his knowledge, no one had stolen from the kitchen in the years since.

Headmistress yawned, then glanced at the timepiece that hung around her neck. She smiled a rare smile. "Dear me, I didn't know it was getting so late. I must let you go to sleep, or there will be no waking you in the morning."

Once Headmistress left the room, the children were quick to settle, each caught up in their own thoughts and wondering what great adventures awaited them. All except one, whose sobs could be heard well into the night.

Chapter Six

It was still dark when Franky and the others were rousted from their makeshift beds and taken in shifts to the water closet. Mistress Scott clapped her hands, drawing the children's attention to the front of the room. "Listen up, children. I want you all to form two lines, boys in one and girls in the other. You're to stand according to height, with the tallest being in the front of the line. Hurry, and be quiet about it."

The children did as told, the process going rather quickly as the children were already used to forming lines in this manner. Franky was near the back of the line, something he'd become used to since moving from the fourth floor. Until then, he'd been accustomed to being at the head of the line. The mistress started down the line, handing the children cotton bags with their names pinned to the fabric.

"There is a fresh set of clothes in the bags for each of you. You're to leave the bags closed until told to open them. The trains can get dirty and you mustn't soil your new clothes before you have a chance to wear them." Someone moaned, then came the unmistakable sound of spewing. Franky twisted his neck and looked toward the middle of the line just in time to see the boy heave once again. Though Franky recognized the boy, he didn't know his name. Mistress Scott shoved the bags she was holding in Mistress Vivian's hands then hurriedly pulled the boy from the line. She felt the back of his forehead with her hand and a frown tugged at her mouth. She looked toward Mistress Vivian and shook her head before pulling the boy from the line.

The door opened, and Headmistress and Clara entered. Headmistress saw the boy standing on his own and ordered him to take his place in line. When the boy didn't respond, Headmistress took hold of the boy's arm.

Mistress Scott made an attempt to warn Headmistress off, but it was too late. The boy turned green, blinked several times, bent over, and emptied the remainder of his stomach, the majority of which landed directly on the headmistress' shoes.

Franky snickered then covered his mouth.

Though her face turned white, Headmistress didn't gag. Franky had to give the woman credit. He was pretty sure he would have heaved himself had he been in her shoes. The thought of Headmistress' shoes covered in vomit evoked another snicker.

"The boy's ill," Mistress Vivian said, stating the obvious. "Shall I send him to the infirmary?"

"Are you sure it is not just a case of nerves?" Headmistress asked, sizing him up.

"Oh, no, ma'am, he's sick to be sure. His head is hot as the dickens, it is."

Headmistress sighed. "You two finish getting the children ready. Clara will see to the boy and find another to replace him. See to it, Clara, and be quick about it," Headmistress said with a wave of the hand. "When you're finished and go to the boys' dorm to choose another boy, make sure to find a child of equal height so the new clothes will fit. We don't have time to go searching for another set."

Clara nodded her understanding then took the boy by the shoulders and guided him from the room.

"Have the children ready when I return," Headmistress ordered before gingerly walking toward the door.

As soon as the door closed behind her, the room exploded with laughter. Much to Franky's surprise, Mistresses

Vivian and Scott were among those laughing.

The gaiety didn't last long, but it helped to relieve tensions of the unknown.

"Settle down, children," Mistress Vivian ordered. "It wouldn't do well for us to be caught up in our hilarities when the headmistress returns."

With the exception of a few snickers, the children grew quiet once more and Mistress Scott resumed handing out the travel bags.

"We have a special treat for you," Mistress Vivian said, drawing the children's attention. "One of our benefactors has seen fit to see you on your way in grand style. It was they who sent over the supplies to make the cheese biscuits you enjoyed before bed last night. They've also seen to it that you each receive a nice ham biscuit for your morning meal."

Her words sent an instant murmur of excitement through the group from those who knew of the delicacy of which she spoke. Franky had not tasted ham, so he couldn't speak to if he'd like the stuff, but the thought of another biscuit made his mouth water all the same. He hadn't even left the building, and already, he felt as if he were on a grand adventure.

Mistress Vivian walked the length of the line, handing the children the biscuit wrapped in cheesecloth and instructing them to place it into their pockets. Franky took the offering, held it under his nose, and inhaled. He tucked the biscuit into his pocket and smiled. If it tasted anything like it smelled, he was going to like it just fine.

The door opened once again and Clara returned with Alfred in tow. Alfred's eyes were red and puffy, and as he caught sight of his brother, tears began to flow anew. Clara bent and dried the boy's eyes with her apron. "Alfred, remember what I told you. Now stop crying before Headmistress returns and sends you back to your dorm."

Franky's mouth fell open. He glanced toward Mistress Scott to gauge her reaction. The woman's face showed a brilliant red. Her scowl deepened as she made a beeline toward Clara.

Mistress Vivian stepped in between them, and for a moment, Franky was worried the two were going to yell. Instead, Mistress Vivian locked eyes with the woman. "You know the girl has the headmistress' ear. You do not want to get on that one's wrong side. I've seen it before. She has the power to have you sent away."

Franky looked at Clara and wondered how a girl who wasn't even a mistress could have such power. A moment later, Mistress Scott dropped the bag she was holding onto the floor in front of Mistress Vivian and walked away in a huff.

Mistress Vivian turned her attention to Clara. "Are you sure this is the only boy who fits the description?"

Clara jutted her chin and pushed the boy into line with others similar in height. She then stepped around Mistress Vivian, plucked the cloth bag from the floor, and handed it to Alfred. Only when she had the boy settled did she turn her attention to Mistress Vivian. "Headmistress told me to collect a boy that matched Johnny's size. Alfred is the same size, is he not?"

"He is, it's just…" The woman held her tongue as the headmistress returned to the room, wearing freshly cleaned shoes.

Clara stepped in front of Alfred. It took a moment for Franky to realize the action had been intentional, as her skirts hid the boy from view. *She's protecting him.* He studied Clara with a new admiration, wondering if he'd be brave enough to do the same if he were in her place.

"We're going to be late if we don't hurry," Headmistress said, clapping her hands. "Come along, children, and remember, we must be quiet."

The second they breached the front gate, Franky felt his stomach clench. He instantly hoped the queasiness was because he'd never stepped outside the gates before and not because he was ill. He took inventory and decided he didn't feel ill. A good thing, because the last thing he wanted was to be sent back to the asylum. By the time he climbed up the trolley steps, he was trembling with a mixture of excitement and fear. The trolley began moving and Franky giggled.

"What's wrong with you? You trying to get in trouble?" the boy sitting beside him whispered.

"No." Franky shook his head, but his giggles persisted.

The boy elbowed him in the ribs. "Stop sounding like a girl."

Franky's giggles increased, and the boy slid as far away from Franky as he could manage, which wasn't very far.

"Do we have a problem?"

Franky recognized the voice even before he looked up. "No, Headmistress. It's just I've never been on anything that moved before."

She smiled. "Yes, well, I am sure you will have a lot of firsts over the next few days. Now do try to control yourself. It wouldn't do to have the whole lot of you giggling like a bunch of girls."

"Yes, Headmistress." Franky didn't know what surprised him more, that she didn't scold him or that she hadn't seemed at all mad.

"I'm not as evil as one might think," she said as if reading his mind. To Franky's surprise, she turned to the children seated across from him and motioned for them to clear a place for her to sit. Once seated, she glanced at the children in her care and began to speak. "Our institution has rules in place for a purpose. It wouldn't do for us to let the children in our care run amok. I'm sure once you get to your new destination, you'll be met with a whole new set of rules. Hopefully, you will find your new situation agreeable. I want nothing more for any of my children than for you to find a new home where someone will love you as much as I do. If not, you'll always have a home here."

The children—Franky included—stared at the woman in stunned silence. Franky wasn't sure if it was because she'd told them she loved them or because she'd suggested they might return to the asylum. Headmistress rose and returned to her original seat without another word.

Franky turned toward the window, his giddiness forgotten as the trolley moved along its way, stopping and starting once more. He watched in utter astonishment as building after building passed by, and people strolled the street seemingly without care. He saw horses pulling buggies and children running after them, many of them laughing and yelling as if they too were without care. Living in the asylum was all he'd ever known and it was a routine of extreme obedience. Deviating from the rules was met with severe consequences. Was this what his new life was to be? He wondered what it would be like to run with abandon and yell until his lungs could stand no more. He'd heard some of the older boys speak of having both mothers and fathers until situations stripped them of both. Was a family really attainable for a child such as him or would he be one of those returned to the asylum because someone deemed him unlovable? No, that wasn't true. Had Headmistress not just told them she loved them all? Surely one could not be unlovable if they were already loved. Then again, if she truly loved him and the others, why was she sending them away? Did he love her? He hadn't really thought of that before. *Do I even know what love is?* He snuck a glance in her direction and watched as her face turned ugly before slapping a boy who'd taken that moment to lick the window pane. He might not know what love was, but in that instant, he knew he had no intention of returning to the asylum.

Chapter Seven

It was hard for Franky to keep focused once the group reached Union Station. Everywhere he looked, there was something new to see and there were people everywhere. While being in a crowd wasn't new, being in a place where so many people spoke at once was rather overwhelming. And yet, everything he saw fascinated him, especially the people. The women wore splendid dresses of various lengths and colors. Up until this point, he'd only seen them wearing the black uniform of the asylum. It wasn't just the ladies; many of the men wore suits that were just as magnificent as the dresses, all topped with some kind of hat. Why, he'd never seen so many hats. Even the children they passed were dressed in the same splendor as the adults. Some of the little girls had grand hats with flowers and feathers protruding from them. If he hadn't seen these things with his own eyes, he would never have believed it.

Headmistress, along with Clara, Mistress Vivian, and Mistress Scott, walked with the children seeing to it they stayed in line and exhibited their best behavior. Like Franky, the others in the group were too enthralled with their surroundings to even think of acting out. After what seemed like ten minutes of walking, they finally came to a stop at the base of the stairs. Headmistress turned and faced them. "We shall wait here until the others arrive. In the meantime, you may take out your ham biscuit. And remember, children, crumbs on our clothes mean less food in your mouth. Do try and take care while eating."

Franky pulled the cheesecloth from his pocket and carefully unwrapped his breakfast. He studied the ham biscuit for a moment before bringing it to his lips, carefully probing the ham with his tongue. As his brain registered the rich, salty flavor, he smiled. Never in his life had he tasted anything so divine. He took a bite, his smile widened, and his gaze darted from side to side ensuring no one was set to steal the savory treat. He wanted to eat slowly and make the moment last, but after the first bite, there was no stopping. He gulped the entire sandwich down in four eager bites, licking the tips of his fingers, not wasting a single crumb. When he finished, it was all he could do to keep from crying, it had tasted so good.

Mistress Scott tugged on Headmistress' arm and pointed across the way. Whispers traveled through the line as another group of children joined them at the base of the stairs. It wasn't long before a third group of children joined.

"We'll walk with you to the doors, and then we'll take our leave. You will be in good hands with the agents from the Children's Aid Society. They've traveled the rails many times over the years. Remember what I said and stay on your best behavior, as I shall hear about it if you do not," she warned.

A woman from another group held up her hand and began leading the children forward.

Headmistress and the other adults departed without a word to the group, leaving the children in the care of two placing agents. As he walked, Franky dared a glance behind him. The only one who looked back was Clara. She waved when she saw him looking. He smiled briefly, then turned his attention back to the group, following as the two lady agents led them outside to the platform. Just before they reached the trains, the agents stopped and motioned for the children to gather close. Both ladies were of similar height and both wore long brown overcoats over their dresses. Wide-brimmed hats covered both their heads. Franky thought of the women they'd passed in the station and frowned. For the life of him, he couldn't help wondering why ladies would choose to dress this way when there were so many other options.

"For those who don't know us, I am Miss Childers, and this is Miss Adams. We are agents with the Children's Aid Society. You children are all old enough to behave yourselves in public and I expect you'll do just that, for if you do not, we'll see you come back with us."

Franky tried to pay attention to what else she said, but it was difficult to hear over the sound of the engine. The terminal doors opened, and a throng of people rushed toward the train, pushing their way around the children as they passed. Franky found himself caught up in the migration and hurried forward to keep from getting trampled. The crowd parted, and suddenly, he was standing directly in front of the massive steam engine. He felt his mouth fall open as he gaped at the shiny black engine idling before him. Until this moment, aside from photos in the picture books, the closest thing he'd seen to a train was the trolley car they rode to the station. While the trolley was not small, it was nothing like the steaming beast before him.

He willed himself forward, intent on placing a hand on the metal just to ensure it was real.

"Not too close, son," a man's voice boomed.

Franky tilted his head to see a mountain of a man towering over him. His dark suit did nothing to hide his bulk. Unlike most of the hats Franky had seen along the way, this man's small hat was round and perfectly flat on top. There was a brim shading his plump face and above the brim appeared to be writing. Franky couldn't read, so he had no clue what the words said. He slid a glance toward his group and wondered how he'd wandered so far — wondering further if they'd hear him if he called. He was getting ready to bolt when the man spoke once more. This time, his tone proved much friendlier.

"My name's Barney. I'm the conductor of this here

train. You slip under her and you'll be a goner for sure. She'll flatten you like a flapjack without batting an eye."

Franky didn't know trains had eyes, nor that the train was a girl. *How could the man even tell?* He also wasn't sure what a flapjack was but had no intention of finding out. "Is she real, then?"

The man smiled. "She's as real as they come, son. I expect this is your first train ride?"

More relaxed, Franky nodded his head. "Yes, sir. I imagine I'll only need one chance to find a family."

Barney laughed, and his round belly shook. "You must be with the Children's Aid Society. It's true our trains help children find new homes, but trains can do so much more. We can take people from one side of this great country to the other. If they want, we can even bring them back again. What do you think of that?"

"I don't think I'd like that much," Franky said, shaking his head.

"Well, why not?"

"Cause if I come back, the headmistress will think I've been bad, and she'll wallop me a good one."

Barney considered that for a moment. "Yes, I can see why that would be a good reason not to return. I guess maybe you should wait and come back when you're a little older. Maybe you can visit with those new parents you're going to find."

Franky scratched his head. "Why would we visit?"

Barney shuffled his bulk from one foot to the other. "Why most people come to see friends and family, I suppose."

"Then I guess I don't need to come back, 'cause I don't have neither."

Barney's face turned serious. "Don't you go worrying about that just now. I've seen a great many children board this train in hopes of finding a new home. I can tell you that most of those children did just that. Find a home, that is. You got a name, son?"

"Yes, sir," Franky said, nodding his head.

"Well, what is it?"

"Franky."

"Now that's a fine-sounding name." Barney rubbed his chin and studied Franky for a moment. "You know, come to think of it, I've seen a child get sent back a time or two, but that's mostly because they caused some trouble. You don't look like a troublemaker to me, are you, son?"

"No, sir."

"Good, then I have faith you'll find a home. If it's all the same to you, I'll say an extra prayer for you just to be safe." He pulled the chain hanging from his pocket, glanced at the silver timepiece, then back to Franky. "It's time to get things moving. You'd better run and join your group. When I get a chance, I'll check on you and see how you're enjoying the ride. It will be a bit, since I'll be pretty busy once we get on our way. Oh, and, Franky, try to get yourself a seat next to the window. There'll be lots to see along the way."

Franky thought to tell him he didn't like windows, but the conductor had already turned and walked away. Instead, he rejoined the group and managed to slip into line without being noticed.

Franky saw movement within the train car. Looking closer, he realized there was a man inside. A second later, the doors opened and the man jumped down, reached inside, and produced a small set of steps, which he placed in front of the opening. The man was dressed the same as Barney; however, that was where the resemblance stopped. He was half the size of Barney in all directions. He wore spectacles and had hair that seemed to grow out of his nose and curl on both sides.

He looked the children over and closed his eyes. Opening them once again, he plastered a smile on his face and extended his arm. “All aboard.”

Miss Childers turned to address the children in a no-nonsense tone. “Come along, children; we’ve no time to dawdle. You’re free to sit where you please as long as there’s no trouble. Find a seat quickly or we’ll find one for you. If you’re disruptive, you’ll find yourself sitting with me.”

Franky hurried to keep up with the line. Though he had no quarrels with the woman, he had no desire to sit with her.

He wasn’t sure what he’d expected the inside of the train to look like, but this wasn’t it. The cabin was about as basic as anything he’d ever seen. So much so that it reminded him of the transition room. Only here, there were windows and rows of bench seats on either side of the cabin to sit upon. There was enough room on each bench for the children to sit two and three deep, depending on their size.

Franky walked through the aisle looking for a seat, not minding that all the window spots had already been claimed. He’d reached the front of the cabin and turned to make another pass when he saw the two brothers who’d nearly been separated.

Alfred was sitting next to the window and George leaned across him, pointing at something on the other side of the windowpane. Though he couldn’t see their faces, he was sure both boys were smiling.

George turned his head, saw him watching, and sighed. He slid closer to Alfred and tilted his head toward the open space. “You can sit if you want.”

Franky hurried to sit before the boy changed his mind.

“You’re the one they call Franky?” George asked.

Franky nodded his head.

“How is it you know’d about the trains before anyone

else?"

"Headmistress told me. She asked me if I wanted to go."

"None of us got asked. What makes you so special?"

Franky swallowed. He'd been asking himself the same thing. "I don't know."

"I heard someone say it's because that girl with the scar is your girlfriend."

Please don't make me move. All the seats are taken. "Mistress Anna is not my girlfriend."

George looked him over. "That's what I said."

Franky's eyes grew wide. "You did?"

"Sure, I did. You're just a runt. You'd have to use a chair just to kiss her."

Franky wrinkled his nose. "Why would I want to kiss her?"

George laughed. "You wouldn't unless she was your girlfriend."

Franky pondered this for a moment. "I ain't never kissed no one. Have you?"

The smile left George's face. "Only my momma."

At the mention of their mother, Alfred, who'd been listening intently to the conversation, began blinking back tears.

George used the boy's shirttail to dry his eyes. "Don't you cry, Alfred. Momma would want us to be strong."

"Okay," Alfred said with a sniff.

"Did your momma die?" Franky's words came out in a whisper.

"No, she's in prison," George said and sighed when Alfred's tears turned to sobs. He draped his arm around his brother and narrowed his eyes. "They took her off just before they dumped me and Alfred at the asylum."

"What…" Franky swallowed the rest of his question when George shook his head. Instead, he looked forward and said, “I don’t have a momma. Never did.”

“I guess that makes you lucky, then,” George replied.

Franky tilted his head, wondering if he’d heard the boy right. “I am?”

“Sure you are,” George said. “Nobody can take something away if you never had it.”

Franky had never thought of it that way, but it made sense. “I guess I am lucky.”

“That’s what I said,” George agreed.

The train jerked to a start, and the train car filled with excited chattering. Alfred turned and faced the window and George kept his arm draped protectively over his younger brother’s shoulder.

George thought him to be lucky because he’d never had a mother. Franky thought Alfred was the lucky one. He’d give just about anything to have a brother like George.

Chapter Eight

As they cleared the city, the train picked up speed, and with the new momentum, the train car rocked back and forth along the tracks. Though he wasn't sitting next to the window, Franky could still see bits and pieces. Mostly he enjoyed listening as George pointed out the changes in the landscape. Much like when Mistress Anna read from a book, George had a way of describing things in such detail, Franky didn't feel as if he were missing anything.

George pointed then leaned back so Franky could get a better look. Franky blinked at the brilliant sparkle of a large lake nearly as blue as the sky. Sitting on top of the lake were large white birds with curved necks. As they passed, one of the birds dipped its head underwater and Alfred laughed.

As the train rolled on, the landscape changed, giving way to large rolling hills covered with trees, some so tall, Franky was sure the tops would reach the tallest building in the city. He wondered for a moment what it would be like to climb one of those trees, further wondering if it was possible to climb all the way to the top. If he succeeded, then what? He'd never climbed a tree before and had no clue as to how he would get down.

He swallowed, deciding it would be best to play under them instead, a thought pushed aside when he realized there were so many trees that in some places he couldn't see the sunlight under their branches. Being alone in a dark room was one thing; being alone in the wilderness was something he could do without. Even the thought of it made his stomach sore.

The forest gave way to lush green pastures. Seconds later, the train cabin erupted with excited chatter as the children made guesses as to what they saw. Franky scrambled to his knees and stretched his neck for a better view. *Horses. No, they were smaller.* Dozens of small brown ponies standing in the field grazing to their heart's content. They appeared a bit on the puny side, but Franky didn't think it was anything to get all excited over. Just as he was about to sit, the train whistle blared and the ponies lifted their heads. Only they weren't ordinary ponies, at least not like any he'd seen. A few had enormous tree branches that appeared to grow right out of their heads.

Alfred sucked in air and pointed.

"What's so funny?" George asked when Franky laughed.

"The ponies have trees on their head." Franky's comment drew laughter from both George and Alfred.

George scratched his head. "They're not tree branches; they're horns. And horses don't have horns, so they must be cows. Though they didn't look like no cow I ever saw."

A head popped up from the seat behind them. "They ain't cows neither. Those be deer. Mighty fine eating they are. I had me some deer sausage once, and boy, I can almost taste it right now."

Franky stared at the kid in disbelief. "You mean to tell me you ate a animal?"

"Sure, people do it all the time. Where do you think meat comes from? Cows. Eggs come from chickens. Why, that ham you had on your biscuit today came from a pig. People don't eat horses so much, but I've had it a time or two. I had dog once, a bit tough if you ask me, but you get hungry enough, you'll eat about anything."

Until this morning, Franky had never eaten meat. At least none that he remembered. Meals at the asylum were a simple mush given several times a day. He thought about the ham biscuit he'd eaten for breakfast and gulped, remembering the story Miss Anna had read about a pig. Had he truly eaten the animal?

The boy leaning over the seat laughed. "What's a matter, kid? You don't look so good."

"Leave Franky alone," George said, pushing him away from the seat. "You okay, Franky? He's right; you do look a bit green."

Franky nodded his head, but in truth, he wasn't all right. He'd felt queasy since leaving the train station but was afraid to say anything for fear of being sent back. Now all he could do was picture the little pig in the book. He couldn't recall the name of the book itself, but he remembered the story just fine. The pig had been the pet of a girl who'd lived on a farm. The girl had loved the pig, who followed her around like a dog. The little girl seemed happy with that pig, and after Miss Anna made the pig sounds, Franky had fallen in love with him too.

The noise in the train car escalated once again as the kids saw something else that grabbed their attention. Alfred and George stayed glued to the window as Franky sat staring at the back of the seat in front of him. He thought of the ham biscuit he'd eaten, guilt gnawing at him as he recalled how tasty the salty ham had been. He closed his eyes and saw Miss Anna turning the picture book around so the children could see the little girl holding her pet pig. His stomach churned as she screwed up her face and emitted an oink. He remembered thinking that one day he too would like to have a pig. All of a sudden, there was no holding back. Franky sat bolt upright and pulled the cloth bag containing his new clothes to his face and hurled. He opened the bag, saw the bits of ham, and repeated the process.

Miss Childers was upon him in a second, pulling him

from his seat and guiding him to the far end of the cabin.

"Wow, he puked even more than Johnny did this morning," someone said in admiration.

"Someone else got sick?" Miss Childers' voice was full of concern.

"Sure did. Puked all over Headmistress' shoes." The boy laughed.

"It's an epidemic!" Miss Adams said, looking at Franky and wringing her hands. "Why, the boy is plumb green. We must demand they stop the train so we can catch the next one home. It won't be long before all the children are ill and what are we to do then?"

Miss Childers looked at Franky and nodded her head. She pulled the soiled cotton sack from Franky and frowned. "Find someplace to dispose of this and then go forward and alert the conductor."

Miss Adams looked at the bag and closed her eyes briefly. Opening them once more, she gripped the bag with the tips of her fingers, then holding it at arm's length, rushed off in the opposite direction.

Miss Childers hurried to move the children in the surrounding seats forward. Franky started to get up, and Miss Childers held up a hand to stop him. "You stay where you are. I'll not have you infecting the whole cabin. Why, they never should've allowed you children to leave your asylum in the first place. They probably thought it best to send you out and let you die on someone else's watch."

Fear crept over Franky. "Am I going to die?"

Miss Childers stopped and looked him over. "No. At least, I don't think so. Though lord knows what kind of sickness you have."

Franky didn't think he was going to die; as a matter of fact, his stomach was feeling much better. Still, how would he know if he was going to die? He was just a little kid and weren't adults supposed to know more than kids? He sank back onto the bench blinking back tears that threatened, wishing he'd never stepped foot on the train.

Moments later, he heard a commotion, peeked around the edge of the seat, and saw Barney's hulk of a frame heading in his direction. Though the train rocked from side to side, Barney navigated the aisle without issue. Franky waved at the man and was rewarded with a brief smile.

"Where's this sick boy you'll have me stop my train for?" Barney's voice boomed for all to hear.

Miss Childers pulled herself from her seat, tugged at her waistcoat, and pointed toward Franky.

Barney focused his attention on Franky, who ducked behind the seat to avoid the man's glare. A second later, the big man was hovering over him and shaking his head. Without a word, he bent and lifted Franky as if he were weightless, standing him on the bench for further inspection.

Franky looked down the aisle and saw every head in the cabin watching. Some stared with curious expressions, others glowering, letting Franky know they were not pleased with the prospect of being returned to the city. Franky turned away from their silent accusations, preferring to face the big man's scrutiny instead.

Barney lifted Franky's head, turning it from side to side. Next, he placed his plate-sized hand on Franky's forehead. Removing his hand, he smiled. "Are you sick, Franky?"

I don't feel sick. "Miss Childers says I may die."

Instantly, the smile was replaced by a deep grimace and Barney cast an accusing glance toward Miss Childers.

"I…I didn't say that," Miss Childers stammered. "Well, not intentionally anyway."

"I know what the woman said to you. But I want to hear

it from you. How do you feel, son?" Barney said, ignoring Miss Childers.

"I feel better now that I threw up," Franky replied.

"Threw up, did you?" Barney asked with a tilt of the head.

"Twice," Franky said, wrinkling his nose.

"He's not the only one," Miss Childers interjected. "The children say there was another boy who got sick before they left the asylum this morning."

"Franky, did you know the boy who got sick?" Barney asked.

"I knew his face."

"Then you didn't talk to him today?"

Franky shook his head. "No, sir, I've never talked to him."

Barney smiled. "I'm going to ask you a question, and this is very important. Do you remember when you first started feeling ill?"

Franky screwed up his face, trying to remember the exact moment. "I think when the train started moving."

"And that's when you got sick?"

"No, sir. It's just when I started feeling ill." Franky lifted his arm and pointed his finger. "I didn't get sick until he told me I ate an animal. I've never eaten an animal before, and well, I guess it just didn't sit well with me. It being a pig and all."

Barney's eyebrows arched. "You don't like pigs?"

"I like pigs alright, but I was thinking of having one as a pet. That boy told me I'd eaten one, and then I thought about the cute little noises they make, and the next thing I knew, I was throwing up. I looked in the sack, saw the pig I'd eaten, and threw up again."

Barney frowned. "Was eating the pig that bad?"

Franky looked down at his shoes. “Actually, I liked it just fine. That was before I knew what it was I was eating. But I can tell you one thing: it tastes much better going down than it does coming up.”

Barney laughed. “I’m sure it did, son. Now, how would you like to go back to your seat?”

“That will never do,” Miss Childers objected. “We have to keep the boy quarantined from the rest of the children until we get back to New York.”

Barney turned and pulled himself up to his full height, which really wasn’t necessary since he already towered over everyone in the cabin. “I will not be stopping the train and there is no reason to keep the boy isolated. He had a queer stomach is all. I’ve seen it at least a hundred times before. The train rocks from side to side and some people don’t handle it too well. Some get over it, others never do, but I can tell you he’s not sick. Not in the way you think anyway.”

“But what about the other boy?” Miss Adams argued.

“Can’t say what was wrong with the other boy, but he’s not my concern. The train has a schedule to keep, and I see no reason to worry the engineer about this. We’ll be stopping to collect water for the engine soon, but it's just a water stop in the middle of nowhere. There’ll be no one getting off the train.”

Barney started to leave and hesitated, turning his attention back to Franky. “Boy, don’t you go worrying about eating animals. Some animals are good for petting and some are good for eating. Take it from a man who knows a thing or two about eating. Pigs taste a great deal better than they smell. You get a chance to eat one again, and you take a big ole bite for your friend Barney, you hear?”

“Yes, sir,” Franky said with a nod of the head, though he wasn’t sure why people would want to eat them since they smelled so bad.

Chapter Nine

Franky was not allowed to return to his seat since Miss Childers and Miss Adams were not as convinced as Barney that he wasn't truly ill. In some respects, it was good news, as he got to have the seat all to himself. While others were cramped with the new seating arrangement, Franky could look out the window or stretch across the seat whenever he grew tired. While he liked the latter, he did find himself missing his seat companions. Especially George and the boy's ability to use words to show him more than his eyes were seeing.

The whistle blared, and the train began to slow. Franky scrambled to his knees to look out the window. They'd made several short stops over the course of the day to collect water for the train's steam engine and he hoped the spigot was on his side of the train so he could watch the men on the platform. While the previous stops had been in the middle of nowhere with a large tank and spout to deliver the water, this stop proved to be more. Several small buildings came into view and he could see people milling around in the street. Franky pushed his face to the window for a better view.

The buildings stood in a straight line and had signs hanging above the doors. Unlike the buildings in the city, not one had more than a second floor. Some of the upper levels even had porches with rails. A man in a gray suit stepped onto one of the upper porches, removed his hat, and waved at the train. The kids thrust their arms out the window, waving in return.

There were several motorcars parked along the street, and just as many horses tied along the front of the buildings. As the train slowed to a stop, he saw several teams of horses with long flat wagons attached. In the back of one of the wagons were three children who looked to be about his age staring at the train in rapt fascination. He smiled, knowing his expression mirrored theirs.

A town. A small one, but a town to be sure.

"Another water stop?" Miss Childers asked when the train porter came into the cabin moments later.

"Yes, ma'am, that and to load more coal. We'll be here for approximately forty minutes if you and the children would like to step off and stretch your legs. There'll be two whistles before we leave. The first, a warning letting you know to head back to the train. The second ten minutes after. See to it all are on board before the second, as we'll be leaving shortly after," he said then left the way he came.

"You heard the porter, children. Off the train and be quick about it. Stay close and mind your manners," she said firmly.

Franky stood, expecting to depart with the others, and Miss Childers shook her head. "You'll be staying on the train this outing, Franky. No need to make the whole town sick."

Franky's heart sank. "But Barney said…"

"I know what the conductor said. I'm sure he's had plenty of experience with train sickness, but I doubt the man's had any dealings with children. You will remain on the train today. If you're still feeling well tomorrow, maybe we'll let you join the others."

Franky sighed and returned to his seat, sulking as Miss Childers and the others departed. He turned to the window; his mood further darkened as the children were marched to the side yard of a stark white building with a steep pointed roof. *Grass; they're actually stepping on grass!* Sure, he'd seen grass when peeking through the bars of the fence that enclosed the play yard, but he'd never actually stepped on it. While some of the older children stood around in groups, many of the younger ones ran in wide circles chasing each other.

Franky sighed. *I wonder what it feels like to run upon the grass.*

He turned from the window, preferring not to watch something he himself could not enjoy. He leaned his back against the window, took off his hat, and tossed it into the air. Catching it, he repeated the process until he grew bored. Next, he laced his fingers together and began rotating his thumb, racing them one way then twiddling them in the opposite direction. He heard a knock on the window and turned, surprised to see the porter peering in at him. Franky looked and saw that the man was standing on a tall wooden ladder. The porter dipped a cloth in the bucket he held then dragged it across the window glass to remove the grime. When the porter finished wiping the window, he motioned for him to lower the window and Franky scrambled to his knees to comply.

"What are you doing in there all alone?" he asked when Franky lowered the glass.

"Miss Childers thinks I'm sick."

"You don't look sick."

Franky shook his head. "No, sir, I feel just fine."

"Who are you talking to, Gilbert?"

Franky turned his head to see Barney heading their way. He stuck out his hand and waved at the big man.

Barney cast a glance toward the group of children. "Why aren't you out getting fresh air with your friends?"

"Miss Childers said I have to stay on the train. Said you may know about trains, but you don't know nothing about children."

Barney's jaw twitched. "Meet me at the door."

Franky thought to object, but Barney was already

heading toward the door. He raced through the aisle, making it to the door just as Barney arrived. He looked over Barney's head and realized he could see neither the side yard nor the children.

"Come along, Franky," Barney said.

"Please, sir, I'd rather stay."

Barney frowned. "You don't want to play with your friends."

More than anything else. "Yes, sir, it's just that I don't want to make Miss Childers angry. If I do, she won't allow me to join the others tomorrow."

Barney looked toward the porter. "Hey, Gilbert, when you're finished there, I want you to go to the caboose and keep a lookout. If anyone from the group near the church heads this way, you're to stall them until I get back. Got it?"

"Sure thing, Barney," Gilbert said, waving his cleaning cloth.

"Come along, son," Barney said and gave him a look that implied it was best not to argue.

Franky hurried down the temporary stairs, surprised when Barney took off in the opposite direction of the others. The man walked fast, passing train car after train car, and Franky found himself running to keep up. As they reached the engine, Barney stopped, stuck two fingers into his mouth, and whistled.

A man stuck his head out of the small window. "Hey ya, Barney, what can I be doing for you?"

"I was wondering if you can give my friend Franky here a quick tour," Barney yelled over the noise of the engine.

The man smiled. "Be happy to."

Franky tilted his head, wondering how he was supposed to get up there, then noticed a thin ladder attached to the side of the enormous engine and heaved a sigh. While he'd climbed stairs, he'd never climbed a ladder before —certainly not one attached to the side of a train engine.

I'll never make it.

Before he could voice that concern, Barney's hands gripped his waist, lifting him high enough that he could grab hold of the sides and climb into the opening.

Franky looked down at Barney. "Aren't you coming?"

Barney laughed. "While you're too small for the ladder, I have the opposite problem. Besides, I've seen it all before."

It was a little quieter and a lot hotter inside the engine. Though the man remained seated, he took off his glove and extended his hand. While Franky had seen it done, this was the first time anyone thought him important enough to warrant a handshake. He placed his hand in the man's and smiled as the man pumped his arm up and down several times before releasing his hand.

"The name's Roscoe. I'm the engineer of this train. Do you know what that means?"

Franky shook his head from side to side.

"It means I drive the train." He took off his cap, exposing a head of white hair. "See, they even gave me this here hat to prove it."

Franky peered at the inside of the engine covered in steel with knobs and lettering and frowned. "How do you see to drive the train?'

The man stood and pointed to the seat where he'd been sitting. "Have a seat."

The seat was simple and sat upon a tall pole with a ring at the bottom to place one's feet. Franky climbed into the chair and laughed when his feet didn't even come close to touching the ring.

The man tapped on one of the glass circles in front of him. "These are my gauges. The numbers in there tell me how the train is running. It tells me when we need more steam and when she's running too hot. That lever above you is for the horn. No, don't pull it, or people will think it's time to come aboard. Now, hop up onto your knees and take a gander out that window there next to you."

Franky stuck his head out.

"Okay, now look to the front of the train."

Franky did as the man said but still couldn't see much, so he leaned further.

"That's how I see to guide the train," the man said, taking hold of Franky's shirt and pulling him back inside.

"But I didn't see nothing. What if something gets in the way?"

"I see enough. You learn to look ahead. You get used to it, and before long, you just know. If I see a road coming, I give a tug on the whistle to let them know to get out of my way. She's big and loud, so most people and animals have done seen her before I sound the alarm. If not…" Rosco shrugged his shoulders. "An engine this big doesn't stop just because something gets in her way. When she gets hungry, we feed her."

Franky felt his eyes grow wide. "The train eats?"

"Of course she eats." Roscoe smiled a wide smile. "Want to feed her?"

Franky gulped.

"Climb on down here. Now pick up that shovel and take a scoop of that coal," he said, pointing.

Franky attempted to lift the coal shovel, but it was long and much too heavy for a six-year-old boy.

Roscoe slipped his hands into his gloves, lifted a shovel full of coal with ease, and turned to face Franky. Franky looked about the cabin for something resembling a mouth but didn't see one.

Roscoe nodded to the front of the train. "See that lever

right there? Grab hold and pull down real hard."

Franky did as told and the steel parted, showing a cavern of brilliant orange and yellow coal. The temperature inside the cabin rose immediately. Franky let go of the lever and fell on his backside as the steel came together with a clang.

Roscoe laughed. "I guess I should have warned you she gets a bit hot-headed when she's hungry. Now pick yourself up and give it another go. Stand to the side and keep your hand on the lever until I pull the shovel free."

Franky stood and placed his hand on the steel handle once more.

"Now remember to keep it open until I bring the shovel clear or she'll eat that too."

Franky pulled the lever and watched with a mixture of fear and awe. Roscoe thrust the shovel into the opening, shaking it from side to side. As the coal landed in the fire, hot embers flew into the air. Franky wanted to let go but, remembering Roscoe's words, held tight until the man pulled the shovel free.

Roscoe dipped the shovel into the coal once more, emptied the coal into a black metal bucket in the corner, returned the shovel to the coal car, and turned toward Franky once more. "Grab you a handful of that coal from the bucket."

Franky walked to the bucket and picked up a large handful. When he turned around, Roscoe's hand was on the lever. He stepped in front of the opening, waited for Roscoe to pull the lever, then stood looking into the embers, his hands trembling.

"You going to feed her or just stand there gaping?" Roscoe said with a chuckle. "Toss it into the firebox and be mindful of any flying embers."

Franky did as told, blinking as the coal fell and a burst of tiny embers sprang to life.

Roscoe closed the opening and smiled. "Want to do it

again?"

Franky nodded and hurried to retrieve some more coal, repeating the process several more times.

"What you're doing is feeding the engine. The gasses from the fire go into the flues and heat the water. Once the water boils, it makes the steam. The steam then enters the valve chests and the valves move back and forth to move the pistons and make the train go. Those gauges I showed you help me to make sure the steam doesn't get built up. If that happens, the whole engine could blow and nothing to be done about it. Does that make sense?"

Franky wanted to say it did, but it was all too complicated. "Not so much, sir."

Roscoe closed the door and shook his head. "Sorry, son, sometimes I think everyone is just as fascinated with the inner workings as I am. I think that'll do her for now."

"Okay," Franky said, hiding his disappointment.

Roscoe handed him a cloth to wipe his face. "You built yourself up a nice sweat there. Best be cleaning yourself up."

Franky swiped the cloth over his face several times. When he handed it back to Roscoe, it was nearly as black as the coal. Roscoe pocketed the rag and handed him a tall green bottle of liquid, then opened a second bottle and took a nice long drink.

"It's a soft drink," Roscoe said when Franky merely stared at the bottle. "It'll help quench your thirst."

Franky tipped the bottle and took three long swallows. On the last pull, the liquid seemed to get caught in the middle of his throat. His eyes watered, and for an instant, he felt as if he couldn't breathe. Franky burped, sending a spray of soda forward, then blinked several times, wondering how coal from the fire managed to find its way into his nose. Slowly, the sensation lessened and he was able to breathe normally once more.

Roscoe's face brightened. "See how that drink got lodged in your throat for a moment. It's kind of what I was just talking about. If the gauges aren't monitored properly or if God forbid one of the gauges gets stuck, then that steam builds up and has no place to go, so it just explodes over everything. Does that make sense?"

It made even more sense when he explained it like that. Franky nodded his head.

Roscoe pointed toward the bottle. "Take yourself another drink."

Franky gaped at the bottle once more.

"Go on now, just a sip at a time," Roscoe encouraged.

Franky gathered his nerve and took a sip, then another and another. While the fizzy drink burned, it was a good burn. Draining the bottle, he burped loud and long.

"There now, that's how it's supposed to work," Roscoe said, taking the empty bottle.

The sound of a shrill whistle drew their attention to the door. Both looked out and saw Barney take an impatient glance toward his timepiece.

Roscoe looked at his own timepiece in return. "Heed my words, Franky. An engineer isn't worth his salt if he doesn't listen to his conductor. That man keeps this train on schedule. If he tells you to do something, you best listen to him."

Franky wanted to ask if that meant Miss Childers was wrong but thought better of it. "Yes, sir. I'll listen to him alright."

"Good. Now turn around and we'll get you off this engine," Roscoe said, lowering Franky into Barney's waiting arms.

Franky's feet had no sooner touched the ground than the horn blared announcing time to return to the train. Franky looked to see Roscoe staring at him from the window. The man tipped his hat and smiled.

"We better hurry," Barney said with a nod to Roscoe. "He's going to be releasing pressure and you don't want to get wet. Roscoe has to do that from time to time, you know."

Franky smiled as he hurried beside Barney. *Yes, he did know.*

Chapter Ten

Franky was sitting in his seat when the group returned to the train. After the children were seated, Miss Adams approached. She took in his appearance and her eyes grew wide.

"Miss Childers, if you'd be so kind as to join me," she said without taking her eyes off him.

"What is it now?" the older woman asked, then she too stood at the end of his seat, mouth agape. "Franky, what in heaven's name have you been doing while we were gone?"

"I dropped my hat and had to crawl under the seat to retrieve it," Franky said and brushed at the soot that covered his clothing. Better her to think him unruly than to find out he'd disobeyed her.

"Crawled under all the seats is more like it," Miss Childers sneered. "This will never do. Why, you look like a little street beggar. Where are your placement clothes?"

"My what?"

"The new clothes you received before you left your asylum," Miss Childers clarified.

"They were in the sack," Franky said, glancing at Miss Adams, whose face turned a tad white.

"What sack?" Miss Childers turned to Miss Adams. "Do you know what sack he's referring to?"

Miss Adams nodded her head. "The sack the boy got sick in."

Miss Childers closed her eyes briefly. "And where is the sack now?"

"You told me to get rid of it, so I tossed it off the train."

The train whistle blared for a second time. Miss Childers placed her fingers at the brim of her nose and blew out a long breath then turned toward Miss Adams. "Pass out the evening meals to the children while I find something to get some of the grime from the boy's hands. If I didn't know better, I'd say he'd been playing in a coal bin."

"But what of his clothes? The child will never find himself a home in his present state," the younger woman said wringing her hands.

The older woman smiled. "There's no need to fret, Miss Adams. This is your first placement trip. Let me assure you, if this is the worse we have to face, then we'll have fared well."

While Miss Childers' words seemed to appease Miss Adams, the same could not be said for Franky. While he'd enjoyed his trip to the engine, he hadn't known there'd be consequences. He hadn't planned on getting dirty. But boy, he'd sure enjoyed throwing the coal into the fire. As the train began to move, he thought about what Miss Adams said about him not finding a home. It would mean he'd get sent back. Going back to the asylum wouldn't be bad; he'd lived there all his life. With the exception of the adventures of the day, he never knew anything else. What worried him was what the headmistress would do if he were sent back. Would she agree that getting sick was out of his control, or would she make an example out of him? She'd made it clear she wouldn't be happy if anyone returned. As he pondered his fate, his stomach began to churn. He swallowed, worried that he was going to throw up once more.

Miss Childers returned with a pail of water and a towel, took one look at him, and handed him the bucket. Franky lowered his head, opened his mouth, and let lose a burp that echoed inside the metal bucket and could be heard throughout the cabin.

Franky pulled his head from the bucket, saw the look of shock on Miss Childers' face, and burst out laughing. To his surprise, Miss Childers joined in. Soon the whole cabin was filled with unrestrained laughter. The only one that didn't find it amusing was Miss Adams, who stared at Miss Childers as if the woman had completely lost her mind.

"That will be enough, children. We've all had a good laugh. Now it's time for us all to settle down," Miss Childers said, regaining her composure. She retrieved the bucket from Franky, dipped the towel inside, wrung out the excess water, and gently scrubbed at Franky's face. After several moments, she took hold of his chin, rotating it from side to side. "You'll do. Now put your hands in the bucket and use the towel to clean them. I'll see you get something to eat. You keep that down and I think it will be safe to move you back to your seat."

Franky went to work on his hands, watching in amazement as the grime turned both water and towel black. As he scrubbed, Miss Childers slid from the seat and called Miss Adams to her.

"You did not approve of my laughing," Miss Childers said when Miss Adams grew near.

"It unsettled the children." A soft pink blush traveled up Miss Adams' neck and covered her cheeks as if she were ashamed of her words. "I was told the key to control is to be firm."

"To be certain, there is a need to guide with a firm hand. But one must also remember that these are children and children have energy. If they are not allowed to release that energy upon occasion, then at some point, they will act out. Now, wouldn't you agree that a child would be best served to release their energy through laughter than anger?"

Though they lowered their voices, Franky was still close enough to hear their conversation. He kept his head lowered so they wouldn't realize he was listening. It surprised him that much like Roscoe, Miss Childers had used his burp as a teaching moment. He wondered if all adults were so smart and thought the answer to be no. The realization surprised him. He slid a glance toward the younger woman, wondering if she'd understood her lesson. Her eyes grew wide and she nodded her head. Franky smiled. He wanted to speak up, tell them about his conversation with Roscoe about the steam, and tell them he too understood. In the end, he kept that bit of knowledge to himself. Sometimes knowing was enough.

***

True to her word, Franky was sent back to his seat as the day turned to dusk. Some might have preferred to remain in a seat where they could stretch out, but Franky was happy to be sent back, preferring the company of his friends to the cold darkness of the rear seat.

It didn't take long for darkness to creep inside the cabin of the train. The lights, dim as they were, didn't do much to illuminate the interior of the train. With nothing to see outside, the children soon settled. For a while, Franky listened to the errant sobs of children who'd braved their fate until finally giving way to their fears. Best to be thought brave than a coward, even though admittedly the so-called coward was likely mimicking how most of the others felt.

Franky didn't cry, not that he was opposed to doing just that, especially if he'd had to spend the night in the seat by himself. But since George and Alfred had welcomed him back without complaint, sitting next to the brothers gave him a small sense of belonging that he'd never felt before. He thought, at least for this night, he would close his eyes and pretend. Pretend that he too was their brother, and they were traveling with their family, a mother, father, and maybe a sister as well.

He woke to the sound of whispers, opened his eyes,

discovering it was still dark. He remained still, wondering if he'd dreamed it, then heard the voices once more.

"Alfred, wake up," George whispered once more.

"What is it?" Alfred's voice was heavy with sleep.

"Shh," the older boy said in return. "Keep your voice down, so we don't wake the others."

"What is it?" Alfred repeated, keeping his voice equally low.

"When we were in the churchyard, I heard some of the other boys talking. They said that sometimes they don't keep brothers together."

"But I..." The rest of Alfred's words were muffled. Franky knew George must have clamped his hand over his brother's mouth.

"You've got to keep quiet," George repeated, lowering his hand.

Franky needed to scratch his nose, but dared not move lest he reveal he was awake.

"I woke you early to warn you it could happen and to tell you I have a plan. If you get picked and I do not, I will come for you. I will find you and see to it we stay together. I swear it, Alfred. I will find you. You believe me, don't you?"

George's words were so intense, Franky found himself nodding in response.

"Good," George said. "Now go back to sleep and never speak of this to anyone. Just know I'm a man of my word."

Franky didn't think George to be a man. All the same, he had no doubt the boy would keep his word. As he drifted back to sleep, he wondered what the boys would do if it were George who was picked first instead.

When next he woke, it was strangely dark. He could hear children chattering about him and wondered why no one was hushing them to allow others to sleep. He got his explanation a moment later when the sun suddenly appeared.

"How'd the sun come out so fast?" Franky exclaimed.

"We were in a tunnel." Miss Childers said for all to hear. "We're in the mountains, and they're too high for the train to climb, so they blasted holes into the rock to make tunnels for the train to pass through."

"What if the mountains fall onto the train?" someone asked.

"That's highly unlikely," Miss Childers replied, then changed the subject. "We'll be stopping in Harrisburg, Pennsylvania tomorrow morning. It's the first official stop on our journey, and God willing, some of you will be leaving us. Do not get discouraged if you do not find a placement at the first stop. There will be others. We rarely fail to find placements for those we bring."

Her words gave Franky comfort. He slid a glance to his seat companions. The boys were holding hands, fingers laced so tightly, their knuckles were white. Neither boy spoke. They just sat there with their hands clasped together as if that simple action could somehow keep them together. He ached to join hands with them. He hoped that someday someone would love him as much as George loved his brother and further hoped that day would come soon.

***

Franky and the others departed the train at the Pennsylvania Railroad Station in Harrisburg. While the station was nice, it was not as grand as Union Station. Once outside, they marched down the four steps that traveled the length of the porch and into the brick-paved street walking several blocks to an ornate structure Miss Childers referred to as a church.

Franky rather liked this building with multiple pitches in the roof. Protruding from one of the points was a chimney-type enclosure, and inside the enclosure was a large bell. Large windows of reds, blues, greens, and yellows sparkled in the sunlight. He and many of the children stared at the building in awe, most agreeing they'd never seen anything so beautiful.

The door opened and a man in a dark suit held the door, welcomed them inside, and led the way to a cavernous room surrounded with more of the colorful windows. At first, Franky thought the windows to have lights but soon realized it was the sun that made them appear so bright. A group of men stood in the center of the room. Miss Childers walked over to greet them and they smiled their welcome.

A woman in shoes that made noise when she walked greeted Miss Adams and then led the group down a small passageway. Halfway down the hallway, the woman stopped and held her arms up, pointing to the doors. "Girls may change in there and the boys are to take this room. We have volunteers who've agreed to help see to the children."

The group split, the girls going to the room on one side of the hallway, while Franky and the boys poured into the other, eager to see what lay inside the room. Several women in dresses short enough to show the bottom of their legs stood just inside the door. Three stacks of chairs sat nestled along the wall and a writing desk sat in front of a blank blackboard. There was another door along the far wall and several framed paintings adorned the brilliant white walls.

Tall, thin windows covered in the same colored glass lined the far wall. Franky smiled. He wouldn't mind sleeping next to a window if it had colored glass.

The lady with the loud shoes cleared her throat. "Listen up, children. My name is Mrs. Spencer. It is time to change into your new clothes. Raise your hand if you require any assistance and one of these ladies will help you. There is a washroom behind that door in case anyone needs it."

Franky kept his hands securely in his pockets as the

other children pulled their new clothes from the bag. Some of the older boys took their bags to the washroom. Franky thought about following them, but the older boys weren't always nice when adults weren't in the room.

Mrs. Spencer looked in his direction and then started toward him, her shoes clicking against the floor as she walked. She took in his appearance and frowned. "You'll never find a home in your current state. Why aren't you changing?"

Franky looked down at his shoes. "I don't have any new clothes."

The woman's frown deepened. "I was told you'd all been given new clothes before you left New York."

"Oh, I got them," Franky said, nodding his head. "Miss Adams tossed them off the train."

The woman's eyes grew wide. "Tossed them off the train? Why in heaven's name would she do that?"

"Cause Miss Childers told her to."

Mrs. Spencer sighed. "Why would Miss Childers tell her to toss your clothes from the train?"

"Because I puked in the bag." Franky lifted his head and smiled at the woman. "Twice."

The woman took a step back. "Are you sick?"

"No, ma'am. I feel just fine. Barney, he's the conductor, said it was because I wasn't used to riding on the train, but I think it's because they made me eat a pig." Franky looked over his shoulder and lowered his voice. "They told me it was ham and so I didn't know it was a pig when I ate it. I like pigs, but I guess my stomach didn't like me eating one. Barney thinks pigs are for eating and not for petting, but I'm not so sure about that. I heard a story once about a girl who had one for a pet. Do you have a pig?"

The woman placed her hand on her chest. "No, I don't and I can't say I've ever thought about having one for a pet."

"Well, why not?"

The woman looked about the room. "Because pigs are not suited for pets."

"But they are," Franky corrected. "The pig in the story was a fine pet. She even liked to kiss the girl. Have you ever kissed a pig before?"

The woman fanned her face with her hand. "I most certainly have not."

Franky was growing bored with the woman. "You got any kids, lady?"

The woman looked down her nose at him. "No, I do not."

Franky nodded his head. "That explains it."

The woman's brows knitted together. "Explains what?"

"Why you're so grumpy. People who don't have kids seem to be grumpy around kids 'cause they aren't used to them."

The woman narrowed her eyes. "I can assure you I'm not grumpy."

"Then why are you yelling?" Franky said with a shrug.

"You certainly are a precocious child," she said, lowering her voice once more.

Franky wasn't sure what that meant, but from the way she said it, he didn't think it to be a good thing. He looked about the room then addressed her once more. "Maybe if you were to adopt one of these kids, you'd be used to kids and wouldn't be so grumpy."

The woman sighed. "I told you, I'm not grumpy. Wait, why not you?"

Franky didn't understand the question. "What?"

"You said I should adopt one of these kids. You didn't say I should adopt you. Aren't you hoping to get a home?"

"Why, sure I am."

"Then why didn't you ask me to adopt you?" the woman questioned.

"Because you're too grumpy," Franky answered truthfully. Apparently, not all adults liked when kids spoke the truth as the woman's face grew red and she stormed off in the other direction.

"Man, you really made her mad," George said after the woman walked away. "What did you say to her?"

"I told her I didn't want her to adopt me because she was too grumpy."

"What made her grumpy?"

Franky scratched his head. "I asked her if she ever kissed a pig."

George let out a laugh. "Yep. I expect that's what did it alright."

Chapter Eleven

Franky stood at the chalkboard drawing pictures with a stick of chalk. Mostly circles and triangles, which was the only thing he knew how to draw. While he enjoyed creating the images, he was not happy about being left out of today's placement proceedings.

He heard clonking in the hall and knew Mrs. Spencer, the lady with loud shoes, was coming to check on him once again. She'd been in several times, fussing over him briefly before leaving again, so he decided to ignore her this time. He kept his eyes on the task at hand, pulling the chalk across the blackboard to make large circles.

"What are you working on, Franky?" Mrs. Spencer asked, coming into the room.

He shrugged his shoulders in response.

She moved further into the room, picked up a piece of chalk, and drew a circle on the blackboard. She moved back, studied the image for a moment, then stepped back to the board and added another circle.

Franky kept his head straight but continued to watch as she added what looked to be eyes and ears. Next, she added some short stubby legs and a squiggly tail. She took another step back and let out an exaggerated sigh. A second later, she snapped her fingers together, moved back to the blackboard, and added a nose. Not any nose, but the nose of a pig.

Smiling, she lowered the chalk, brushed her hands together to remove the dust, and stepped back once again to admire her work. She glanced at Franky, who pretended not to notice.

"Now that's a pig I wouldn't mind kissing," she said, and much to his surprise, she leaned in and did just that, kissing the pig straight on the snout. When she lifted her head in his direction, her nose was covered with chalk.

Unable to ignore her silliness, Franky giggled.

"Ah, so you were watching," she said, wiping the chalk from her nose. "I know you're upset that you're not out with the others, but we're going to fix that soon."

"You mean I get to join them?" Franky's voice was filled with hope.

Mrs. Spencer dusted the chalk from her hands once more. "No, I'm afraid not today. But I've sent someone to find you some clothes to wear. That way, you'll look more presentable at your next stop."

"Oh," Franky replied.

"Don't sound so disappointed. I've seen the people that are here seeking children today. You wouldn't have liked any of them."

Franky turned to face her. "What's wrong with them?"

"What's wrong with them? Well, they're all wrong for you."

Franky scratched his head. "What makes them wrong for me?"

Mrs. Spencer pushed a strand of hair behind her ears. "Why, I can tell by looking at them that there is not a one in the room who'd be open to having a pig as a pet."

Franky sighed. "You're just teasing me."

She shook her head. "I most certainly am not. I may not be the smartest person in the room, but I know what a person looks like that would allow a pig in their home."

Franky looked the woman over to see if she was pulling his leg. She seemed serious enough. "What do the people out there look like?"

She smiled once more. "Why, they look like me."

"Ah, you were fooling."

"No, I told you I'm not. You see, you had me figured out all along. That's why you didn't want me to adopt you. You're smart that way. The way I see it, you're lucky that you don't have any clean clothes."

I don't feel lucky. Franky scratched at his head. "I am?"

"Sure you are. If you'd have had clean clothes, then one of those folks in the other room may have wanted to adopt you, and that would have been bad."

"It would?"

"Of course it would. Then you'd never have a pig."

He hadn't thought of it like that. "You really think they're all like you?"

She nodded her head. "Every last one of them."

"And you wouldn't let me have a pig?"

"Never," she assured him.

Franky walked to the blackboard and ran his hand over the board. When finished, he wiped his hands onto his pants.

Mrs. Spencer tilted her head. "What are you doing, Franky?"

"I'm making sure I don't get adopted. Not today anyway," he said, grinning. "Do you think this will work?"

Mrs. Spencer bit at her lower lip. "Franky, I think that will work just fine, but no more, okay?"

Franky looked at the white lines on his pants. "You think this is enough?"

She looked him over for a moment and frowned. Moving to the blackboard, she traced her finger across the pig nose she'd drawn then rubbed the chalk dust onto Franky's nose. "There. Now I think it's just right. I have to go check on things. Will you be all right until I return?"

"Yes, ma'am. Mrs. Spencer," he called just as she was leaving the room.

"Yes, Franky?"

"It's too bad you don't like pigs. You don't seem nearly as grumpy as I thought."

"Thank you, Franky. You don't seem all that bad yourself," she said.

Franky listened to her steps as she walked down the hallway. When at last he could hear her no more, he wiped a tear from his eye.

***

Much to Franky's chagrin, Barney was nowhere in sight and the new conductor couldn't be bothered with questions. After pestering the new porter with questions, Franky learned this to be a different train than the one on which they'd arrived. While the train cars were identical, their cabin was considerably less crowded the next morning when the children took their seats, with most able to sit two to a seat. Franky's seat was also lighter by one.

Alfred was gone.

They'd all spent the night in the church. Mrs. Spencer had seen to it Franky had a sponge bath, and he'd been given a brand new set of clothes, complete with a new hat and shoes. He'd been so busy, he hadn't been able to speak with George. Though from a distance, the boy didn't seem at all upset that his brother was not by his side. He'd wanted to ask him about it during the walk back to the train, but each time he'd tried, the boy had changed the subject. Franky slid into the seat beside George, but he didn't seem in the mood to talk, so Franky decided not to pester him about his brother.

The train horn sounded their departure and George leaned in close to Franky and kept his voice low. "I've got to go, kid. Don't you worry about me; I've been on my own before."

"Where are you going?" Franky whispered.

"To find Alfred. I'd take you with me, but I can't risk it. Take it easy, kid, and don't let anyone push you around." Franky wasn't sure who would be pushing him around, but he nodded his head, and George stood and moved into the aisle.

"Where are you going?" Miss Adams' voice drifted over the seat.

"I've got to use the water closet," George said, looking to the front door of the cabin.

"We've only just left the church. Why didn't you go there?" Miss Adams sounded annoyed.

"I did," George insisted. He made a show of dancing from foot to foot and scrunching up his face. "I really need to go, or I'm going to mess up my good clothes."

"Then be off with you. Straight there and straight back. No talking to the other passengers and no dawdling," she said firmly.

"Yes, ma'am," George agreed.

George made his way to the front of the cabin. Just as he reached the door, the train began to move. George cast a glance over his shoulder. As Franky looked on, one of the older boys began to cough. George smiled and gave a slight nod of the head.

"He's choking," another boy cried out.

Miss Adams and Miss Childers were out of their seat in an instant, rushing past Franky's seat and hovering around the boy who continued to cough. The forward door opened and Franky watched as George stepped onto the small platform that connected the train cars. Just as the door shut, George jumped from the train, raced a short distance, and hid behind a post. Franky hurried to his knees and peered out the window. As the train passed him by, George peeked from behind the post and tipped his hat. Franky pressed his face to the glass and watched until he could no longer see his friend. He pulled away from the window thinking that maybe he should say something now that the other boy had stopped coughing. He looked across the aisle and saw an older boy staring at him. As if reading his mind, the boy narrowed his eyes and shook his head.

Franky gulped and leaned back in his seat.

"Dear me," Miss Adams said to Miss Childers as they returned to their seat. "I thought we were going to lose the boy."

"Nonsense," Miss Childers said. "I've not lost a child yet."

Franky looked at the boy in the opposite seat once more. This time he was met with a grin. Not wishing to be labeled a snitch, Franky took advantage of his situation and slid next to the window for a better view. It wasn't long before he started seeing steep mountains in the distance. He leaned his head against the window staring in wonder at each new thing. Every now and then, he'd see a deer or some other animal he didn't recognize. Sometimes someone would call out the name, other times the train passed without him knowing what it was he saw.

The trees fascinated him just as much as the animals. He'd never seen so many trees in one place and now they were getting into the mountains, many of the leaves were brightly colored in yellows, reds, and oranges. When the sun caught them a certain way, it reminded him of the painted windows in the church. It occurred to him during one such time that in the last two days he'd seen more colors than he'd seen in all the years he'd spent in the asylum. He decided he much preferred a mix of colors than the blacks and blues he and the others were made to wear in the asylum.

The train started up an incline, slowing to where Franky thought it would be faster to walk than ride. He imagined himself jumping from the train and racing it up the mountain.

He pictured George jumping from the train and wondered of the boy's fate, further wondering how long it would take him to find his brother. He smiled, knowing George wouldn't stop until he'd done just that.

The mountain was closer now, so close Franky thought he might be able to touch it if his arms were just a little longer. He thought about lowering his window to try, quickly changing his mind when the train suddenly plunged into darkness. Franky was glad he wasn't running alongside the train. He did not like tunnels. He didn't like the dark, nor the smell, and certainly would not like to be alone on foot in one.

How did people get over the mountain before tunnels? He was still pondering that thought when the train made its way back into the sunlight. A moment later, the view opened, and he could see a valley far below the tracks. Speckled with houses, Franky knew it to be a small town. He looked for any sign of a road to explain how the townsfolk could reach the houses but didn't see one. After several more attempts, he decided it was just another mystery of which he might never know the answer.

A shadow fell over his seat and he turned to see Miss Adams hovering over him.

Her brow wrinkled as she searched the cabin. "Franky, where's your seatmate?"

"I don't know." He felt his face flush from the lie and hoped she wouldn't notice.

"You did have a seatmate this morning, did you not?"

"Yes, ma'am."

"Then where'd he go?" Her words seemed strained.

"He said he was going to the water closet." There, he hadn't told a lie.

Her eyes opened wide. "The water closet. Why that was hours since."

"Yes, ma'am." Franky frowned, trying to match the

look of concern on her face.

She peered around the cabin once more. "And he hasn't come back?"

He's not coming back. "No, ma'am."

She placed her hand on her chest. "Oh, my."

"What is the problem?" Miss Childers asked, approaching the seat.

"I'm afraid we may have lost a child," Miss Adams said, wringing her hands.

"Lost a child? Don't be ridiculous. All the children were here when we left this morning. I counted them myself."

"Yes, the boy was here, but he went to the water closet this morning and hasn't returned. I'm afraid we may have lost him."

"Nonsense, Miss Adams," Miss Childers chastised. "Children don't just jump off a moving train. You're getting yourself all worked up over nothing. Alert the porter to do a search for him. The boy's got to be around here somewhere."

For the second time that day, Franky realized that just because someone was in charge didn't mean they knew everything. He turned toward the window so they couldn't see his smile.

Chapter Twelve

Oct 1926, Fort Wayne, Indiana.

It was well into the night, but Franky couldn't sleep. The procession of children was smaller than when they'd first arrived. Two days had passed with children getting chosen and taken away, yet he was not amongst those chosen. At first, he'd told himself he wouldn't wish to go home with any of the people he'd spoken to, but now as the procession dwindled, he was beginning to fear no one wanted him. His only consolation was that he was not the only one left. Though he couldn't count, he knew the number of children left to exceed all his fingers and some of his toes. They were sleeping at the church, as they'd done the previous night. Tomorrow, those left were to board the morning train for a place called Chicago. Franky didn't know where Chicago was, but he'd been told it was to be their final stop before heading back to the asylum.

He was just drifting off to sleep when he first heard the whimpers.

Someone's crying.

He lay there trying to determine the direction of the sobs when a rustle of skirts told him one of the mistresses was up and seeing to the crying child. As the figure passed by the pew he lay on, he scooted to the end and peered down the aisle. It took him a moment to realize she was moving away from the sobbing, not toward it. He heard the church door open and shut once more, then the church was silent except for the sounds of sobbing.

Franky rolled off the bench and crouched near the end

of his pew, debating. Finally, unable to restrain himself he stood and made his way toward the sobs thinking to comfort the child.

As the sobs grew louder, his mouth went dry. He'd heard boys and girls crying, and this was neither. He trembled as he reached the final pew. Holding his breath, he peeked. He inhaled as his suspicions were confirmed. The sobs did not belong to a child.

Miss Childers!

She was lying on the pew, her knees pulled to her chest, sobbing as if her heart were breaking. Franky wanted to race back to his pew, close his eyes, and pretend he'd never seen the woman, however, his feet appeared frozen in place. He'd never seen a grown person cry before, and it was terribly unsettling. It wasn't until he heard his own sobs that he realized he too was crying. He closed his fists and placed them to his eyes in a desperate attempt to squelch the tears.

"What is it, Franky?" Miss Childers asked. She made an attempt to get up then blew out a ragged sigh.

"You're crying," Franky sobbed.

Miss Childers reached a hand toward him, her face screwed up, and she clutched her stomach, crying out in pain.

Franky bolted, running between the pews as if being chased. He ran to the door he'd seen Miss Adams use, frantically searching for the woman in the dark. He ran the length of the dirt path that led to the road and hesitated. He'd never been outside by himself before.

Miss Childers needs help.

He searched from side to side, wondering where he should go, saw a row of small houses, and decided to go in that direction thinking to knock on the doors until someone answered. He'd barely taken a handful of steps when he saw lights coming toward him.

A motorcar!

He took a breath and stepped into the street, waving his hands. The motor car swerved and came to a stop in front of the church.

He ran toward the motorcar, hoping to find help. The doors opened, and two people clambered from the car. Though it was dark, he could tell from the clothes that one of the figures was a man and the other female. The man reached inside, grabbed a bag, and ran toward the church. The woman rounded the car and hurried in his direction.

"Franky! What are you doing outside the church?"

Fresh tears sprang to his eyes at hearing Miss Adams' voice. "It's Miss Childers! Something is terribly wrong. I must get help."

Her expression softened, and she reached a hand toward him. "It's okay, Franky. The man who came with me is a physician. Come inside, and we'll see what he has to say."

Franky breathed a sigh of relief and took the offered hand.

The lights were on when they entered. The doctor hovered over Miss Childers, and most of the children were leaning over the pews watching as he examined her. The doctor placed a hand to Miss Childers' forehead and frowned. Placing his hands on her stomach, he poked and prodded until Miss Childers could bear it no longer.

"For the love of all that's holy, please stop," she said through tears and gritted teeth.

The doctor turned and faced Miss Adams. "We shall have to take her to the hospital."

Miss Adams wrung her hands. "We are such a long way from home. Can't you give her something to tide her over?"

The man shook his head. "I'm afraid the woman's condition is much too grave. If she doesn't have an operation soon, she will surely die."

At his words, several children burst into tears.

"There there, children, Miss Childers will be just fine," Miss Adams didn't sound as convinced as her words.

The doctor placed his stethoscope in his black bag, took out a pad of paper, and jotted something on the pad. He then turned to one of the older children. "You, boy, run to the house next door and see if they have a telephone. If not, go to the next one and the one after that. Someone must have a phone. If they say yes, give them this note and tell them to phone this number and repeat what I wrote."

Miss Adams grabbed the boy's arm. "You are to do exactly as the man said and come straight back, understand?"

The boy nodded his agreement and raced off.

"Miss Adams?" Miss Childers' words came out in a whisper.

The doctor moved aside, and Miss Adams sank to her knees beside the ailing woman.

"You must take the children back to New York."

Franky's heart sank as the meaning of her words registered. *I'll not be getting a new home.*

"But the children..." Miss Adams said, echoing Franky's inner thoughts. "Surely we could stay here until you are well enough to travel."

Before Miss Childers could respond, the doctor shook his head. "I have my suspicion of what it is."

"And that is?" Miss Adams pressed.

"I believe the woman has a ruptured cyst, but we won't know for sure until we get inside and have a look-see. Either way, she'll be cut open and will be bedridden for weeks afterward."

Miss Adams face turned white. "Weeks?"

The door burst open once more, and the boy who'd been sent for help returned, followed by two men who removed their hats upon entering the church.

"I called the hospital as your note instructed. I'm afraid both ambulances are out on other calls. Your note seemed most urgent, so we came to help you get the woman to the hospital," one of the men said as they neared.

"Yes, yes, most urgent indeed," the doctor agreed, motioning in the direction of Miss Childers, who was looking more distressed each time Franky glanced in her direction.

The men hurried to help her off the pew and onto her feet as they helped support her weight. As they neared Miss Adams, Miss Childers clutched her arm.

"You must take the children home," she said breathlessly.

Miss Adams looked past her to the children peering over the pews, then nodded her head. "I will see to it the children make it home."

***

Franky heard the rustle of a skirt and turned to see Miss Adams making her way down the center aisle. Angry with the woman, he turned his head, hoping to avoid conversation. The rustling stopped, and he sighed as she motioned the boy next to him out of his seat. The boy hurried to oblige, sliding into the seat across from him.

"You haven't said two words to anyone since we left the station," she said, taking the boy's place.

Franky shrugged but remained silent.

"I can't fix what's ailing you if you don't tell me what it is," she said softly.

"You lied. You told Miss Childers you would see us home," he replied.

"Oh, so that's it. I thought you'd be happy to be heading to Chicago. Don't you want to find a home?"

He almost laughed at the absurdity of the question. Sure

he was happy, but that didn't change the fact that she'd lied. And with Miss Childers being so sick and all. "Of course I do, but that's not the point."

"I didn't know you were so loyal to Miss Childers."

He wasn't. He barely knew the woman. But he'd tasted enough soap to know a person was not supposed to lie. Why go through the process of teaching a kid to tell the truth when it didn't matter? "You told a lie."

"No, not really."

She had, and now she was lying to him as well. He narrowed his eyes. "I was standing right next to you when you promised Miss Childers you would take us back."

She shook her head. "No, I specifically remember telling her that I would see you all home. If I can get you all placed, I will have kept my word, won't I?"

When she said it that way, it didn't sound like a lie. He thought about that for a moment. "What if you don't find us homes?"

"Chicago is a big city, and there are only a dozen of you left. I think the odds are in my favor."

Franky felt a tug of hope replacing the anger. "You really think I'll find a home?"

"I do," she said, and started to rise.

"Miss Adams?"

She pressed back into the seat. "Yes, Franky?"

"Does that mean it's okay to lie sometimes?"

She tilted her head as if thinking about his question. After several moments, she answered, "No, lying is wrong, but sometimes there may be a very good reason to stretch the truth."

"Like what you said to Miss Childers?"

"Yes, like that."

"Why?" he pressed.

"Franky, what would have happened if we would've

taken a train back to New York?"

"I would have gone back to the asylum."

"Did you like it there?"

He shrugged. "I didn't not like it."

"Yes, well, my decision wasn't just about you. I had twelve children to think about. Had we taken the train back to New York, each of you would have had to return. Lord knows if or when you'd get another chance."

"I guess."

"How old are you, Franky?"

"Six."

"If I were to take you back, there is a very good chance you would spend the next twelve years there. Do you know how many twelve is?"

He nodded his head, held up both hands, extending his fingers. Closing his hands, he held up two more fingers as he'd been taught.

Miss Adams smiled, showing he was correct. "You wouldn't want to stay in the asylum for that long, now would you?"

If she'd have asked him that question before he left for the trains, he might have told her it didn't matter. But now that he knew there was so much more to see, he knew his answer to be no. He would be the one telling the others what it was like on the outside. He who watched their faces knowing they no more believed him than he'd believed the others who told such tales. Now he wanted nothing more than to go to a home where he would have people who would look after him. Suddenly, he realized he would do almost anything to find a home where he wouldn't be trapped inside the cold walls of the asylum.

"Well?" she said when he failed to answer.

"I'd like to find a home in Chicago." *Even if it means going to a home that won't let me have a pig.* He thought to voice that aloud but decided against it. It was a lie, and at the moment, he couldn't think of a good enough reason to tell it.

Chapter Thirteen

Chicago, 1926

Franky stood shoulder to shoulder with the remaining children as Miss Adams told the people sitting in the seats about the placing-out program. Her voice trembled as she spoke, leading Franky to wonder if something was ailing the woman.

Miss Adams' skirt rustled as she walked the stage speaking of all the children she'd helped to place over the years, mentioning a specific child she'd helped and pausing as if waiting for a reaction from the crowd.

Franky slid a glance in her direction. *She's lying again, repeating Miss Childers' words. Miss Childers said this was Miss Adams' first trip on the trains. How could she possibly have been there to help the same children?* He glanced at the others, amazed that none of them seemed to notice or care.

Scowling, he turned his attention back to the people sitting in the chairs in front of him, wondering what they thought of her lies. To his surprise, not one of the onlookers appeared the wiser. *Is it that easy to tell a lie? Even if it's easy, why would she not just tell the truth?* As he stood there, his mind began to wander, taking him back to the transition room to the day he'd learned his lesson about lying. He'd spent the morning on the rooftop playing with the other children. It was hot, and Mistress Vivian had sent the children to the washroom to clean their faces, reminding each of them to wash behind their ears. While Franky washed his hands and face, he'd neglected to wash behind his ears, doubting anyone would notice. Mistress Vivian had pulled him aside, asking if he'd washed thoroughly, to which he promptly nodded his head. Mistress Vivian pursed her lips and sighed. Removing her handkerchief, she ran it the length of the area behind his ear then peered at the cloth. Frowning deeper, she turned the fabric for him to see the grime. She'd scolded him, not for his lapse in hygiene, but for the lie itself. He'd paid dearly for that lie: ridiculed in front of his peers, soap to wash the filth from his mouth, and made to stand against the wall while the others got to play. All for a single lie told to one person. He clenched his fist and stared at Miss Adams. *Why is it okay for her to tell a lie and to so many people? Shouldn't adults get into trouble just the same as children?*

Miss Adams looked in his direction, stumbled on her words, and for a moment, he worried she'd been privy to his inner thoughts. She turned away, addressing the audience once more. "You are welcome to come up and speak with the children. Oh, and remember to take note of the numbers on the children's clothes as they will help you identify the child."

With that, the people made their way to the stage, approaching the children in groups, asking questions, and waiting for their answers.

Franky's heart skipped a beat as a couple climbed the steps, moving in his direction. Disappointment washed over him as they passed by without comment. A large lady carrying a small dog narrowed her eyes at him, then leaned in and whispered something to the dog as she passed. As the morning wore on, the people began returning to their seats. Much to Franky's dismay, by the time the stage had cleared, not one person had approached him.

Miss Adams walked to the center of the stage and addressed the crowd once again. "If you've made your selection, place the child's number on the application you were given. It would be wise to have a second or third choice in case your first selection is not available. The committee will review your applications and give their verdicts after the noon meal. The committee should have its recommendations in about two hours."

***

Franky sat, arms crossed, waiting for the door to open once more. The boy sitting beside him had tried to strike up a conversation, but Franky would have nothing of it. They were the only two left in the room, and Franky had long given up hope of finding a home. Every few moments since they'd returned from lunch, Miss Adams would stick her head inside and call out a number. The child wearing that number would rise, collect any belongings, and follow her from the room, not to return. The door opened, and Franky held his breath, only to let it out once more when she looked at the other boy. He leaped to his feet without waiting for her to call his number, turned to Franky, and stuck out his tongue.

Franky waited for the door to close, and then kicked the boy's chair, sending it sliding across the floor. *I don't need a stupid home anyway. I liked the asylum just fine. I may not have any friends left there, but Miss Anna treated me just fine. I don't mind going back, not really.* Tears sprang to his eyes, and he batted them away, angry at himself for daring to think he could find a home. He was still trying to stifle his tears when the door opened once again; only this time, Miss Adams wasn't alone. With her was a man with greying hair and large ears that stood out from the sides of his head. The man limped as he followed her into the room, leaving Franky to wonder if he'd hurt his leg.

"Franky, this is Judge Doty. He was one of the men on the committee that helped place all the children."

"Not all of them," Franky said, staring at the man.

Miss Adams ignored the comment. "Judge Doty has a proposition for you."

Franky waited, not sure what he was supposed to say.

The man limped to a chair and sat, then motioned for Franky to do the same. Once Franky was seated, the man looked at Miss Adams. "I'd like to speak with the boy alone if you'd be so kind as to give us a few moments."

"Yes, of course," Miss Adams agreed, then left, closing the door behind.

"I've asked to take you home with me. What do you have to say about that?" the man said the moment they were alone.

Franky wrinkled his brow. "What am I supposed to say?"

The man chuckled. "You can say yes, or you can say no. There's not really anything in between."

Franky thought about that for a moment. "You want to adopt me?"

The man stretched out his bad leg and rubbed at his knee. "No. But I'll agree to be your guardian so you don't get sent back."

"What does 'guardian' mean?"

"It means I'll agree to look over you and protect you." The man let out a belly laugh. "Don't look so disappointed. It's not like you got a better offer. Though I can understand why none of the others wanted you, you having an attitude and all."

What's that supposed to mean? "I have an attitude?" Franky asked, looking at the man.

Judge Doty sat back in his chair and crossed his arms. "Son, the anger radiating from you this morning could have frozen Lake Michigan. I wasn't the only one who noticed. Why do you think no one spoke for you?"

Franky blinked his surprise. Sure he'd been angry, but he hadn't said anything. "You mean people can tell when you're mad even if you don't tell them?"

"Sure. I've made a good living reading people. Though I have to admit, I may have misjudged you. I had you pegged as a fighter, and now I'm not so sure that's the case."

Franky sighed. "Does that mean you've changed your mind about taking me home?"

"Did I say that?" the man asked with a tilt of the head.

Franky looked at the ground. "No."

"Look a man in the eye when you talk to him, son. That way, he knows if you're telling the truth. A person is only as good as their word, and I won't abide lying."

It was Franky's turn to laugh.

"Did I say something amusing?"

Franky looked to his feet once more.

"Franky, we need to get something settled. If I ask you a question, I expect you to answer me. And I expect proper courtesy. You will say yes sir or no sir. Now, I ask you again, did you find what I said funny."

"No." Franky looked up and saw Judge Doty staring at him. "Sir."

"Then it's telling the truth you have a problem with."

"Yes, sir."

The man's eyebrows arched. "You don't think a person should tell the truth."

"I used to. Now I'm not so sure."

Judge Doty leaned forward and intertwined his fingers. "And why's that, son?"

"Cause Miss Adams lies all the time," Franky blurted. "First she lied to Miss Childers telling her she'd take us home, and then she lied to the people today, telling them about all the children she's helped."

Judge Doty pressed back in his chair once more, a slight smile playing at the corner of his mouth. "And you know this to be a lie?"

Franky stood and faced the man. "Course I do. All us kids knew. Miss Childers said it was Miss Adams' first trip on the trains. Why, she wasn't doing nothing but repeating Miss Childers' words."

The man's smile spread. "Are you telling me that's what had you so riled this morning?"

Franky narrowed his eyes at the man. "Course it made me mad. If I'd of said it, she would have put soap in my mouth. Ain't nobody going to put soap in Miss Adams' mouth 'cause she's too big. How come it's okay to tell lies when you're grown anyhow?"

Judge Doty tapped his thumbs together. "I wish I could tell you that isn't the case, but it is. Why, I've had people come into my courtroom so good at lying, you'd swear they were telling the truth. Sometimes I believed them, but most of the time, I'd get a gut feeling and know they were lying through their teeth. Then I would throw them in jail."

Jail? Is Judge Doty a policeman? He remembered the headmistress threatening to throw him in prison if he didn't tell the truth. He swallowed. "Are you going to throw Miss Adams in jail?"

Judge Doty shook his head. "No, I'm afraid I don't have the authority I once did. Besides, I think what Miss Adams said was a white lie."

"What's a white lie?"

"It's a lie that's intended to do good. In this case, Miss Adams was hoping her words would help you children get new homes."

Franky scratched his head. "You don't think kids would have got homes if Miss Adams would have told the truth?"

"The people were eager. I think they'd have taken a child either way. But her lying did do some harm now, didn't it?"

Franky shrugged.

"Her lying made you mad. Because you were mad, people thought you were a bad seed, and therefore no one wished to choose you. Had she have told the truth, you might be sitting in a house with a new mother and father instead of contemplating going home with an old man. Now can you see the value of telling the truth?"

"I guess."

"Good, then you've learned a valuable lesson today. Now, back to the original question. Do you think you'd like to come home with me?"

Franky studied the man for a moment, noticing his pressed suit and shined shoes. Not a man likely to have a pig for a pet. Then again, he didn't look likely to take in a kid like him either. "Mister?"

"Yes, Franky?"

"What do you think of pigs?"

The man's eyes grew wide. "Why, I've never given them much thought. Why'd you ask?"

"Cause I thought maybe I'd like to have me one someday. Barney, he's a man I met on the train, he said some people think pigs are good for eating, but I don't want to eat it. I just want it for a pet."

Judge Doty ran a hand through his hair. "Is it a deal-breaker if I say no?"

At one time, Franky would have said yes; now it didn't seem like such a big deal. "No, I was just asking is all."

The man blew out a sigh. "Good. Let's see about getting you settled, and we'll debate the pig later. How does that sound?"

Franky didn't know what "debate" meant, but the man hadn't said no, so he could deal with the answer. "It sounds good, sir."

The man stretched his hand out to Franky. "It's always best to shake hands when making a deal."

Franky placed his hand in his and watched as it disappeared within the man's grasp.

"I guess you two came to an agreement," Miss Adams said, coming into the room. "Shall I draft a letter to the asylum letting them know Franky is going home with you?"

Franky hadn't realized she'd be letting those at the asylum know where he'd gone. He thought of Mistress Anna and wondered if she'd be disappointed to hear he'd not been placed with a family. Somehow he thought she would.

"Yes, that would be fine," Judge Doty said, pushing from his chair.

"No, wait," Franky blurted. "Can you say I'm going to a family and will have plenty of brothers and sisters? No, tell them I'm going to a nice family with a dog?"

Miss Adams' mouth dropped open. "Why, Franky, that would be telling a lie!"

"Only a white one," Franky said, glancing at Judge Doty.

"While you are at it, I guess you can officially tell Miss Childers you didn't lie to her," Judge Doty said, and winked at Franky.

Miss Adams cast an accusing glance toward Franky, and he smiled.

Chapter Fourteen

Franky followed Judge Doty from the building, surprised when the man walked to a nearby motorcar. Vibrant red with a black roof and fenders, there was a small ledge below the doors to help one step inside. The paint was polished to a high shine, and Franky smiled at seeing his reflection in the door.

Judge Doty pulled the door open and Franky was amazed to see the seats and door panels were nearly as red as the outside. If Franky could have whistled, he'd have done just that.

Judge Doty saw his expression and chuckled. "Surely you've seen a motorcar before."

"I have," Franky agreed. "But none as pretty as this one. Is she new, then?"

"Naw, I've had her a couple of years. She's a 1924 Cadillac, what you call a V-63 coupe if you want to get technical. I just call her Trudy."

"Named after your first love, then?" Franky asked, remembering his conversation with Roscoe.

"As a matter of fact, she is and just as feisty to be sure. Purring one moment and ready to scratch someone's eyes out the next. The moment I saw her, I knew she was the girl of my dreams."

Franky watched the man's eyes twinkle as he spoke, and for a moment, he wondered if he was talking of the car or the girl. His face turned nearly as red as the car, and he stopped as if he'd forgotten Franky was there.

"We'd best be getting on home now, son. Hop on inside, and we'll be on our way."

Franky stepped onto the running board and scooted across the seat as Judge Doty slid behind the large wooden steering wheel, pulling his leg to help him maneuver inside the car. Once fully inside, he wiped his brow with a handkerchief and turned the key, smiling as the engine rumbled to a start.

"Mr. Judge, how is it that people know things to be girls or boys?" The question had plagued him since the conversation with Roscoe.

"What do you mean, Franky?"

"Roscoe, he was the engineer on the train. He said the train was a girl and you say your motorcar is a girl. How do you know?"

Judge pressed his lips together for a moment. "You see, son, women are known to be temperamental. You don't treat them right and, well, they can cause a fellow a lot of grief. Same with machines. You got to check the oil, put gas in her, and talk to her real nice on cold winter days to make sure she won't let you down. And then there's the beauty of the machine. Why, I could shine and polish her all day; a man does that, he better be in love. Oh, and it's not Mr. Judge. It's just Judge."

"Oh no, sir, I couldn't call you by your first name. It wouldn't be proper."

"Judge is not my name; it's my title," he said, turning the corner and veering around a horse and buggy. "My given name is James Forest Doty."

Franky didn't know what a title was, but he guessed it was okay to address him that way if the man said so. "Okay, Mister, I mean Judge."

It didn't take long to get where they were going. Judge pulled into the grass beside a two-story dark brown brick house with a covered porch. Matching brick pillars sat on a small brick wall and held the roof of the porch in place. Three steps led up to an opening in the center. The house looked much the same as the rest of the houses on the street, except for the one sitting next to it, which was a bit more rounded and reminded him of some of the barns he'd seen along the way. There was a large tree at the side of the house, so close the branches nearly touched the roof. The lawn was brilliantly manicured except for the spot where Judge stopped the motorcar, showing it wasn't the first time he'd parked there.

Franky waited for Judge to get free of the seat before sliding out behind him, closing his eyes as his feet touched the grass. Even through the soles of his shoes, he could feel the spring of the lawn. For a moment, he thought to toss off his shoes and run through the lawn like the horses he'd seen romping in fields. The only thing stopping him was fear of being laughed at by the man who'd already reached the front steps and had turned to see what was keeping him.

Franky hurried to catch up and followed him inside the house, stopping just inside the doorway to take in the room. A large brick fireplace adorned one of the walls. Hanging on the brick above the fireplace was a painting of a woman in a green dress. The woman sat on a matching chair that matched her dress and stared out at him as if wondering why he was there.

The rest of the walls were covered in shelves that housed books. Not just a few like he'd seen in the asylum, but seemingly all the books ever written. Multiple oversized chairs upholstered in luxurious leather that matched the color of the brick sat around the room. Each had a side table placed near, and even the side tables had books sitting on top. A dark wooden staircase stood to the left of the room. Franky gazed upwards, but all he saw were more stairs.

Judge shrugged out of his suitcoat, placing it and his hat on a hook just inside the door and motioned for Franky to do the same. Once Franky had obliged, Judge moved to the stairs and began making his way upward, leaning heavily on the rail.

"Does it hurt?" Franky asked.

"My leg? Only when the weather turns. It's more of a nuisance than anything," Judge said. He breached the top of the stairs, hobbling a few steps until his limp decreased. "There, that's more like it. These doors go to bedrooms. There are four of them. I sleep at the end of the hall on the right. You can have your choice of any of the others. The facilities are at the end of the hall. There's a closet behind the door where you'll find towels and toiletries. I didn't have such niceties when I was your age. Got my fair share of splinters from sitting in the outhouse. Then, you being from the city, I guess you've never had to deal with things of that sort, have you, son?"

"I used an outhouse at one of the train stops. It smelled pretty bad, so I don't think I'd be happy to sit in there for too long. I was standing and holding my nose with one hand. The other hand was busy," Franky said with a shrug.

Judge smiled his understanding. "You'll be thankful for the indoor plumbing once the weather turns. Have a look-see in those rooms and see which one suits you."

Franky opened the first door and looked around. The room was painted white, had a bed, a straight-back chair, and a tall wooden dresser pressed against the wall. Long heavy blue curtains that matched the spread on the bed draped each side of the window. The room across the hall was much the same. He bypassed Judge's bedroom, checked out the washroom, then opened the door to the next room. No surprise, it was nearly identical to the previous two. He walked inside the room and peered out the window and smiled when he saw the huge tree just within reach. He turned to see Judge watching him, an unreadable expression on his face.

"Is this the one, then?"

"Yes, sir."

The man tilted his head to study the room. "Why'd you settle on this one?"

Because it is the closest to your room and I've never slept alone before. And because of the tree. Franky thought to tell him the truth but decided to take a different approach. "It's closer to the washroom."

Judge laughed a hearty laugh. "Boy, that's the worst lie I've ever heard. You picked this room because you can picture yourself climbing down that tree and running off into the night."

Franky felt his eyes spring wide. The thought had never entered his mind. "No, sir, I'd never run off. Why, where would I go?"

Judge leveled his gaze at him. "You're going to stand there and tell me the thought never crossed your mind?"

"Not of running off," Franky answered truthfully.

"But you did think about scurrying down that tree."

"Oh, to be sure," Franky said, bobbing his head.

Judge crossed his arms, rocked back on his heels, and considered Franky for a long moment. "I'll agree to your having the room if you make me a promise."

"What promise?"

"Promise me you'll wait a couple of years until you take it upon yourself to climb out that window. You get a little older and build up some muscle so your arms will hold you up. You try it now and you'll end up in the hospital with a broken leg. Something like that's bound to mess up a boy of your age, and you'll likely hobble around for the rest of your life." Judge led the way from the room and began making his way downstairs.

Franky followed. "Is that what happened to your leg?"

"It is. I wasn't much older than you, and I'd had a spat with my dad. Looking back, what we fought about wasn't a big deal, but at the time, boy howdy, I was going to show him by running off. I don't recall where I had a mind to go, not that it matters since I never made it. I guess I'm lucky it happened in the fall, as there was a cushion of leaves to help soften the blow. But I lay there in agony for some time before anyone heard my cries. The doctor said the leg was broken so badly, he didn't think I'd ever walk again. At one point, it got infected, and the doctor said it might be best to take it off completely, but my pop wouldn't hear of it. We lived on a farm, and he needed my help. My pop wasn't a small man, so I think he put a bit of fear into that doctor. He told the doctor to fix it and fix it well. I was laid up for months. Can you imagine being in the same room all day and never being allowed outside?"

Franky thought about his time in the asylum prior to being allowed to leave the confines of the room. Then remembered the thrill he and the others had felt when finally being allowed onto the rooftop and then later into the play yard. He thought about telling Judge about that time, but the man continued with his tale before Franky could gather his words.

Reaching the first floor, Judge sat in a chair and tapped one of the many books that adorned the side table beside him. "That's when I first learned to read. Before that, I didn't have a mind for any learning. We lived on a farm, and I thought I would never have a need for such things."

A farm? Franky hung on the man's words.

Judge picked up the book and closed his eyes briefly before speaking. "A book can take you places you'd never be able to travel, especially when you're too lame to go on your own. I never was able to climb another tree, not that I had a mind to after what happened. But I couldn't ride a horse either, and I wasn't any use on the farm. Pop never made me feel like I was a burden. But after a while, he made me get off the bed. He fixed me up a special buggy and trained that horse of mine to pull it. She was barely saddle broke, but she took to it well enough. The buggy was low enough I could get inside but tall enough I didn't have to worry about stumps and brush along the way. I loved getting outside. Mostly, I'd take the buggy out to a stream that was near and sit on the bank and read. I guess once my mind opened to reading, there was no closing it."

Franky didn't understand everything the man was saying, but he had a way with words, and Franky enjoyed listening to him.

"One day, I was in town with my pop. He needed something from the store and had made me come along for the ride. I was sitting in the buckboard reading when a man in a fancy suit walked by. I'm not sure what made him stop, then again maybe it was because I was reading *Twenty Thousand Leagues Under the Sea* when most of my friends were working in the fields. Anyhow, he spoke to me a few moments and learned of my situation. He asked me what other books I liked to read. I told him I didn't know because we only had a few books at the house and I just kept reading them over and over. Well, he told me he was a lawyer and had a whole library full of books. Then he went further, telling me I could stop by his house anytime I wanted, and he'd lend me a book."

Judge looked up, and Franky was surprised to see a broad smile take over his face. Franky returned his smile, though he didn't know why the man was so happy.

"I'm not sure what surprised the man most, that I actually took him up on his offer or that the first book I borrowed was *War and Peace*. I guess I was just hungry. Not for food, mind you, but for knowledge. Mr. Jackson, that was the man's name, took me under his wing and even saw to my education. I became a lawyer and later moved to Chicago and served as a judge. When Mr. Jackson died, he left me all these books."

The smile left Franky's face. "Weren't you sad Mr.

Jackson died?"

"Yes, of course I was. Why would you think I wasn't?"

"You don't seem sad is all."

"Franky, Mr. Jackson died long ago. I've had many years to get over his death. Now I keep his memory alive by reading and taking care of his books."

Franky gasped. "You mean to tell me you've read all of these books?"

"I have. Most of them more than once. I'm going to teach you how to read them as well. What do you have to say about that?" he said, offering Franky the book he'd been holding.

Franky pushed from his chair, walked over to where Judge sat, and took the book, thumbing through the pages. To his dismay, there wasn't a single picture. "These are just words. Where are the pictures?"

Judge lifted his hand and tapped Franky in the middle of his forehead. "The pictures are in there, son."

Franky tried to see where Judge pointed, and the man laughed. "You can't see them that way, son; they are in your mind. You see, when you learn the words, you'll be able to see them inside your head. When you get to that point, they will appear more beautiful than anything printed on a page. When that happens, you'll gain a wealth that no one will ever be able to take from you. Even if you haven't any money, you'll be able to travel anywhere in the world just by opening a book."

"Are you rich, then?" Franky asked, motioning toward the shelves of books.

Judge nodded his head. "I think I'm wealthy beyond compare."

Franky handed Judge the book he was holding, dragged one of the chairs closer to the man, and sat. "Will you teach me to be rich too?"

Judge smiled a wide smile. "Franky, I'll teach you anything you wish to know."

***

Cindy reached for another stack of papers and noticed Linda staring into space. Leaving the papers where they sat, she turned to her mother. "You okay?"

Linda shook her head.

"What is it? Don't you want to read anymore?"

Linda sighed. "I don't think I do."

Cindy hadn't expected that. "What's troubling you, Mom?"

Linda wrung her hands. "Franky is in a good place. If I stop right now, then I can keep him there."

Cindy placed her hand on her mother's. "Mom, you know these journals were written long ago. Anything that we read has already happened."

"I know, but the Judge seems so nice, and he could have been so good for your uncle."

"I agree, but don't you want to know what happened?"

Linda pulled her hand away and pushed off the couch. "No, I don't think I do. I think I'll go and sit with Frank for a while."

"Okay, give me a moment to get ready, and I'll drive you."

Linda put up a hand to stop her. "I'm perfectly capable of driving myself."

Cindy hesitated. While she was happy her mother had regained some of her independence, it was also clear her mother was on edge. "Are you sure you'll be all right?"

"I'm sure."

"Okay, promise you'll drive carefully."

Linda's lips pinched together. When she spoke, Cindy could see she'd touched a nerve. "Why do people say that?"

"Say what?"

"Why do people insist on telling people to drive safe?"

"I don't know. You used to say it to me every time I left the house."

"Yeah, well, maybe you should have argued with me."

"What would you have rather I said?"

"I don't know, tell me you'd planned on grabbing a six-pack and driving blindfolded down a one-way street or something. It's just plain idiotic to tell someone to drive safe. It's like telling someone something they already know."

"Mom, you're starting to worry me. Are you sure you're all right?" Cindy said, mirroring her inner thoughts.

Linda blew out a breath. When she spoke, she sounded calmer. "I'm fine. It just frustrates me that I can't help the boy."

"I know, Mom. I feel the same way." She followed as her mother went into the kitchen to retrieve her purse and keys and resisted the urge to tell her mother to be safe once more.

"I won't be long," Linda said, reaching for the doorknob.

"Mom," Cindy said softly.

Linda looked over her shoulder. "Yes?"

"Give Uncle Frank a kiss for me."

"I will," Linda said and pulled the door closed behind her.

Chapter Fifteen

Cindy was just pulling the pan of roasted red potatoes from the oven, when she heard Linda's car pull into the driveway. Placing the tray on top of the stove, she went to unlock the door for her mother.

"You cooked." Linda sounded surprised.

Cindy thought to remind her mother that she'd cooked all of her own meals before inviting her to come live with her but opted for a more civil response. Truth of the matter, she was lazy and was in no hurry to disrupt her current way of life. "Yes, I can still manage a meal or two when I set my mind to it."

Linda walked to the sink and washed her hands before lifting the lid on the skillet simmering on the stove. She glanced at the contents and raised an eyebrow. "Sloppy joes?"

Over the years, Cindy often regretted not joining her mother in the kitchen when the woman had offered to teach her to cook. While she'd learned to get by, she was often envious of her mother's ability to fix an elaborate meal without the aid of a cookbook, often forgoing measuring cups or spoons as well. *Maybe I should ask if the offer is still on the table.* Cindy shrugged. "I didn't say it was a gourmet meal. How's Uncle Frank today?"

Linda sat at the table, obviously content to let Cindy serve her for a change. "He didn't even know I was there, just sat in the chair watching the birds at the feeder. He's declining. I spoke with his nurse before I left. She agrees with my assessment."

"As do I," Cindy said, placing the buns and ranch

dressing on the table. She returned for the plates and silverware, putting them on the table as well. "You want cheese?"

"No, I'm good," Linda replied.

Cindy grabbed a couple cheese slices for herself, then brought the skillet over and placed it on the hot pad. She scooped some potatoes onto her plate and did the same for her mother. Taking a seat, she squeezed some ranch onto her plate and dipped a potato into the creamy sauce.

Linda shook her head. "You know that's for salads."

Cindy dipped another potato and took a bite. "It's good. You should try it. Besides, potatoes are vegetables."

Linda forked a potato and dipped it into the dressing on Cindy's plate then took a bite.

"See what you've been missing all these years," Cindy said when Linda grabbed the bottle and added some to her plate.

"Have you thought about where you'd like to be buried when you die?" Linda asked.

"Sheesh, Mom, my cooking isn't that bad."

"I'm being serious. I'm going to be right next to your dad, and I'm guessing we'll try and bury your Uncle Frank nearby. I was thinking of going to look at plots this week, and well, if you want to be close, I could get you one too."

"I guess it depends on what life throws at me. I mean, who knows, I could get married and have a dozen kids between now and when I die." It wasn't in character for her mom to be so morbid, so Cindy threw in the last part to cheer her up.

Linda looked over her sandwich at her. "I thought you didn't want kids. Are you telling me you're waiting until I die to give me grandchildren?"

So much for cheering her up. "Mom, I was being facetious. I'm just saying I'm young and don't know what will happen in the future. Heck, you could end up outliving us all."

"So you'll leave me to figure it out?" Linda chided.

"Think back to when your father died. If he and I would have seen to the arrangements when we were younger, it would've made that time so much easier."

Cindy did remember that time and how painful it was to make the decisions that came with her father's untimely death. "How about this? I don't plan on dying anytime soon, but if I do then yes, you can bury me next to Uncle Frank."

"Good, we'll go this week, and you can help me pick out the plots. Afterward, we will go to Marsh and go over your and Frank's arrangements. We can even go to Sandtown and pick the flowers. We'll make a day of it."

"Do you really think that's necessary? I mean, I can understand Uncle Frank, but I think this is going a bit too far."

"Quit being so melodramatic. Making funeral arrangements doesn't mean you're going to die any more than opening a bottle of salad dressing means you're going to eat a salad," Linda said, then dipped another potato and took a bite.

Cindy had to give it to her mother; the analogy worked. "Fine, I'll go with you to make the arrangements."

"Good, how about we get this mess cleaned up so we can get back to reading Frank's journals."

"What made you change your mind?"

"Morbid curiosity, I guess."

"Good a reason as any, I suppose," Cindy said, gathering the plates. "I've got this, Mom. You go on and get everything ready. I'll be in in a bit."

Linda left the room without argument, leaving Cindy to clean up. As she moved around the kitchen, she couldn't help but replay their conversation in her head. As much as Cindy hated to admit it, her mother was right in insisting she get her affairs in order. If something happened to Linda, she would be all alone. If she didn't put something in place now, who'd see it done? *Uncle Frank has Mom and me to look after him. Mom has me. But if Mom goes, then who do I have?* Cindy had often joked about being an old maid and living out her life as a spinster. She'd lived on her own most of her adult life and had been comfortable in her solitude. Lately, the reality of her situation didn't seem as funny as it once had. *Is it reading the journals that is changing the tide, or could it be that I actually enjoy having Mom living here?* She didn't have to ponder the question long to know the latter to be the reason. *Huh, I spent years dreaming of getting out of my parents' house and living on my own. My, how times have changed.*

***

Franky woke from a troubled sleep to the feel of the train rocking back and forth as it hurried down the track. He looked about the darkness and felt sadness grip him as he realized he was still on the train. Worse yet, he was headed back to New York, destined to return to the asylum. He wondered what the others would say upon his return. Would they welcome him back with open arms or ridicule him for not being worthy of finding a home. He closed his eyes, letting sleep engulf him once more.

***

Even before opening his eyes, Franky could tell daylight had overtaken the darkness. Lifting his eyelids, he looked about the sun-filled room, studying his surroundings. The window was raised just a bit to allow some of the cool evening air to seep inside. The curtains moved ever so gently against the breeze, allowing the sunbeams to dance along the wall. Just past the window glass, he could see the giant tree standing steady against the wind. He realized he'd been so tired when turning in that he'd given nary a thought to sleeping on his own, falling asleep within moments of pulling the covers to his chin.

It was only a dream.

He tossed the plaid quilt aside and slid from the bed. A

shiver raced over him as the bottom of his feet came to rest upon the hardwood floor. He walked to the window and looked at the large branch that reached out from the tree and curved just before it reached his window. He smiled, knowing that one day he would be straddling that very branch looking in. But not yet, Judge's story had cautioned him. At least for now.

Franky closed his eyes. Stretching his arms wide, he took a step, then another, and another. Opening his eyes once more, he spun in place, arms wide. It was a real room with plenty of space, and it was all his. Furthermore, it felt good to not only walk a steady line without being sent into the nearest seat but to be able to walk without swaying. While he'd enjoyed the train ride and the newness brought with each mile traveled, he was pleased his journey was over. He had a new life now and someone new to share it with. *Judge*. Maybe the guy wasn't ready to be his dad, but he was all Franky had, and Franky was happy for it. He hurried to dress in the only clothes he owned and went in search of the man who called himself his guardian.

As he exited his room, he heard Judge talking to someone and wondered if they had company. Not wishing to interrupt, Franky crept down the stairs. As he reached the bottom, he saw Judge standing in front of the fireplace, speaking to the woman in the green dress above the mantel. Franky froze in place, listening to the one-sided conversation.

"I hope I'm doing the right thing, Beth," Judge said, looking up at the portrait. "The boy seems like a good kid. Not like some of the ruffians you and I took in in the past. Still, I sure do wish you were here with us. The boy could use a mother's touch. Something tells me he's been lacking in that department and I'm not sure what's to be done about it. Maybe I should have left him be and saw him returned to New York. At least if I had, he might have had a chance at a normal life with both a mother and father to see him through life."

Franky stood rooted in place, a lump forming in his throat. *Was the man not happy he was here?* He swallowed the lump and spoke. "Are you going to send me back, then?"

Judge spun around as if caught doing something he shouldn't have and looked at Franky with questioning eyes.

"I heard you talking to the woman on the wall, and it sounded like you're going to send me back."

"The woman on the wall was my wife, a likeness of her anyway. She died a few years ago. Three to be exact. I still talk to her from time to time; she listens pretty well." A sly smile crossed his face. "A lot better than she used to."

Franky slid a gaze toward the portrait. "Does she answer you?"

"She mostly listens," Judge said with a shake of the head.

Franky cocked a brow. "Mostly?"

"How'd you sleep last night? The room warm enough for you?" Judge asked, ignoring the question.

"Oh, plenty warm." Franky thought to tell Judge about the dream he'd had, but in light of the man's misgivings about bringing him home, decided against it. He nodded toward the portrait instead. "Do you miss her?"

"With every beat of my heart."

Franky thought that to mean yes. "You're not crying. When kids at the asylum talked about missing someone, they cried."

"I've shed my share of tears, son. When I get sad, I try to think of our happy times together, and that seems to help ease the pain of losing her. You want some breakfast?" Judge asked when Franky's stomach rumbled.

Franky wrinkled his brow. "Who's going to fix it?"

"Why, I am, of course."

Franky felt his eyes grow wide, and Judge laughed.

"Don't worry, boy. I've been cooking my own meals ever since Beth passed, and I haven't managed to poison myself yet. Come on in the kitchen, and I'll show you how it's done."

"I have to go to the washroom first," Franky said, wishing he'd done so before coming downstairs.

"See to it, then, and don't forget to wash your hands when you're done," Judge said, heading toward the back of the house.

Franky waited until the man had left the room before walking to the fireplace and addressed the lady in the painting. "Mrs. Beth. I know you don't know me none because you're dead and all, but if you do talk to Judge, please don't tell him to send me back. I like it here just fine."

Chapter Sixteen

"Look at all that water!" Franky exclaimed. While he'd seen the lake when arriving in the city, he hadn't realized he now lived so close.

Judge laughed. "We drove by it yesterday. I was wondering why you didn't mention it then."

"I think I was too scared to see anything," Franky said, staring out the window.

Judge blared the horn on the Cadillac as a yellow motorcar darted in front of them and then came to a stop. Judge looked over his shoulder then pulled around the motorcar, glaring at the driver as he passed. "Confounded yellow cabs are taking over the city. Between them and the busses, I'm afraid there may come a day when there won't be a reason for a man to own an automobile."

Franky pulled his head in the window and looked at Judge. "You don't look scared."

Judge glanced over at him, then turned his attention back to the road. "Me, scared? Why, what's there to be afraid of?"

"You just said you were afraid of the busses and yellow cabs," Franky reminded him.

Judge chuckled. "It was just a figure of speech. No, with so many people living in the city, having a way to get where you're going is a good thing. Can you imagine if everyone in this city owned an automobile? If that were the case, it would be a log jam of no one going anywhere. As it is, a person can get anywhere in the city if they are willing to pay for the trip.

Say you need to go somewhere and I'm not there to drive you. You have the yellow cabs, and the green, or checker cabs. They are all good, but stay with the yellow cab; they have a better reputation. You'll need money because they'll charge you to take you where you need to go."

"How much money?" Franky asked. Not that it mattered, as he was a boy of no means.

"Twenty-five cents for the first fifth of a mile. If you go another fifth of a mile, it'll cost you another ten cents and ten cents for each fifth of a mile after that. You don't want to keep them waiting because they'll add on another ten cents if you do. If you have the money, you can ride around for a whole hour."

"Have you ever ridden around for a whole hour, Judge?"

"I have, but I don't recommend it unless you have three dollars to part with," Judge replied. He looked around and pointed to a red bus. "Now there's another way to get around that doesn't cost so much, but you need to know where you're going so you know which bus to ride. The red bus will take you to the south side of town. The brown goes to the north side and the green bus to the west side."

"What if I get on the wrong bus?"

Judge looked in his direction once again. "There now, boy, wipe that frown off your face. I wasn't trying to worry you any. I was just making conversation. I don't think you'll be heading off on your own anytime soon. I'll see to it you know your way around the city long before you venture out on your own."

"Is this the Loop?" Franky asked when Judge pulled the Cadillac to the curb in front of a large square block building. He wasn't sure what he'd expected when Judge told him they were going to the Loop, but it looked like an ordinary building to him.

"This whole area is considered the Loop," Judge said,

opening his door and extending his arms to encompass the surrounding buildings. He nodded to the building in front of the Cadillac. "This is Marshall Fields, where I have no doubt we'll be able to find you some clothes."

Franky slid across the seat and stood next to Judge. "What's wrong with the clothes I have on?"

Judge smiled. "The clothes you have on are fine, but you can't wear them every day. We'll get you a few pairs of trousers and a good sturdy coat to get you through the winter."

"My own coat? You mean I won't have to share?" The coats at the asylum were all hung near the door to the play yard. Larger coats were hung on high hooks and smaller coats a row lower. When going outside, a child simply picked a coat from the wall. As a result, the coat rarely fit and often smelled like the inside of an old shoe.

"No, son, I'll not be wearing your coat," Judge replied and led the way to the store. He removed his hat upon entering and motioned for Franky to do the same.

Franky felt like a lizard as he followed Judge into the department store, his eyes moving in all directions, trying to take in all the colors, sounds, and smells at once. Even at the early hour, there were clusters of people milling about the store. And for every customer, there appeared to be a salesman or woman ready to attend to them.

A salesman in a white shirt and tie headed in their direction the moment they entered. As he neared, his smile broadened. "Good morning, Judge, I see you brought a friend with you today. Introducing the lad to the third floor, I presume."

"In due time," Judge said, embracing the man fondly. Stepping back, he gave a nod toward Franky. "The boy is staying with me and will need some items other than the clothes on his back. Pants. A couple of shirts and a fine coat to keep him warm. "

The man's smile faded. "I didn't think you'd be taking in any more strays."

Judge's gaze flicked to Franky then back to the man standing in front of them. "The boy was in dire straits, and I thought that maybe I could be of help. And, Nathaniel, you'll do good to remember you too were once one of my strays, as you call them."

"You're one of the few who's ever called me by that name." The man's smile returned, and he turned his attention toward Franky, extending his hand. "Most call me Nathan. What shall I call you?"

Franky hesitated. He wasn't sure he liked the man but didn't want Judge to think him rude. Reluctantly, he reached his hand up, and Nathan's enthusiastic grip instantly consumed it.

"You got a name, don't you, boy?" Nathan asked when Franky failed to reply.

"Course I got a name. Doesn't everyone?" Franky said, pulling his hand free.

"Well, what is it, then?" Nathan pressed.

"It's Franky."

"Is that all?"

"It's been enough so far," Franky said with a shrug. Something about the man irritated him.

"Trust me; it won't be long before the old man here starts calling you Franklin. Just you wait and see."

"The old man is still sound enough to give you a what for if you don't watch yourself," Judge said firmly. "Or do you not remember?"

Nathan's face turned a brilliant shade of pink. "Oh, I remember, alright. Watch yourself, Franky. Don't let the man's limp fool you. He can outrun a rabbit if he's a mind to it. Chased me around the yard a time or two."

Franky opened his mouth to ask why the man needed chasing when Judge spoke instead.

"Teach you to sass your mother. You're lucky it was me chasing you instead of Beth."

"The woman over the fireplace is your mother?" Franky asked, recognizing the name.

"Not any more than the Judge here is your dad. Take heart, though, kid, he may not be your real pop, but he'll do right by you."

Franky felt his eyes grow wide. "You mean you came over on the trains too?"

"The trains?" Nathan asked and looked to Judge for clarification.

"Franky here rode the train from New York. He was in an asylum there, and they sent the kids out looking for a home."

"All the way from New York?" Nathan said, looking at Judge once more. "Don't tell me you couldn't find any strays in Chicago."

"I wasn't looking for another charge. It just sort of happened," Judge replied.

"So if you didn't get off the trains, why'd you need a home? Didn't you have a mom and dad?" Franky pressed.

Nathan's jaw tightened, and he narrowed his eyes. "Yeah, I had a mom and dad, but just because you've got them don't mean they're any good. Consider yourself lucky you didn't have parents like mine, kid."

Seeing the set of Nathan's jaw, Franky took a step back. He'd seen that look on some of the kids in the asylum right before they'd gotten into fights.

Judge clamped his hand on Nathan's shoulder, and they locked eyes. After a moment, Nathan's jaw slackened, and he blew out a long breath.

"Sorry, Judge, I guess you didn't get all the fight out of

me after all," Nathan said softly.

"Beth would be proud of the man you've become, son." Judge released his grip and nodded toward Franky. "I just hope she will guide me with this one."

"I have no doubt she's still in the house looking over you," Nathan assured the man.

"Sure she is, ain't she, Judge?" Franky interjected. "She's hanging over the fireplace. Why, just this morning, I came downstairs and heard Judge talking to her. Isn't that right, Judge?"

Judge's face turned a brilliant shade of red.

"Why don't we go find you some clothes?" Nathan said, whisking Franky away before Judge could answer.

Franky shrugged out of Nathan's grip and looked over his shoulder, expecting to see Judge limping after them.

"He'll be along," Nathan said. "Soon as he collects himself. You can't call the old man out like that. Understand?"

Franky shook his head.

Nathan stopped and leaned against a counter. "It's like this. Judge and Mrs. Beth, they were something. For some reason, they never had any kids of their own. Instead, they took in kids—boys, who, for one reason or another, found themselves in need of a home. Judge adored Mrs. Beth and nearly came unglued when she died. You see, they'd taken in another kid, only this boy was filled with hate. He would scream and shout and did everything he could to cause friction between Judge and Mrs. Beth. I'd never heard them raise their voices to each other until Garret showed up. But afterward, they were at each other's throat daily. Mrs. Beth knew Garret was stealing them blind, and he was mean to her whenever Judge wasn't around. I tried to help, but Garret was bigger than me. More than that, he was mean, and to be truthful, I was scared of him. But Judge, he was determined to fix the boy. Judge went to work one day and took me with him. I'd been begging to go as I enjoyed sitting in the courtroom when Judge heard cases. That wasn't the only reason. I didn't want to spend another day with Garret. "

Nathan closed his eyes momentarily before continuing. "When we came home, Mrs. Beth was lying at the bottom of the stairs. She'd been there a while. At least that's what the doctor said. He said she'd most likely fallen, but Judge and I knew different. Only it was our word against Garret's, and with no proof…"

"Proof of what?" Franky asked. "And why was she lying on the floor?"

"Proof that he'd killed her." Nathan's jaw twitched as he spoke. "She was on the floor because she was dead."

"Oh," Franky replied. "What happened to Garret?"

"Judge made him go. Garret wasn't happy about it neither. Swore his revenge as he was walking out the door. I guess Garret was all talk; no one's seen him since he left. Judge retired shortly after that. Said he just didn't have the stomach for it anymore. I think he was tired of seeing the guilty get set free. I think he also felt bad he wasn't there when Mrs. Beth died. For a while, I thought he'd send me away too, but he didn't. I heard him talking one night and snuck downstairs, thinking maybe Garret had come home. Judge was standing near the fireplace talking to that painting. It was as if he thought Mrs. Beth was standing right there. I turned and ran back to my room. I figured if he could see Mrs. Beth, then maybe she could see me. Thought if she could, she wouldn't be happy about me listening to them. You keep that in mind if you hear him talking and leave them be, understand?"

Franky nodded his head. The last thing he wanted was to get on Judge's wrong side and be sent away like Garret.

"Good, now let's get you some clothes before Judge

comes and wants to know what we've been doing all this time. Oh, and kid, don't let on I told you about Garret. I probably shouldn't have, but then again, if you're going to live there, I thought maybe you should know."

"Nathan? Why don't you live with Judge anymore?" Franky asked as Nathan plucked clothes from a rack and held them next to him to evaluate the fit.

Nathan blew out a sigh. "I guess it just wasn't the same after Mrs. Beth died. I stayed on for a while, but then I decided it was time to go. I had a job, and well, there comes a time when a man's got to take responsibility. I figured since I had my own money, it was time to strike out on my own. Judge must have thought so too on account he didn't push back when I told him. I worried about him for a while. I'd go see him and make sure he was eating. After a while, he told me to stop fussing over him. He seemed to be doing better, so I stopped dropping by. Judge knew where I worked, so I knew he'd know where to find me when he was ready. He used to come here every day, but it was months before I saw him again. Then one day, he just showed up and talked to me like nothing had happened. He looked good. I think he'd gotten to where he was okay living on his own. He comes in from time to time, but not as often as he did before Mrs. Beth died."

Franky looked around the vast store. "Why would Judge come in here every day?"

Nathan shoved the clothes into Franky's arms. "Let's go find Judge. He'll be happy to show you around the third floor."

Franky looked toward the ceiling. "What's on the third floor?"

"According to Judge, the whole world is up there. But I'll say no more."

"Why not?"

"Because that, Franky, is Judge's story to tell."

Chapter Seventeen

"Would you like me to hold your purchases until you're ready to leave?" Nathan asked.

"That won't be necessary," Judge said, and handed Franky the bags. "We'll not be long."

This elicited an eye roll from Nathan. "You know as well as I do that time stands still when you visit the third floor."

"Yes, well, be that as it may, we have other things on our list today. I'm taking the boy to the south side," Judge said, pocketing his change. "Care to join us, Nathaniel?"

Nathan wrinkled his nose. "I haven't lost anything on the south side."

"Good boy," Judge replied. Plucking his hat from the counter, he placed it under his arm, then pressed his cane to the floor. "Come along, Franky, the day's a wasting."

Franky frowned his confusion as Judge led him into a wide, brightly lit hallway, walked to the wall, and stood in front of a large silver door. He waited for Judge to open the door, but looking further, realized there was no handle. Instead, Judge pressed a button on the wall with the tip of his cane and continued to stare straight ahead. A moment later, the wall rumbled from within. The rumble quietened as the door slid open, exposing a handsomely dressed woman behind a gated cage. The lady's painted lips parted as she placed a slender hand on the doorframe and slid the gate open.

"Good morning, Miss Greene," Judge said warmly and motioned for Franky to step inside the box.

"Why, good day to you, Judge." The woman's smile

broadened. Tall and thin, dressed in a light blue skirted suit with a white collar, her blonde hair was pulled tight on top of her head. Her face was painted, enhancing her eyes, lips, and a rosy glow on her cheeks. Even at his young age, Franky thought her very becoming. As he passed through the doorway, he noticed the woman smelled just as pretty as she looked.

Judge stepped in after him and turned, placing his back to the wall.

Miss Greene slid the metal barrier across the opening and pushed a button to close the outer doors. "Third floor?"

Judge nodded his reply.

As the doors came together, Miss Greene wrapped her fingers around a lever and pulled. A second later, the box they were standing in jerked, the floor began to shake, and a loud rumble came from beyond the walls of the box. Frightened, Franky took several steps backward, his body pressing firmly against the back wall of the box. Franky glanced at Judge, who didn't seem the least bit concerned.

Miss Greene glanced at Franky and gave a reassuring smile. "First time in an elevator?"

"Yes." The word came out as a croak.

"Don't worry. I haven't crashed one yet."

The rumbling quieted as the elevator came to a jarring stop. The woman's voice was like a song as she announced their arrival on the third floor. The door opened, and the woman slid the gate out of the way. As Franky left the elevator, he noticed the box was not even with the floor. He looked to the woman, who simply shrugged her apology. He followed Judge into the hallway and turned, expecting Miss Greene to follow. To his surprise, she slid the gate closed once more and gave a finger wave as the outer doors slid together.

"What was the lady doing in the box?" Franky asked.

"Miss Greene's the elevator attendant," Judge said, "It's

her job to take people to their floor. She dropped us off at the third floor and will now go to see to other customers."

Franky stopped mid-step. "You mean to tell me we made it to the third floor and didn't have to climb a single stair?"

"Amazing times we live in, aren't they, son? We could ride all the way to the top floor if we wanted. Not only that, but we get to do so in the company of a pretty lady."

Franky stopped and looked about the hallway, turning in all directions, searching for something to verify they were indeed on another floor. He saw nothing. The hallway was exactly the same as the one they'd just left. He started to say as much when he noticed Judge rounding the corner at the far end of the hall. Franky shoved aside his disappointment and ran to catch up. Judge walked to a table and lifted a book off the counter. Franky gazed around the room, further disappointed to find the entire space filled with tables of books. He hadn't known what to expect, but this was the furthest thing he would have imagined.

"Don't sound so disenchanted," Judge said when Franky blew out a sigh.

"But it's just a lot of books. Don't you have enough books at home?"

Judge's brows lifted. "Son, one can never have enough books. Besides, I didn't come here for myself. I brought you here so you could pick out a book."

Now that's more like it. "You mean it will be my very own book?"

Judge peered down at him and gave a nod. "The first of many if you play your cards right."

"Oh," Franky said, looking at his shoes.

Judge placed a finger under Franky's chin, lifting until their eyes met. "What do you mean, oh?"

"I don't know how to play cards. I can't roll dice neither, but I've seen it done before."

Judge chuckled and released Franky's chin. "Do you always take everything you hear so literally?"

Franky hadn't a clue what the man meant. "I don't know."

"I forget you are but a boy. I can see I have my work cut out for me, but rest assured, I'm up for the challenge."

Franky still didn't know what Judge was talking about, but the man was smiling, so he wasn't worried. "What kind of book are you going to buy me Judge?"

"That, son, is entirely up to you. Have yourself a look about and see what strikes your fancy. When we get home, I'll teach you to read it."

Franky looked about the room with his mouth agape. "You mean to tell me I get to pick it?"

"You do."

"All by myself?"

"That's right. All you have to do is find the book that best suits you. I'll be over by that cluster of chairs. Take your time. Pick the one you want and come find me. Franky," Judge called as he started to walk off, "give me the bags so you'll be able to give the books their proper attention."

Franky handed Judge the bags and watched as the man limped off toward a table on the far side of the room.

While Franky was excited with the prospect of having a book to call his own, he had no idea which one to choose. Since he couldn't read, he had no way of knowing what book best suited him. A part of him wished to call to Judge, asking him to help navigate the tables of books. The other part was pleased to be saddled with such an important decision. He moved through the room, picking books from the tables and leafing through them, pretending to know the words within. He was glad Judge took the packages, as some of the books were much too heavy to lift with one hand. He'd just arrived at yet another table when a book with a dark maroon cover caught his eye. As he lifted the book, he knew the reason it had captured his attention; it was the same color as the lips on the lady in the elevator. He opened the book, peered inside, and found himself just as mesmerized by the photos within.

"That's a mighty big book for a lad your size," a man's voice whispered over his shoulder.

Startled, Franky nearly dropped the book. "Sheesh, Mister. You scared me."

The stranger helped to right the book then took a step back, peering at Franky through light blue eyes. "You must have been absorbed in your reading. I cleared my throat as I approached the table and you didn't flinch. I haven't seen you in the store before. Do you come here often?"

"Nope. Just today," Franky replied.

The man nodded toward the book. "You planning on reading that here, or are you going to take it home?"

"I haven't decided yet," Franky said with a shrug.

"The Great War in the Air: Volume II," the man said, glancing at the cover. "Know much about the Great War, do you?"

"I've heard of wars." He had too; some of the boys in the asylum talked about them. A few had lost their fathers in the Great War. Of course, they didn't tell that to Franky directly. He'd overheard the boys whispering about such things late at night after they were all supposed to be sleeping.

The man pulled a chair to the table and placed his jacket over the back before using crutches to help him maneuver into the chair. It was then Franky realized the man was missing his right leg. He saw Franky gaping but didn't acknowledge the missing limb. Instead, he pulled another book from the pile, opened it, and tapped a picture to get Franky's attention. "See this picture?"

"Yes, sir," Franky said, peering at the page.

"The real war was fought on the ground. At least that's what anyone who was there would say. This picture shows the battle of Saint-Mihiel; over 500,000 troops fought in that battle. A lot of good men died. It rained for days, sopping the ground so that the tanks couldn't make it through the mud. The trenches would fill with water as fast as we dug the holes. A lot of the men developed trench foot and could barely walk." The man closed his eyes and grew silent.

"Is that where you lost your leg?" Franky asked

"No, that's where your friend here got his battlefield commission," Judge said, coming up behind them. "His whole regiment was under attack, and their officer killed. Instead of diving into the trenches and waiting for direction, the private here took charge and guided his men forward, arriving at the front in time to help Colonel Patton and his subordinates break through the enemy's front line. Patton was so happy for the victory, he gave him a meritorious promotion to lieutenant."

The man laughed. "To hear you tell it, I singlehandedly won the war. Besides, like most battlefield commissions, the Army rescinded it as soon as the war was over."

"Just giving credit where credit is due," Judge said and placed his hand on the man's shoulder. "You're smart, and from what you said, Colonel Patton liked you. If not for your leg, you'd have followed him instead of sitting here filling my boy's head with stories."

Hearing Judge refer to him as his boy caused Franky's heart to skip a beat. *Had Judge decided to adopt him after all?*

The man sat back in his chair and pressed his fingers together. "I didn't know you were still taking in boys. What did this one do?"

"Mind your manners, Joshua. Franky didn't do anything. He required a home, and I happened to have room. He chose your old room, you know."

A knowing smile crossed the man's face as he studied Franky. "You picked it because of the tree, didn't you?"

Franky nodded.

"So did I. Didn't get a chance to climb it, though I always wanted to." He frowned and looked toward his missing leg. "I guess some things are just not meant to be."

There was an easy casualness to Joshua that Franky liked. It bothered him that the man seemed sad about not having climbed the tree. Hoping for a solution, he thrust his hand toward Joshua, hoping to make a good impression. "I'll climb that tree for both of us one day."

Instantly, Joshua's frown transformed into a smile. He gripped Franky's hand and gave it three firm pumps before releasing it. "It's a deal, but not before Judge gives the okay. Understood?"

"Yes, sir," Franky agreed.

Joshua gave a nod toward Judge. "You're lucky to have a man like Judge here to watch over you."

Joshua was not the first to tell him that, and so far, Judge hadn't done anything to make him disagree. Franky looked at Judge and then returned Joshua's smile. "Yes, sir."

Judge cleared his throat. "Did you settle on a book, then, lad?"

"I'd like this one," Franky said, turning the book so that Judge could see.

Judge sighed. "Of all the books in the room, you picked one about war."

"I can think of worse subjects," Joshua said, rising from the chair and grabbing the crutches to steady himself.

"As can I," Judge agreed.

"Hang on a moment." Leaning on the crutches, Joshua hobbled to a nearby table. Franky watched as the man plucked two books from the table. When he returned, he offered them to Franky. "These are two of my favorites."

"Oh, no, I couldn't take them. Judge said he would buy me only one book," Franky objected. He hated refusing the books, but he didn't wish to take advantage of Judge's generosity.

Joshua gave a hearty laugh. "Franky, when it comes to Judge, you can never go wrong asking for books. Isn't that right, Judge?"

Judge took the books, looked at the covers, and leveled his eyes at Joshua. "Where did I go wrong with you?"

"Sorry, Judge. I know you tried, but fine literature was never my thing. Besides, it was much easier to travel the world with these. And how can you think you went wrong when I come to the bookstore nearly as often as you?" He offered Franky the books once more. "Go ahead and take them. Judge will give you a hard time about reading dime novels, but I think you'll find them enjoyable."

Franky looked to Judge to see his reaction and was rewarded with a nod of the head. Taking the books, he studied the brightly colored covers. Opening one, he was amazed that the pages were just as graphic. He smiled.

"And just like that, you've managed to corrupt the lad," Judge grumbled.

"Not corrupting, just showing him a different world," Joshua said in return. He steadied himself and placed a hand on Judge's shoulder. "You're a good man, Judge. What you did for me, the others, and now Franky here. Not many would take on such a challenge. I know you didn't formally adopt me, but I've always considered you my pop."

"I'm proud of you, son." Judge's voice quivered when

he spoke. "You had your moments when you were young, but you listened, and in turn grew into a fine man. You've done an old man proud. I'm sorry the war took your leg. I know you've struggled with the fact that you're no longer a whole man. I know there've been times when you wished yourself dead. But, praise be to God the ravishes of war took only your leg and left the rest of you."

Franky sighed. Judge obviously liked the guy. If he didn't see fit to adopt Joshua, then Franky doubted he'd change his mind about adopting him. It didn't matter. Not really. He was pleased Judge had agreed to become his guardian. Franky lifted his chin and stared at Judge.

Someday I will make you proud of me as well.

Chapter Eighteen

"I liked the bookstore," Franky said as they returned to the Cadillac. He climbed in and hoisted the bags over the back of the seat. "Maybe when I learn to read, I'll go there every day too."

Judge slid behind the wheel, started the engine, and turned the wheel, steering the car in the opposite direction from which they'd arrived. "You certainly could find worse ways to spend your days. This area is full of bookstores, but Marshall Fields is the largest. Wait until you see the store at Christmas. It's about as busy as a store can get with over a hundred clerks in the book department alone."

Franky wasn't sure what Christmas was, but it sounded like a lot of clerks. "What do the clerks do?" Franky asked, watching out the window at the shops that lined the street.

"A clerk is an employee of the store. Their job is to help the customer find what they're looking for."

"Like when Nathan helped me find new clothes?"

"Precisely," Judge said as he turned onto a different street.

"A hundred is a lot, right? People must buy a lot of books."

"At Christmas, people buy a lot of everything."

"Where do they get the money to buy things?"

"Why, they earn it. People go to work, and when they do, they get paid."

"Do you go to work?" Franky asked.

"I used to. I'm retired now."

"Oh." Franky wasn't sure what "retired" meant, but he didn't want Judge to be sad that he didn't go to work where he could get money to buy books, so he decided to change the subject. "Why don't you like Nathan as much as you do Joshua?"

"What makes you think I don't?"

Franky wasn't sure how to explain it. Even he preferred Joshua over Nathan. Still, he wanted to find out what made Judge like Joshua best so that he himself could get in Judge's good graces. "You told Joshua you were proud of him."

"Yes, and I meant it," Judge agreed.

"You didn't say that to Nathan," Franky reminded him.

"You certainly are astute for your age. That means you're perceptive. You don't miss much," Judge explained.

A piano in a store window caught Franky's attention, and he thought of the dark-haired girl that played the piano at the asylum. "I think I miss Mistress Anna."

Judge glanced in his direction. "Mistress Anna, was she one of your guardians?"

"No, she was a just a mistress. She played the piano real good." Funny, Franky hadn't thought of her in a while, but suddenly, he could clearly picture her face and almost hear the sweet music she played.

"Real well," Judge corrected. "One does not play the piano good; they play it well."

"Oh, no," Franky argued. "She was really good."

Judge sighed. "Do you wish to learn to play the piano? I could get you lessons at Lyon & Healy."

Franky hadn't thought about learning to play. He just liked listening to the sounds Mistress Anna made when her fingers danced. He looked at his hands and frowned. "No, I don't think my fingers would sound that pretty."

"Don't ever discount something before you try. You'll

never find what you are good at unless you put forth the effort to learn."

Franky studied his fingers once more. *Could I really learn how to play like Mistress Anna?* It was a fleeting thought. "What are you good at, Judge?"

Judge drummed his fingers against the steering wheel. "I guess I haven't given it much thought."

"I think you're good at being nice," Franky said cheerfully.

Judge chuckled. "Oh, you do, do you?"

"Yes, sir."

"Let's see if you still think so after living with me for a spell." Judge turned the wheel and steered the Cadillac to the curb in front of a massive building. Letting go of the wheel, he ducked his head and gave a nod toward the window. "See that building?"

Taking up more than a city block with its thick brick walls and arched windows, there was no missing it. Lengthwise, it was without a doubt the largest building Franky had ever seen. "Yes, sir."

"That's the Coliseum. Before that building was erected, the Libby Prison stood there. It was used by the Union Soldiers during the Civil war."

Franky shuddered at the word "prison," remembering what the headmistress had told the children, and wondered if a Civil War prison was as bad as the one headmistress described in New York City. *Surely not.* "That building there?"

"No, Libby Prison. It originally stood in Richmond, Virginia. A man named Charles F. Gunther purchased the prison and had men tear the building down."

"Oh." Franky sighed. Though he was disappointed he wouldn't be able to see it, a part of him was glad he didn't have to worry about being sent there.

"That's the thing. Gunther had the workers dismantle the prison brick by brick and put those bricks on trains. It took a hundred and thirty-two railroad cars to bring the building to Chicago. Then they put all those bricks back together again to be used as a museum. I visited there a few times and found it most impressive. Why, you'd have thought the building was built on this very spot. I guess he thought it would be a big thing for people to see, but most people were not as interested as he'd hoped. A few years later, they tore down the prison for the last time and built this here building in its place. We'll come back someday and I'll show you one of the original prison walls. I guess they left it so that at least some of the history of the building could be preserved."

Franky sighed once more.

"Don't sound so defeated. The Coliseum itself has a rather robust history. Presidents Roosevelt, Taft, and Harding have all gotten their start in that building, with their committees giving them the presidential nomination."

Not knowing anything about presidents, Franky was far from impressed. He remained silent as Judge maneuvered the Cadillac back into the street. A few moments later, after pointing out a street of enormous houses he referred to as mansions, Judge brought the motorcar to a stop once again. This time, Judge got out and motioned for Franky to follow. As they approached the railroad tracks, Judge turned his attention to a large statue.

"This here monument was erected to commemorate the Battle of Fort Dearborn." Judge pointed to a man without a shirt holding his hand in the air while another man attempted to use a knife on the woman standing between them. A child sat on the ground behind the woman, her arms outstretched as if begging someone to pick her up.

Franky searched the area for signs of a struggle. "There

was a war here?"

"Yes, many years ago in 1812. The man on the right is Chief Black Partridge. His Potawatomi Indian name was Mucktypoke, and he was a friend to the settlers who came to the area. He was an advocate for peace between the settlers and the Indians. See how his hand is raised?"

Franky nodded.

"He went against his own people to protect this lady. Her name was Margaret Helm. Chief Black Partridge saved both her and her daughter."

Franky walked over and studied the child. "What was her name?"

"I'm afraid I don't recall the child's name," Judge answered.

"But the Indian saved her?"

"He did. He saved the child and her mother. Later, he rescued her father as well. The president even gave him a silver medal, though he later gave it back."

Franky cocked his head in surprise. "Gave it back? Why would he do a fool thing like that?"

"Because, while Chief Black Partridge was fighting to save this mother and child, the Illinois Rangers were at his village – his home – burning it down. In doing so, his daughter and granddaughter were among those killed." Judge's voice softened. "I'm not opposed to war, Franky – people must fight to protect what's theirs – but you need to know in every war there are always casualties on both sides."

Franky walked around the statue, memorizing each detail until Judge motioned him back to the Cadillac. Franky slid across the red leather bench seat, and Judge took his place behind the wheel once more.

"Judge," Franky said once they were moving. "What did the men do to get sent to Libby Prison?"

"Mostly for picking the wrong side. You see, during the Civil War, you had Confederate and Union soldiers. The Confederates thought they were right and the Union soldiers thought they were right. Whenever either side caught someone from the other side, they would take them as their prisoner. You had regular prisons for the lower-ranked men, and officers' prisons like Libby for the men in charge. If the Confederates captured a Union officer, it was very likely they would send that man to Libby Prison," Judge explained.

"Do you think Libby Prison was worse than prisons are in New York?" Franky asked, voicing his earlier thoughts.

"From what I've read, Libby Prison was only second to Anderson Prison in Georgia. And Anderson Prison was as bad as they get. A lot of men died in that prison. How come a boy of your age would know about prisons in New York?"

"Headmistress told us about them when she sent Rat there."

"You had rats at the asylum?"

"Yes, but that's not the kind I'm talking about. Rat was a boy who got caught stealing food. The police came and got him and took him to prison." An image of the boy being hauled away by the police came to mind, and goosebumps ran the length of his arms.

Judge looked at Franky. "Did they not feed you enough in that asylum?"

"I got enough." Franky wanted to add that Mistress Anna had snuck food to him, but she'd made him swear never to tell anyone, so he refrained. He thought about the woman for the second time that day and wondered why she'd taken such an interest in him. He was still pondering that when a dreadful smell invaded his nostrils.

"The wind is not in our favor this day," Judge said, pulling the Cadillac to a stop in front of a small building. "This is the Stockyard Inn. Rest assured, the food in this establishment will take your mind off the smell."

Franky thought it more likely the smell might ruin his appetite altogether. That is until they entered the building where an entirely different aroma filled the air. He followed his nose and realized the perfume was coming from a large vase of freshly cut roses. He'd seen roses in picture books, but never had he seen one in person. Neither did he know how beautifully they smelled. Just as he reached to touch one of the roses, Judge drew his attention, calling for him to follow. Franky's hand grazed the rose, and several petals lost their hold, drifting onto the table. Upset he'd broken the flower, he scooped up the petals and shoved them into his pocket unseen. Turning, he followed Judge to the back of the building and into a quaint dining room.

Covering the walls were stately paintings of men on horseback with dogs chasing birds. One of the paintings showed a man sitting high on top of a horse as the horse jumped a tall fence, a colorful bird flying just out of reach. Franky wondered for a moment what it would be like to ride a horse. Then, noticing all the men held guns, he wondered if the men were at war with the birds.

Around the room were numerous small round tables covered with white linen cloths that nearly touched the floor. As they walked further into the room, new smells caused his stomach to rumble.

"Did I not tell you the aroma would be better inside?"

"Yes, sir," Franky said and inhaled deeply. He'd never smelled anything so divine. "What is it?"

"Pork tenderloin," Judge said, settling into a chair. "Cooked to perfection with a hint of rosemary and garlic."

Franky was impressed. "You can tell all of that just from the smell?"

"That and the fact that it says so on the board over there. Not to mention it's Thursday, and they always have pork tenderloin on Thursday," Judge said and winked.

A woman in a white dress and matching apron approached. She seemed a tad nervous as she cast her gaze over Franky. When she spoke, she lowered her eyes and directed her comments to Judge. "Good afternoon, Judge. What can I get for you today?"

Judge smiled a full smile. "Afternoon, Gloria. How's that son of yours doing? Keeping out of trouble, is he?"

A red hue crept over the woman's face. "Oh, yes. He learned his lesson well. He knows what a help you were in seeing him get his life in order."

"Good," Judge replied. "Always glad to help. We'll have two of the seventy-cent plate luncheons and two glasses of cold milk."

"It'll be right out," the woman said then hurried away.

"Boy, you sure know a lot of people, Judge," Franky said after she'd gone.

"I've lived in this town a long time."

"But it's such a big town," Franky replied. "Surely you don't know everyone."

"I certainly do not. But in my line of work, you get to know people and they you. I've been in the paper a time or two; most of them only know that I'm a judge. Sometimes that is a good thing; sometimes it's not. If I've put away someone they love, then that person might not be so happy with me," he said, his gaze trailing in the direction the woman had gone.

"What does it mean to put someone away?" Franky pressed.

Judge stared at him for a long moment. "It means I sent them to prison."

Franky felt his eyes grow wide. "You mean with the

murderers and rapists?"

"That's right."

Franky swallowed, remembering the rose petals in his pocket. He hadn't meant to take them, but he was afraid to let on he'd broken them. *I've ruined everything. Judge won't want me to live with him now. He'll have no choice but to send me to prison for stealing. I didn't mean to break it. Maybe if I tell him, he won't be mad.* Before he could confess his wrongdoing, the waitress arrived, setting before him a plate filled to the edges with food.

"Will there be anything else?" she asked.

"No, thank you, Gloria," Judge said, unwrapping his silverware.

Franky mirrored Judge's actions, cutting his meat and placing it into his mouth. It was savory and tender, unlike anything he'd ever tasted before. He was glad to be enjoying something so delicious, knowing his next meals would consist only of bread and water.

"You confuse me," Judge said a few moments later. "Your face is one of total mortification, and yet you are shoveling the food as if it were to be your last meal. I am not an ogre, Franklin. If you dislike the food, just say so, and I'll have something else brought to the table."

"I like it very much, sir," Franky insisted. The fact that Judge had called him Franklin made the situation even worse. It wasn't so much the name, but what the lengthened name represented. According to Nathaniel, Judge only did that to boys who were in his care. As soon as Judge found out what he'd done, he'd go back to calling him Franky once again. While he liked the name Franky, he also liked feeling as if he belonged. Sitting his fork down, he decided it was best not to prolong the inevitable. If he was going to prison, he might as well go there now. "I need you to take me to prison."

"You wish to visit a prison?" Judge asked, taking a bite of his meat.

"Not visit. I wish to be locked up." That was a lie, but he knew it was what Judge had to do. "I stole something, and I must pay the price."

Judge's face showed no emotion as he lowered his fork. "Just what is it you stole that will have you wishing to go to prison?"

"Oh, I don't wish to be sent to prison. But it's your job. Course I won't be happy living with the murderers and rapists, but I won't cry any." *At least not where you can see me*. The last thing he wanted was for Judge to be sad over doing his job.

Judge leaned against the back of his chair. "Why don't you start from the beginning and we'll see if we can sort this thing out."

Franky dug into his pocket and retrieved the red petals. Opening his hand, he watched as they floated toward the table. He would have smiled at how pretty they looked against the white linen tablecloth if not for the seriousness of the situation. "I broke them. I didn't mean to. I only wanted to smell them. They smelled so good, but when my hand hit them, they broke. I was scared I'd get in trouble for breaking them, so I put them in my pocket. I'm sorry, Judge. I really am."

Judge placed his hand in front of his mouth for a moment, then laced his fingers together, lowering them to the table. He stared at Franky for a full moment as if considering his words. "I'm not going to send you to prison."

Franky let out the breath he was holding. "You're not?"

"I'm retired. I don't send anyone to prison anymore. Even if I were still working, you would not go to prison over something like this."

"I wouldn't?"

"No, something like this would only get you a strap

across the backside," Judge said evenly.

Franky sighed. Getting the strap was much preferred to going to prison.

"Sit down, Franklin," Judge said when Franky stood, ready to take his punishment. He picked up one of the petals. "You didn't break the flower. Their beauty is fleeting. If they're cut and stuck into a vase, they die even sooner. The petals would have most likely fallen off today at any cost."

This came to a great relief to Franky. He looked at the petal in Judge's hand. "Then why do people cut them?"

"For the same reason you were drawn to them. Their beauty and fragrance fill the air and drown out other, less enjoyable aromas."

"You mean like the smell I smelled outside?"

"Indeed," Judge said with a nod of the head. "It wouldn't do for people who frequent this establishment to smell that retched odor while they were dining on the end product now, would it?"

"What do you mean, end product?"

Judge leveled his gaze at Franky. "That stench is from the stockyards. You curl your nose at the smell, but if not for the stockyards, you would not have that fine meal you just ate. Why, I assure you the pig that provided you your pork loin was alive this very day."

Franky cast a glance at his plate. "I ate a pig?"

"Most likely a hog, but that's just semantics."

"Do all pigs smell that bad?"

"Well, to be fair, the smell is an accumulation of many animals. Pigs, hogs, sheep, and beef cattle. A great number of them. Last I read the stockyard can accommodate nearly eighty thousand hogs."

"So one pig wouldn't be bad." *Surely not or the girl in the book wouldn't be kissing it.*

"One pig would not smell as ripe as the ones we smelled today. But pigs eat slop, and slop has an odor that will make you lose your breakfast if you don't stay on top of it. But if you want a pig, then a pig you'll get. That's why we are here today. It was to be a surprise, but we can go right over to the stockyards and pick you out one if you're ready."

Franky hadn't expected this. Nor had he expected a pig to smell so bad. Then he remembered what Barney had said about pigs. '*Take it from a man who knows a thing or two about eating. Pigs taste a great deal better than they smell.*' Then he thought about how good the meal he'd just eaten had tasted and knew Barney had been right. "Judge, if it is all right with you, I'd rather eat a pig than keep it as a pet."

Judge's lips curled slightly. "If you're sure that's what you want."

"Yes, sir, it's what I want," Franky answered, knowing he'd never be inclined to kiss something that smelled that bad. "Judge, I'm glad pigs taste better than they smell."

"So am I, Franklin," Judge said, pulling some coins from his pocket and laying them on the table.

Judge stood, and Franky did the same, following him from the dining room. As they exited the building, the stench hit his nostrils, leaving little doubt he'd made the right decision. Judge opened the door to the Cadillac and Franky stepped onto the sideboard, sliding across the leather seat.

"Where are we going now, Judge?"

"We're going home, Franklin. We still have a serious matter to address."

"What's that, Judge?"

"The fact that you stole the petals."

Franky's heart skipped a beat. "But you said I didn't break the flower."

"That's right. But you didn't know that at the time.

Instead of owning up to your mistake, you took the petals so no one would know. If you are going to live under my roof, I'll not abide dishonesty. Is that clear?" Judge said sternly.

It was clear Judge was disappointed with him, but even though he might have to face the strap, he also knew Judge still wanted him to share his home. Franky sat up straight and looked the man directly in the eye. "Yes, sir, Judge."

Though Judge didn't respond, Franky knew the man was pleased, as he once again showed the barest of smiles.

Chapter Nineteen

June, 1928

Franky sat on the porch next to Judge reading aloud from *The Great Gatsby*, by F. Scott Fitzgerald. The day was one of the warmest of the season, but the breeze that swirled around the covered porch was delightfully crisp. *Gatsby* was not his preferred read, then again, most of the books in Judge's library were not. His finger slid under each word as he read. "The automatic quality of Gatsby's answer set us all back at least another minute. I had them both on their feet with the desperate suggestion that they help me make tea in the kitchen when the demonic Finn brought it in on a tray. Amid the welcome confusion of cups and cakes, a certain physical decency established itself. Gatsby got himself into a shadow and, while Daisy and I talked, looked con… conscien,"

"Sound it out," Judge said when Franky struggled.

Franky ran his finger over the word, trying to sound it out. "Conscientiously," he said, then resumed reading. "Conscientiously from one to the other of us with tense, unhappy eyes."

"Good job. You can stop there for today." Judge pointed to the page. "What do you think the word 'conscientiously' means?"

Franky scanned the paragraph once more, reading it silently this time. "Careful?"

"Splendid." Judge beamed. "Only in this case, since the word is an adverb, it would be carefully."

"Oh." Franky sighed.

"There now, don't sound so discouraged. I don't know many eight-year-olds who have the comprehension skills you have. Why, I doubt even I would have been able to figure it out at your age. I just wish you enjoyed reading as much as I," Judge said, placing the bookmark between the pages and closing the book.

"I like to read," Franky said at hearing the disappointment in the man's voice.

Judge snorted a laugh. "Son, those dime novels you prefer reading are nothing more than fodder for such a gifted mind. You should be reading masterpieces, not trivialities."

Franky wondered if Judge was upset that he was reading Harry Moore's *The Liberty Boys Running the Blockade* or more books about his newfound interest in the American Revolution. "Why don't you like me reading about the war, Judge?"

"It's not the war, son. It's how you romanticize it."

"I'm not in love with the war, Judge."

Judge smiled. "Not romance, romanticize. You idolize war as if you wish you'd lived it."

"Well, what's wrong with that?"

"Killing a man isn't as easy as it sounds, Franky."

"Sure it is. You just point the gun and pull the trigger," Franky argued.

"That's true, but then you have to deal with what comes afterward."

"You mean the blood?"

"No, I mean in here," Judge said, thumping the side of Franky's head with his finger. "A man's got a conscience. You know what that word means?"

"It means you think about stuff."

"That's right, so say there's a man walking up the porch right there. Now let's say something about that man causes the hairs on your arms to stand up, and you know that man is up to no good. So you do what comes naturally, and you raise your gun and shoot that man."

"If he's up to no good, I'd say he deserves to be shot," Franky agreed.

"What if your feeling was wrong? Say he only looked like he was up to no good."

"Why did he look like he was up to no good?" Franky pressed.

"Maybe he'd fought with his wife, and he was thinking of the fight when he walked onto the porch. Or maybe he had a toothache, and it was hurting something fierce, and that was what made his face screw up. You'd feel bad if you shot him just because he was having a bad day now, wouldn't you?"

"What does that have to do with the war, Judge?"

"It has a lot to do with the war. You don't know the man you're about to shoot. All you know is you're supposed to hate the man and he you. So you pull the trigger before he does and stop him in his tracks. Later, when you're left to your thoughts, you might see that man again in your dreams. And maybe when that happens, it is he who kills you instead of the other way around. You wake from that dream thinking, *Why'd you kill me? I did nothing wrong*. Killing a man, whether in war or anger, is something that can rot a man's soul if he's not careful. You ever have to pull the trigger; you'd better be sure you're ready to live with the darkness it leaves behind."

"Have you ever killed a man, Judge?"

"Have I ever shot a man, no, but I've been responsible for many deaths," Judge said solemnly.

"How can you kill a man if you don't shoot him?"

"It was part of my job, Franky. Some men I'd send to jail; others who'd committed more heinous crimes would get the noose. It didn't matter that I wasn't the one who placed the rope around the man's neck. I ordered it done."

Franky scratched his head. "You said juries decide who's guilty."

"That's right, but it's up to the judge to pronounce the sentence. A gun. A rope. Killing is killing, and in the end, there's almost always a little nag in the back of your mind wondering if you've done the right thing."

"Almost?"

"Yes, there are some men that are just from a bad seed. You try to do right by them, but they're already too far gone." Judge's voice had turned to a whisper as he looked out at the yard.

"Have you known men who were a bad seed, Judge?" Franky asked, equally low.

"I have."

Franky waited for the man to say more, but he never did. Instead, Judge took the tip of his finger and wiped away the moisture that had formed in the corner of his eye. The moment passed. Judge slapped his hands against his thighs and stood, stretching as he rose.

"Enough fun for now. It's time to get back to work." For a man who claimed not to work, Judge found plenty to keep them busy, the latest of which was stripping and painting the small shed in the backyard. They'd put on a coat of paint just this morning before taking a break during the heat of the day so Franky could practice his reading.

Franky followed Judge to the backyard and mimicked him as he walked around the shed, inspecting their handiwork. Now and then, Judge would lean closer as if to get a better look. Franky followed his actions, trying in vain to see what had captured Judge's scrutiny. After circling the shed twice, Judge nodded his approval.

"Are we done, then?" Franky inquired.

"With the outside," Judge replied.

Franky heaved a sigh. "You mean we have to paint the inside too?"

"Not me, you," Judge answered. "And you don't have to; you get to."

Franky laughed. "You say that like it's a good thing."

Judge cocked his head and raised an eyebrow. "Isn't it? Why, when I was a boy, I would have jumped at the chance to paint my own fort."

Franky looked at the shed more closely. "What do you mean 'fort'? It's just an old shed."

"Tsk, where's your imagination, boy?" Judge replied. "This here shed's no different than those books you read."

Franky scratched at his head again. "How's that?"

"Why, when you read a book, really read it, you immerse yourself in another world. The writer writes the words, but it is up to you to see the picture he or she paints. You've done that, haven't you?"

"I think so."

"You think so. Tell me you haven't imagined yourself in the stories we've read."

Franky thought of the book they were currently reading. No, he didn't think he'd ever imagined himself as the Great Gatsby. Then he thought about the dime novels he'd read and how he'd often imagined himself marching along with the soldiers or fighting the Indians, though sometimes it was he who was an Indian, sneaking around in the dark while the cowboys were sleeping. He smiled at Judge. "Yes, I have imagined being in the book."

Judge opened the door to the shed and waved a hand. "You've lived a sheltered life, Franklin. It's okay to be a boy now and again. Get this place cleaned up a bit, add a fresh coat of paint, and let your imagination do the rest."

Franky looked inside, letting his gaze fall over the

contents within the shed. A push mower—basically a long stick with sharp blades that turned when you pushed it across the yard. Cutting the grass held excitement the first few times, but quickly became nothing more than a weekly chore. The shelves held several buckets and tin cans along with a small metal box filled with tools. On the far shelf sat a few lamps they'd used multiple times when storms had rendered them without electricity. Beside them sat a stack of newspapers. Judge liked to keep the papers, as when crumpled into a ball, they made short work of starting a fire in the fireplace. Various yard implements were leaning against the wall, along with a new wooden ladder Judge had purchased from the hardware store when they bought the paint. Franky had been introduced to most of the implements over the last two years. He'd spent enough time with the rake, that at one point, he'd wished to cut down the large tree that drew his attention when he first moved in. Once the leaves were finally disposed of, he'd forgiven the tree for shedding her fall foliage, especially once Judge had deemed his work worthy of something called an allowance. Judge often called on him to do one task or another, but in the end, he always rewarded Franky with what he called honest wages. Franky wiped the sweat from his brow and rubbed his hands on his trousers. "I best be getting to it, then."

"Splendid," Judge said, a victorious smile spreading across his face. "You'll find the paint where we left it. I'll go in the house and make up some lemonade."

Franky went to work, pulling everything from the shed, leaving the ladder to help reach the upper walls and ceiling. He then pulled some of the newspapers from the stack, and using some adhesive tape, covered the windowpanes to keep from splashing paint onto the glass. He was careful to use single layers so to allow light to seep through. He soon discovered it was much easier to paint the inside of the shed, as it had never been painted before. Since the walls didn't need scraping, it didn't take much time at all to get everything covered.

As he finished with the last wall, he thought about his conversation with Judge and how the man had made painting the shed seem like a good idea. While the white paint made the shed look more cheerful, he still couldn't see any potential of using it as a fort. Never in all the books he'd read did any of the forts have white walls. White was a woman's color, used for houses and picket fences. As the thought came to him, he realized he'd been played. *Judge used his smarts to get me to paint this shed just like Tom Sawyer got his friend Ben and the other boys to do his work for him. But Tom had to paint the fence because he'd gotten in trouble. Am I in trouble?* He pondered that thought for a moment but couldn't think of anything he'd done to raise Judge's ire. *Then why make me paint the shed by myself?*

"I figured you'd be about finished. I brought you some lemonade," Judge said, bringing him out of his musings.

"Are you mad at me, Judge?" Franky asked, taking the glass and lifting it to his lips.

A frown fleeted across Judge's face. He peeked inside the shed then tilted his head at Franky. "Should I be?"

"I don't think so," Franky answered, then drained the contents of the glass. He used the back of his arm to wipe his mouth then handed the glass back. "I can't think of anything I've done wrong. But you made me paint the shed."

"I thought you wanted to paint the shed. Remember what we talked about."

"Yes, that's why I thought you were mad."

"Franklin, I'm beginning to think the heat has gotten to you. You're not making a lick of sense."

"It's just like in the book. Aunt Polly made Tom Sawyer paint the fence because he was in trouble. Only Tom didn't want to paint the fence, so he convinced his friends that they really wanted to paint the fence."

"So you think I tricked you into painting the fence?" There was a twinkle in Judge's eye as he spoke. "Franklin, I must admit I did use a bit of persuasion to get you to paint the shed, but not because you were in trouble. I did it because I'm not the young man I once was, and truth be told, I was tired, and you being a young fella and all, I thought you'd be able to make short work of it. And I was right. You're finished in half the time it took to paint the outside. And a fine job you did at that. Why, it hasn't looked this good in all the years she's been standing. I'm proud of you, son, and you should be proud as well, especially knowing you did it all by yourself."

Franky hung on each word as the praise poured out of his caregiver's mouth. He was tired, and his shoulders ached from moving the ladder and stretching to reach the upper corners of the small shed. But Judge had said he was proud of him, and at the moment, that was all that mattered.

Chapter Twenty

Franky pulled the checkered quilt over his bed, fluffed the pillow as he'd been shown, and raced from his room, sprinting down the stairs, eager to get started on his daily chores. First on his list, mow the yard. Rain had kept him from cutting it for nearly a week. Between the rain and the warm temps, the yard was looking like a jungle. If he didn't get it cut soon, he'd have to spend even more time raking it. He didn't mind mowing; it was the raking he detested. So much so, he often walked around the yard with a mower twice in the same week. Not for the first time, Franky wished Judge would invest in a new gas mower like their neighbor had. Franky knew the man was away visiting his son and gave a moment's thought to sneaking into the man's shed and borrowing it, a thought he immediately dismissed, knowing Judge wouldn't approve. Borrowing without asking was stealing, even if one brought the item back. Besides, Judge argued the push blade mower they had did a better job, further saying a man could think better without all that noise. Franky had argued that he didn't want to think—he wanted to cut the grass and be done—but Judge hadn't wavered, saying a man could get further in life by being a thinker. That was the thing about Judge; he was logical.

"You seem to be in quite the hurry this morning," Judge said as Franky bounded into the kitchen. "Think you could slow down long enough to eat breakfast?"

"Sure, I can. A fella can't do a good job without the proper fuel," Franky said, repeating what Judge had told him numerous times.

Judge stood in front of the stove, watching over a cast-iron skillet, and nodded toward the cupboard.

Franky understood the gesture, having witnessed it many times over the years. He opened the cabinet, retrieved two glasses, and walked to the icebox, retrieving the glass bottle of milk. Unscrewing the metal cap, Franky poured a glass for each before returning the container to the icebox. He gathered the glasses, placing them on the table before taking his seat.

Judge nodded his approval as he placed a plate of blueberry hotcakes in front of him, then set a second plate on the opposite side of the table. He let out a long sigh and took his place at the table, closing his eyes briefly. After a moment, Judge looked up and cocked an eyebrow. "What's got you all fired up this morning?"

He forgot. Franky's heart sank. They'd spent the better part of the evening discussing the Great Chicago Fire, and Judge had promised him he would take him to De Koven Street to show him where the fire started. He'd been awake a great deal of the night thinking of Mrs. O'Leary's cow and how the thing had knocked over a lamp, causing such destruction that was still talked about to this day.

All that missed sleep for nothing.

Franky picked up his utensils, somberly cut his hotcake, then drizzled warm syrup over his plate. Stabbing a piece with his fork, he took a bite and thought about reminding Judge of his promise. Something about the man seemed off, maybe because his face seemed to be lacking color this morning. Knowing Judge hadn't been feeling well of late, Franky decided it could wait until Judge felt more like himself. Hoping not to let his disappointment be known, he kept his eyes lowered as he slid the syrup across the table.

"Why, if I'd known blueberry pancakes would put the fire out that fast, I would've chosen something else for breakfast. You're not going to have enough energy to do your chores much less take a ride about town."

He didn't forget after all. Franky looked up and gave a sheepish grin. "I thought you'd forgotten. You having been ill and all."

"The doctor said I'm not to get excited is all. The body might be slowing down a bit, but the mind is still pristine," Judge replied. "When you're finished eating, you can help me put the top down on the Cadillac before you start your chores."

"Sure thing, Judge," Franky said between bites. Not knowing anything about automobiles, he'd been stunned at the beginning of spring when Judge first enlisted his help lowering the top on the Cadillac. Now he preferred riding around with the wind zipping around his face.

Franky finished his meal, guzzling the last of his milk before taking his dishes to the sink. He dipped them into the waiting water, used a cloth to clean each before rinsing everything under the faucet, and set them on the towel to dry. He then collected Judge's flatware and repeated the process. When finished, he turned to Judge, who had removed the handkerchief from his pocket and was in process of wiping sweat from his face. Odd, since it was early in the day, and the temperature seemed pleasant enough in the house. *I'm glad he didn't forget about our outing. The fresh air will do him good.* Franky managed a smile. "Are you ready?"

"Yes, yes. Ready," Judge said, pocketing the hanky.

Franky led the way outside, and Judge followed him onto the porch. An automobile pulled in front of the house, the door opened, and a man stepped out. His hair was the color of a rusty pipe and he was dressed as if he hadn't a penny to his name. As the guy made his way across the yard, Franky could smell the liquor that leached from the man's pores. Franky had seen men like this while touring what Judge referred to as the lower-class section of Chicago. Aside from the way he dressed, Franky knew there was something off about the man. Maybe it was the way his eyes darted from side to side as he approached.

Judge took in an audible breath, and Franky shot him a questioning look. Judge's face paled further as the man neared the house.

"Go back in the house, Franklin," Judge said under his breath.

What? And leave you alone with this guy? "But…"

"Now," Judge said, leaving no room for argument.

Franky chanced a glance over his shoulder before doing as told. Once inside, he scrambled to the floor and moved to the window, pulling the curtain aside so he wouldn't miss anything.

"Don't look so surprised to see me, Old Man. I told you I'd be back," the newcomer said as he started up the steps.

"That's far enough, Garret." Judge's voice was so cold, it made the hairs on Franky's arms stand on end.

So Judge knows the man. Not someone close, or I would have met him at some point. Garret. I'm sure I've heard that name before.

The man laughed but stayed in place. "Easy, Pop, I just came to see how you're doing."

"You've seen me. Now go away and take your friends with you," Judge said firmly.

Friends? Franky moved to the other window to get a better look inside the automobile. Sure enough, there were several people sitting inside.

"Yeah, I see you. I also see that fine ride in the driveway. A much better choice than the coupe you had when I lived here. A beauty like that must have set you back a buck or two." Garret lifted his eyes. "Tell me you still have more in that chest you keep hidden in your closet."

Garret. That was where he'd heard the name; the boy

Nathaniel said pushed Mrs. Beth down the stairs. Not a boy any longer, but Franky could see the wickedness behind the man's eyes. Franky sucked in a breath as Judge balled his hands into fists. He'd never seen the man so angry.

Judge pulled himself a little taller. "Get off my property before I throw you off."

"Now see, I thought we'd be able to do this the easy way," Garret said, looking toward the house. "Just look at the example you're setting for the kid. Why, he's standing right behind you watching everything."

He's lying; I'm not behind you. He's trying to trick you! Just as he opened his mouth to say as much, Judge cast a glance over his shoulder. From the look on his face, Franky knew Judge realized his mistake at taking his eyes off the man. He turned his attention back to Garret just as he slammed into him, knocking him into the door frame. Judge tried to fight back, but Garret was younger and faster. Within seconds, Judge lay on the cement porch gasping for breath. Franky pushed out the door ready for a fight and soon discovered he too was no match for Garret. The man didn't seem to mind hitting a child. In fact, it was as though he was enjoying using Franky as a punching bag. It felt as if the beating went on forever; in reality, it was probably only seconds. Time didn't matter; it wasn't as if the length of the pounding made it hurt any less. When at last the beating stopped, Garret gave Judge a final kick. Satisfied, he spat on the ground next to him and disappeared inside the house.

Franky tried to control the sobs as he made his way to Judge, who hadn't moved. Laughter drifted overhead as several people joined them on the porch. Franky wondered what they found so funny and further questioned why no one offered to help. He thought about asking, but instead, he laid his head on Judge's chest and closed his eyes.

The sun was high in the sky when Franky woke and found himself lying on his bed on top of the quilt. Regret washed over him as he felt the heaviness of the air and realized he'd slept in. *I was supposed to cut the grass. Judge is going to be disappointed. Why didn't he wake me?* He moved to get up and felt the effects of his earlier beating. Only then did the events of the morning come rushing back. The last thing he remembered was crawling over to Judge and placing his head on the man's chest.

Judge!

Breathing through the pain, Franky gingerly made his way to the door to his bedroom. He pulled it open and checked for any signs of Garret or his friends. Not seeing them, he walked to Judge's room and placed a hand on the doorknob, hesitating. Uncertainty kept him standing there for several moments until, at last, he turned the knob, pushed open the door, and searched the room. At first, he didn't see the man, as the sheet covered his entire body. Odd, since the room felt like the inside of a furnace. He swallowed his fear, walked to the bed, and touched the man through the sheet.

"Judge?" When he failed to answer, Franky poked him a bit harder. It wasn't like him to take an afternoon nap. "Judge, it's hot in here. Why do you have the sheets over your head?"

Still no answer.

Franky bit at his lower lip as he gripped the sheet with his fingers and pulled it down. Judge's face was cut and bruised, but his eyes were open, staring at him. Franky smiled. It hurt to do so, but the relief won out over the pain. "Boy, Judge, you sure scared me. Did you carry me to bed? You must have. I don't recall walking there myself."

Judge didn't answer. He just continued to stare at Franky with unblinking eyes.

"What is it, Judge? Why won't you talk to me? I did

what you told me and stayed inside." Not true; he'd come out when Judge fell to the ground. *Was that it? Was Judge mad at him?* Tears rolled down Franky's cheeks as he shook the man and tried to make him understand. "Don't be mad, Judge. I didn't mean to disobey you. It's just that the guy kept hitting and kicking you. I was afraid. I had to come out."

When Judge still didn't answer, Franky stared at his chest, waiting for movement that never came. In the recesses of his brain, Franky knew Judge was dead. But he'd never dealt with death before, and it was easier to think the man angry than face the reality of the situation. A fly circled Judge's face then landed on the tip of his nose. Franky willed Judge to brush the creature away. When he didn't, Franky shooed it with his hand and then carefully pulled the sheet up to keep it from landing again. He stood staring, wondering what he should do next. An image of Nathan came to mind. Franky knew how to get to the department store. He'd been there with Judge enough to know the route. He would take the Cadillac. He'd watched Judge enough to think he'd be able to drive. *Ha, you can't even reach the pedals,* he chided himself. *Maybe if I sit on the edge of the seat, my feet will reach. It's worth a try. I can't leave Judge here all alone. Are we alone?*

He didn't hear any noise, but maybe Garret and his friends were being quiet, waiting for him to come downstairs. He struggled with his emotions for several moments, trying to decide his next course of action. Finally, not knowing what else to do, Franky crept from the room. He stayed silent, even though it hurt to walk, edging down the stairs and stopping on each one to listen for any sign he wasn't alone. When at last he reached the bottom, he looked around the room. His gaze sought out the open window, forgot his need for silence, and cried out his anguish.

The Cadillac was gone!

Chapter Twenty-One

Franky sat on the floor just outside Judge's bedroom hugging his knees to his chest. As much as he wanted to check on the man, he couldn't bring himself to go inside. Never having dealt with death before, he wasn't sure what he was supposed to do.

A fly buzzed past, circled his head, then landed on one of his many wounds. He winced as he lifted a hand to usher it away. It took flight, circling once more before landing on the other arm. He thought about brushing it away once more, then decided the pain wasn't worth the bother. It was easier to close his eyes.

***

Franky opened his eyes, lifted his head, and wiped the drool from his face. Just the simple movement made him wish to cry out. A tear trickled down his cheek, and he could hold back no longer. Opening his mouth, he wailed his sorrow, letting the tears flow without trying to stifle them. When at last they ebbed, he realized just how vile he looked and smelt. On a sob, he stood and stripped the clothes from his body, tossing them onto the floor without a care. He walked into his bedroom to retrieve another set and remembered one of the chores of the day was supposed to be washing out his dirty laundry and hanging them on the line.

He stood staring at the nearly empty drawer for several moments before deciding underwear would suffice. Lifting a pair from the drawer, he walked from the room without bothering to close it.

Judge had often taken baths with Epson salt to alleviate the pain from his leg. Franky decided to do the same. He made his way to the water closet, took hold of the chain, and pulled the rubber stopper into his hand. Securing the plug in the hole, he turned on the water. He couldn't remember what temperature Judge liked his bath for soaking out the pain, so Franky adjusted it to his liking. As the tub filled, Franky went to the closet and brought out a fresh towel and the container of Epson salt. He loosened the lid and poured some into the tub, then started to return the container to the closet. Pain surged through his body, so Franky decided to add some more for good measure. Once the tub was nearly full, he turned off the water. As he sank into the bath, some of the water overflowed onto the floor. Franky looked over the edge, thought about getting out and cleaning the mess, then decided he didn't care.

His stomach rumbled, and he wondered what Judge would make for supper. Then he remembered, and tears trickled once more. Franky closed his eyes and retraced the events of the morning. Odd how having breakfast was the only normal thing that had occurred that day. He remembered walking onto the porch, watching as the car pulled to the curb, and recalled the shock at seeing Judge clench his fingers into fists.

Judge didn't have his cane with him.

Franky's eyes opened wide. It wasn't abnormal for Judge to move about the house without his cane. Still, Franky wondered if having the stick would have made any difference. *Probably not. Probably Garret would have taken it from Judge and used it on him. That could have made matters worse.* Franky laughed a hollow laugh. *Judge is dead. How could it get worse?*

As if in answer to his unvoiced question, Franky heard the muffled sound of voices drifting up the stairs. Forgetting his pain, he scrambled from the tub and quickly brushed the water from his bruised body with the towel.

Clad only in underwear Franky tiptoed from the washroom without a sound.

"Well, look who's still among the living," a man he didn't know said as he reached for his pile of clothes. Dressed in holed trousers and a once-white crumpled shirt, the man smiled, showcasing several missing teeth.

Franky left the pile in place and inched back toward the washroom as Garret breached the top of the stairs and joined them in the hallway. Garret stopped just before reaching him and opened the door to Judge's room and looked inside.

"He's the only one. The old man's a goner," Garret said. "Heck, if I knew it would be this easy, I'd have done him when I did Ma. It would've saved the hassle of living on the streets all these years. Course I'd have done it upstairs so I wouldn't have to drag the old man up the stairs again."

"You should have left the old geezer on the porch," the other guy chided.

"What and let him fester in the sun? Why, JT, whatever would the neighbors say?" Garret replied.

"Better out there than in the bedroom," JT said, wrinkling his nose. "All I know is I'm not sleeping in there."

"Ain't no one sleeping in there," Garret said, closing the door once again. "Keep the door shut. The flies are already swarming. Gonna get real ripe in there pretty soon. Let him rot for all I care."

Franky felt the blood rise in his cheeks. He sprinted toward Garret, aiming to sink his teeth into the man's arm. Garret moved out of the way and shoved Franky, sending him headfirst into the wall. Dazed, Franky dropped to his knees, blinking to clear his vision.

JT pulled a cigarette from behind his ear and a matchbook from his pocket. He lit the tip of the cigarette and let the match fall to the floor. "Maybe we should take out the kid as well."

"Na, the kid has some spunk. I say we keep him around and have some fun with him," Garret replied. "What do you say, kid, ready to have some fun?"

JT's frown transitioned into a smile as he flipped the cigarette onto Franky's discarded clothes and took a step in the boy's direction.

Garret caught hold of JT's arm. "Put that out before you catch the house on fire. I ain't sleeping on the streets another night."

JT pulled his arm free and walked over to where the cigarette lay smoldering atop the clothes. His smile broadened as he unzipped his pants and began urinating on the pile of clothes.

"Nice," Garret touted. "It's not bad enough we have a body in there festering, now the whole house is going to smell like piss."

JT said, shrugging off the comment, "You said to put it out. Besides, who made you boss?"

"My house, my rules," Garret replied.

Franky had heard enough. "It's not your house. You don't belong here. Judge said so."

Garret grabbed hold of Franky and pulled him kicking and screaming toward Judge's bedroom. Once inside, he yanked down the sheet and pushed Franky's head close to the unmoving body. "Hey, Old Man, the kid here thinks you want me to leave. Say something if you agree."

Franky choked back a sob as Garret waited for his answer. After several moments, Garret jerked him away. "You see there, kid; Judge doesn't mind if we stay."

Seething with rage, Franky twisted, and this time managed to tear into Garret's arm with his teeth. He bit down, tasting blood as Garret tried to shake him off. When at last Franky let go, there was a gaping hole in Garret's arm.

JT tripped him as he ran from the room, sending him sliding across the floor. Franky crawled to his bedroom, and both men followed. Fear surged through his body as JT shut the door behind them.

***

Franky sat in the corner of the room, trembling and staring at the closed door. There wasn't a part of his body that didn't hurt, nor a part of his heart not filled with anger. As nightfall dimmed the room, he welcomed the loss of light. He was tired. Tired of fighting, tired of loathing the men who'd destroyed his chance at happiness, tired of hearing the laughter of his attackers, but mostly tired of seeing the indignities done to him. He closed his eyes and willed his life away. If he were going to die, he wished it to be today.

***

It was still dark when next he heard voices. More of them this time, all laughing. He heard the unmistakable lilt of women's voices mingled with the rest. For a moment, he thought of going in search of the voices, but fear prevented him from doing so. Instead, he pulled himself to his feet and went to secure the lock on the door. The voices grew louder. Franky's heartbeat quickened when they stopped outside his door. He heard the unmistakable rattle of the doorknob. And then the door vibrated against its hinges.

Franky jumped as fists pounded the door. He searched the blackness, looking for a place to hide. Pointless, as the second the light flicked on, he would be discovered. It was as if he were at war, and the enemy was coming for him. *I need a fortress.* As the thought came to him, he heard Judge's voice so clear for a second, he thought the man to be standing next to him. *Go to the shed!* But how? He'd never make it without getting caught. If only there were another way out.

The tree. Judge made me promise to wait until he gave permission. Judge is dead. His head throbbed as he struggled with his indecision.

A renewed pounding against his bedroom door gave him all the permission he needed. He pushed the screen from his window and swallowed his fear as he climbed onto the window frame. It was a long way down, he knew, as he'd judged it often enough. The only light was from the full moon, which was drifting in and out of the clouds.

"Hey, Garret, come help me kick in this door. The blasted kid's got it locked," JT's voice called from the other side.

I'd rather die from the tree than stay here.

Franky jumped and somehow managed to land on a limb. Once he latched on, he didn't stop to gather his courage. He'd scurried down the tree a million times within his mind. As he descended, each branch was precisely where he pictured it to be. Leaving the tree turned out to be trickier than he thought as the branches were higher than he'd imagined. After a bit of consideration, he landed on the ground with a jolt. He stood, waited for a wave of nausea to pass, then ran the short distance to the shed.

It was padlocked, but he knew one of the windows to be easy to open. It wouldn't be the first time he'd use it to gain entrance. As he reached the back of the house, he heard agitated voices from within. He started to cross the lawn, realized the moon was illuminating the whole yard, and paused. He remembered one of the books he'd read and how the regiment had waited for cloud cover to sneak through the enemy lines, and willed himself to wait. All the while, he was aware of the voices growing louder.

Please don't let them find me.

A cloud captured the moon's light once more, and Franky sprinted across the yard. It hurt to run. He imagined himself shot by enemy troops and reminded himself it was only a short distance to safety. He rounded the shed just as the cloud passed, pushed the window open, and clawed his way inside the small shed.

Once inside, he locked the window and tested the latch on the other. Satisfied, he opened the drawer to the toolbox and used his fingers to procure a screwdriver. Clutching his weapon, he crouched in the far corner, waiting.

It wasn't long before he heard the voices outside of his hiding place. He was glad he'd left the paper on the windows, telling Judge it would help to keep the shed cool. In truth, he'd been too tired to remove it. However, since Judge agreed with the farce, the paper had remained taped to the window.

A shadowy face pressed against the other side of the glass. "Hey, kid, you in there?"

Franky held his breath.

"Come on out, kid. We want to play some more."

Franky cringed at hearing JT's voice so close.

"The kid's not in there," Garret called from the front of the shed.

"How can you be so sure?"

"The door's locked."

"Yeah, well, maybe he locked it after he got inside," JT argued.

"Not unless he's a magician. It's locked from the outside," Garret said.

Someone jiggled the lock once more, and then the voices drifted away.

Trembling, Franky breathed out a sigh of relief. A short time later, Franky curled into a ball and silently cried himself to sleep.

Chapter Twenty-Two

Franky jumped to his feet, teetering back and forth a second before extending a hand to steady himself. He remained quiet, listening for the sound that woke him. An engine started then motored down the street, stopping once again. He instantly recognized the stop and go sound – *the milk truck.* It rumbled down the street each morning before dawn, while most people were still sleeping. In the summer months, when the windows were open, the motor would wake him. He would lie there listening for the subtle clang of the jars as the milkman retrieved their order of fresh milk – two fluted jars each day – and then drift back to sleep as the truck motored toward its next delivery.

Franky's stomach rumbled at the thought of fresh, chilled milk. He hadn't eaten or drank anything since breakfast the previous day. If only he could get to the milk before anyone else. *Why couldn't I? They're probably sleeping. Maybe they're gone. Doubtful; Garret had called this his house. But if they are sleeping, I can get the milk and climb back into the shed before anyone sees me.* Once he'd made the decision, there was no turning back. His stomach growled its insistence.

Unlocking the window, Franky climbed onto the ledge before jumping the short distance to the ground. The jump reminded him of his injuries. Closing his eyes, he waited for the pain to pass then made his way to the front porch, making sure to stay close to the house, ducking beneath the windows so as not to be seen. The front porch would be trickier. He stopped at the edge of the brick, wondering if it would be better to climb over the side or boldly walk up the front stairs. He studied the brick ledge for a moment, considering. He'd climbed it many times in the past without difficulty. Realizing his body ached with each breath, he decided to take the stairs. The best plan was to run up the steps, grab both bottles of milk, then speed back to the safety of his fort. But running wasn't an option. He was entirely too sore. He kept low so as not to be seen over the brick railing and slowly made his way to the stairwell. Once there, he gathered his courage, taking the steps one at a time. He picked up the first container, reached for the second, and hesitated. *Garret used to live with Judge. He'll be expecting the milk.* Franky decided to leave the second container, hoping to alleviate the man's suspicions.

Retracing his steps, he returned to the shed and raised the window. Only then did it occur to him, he would not be able to climb inside while holding the milk. Nor could he toss it in without risk of breaking the glass. *I could drink it here. No, I'd never be able to drink it all right away.*

He placed his back to the shed and closed his eyes, his mind searching for a solution. If I had a rope, I could use it to lower the bottle. He tried to remember if there was any rope in the shed but couldn't remember seeing any. He opened his eyes and found himself staring at the neighbor's shed. Mr. Callahan would have some. He had everything. Franky set the bottle on the ground, walked to the shed, lifted the sign on the door, and retrieved the key to the lock. Why the man locked the door, he didn't know. He never bothered to hide where he kept the key. Franky found a length of coiled rope hanging just inside the door, plucked it from its hook, closed the door, clicked on the padlock, and returned the key. He was just about to leave when he remembered the blueberry bush that grew at the back of the shed. He knew them to be ripe, as he'd picked some a few days earlier, presenting them to Judge to make a pie. His heart ached at the memory. Shaking it off, he retrieved the bucket from the hook aside the shed, and began pulling berries from the bush.

It was nearly daylight when at last Franky returned to the shed with his coveted breakfast. He tied the rope around the jar and lowered it through the window, setting it upright on the ground. It was only then he realized he still needed to get the bucket of berries inside. *I could drop them to the ground. It's not like they'll break. No, I'll squish them when I climb inside.*

His head throbbed, making it difficult to come up with a plan. Hearing the back screen door slam, he scrambled into action, tossing both the rope and bucket through the window. The bucket tipped, and the berries rolled across the hard-packed dirt. He clasped the windowsill and, ignoring the pain, used his feet to climb inside. He'd just managed to lower the window and flip the lock into place when he heard someone fiddling with the window.

Franky froze in place as a shadowy figure moved forward as if trying to see through the light layer of newspaper. The shadow disappeared, and Franky heard the sound of the padlock rubbing against metal. The rubbing stopped. He froze, only taking in a full breath of air when he heard the screen door slam once again.

Franky dropped to the ground, unscrewed the lid from the glass, and tilted it to his lips, drinking in greedy gulps, not caring that some of the liquid ran down his chin. It was sweet and delightfully cool to his parched throat, adding a much-welcomed fullness to his empty stomach. He drank nearly half of the container before finally pulling the glass from his lips. Only then did he lower into a squat and spread his fingers in search of the tart berries.

The meal, as simple as it was, helped. While it still hurt to move, the throbbing in his head was less, and he could think much clearer. Unfortunately, it also meant he could remember things he'd managed to push aside. He thought of Judge and wondered if that pain of losing him would ever go away. *I don't think so.* For lack of anything better to do, Franky returned to his corner and closed his eyes.

***

It was much brighter inside the shed when next he woke. Even with the papers covering the windows, it was stifling hot inside his little fortress. Franky pressed his face to the papers, surprised he could make out the image of the house.

If I can see the house, maybe they can see me.

He pulled the adhesive tape from the drawer, gathered some papers from the stack, and went to work adding several more layers to the windows. It didn't matter that he could no longer see anything inside the shed. If he couldn't see out, it was very likely they couldn't see in either. Satisfied with his handiwork, he lay on the dirt floor, welcoming what little coolness it offered.

With his most crucial need met, Franky fell into a routine of sleeping, waking for brief periods, and falling asleep once more. He didn't know how much time had passed when, at last, he woke feeling the need to relieve himself. Afraid to venture outside, he emptied a large tin can then took a stack of newspaper to the opposite corner of the shed. He thought of the shovel and wished he could dig a hole to dispose of the waste as they did in several books he'd read, but it was dark in the shed, and he was afraid he'd accidentally bump into the can, spilling the contents.

He wished for something to read to take his mind off his current situation then realized he would not be able to light a lamp without being discovered. Someone laughed, and he scurried back to his hiding place as voices filled the air. After several uneventful moments, he crawled to the far wall and stood. Feeling his way to the window, he dared pull back a small corner of the paper, surprised to discover darkness had returned.

A group of people stood in the backyard near the stoop. Bile rose in his throat as he heard both Garret's and JT's voices amongst those standing around. They were smoking something, and as the night wore on, their laughter increased. Every now and then, someone would take hold of another's hand and lead that person inside the house. Moments later, a light would switch on in one of the upstairs rooms. The routine continued until, at last, the yard was empty once more. Having nothing else to do, he stood at the window, staring out through the peephole until the house grew dark, and there was nothing more to see. He was just entertaining going to sleep when he remembered the empty bottle of milk. *The milkman will not replace it unless the bottle is there.* He doubted Garret had thought to leave the other by the front door.

Groping the ground for his empty bottle, he went to the far window and raised it, sucking in the night air. Though humid, it was far better than the stale air inside the shed. He used the rope to lower the bottle and climbed out after it. Crouching low, he untied the line and set it to the side. He thought about lowering the window but decided to leave it open until he returned. He kept to the shadows once he crossed the yard, but this time, he only crouched when he neared a window. He walked up the step, placing the empty bottle near the door. His stomach grumbled, and he gave a moment's thought to sneaking inside the house in search of something to eat. The memory of Garret and JT's laughter convinced him to turn around and return to the shelter of the shed.

***

Franky was awake and hiding in the bushes near the house when the milkman made his delivery. It never occurred to him to ask him for help. Instead, he waited for the man to return to his truck before sneaking onto the porch and retrieving the milk. Famished, he had most of the contents drunk by the time he returned to the shed. He gathered some berries, sitting with his back to the shed while he ate. As the sun rose, he stood ready to head back into his sanctuary. He heard a door slam and dared peek around the building. A car idled in front of the house, and to his surprise, Garret, JT, and several others piled inside. A moment later, the vehicle sped off.

He stood in place for some time before gathering the courage to venture toward the house. Finally, he placed one foot in front of the other, repeating the process until, at last, he was at the back door. He twisted the handle, surprised to find it unlocked. As he entered, his senses were on high alert. Franky knew he should look for food and leave, but he'd just eaten, and food was not a necessity at the moment.

Almost unconsciously, he made his way up the stairs, turned the doorknob to his bedroom, pushed open the door, and looked inside. The room was a mess and reeked of nothing he'd ever smelled before. He closed the door and walked to the room across the hall. His breath caught when he opened the door and looked inside. Three ladies were lying naked across the bed and appeared to be sleeping. A man he didn't recognize sat on the floor, holding a round glass bottle in his hands. The bottle seemed to be on fire as smoke drifted from the clear liquid inside. He smiled and offered Franky the bottle, and Franky shook his head. The man shrugged and sealed the bottle with his lips. Franky closed the door.

He made his way to the next door and willed himself to turn the knob. His hand trembled as he twisted the doorknob. Even as he pushed the door open, his mind was screaming for him to run. Except for his near visit to the stockyards, he'd never smelled anything so foul. Struggling for control, he walked to the bed and lifted the sheet. He screamed and let the cloth fall back into place. He was halfway down the stairs when he looked out the front window and saw the car that had carried Garret and JT away pull into the driveway. He rounded the stairs without stopping, ran through the kitchen, and pushed through the screen door, which slammed in his wake. Running as fast as his feet would carry him, he sprinted across the yard and climbed through the open window without stopping to gather his belongings.

His heart pounded within the walls of his chest, nearly stopping when he heard Garret and JT calling for him. He heard the men at the window and realized in his haste he'd forgotten to lock it.

"Check it out. The kid's been stealing our milk." Garret was right outside the window.

"It's not nice to steal. Time to come out, kid; we know you're hiding in there." JT said. "Hey, look at this. The chump left us a rope to tie him up with."

The window slid open, and Garret stuck his face inside. "You like to play games? We've got some to teach you."

Fear gripped Franky as he looked for something to use as a weapon. Spying the screwdriver, he jabbed it toward the window, just missing Garret as he ducked out of the way.

"Want I should go in after him?" JT asked.

"No, he's got too much fight left in him. I say we heat things up a bit. By the time we come back, he'll be ready to play real nice," Garret said and closed the window.

Relief washed over Franky as he heard their laughter drift toward the house. He'd just settled onto the ground when he heard the sound of breaking glass. He jumped to his feet and peeled back the paper to get a better look. Though he couldn't see the men, he could tell they had broken into Mr. Callahan's shed. Garret and JT came back into view, and Franky hurried to lock the window. He needn't have bothered, as when they returned, they proceeded to nail the window shut. Seconds later, they repeated the process on the other side.

"Don't even think about breaking the glass, kid. If you do, we'll come running, and you won't like the things we do," Garret promised.

After they left, Franky tested the windows and found them securely closed. He smiled. *They'll never get in now.*

Chapter Twenty-Three

As the day wore on, the temperature inside the shed skyrocketed. Franky felt the ground beneath him and wondered for a moment if he'd unknowingly wet himself then realized it was only sweat. Rising from his resting place, he wiped the moisture from his face, wishing he hadn't left the remainder of the milk outside. He wondered if Garret and JT had taken the bottle with them and decided to check. He went to the window, unfastened the latch, and pushed. *It won't open.* He made several attempts before remembering the events of the morning. *They nailed the window shut.* He'd been so relieved at having been left alone, it never dawned on him to consider the consequences. While Garret and JT couldn't get inside, it also meant he had no way of leaving.

But it's so very hot in here.

He thought about breaking the glass but remembered what'd they'd said. *"If you do, we'll come running, and you won't like the things we do."*

A chill ran through him, and he rubbed at his arms, wondering how it was possible to be cold when it was so hot in the small room. Not knowing what else to do, he returned to his corner and closed his eyes. As he drifted off to sleep, Garrett and JT joined him in his dreams.

***

The sound of rolling thunder woke him from his nightmare. He opened his eyes, grateful for the reprieve. He lay there in the dark, watching as the lightning danced its way through the layered newspapers covering the windows. It wasn't long before the patter of rain danced on the roof. *If only I could open the window and stick my head out.* He remembered when he lived in the asylum and how he was afraid to sleep near the window. Now he'd give anything if he could open it and stick his head outside. He sneered at his silliness. Oh, what he'd give to have that chance again. He hadn't thought of his days at the asylum in years; funny how having a real home made one forget the troubles of the past. *But I don't have a home. Judge is dead, and Garret and JT want to do bad things to me.* He remembered his dream and quickly pushed the image away. *There's no way of stopping them. I'm going to die.*

An image of Judge, bluish-grey and lying on the bed covered with flies, replaced Garret and JT. Just as disturbing, only Judge didn't want to hurt him. Judge couldn't help it that he was dead.

If they kill me, I'll look and smell like that too. The realization hit him like a slap across the face. Sinking further into his corner, he thought about what he'd seen when he pulled back the sheet. He'd never seen death before, but now he had trouble unseeing it. Worse than seeing it was the way the room had smelled. The only thing he could remember smelling anything even close was when he and Judge had driven near the stockyards.

Does death hurt? He didn't think so because even though Judge looked and smelled terrible, he hadn't made a sound. Suddenly, dying didn't sound so bad. *At least I won't hurt when I'm dead.*

Resigned to his fate, Franky pulled his hands around his knees and waited for death to take him.

***

Once again, Franky woke to the sound of the milk truck puttering down the street. He waited for the engine to slow, but it continued past the house. *Garret must have forgotten to place the jugs outside.* Pulling to his feet, he winced as his body fought the movement. He licked his lips, tasted dried blood, and wished for something to wash away the taste. Stifling a sob, he lowered to the dirt floor of the shed. As the storm drifted away, he succumbed to sleep once again.

Sometime later, he thought he heard a car door slam. It sounded close and he wondered if Garret and TJ were leaving or if they'd just returned. He gave a moment's thought to pulling back the edge of the paper and taking a look then decided he didn't care. If they were leaving, they were sure to come back. If they'd returned…well, he'd find out soon enough.

The air was so hot, he found it difficult to breathe. The smell coming from the can filled the air. It wasn't that he'd needed to use it often, but he'd neglected to empty it when he'd had the chance.

Sweat trickled down his arm, and in desperation, he chased the liquid with his tongue. The salty dribble did nothing to satisfy his thirst.

Am I dead? He didn't think so, but he poked some of his wounds just to be sure. Touching a particularly painful spot, he called out against the pain. *Nope, not dead yet.*

He had no way of knowing how long he'd been locked in the shed, but it surprised him it was taking so long to die. After all, Judge died in only a matter of moments. He pictured the man's face and angrily pushed the image from his mind. His anger caught him by surprise. He had no reason to be mad at the man. Did he?

The screen door slammed, bringing him to his senses. They were coming for him. A part of him welcomed the release, but something deeper inside was still willing to put up a fight. He groped the ground for the screwdriver, found it, and wrapped his hands around the tool. Trembling with a mixture of fear and anticipation, he waited.

Whoever was outside tried the lock. A second later, a faint shadow fell over the window, and Franky heard someone breathing just beyond the glass. He closed his eyes when he opened them again; the shadow was gone.

Franky jumped when a loud bang pierced the air. The noise caught him by surprise, causing him to lose his grip on the screwdriver. The door opened, and sunshine flooded the small shed. He'd been sitting in the dark so long, the light hurt his eyes. He raised a hand to shield the sun. As his eyes adjusted, he realized the man was brandishing a gun.

Smartly dressed in a dark suit and shiny black shoes, the man looked under the brim of his hat, studying him briefly before stepping inside.

Franky clutched the screwdriver once again, holding it like a knife. Trying to appear more menacing than he felt, he clenched his teeth as he spoke. "Come near me again, and I'll kill ya."

The man hesitated, then holstered his pistol and lowered into a squat. He raised his hands, and when he spoke, his voice was calm. "Easy, boy, I'm a friend. I'm not here to hurt you. Your name is Franky, yes?"

Maybe it was the way the man was dressed. Perhaps it was the fact that he called him by name. But something told Franky he could trust the guy. Tears of relief sprang from his eyes as he tossed the screwdriver to the ground and ran into the stranger's arms, clutching him as if he were a long lost friend. After he'd cried himself dry, he released his hold on the stranger and rubbed at his tear-filled eyes.

The man looked him up and down, his dark eyes narrowing as they took in his bruised and battered body. "Who did this to you, boy?"

"I don't know their names," Franky said, looking

toward the house. He didn't mean to lie, but now that he was rescued, he didn't wish to speak of them.

The stranger's jaw twitched. "Do you know faces?"

He wanted to tell the man that he couldn't stop seeing their faces. He could see them in the dark, when he closed his eyes, and especially in his dreams. He was beginning to think he'd never stop seeing Garret or JT. Nor could he forget the evil things they'd done to him. Instead, he merely nodded.

"Show me." The man sounded agitated, and for a moment, Franky thought the man knew he'd told a lie. Before he could ask for forgiveness, the man took hold of his hand and led him from the shed. Franky filled his lungs with the humid air. Though it was muggy, the air was clean and didn't burn his nostrils. They started toward the house, and Franky thought to argue. How could one man be a match for so many? He thought about what they did to Judge and worried they would do the same to his rescuer. Then he remembered the gun. He didn't recall seeing any of the others with a weapon. Besides, this man didn't look like someone who would take too kindly to being argued with.

They entered through the back door, searched the bottom floor, and found it empty.

Maybe they left. The man kept hold of his hand and started toward the stairs. Franky wanted to tell the man he wasn't a baby and didn't need his hand held, but something about the confidence in the way the man walked – as if he weren't afraid of anything or anyone – kept him silent. He'd been alone and scared too long. This man's touch felt safe.

As they climbed the stairs, the stench invaded his nostrils. Franky wondered if the man smelt it too, then knew he did when he coughed and covered his nose with his hand. Franky wondered if the man knew he was smelling death, and started to ask, but there were so many flies, he decided to keep his mouth closed.

The man opened the first door and stepped aside as another familiar odor filled the hallway. Franky remembered the smell from the last time he'd ventured upstairs. He looked inside and saw the man who'd offered him smoke from the bottle. The ladies were still with him. However, they were no longer asleep. In fact, they were very much awake and still not wearing any clothes. He took another look, gulped, and quickly shook his head.

He did the same with the two additional rooms.

The man led him to Judge's door, which, to his surprise, was fully open. Franky looked closer and wondered who'd broken the door. He planted his feet, pulled at the man's arm, and shook his head, silently pleading the man not to make him go inside. "That's not him."

The man seemed relieved at not having to enter. Instantly, Franky knew he had smelled death before.

The stranger pulled the door closed. "Where are your clothes, kid?"

Franky blinked back tears as he pointed to his urine-soaked clothes still lying in the middle of the hallway.

The man's jaw twitched once again as he took hold of Franky's hand and led him down the stairs.

Seeing a second man sitting on the porch railing, Franky hesitated at the door.

The man waved a pistol and tilted his head as he spoke to Franky's rescuer. "I heard the shot and thought I'd keep these two company until you returned. Everything okay in there?'

His rescuer shook his head and moved aside.

Franky gulped when he saw Garret and JT lying in the shade of the porch. They smiled when they saw him, and fear raced up his spine once more. Mustering his courage, he stepped outside and pointed at both men.

JT licked his lips and elbowed Garret in the side. “Look who's finally come out to play.”

Without warning, Franky’s rescuer pulled his pistol, firing a single round at each man. It was over in a flash, and Franky knew them each to be dead.

His rescuer holstered his gun and turned to Franky. “You are not to speak of them. You are not to allow them to invade your dreams at night. They are dead and can never hurt you again, understand?”

Franky wanted to tell him that they’d already invaded his dreams. Instead, he nodded.

His rescuer took him by the hand once again and turned his attention to the other man. “I guess we’re done here.”

Looking at Garret and JT lying dead on the porch, Franky only had one thought, that it was too quick. For what they’d done to him, dying should have taken longer.

Chapter Twenty-Four

Franky sat in the backseat of the green car feeling better than he had in days. The driver, a guy called Joey, had driven them to an apartment where he'd been fed and allowed to take a shower. His rescuer, a man he only knew as Mouse, had doctored his cuts and Joey had given him a shirt to wear. The shirt wore like a dress, hanging well past his knees, but he was clean and so was the shirt. Besides, from what he'd seen, he didn't think either man to be in the mood for argument. As a matter of fact, there'd been very little conversation since leaving Judge's house. Franky himself hadn't uttered a sound. After being ushered to the car once more, Joey drove them a short distance to the department store where they were currently parked.

Mouse opened the door and Franky moved to follow.

Mouse put up a hand. "You stay here with Joey while I get you some decent clothes to wear."

Franky didn't want him to leave. He thought to protest being left behind but decided against it. Leaning against the seat, he stared out the window, watching as Mouse went into the store.

Joey waited for Mouse to enter before turning and looking over the rear seat. "You okay, kid?"

Franky kept staring out the window, preferring not to answer.

"Things looked pretty bad back at the house. How long's it been like that?"

Franky remained silent.

Joey lit a cigarette, inhaled and then blew the smoke out in a slow and steady stream. "I gather Judge is dead?"

Franky's head snapped around as if he'd been punched. "How do you know about Judge?"

Joey glanced at the store before speaking. "I knew Judge well. I used to be one of his boys. He took me in a few years ago, although I wasn't what one would call a faithful student. The old man tried, but I guess I was already too far gone."

Franky glared at Joey. Mouse had told him not to speak of the men, but he couldn't stop himself. "The man that…the one with the missing teeth, he was also one of Judge's boys. Did you know him?"

"No, Judge must have taken him in after I left."

Franky narrowed his eyes. "He's the one that killed him. Did you want to see Judge dead too?"

Joey took another drag from the cigarette and blew it out slowly. "No, I admired the man. Not many people will take in a stray dog knowing the dog might bite. But Judge, he could see past the anger and hate and could whittle away the fear. Most of the time anyway. He did the best he could with me. In the end, I guess I was a dog he couldn't tame. Al – Mr. Capone – the man I work for – was able to reach the part that Judge never could. He knows how to take a mad dog and use them to his advantage. Fuel the fire, so to speak, and sic the dog on his enemies. It keeps us both happy. How about you, kid, did Judge manage to knock the chip off your shoulder?"

Franky looked at his shoulder, trying to see what chip Joey was referring to.

"I was speaking metaphorically, kid." Joey laughed. "Maybe the old man did some good after all. If it wasn't for Judge teaching me to read, I'd have never known how to use that word in a sentence."

Franky narrowed his eyes. "You stayed on the porch. If

you knew Judge lived there, why didn't you go in and check on him?"

"I guess I already knew. I recognized the address as soon as Mouse showed it to me, though I didn't let on at the time. I pulled up and knew something bad had happened. The man I knew never would've let his yard go to seed like that. He was a stickler for having the best lawn on the street. Even with his gimpy leg, he managed. So, yes, I knew and couldn't bear to face the truth."

"So you're a coward, then?"

Joey took a long pull from the cigarette and smiled. "I guess Judge still had some work to do with you. Am I a coward? Maybe, but not in the way you think. I wasn't afraid of those people at the house, but I have a reputation to uphold. It wouldn't be good for Al – Mr. Capone – to know I'd spent time living with a judge. A person could be considered a rat for much less. I would not wish the man to question my loyalty, so I waited in the car until Mouse went inside. I saw the men on the porch and we had a chat. After speaking with them for a moment, I decided to stay with them to make sure they didn't get away. I couldn't just kill them, as that would've raised questions. If Mouse hadn't taken care of the matter, I'd have dropped by later and seen to things. My only regret is that it wasn't my bullets that vindicated Judge."

Franky thought about what Joey had said about using the dog to his advantage and knew the man was talking about the anger inside himself. He looked Joey in the eye.

Joey met his gaze and took a puff from the cigarette. "You got something to say, kid?"

"There are more people inside. They were there when Judge…" Franky's voice cracked, and he hesitated. Swallowing, he continued. "They were in the car, but they had to have seen what was going on. They could have stopped it, but all they did was laugh and say Judge had gotten what he'd deserved. Judge didn't deserve to die. He hadn't done anything wrong. All he did was try to help them, the way he helped me. The way he tried to help you."

Franky lowered his eyes and swallowed once again, hoping Joey wouldn't see through his lies. Judge hadn't tried to help any of them. He'd stood at the door, insisting they leave. At first, Franky had thought him to be rude, but in retrospect, he had no doubt Judge knew them all to be bad seeds. Sucking in his courage, Franky locked eyes with Joey once more.

Joey flung the cigarette butt out the window without taking his eyes off Franky. His jaw twitched and he bared his teeth ever so slightly. He didn't reply to what Franky had said, but then again, he didn't need to. There was no doubt in Franky's mind that they'd reached an understanding.

***

Opening his eyes, Franky saw a man sitting in a chair in the corner of his room. Throwing the covers aside, he was halfway to the door when the man caught him. Franky screamed and clawed at the man, but he was no match for the guy whose laughter sent waves of fear through his small body. A hand covered his mouth and he fought to get away.

"Easy, Little Man, it's only a dream."

Franky fought through the fog, trying to remember where he'd heard the voice.

"Let it go, Franky. They can't hurt you now. They're dead. Dead men can't hurt you." The voice was calm, reassuring.

Mouse. Franky opened his eyes and looked around the room. A small lamp on a side table beside the sofa put out just enough light to see the sparsely furnished room – the main room in the apartment Mouse called home. He instantly remembered the events over the last couple of days – being rescued, the drive to Detroit, and being given a pallet of blankets on the floor of the main room. *I'm safe.*

"You're safe here," Mouse said, echoing Franky's thoughts. "Go back to sleep."

Franky closed his eyes until Mouse walked away, but fear of what lingered in his dreams kept him from falling asleep. He lay there, thankful for the low light waiting for morning to come.

A short time later, the door to the apartment opened and a man entered without knocking. Instantly alert, Franky wished he had a weapon to ward off the intruder.

"Leave the light off," Mouse said quietly when the man reached for the switch.

Franky relaxed.

The man lowered his hand and looked in Franky's direction. "How's the kid?"

"He had a nightmare, but he's sleeping now." Mouse said, keeping his voice low. "How'd you know he was here?"

Though dark in the room, Franky could tell the man to be well dressed, and from the sound of his voice, close to Mouse in age. He entered and took a seat on the arm of the sofa. As he spoke, his knees bounced up and down. "I ran into Mac. He told me there was some trouble in Chicago and you brought back a kid. Said the kid was pretty messed up. You going to tell his mother?"

Mother? Whose mother?

"No," Mouse said firmly.

"She has a right to know. Have you told the kid about her? He has a right to know too." Tall and thin, the man rose to his feet and moved around the room as if he had ants crawling up his legs. "Maybe if he knew, he'd take going back to the asylum a little easier."

How do they know about the asylum? It doesn't matter.

I don't care what they say; I'm not going back! Franky thought to let that be known but recalled how intense Mouse could be. If the man wished to send him back, Franky would have no option but to go. *If they try to send me back, I'll run away.*

"What makes you think I'm sending him back?" Mouse asked. His voice seemed agitated.

The man laughed. "Don't tell me you're planning on keeping him. He's not a stray pup you found on the street. He's a kid. And he has a mom who's worried about him."

I don't have a mom. I've never had a mom. While Franky wanted to jump up and say as much, it had been his experience that adults stopped talking if a kid was near. Especially if saying things they didn't want the kid to hear.

"My sister was never a mother to him," Mouse said firmly.

"She cares about him, Mouse. You have to know that. If not for her asking you to go, you never would have found the kid in the first place."

"The kid has a name. And you're proving my point. She didn't ask me to look for him. She told you to ask me. And when I said no, she didn't give it another thought."

"You don't know that to be true," the tall man replied.

"Don't I? Did she ask you to go? She's old enough to leave the asylum. Did she bother to go herself? If she was so worried about the boy, why didn't she check on him? She knew the address."

Leave the asylum? What's my mother doing in the asylum? Was she there when I was there? If so, why didn't she tell me?

Franky watched as the tall man shook his head in response.

"I don't know. Maybe Anastasia…"

"Maybe nothing," Mouse fumed. "Anna doesn't care

about anyone but herself. She never did and never will. She knew what our father was doing to my family and me, and yet she left anyway. Because of her, our mother is dead. I ended up on the streets and Ezra… I'll never know what happened to him. You don't know her like I do, Slim. She lies and manipulates everyone around her just to get her way. The last time I saw my sister, her tongue held the venom of a snake, and yet the letter you gave me purred like a kitten. Anna's not to be trusted. She's not fit to be a mother and I'll not send Franky to her."

The man named Slim looked in his direction once more. "How many times have you told me not to get involved with the Purples? And yet you think he's better off being brought up in your world?"

"He won't be working for the Purples; he'll be working for me," Mouse said. "I can guard the kid."

"And just how do you propose to do that?"

"With your help."

Slim was moving so much, Franky wondered if there was something wrong with the man. "My help? You want me to be his bodyguard?"

Mouse laughed. "Only if it comes to that. For now, I just want you to keep your mouth shut. No one is to know who the kid is to me, not even Franky. People find out and they will use the boy to get to me."

"So we make up a lie?" Slim asked.

"No, his story is legit. No one will blame me for taking him away from that. But that is where the story stops."

"Seems a shame the kid's never going to know you're his Uncle Tobias."

"It's for his own good."

"What do I tell Anastasia?"

Mouse was quiet for so long, Franky didn't think he would answer. When he did speak, his words sent chills down

Franky's spine. "Tell her I was too late. Tell her when I found him, the boy was already dead."

"To what purpose?" Slim asked heatedly.

"She had plenty of time to come clean with the kid and never did. Tell her what you want, but if she ever mentions the kid, well, you'd better make sure that doesn't happen," Mouse said tersely.

"Don't worry, Mouse. Your secret is safe with me." Slim started toward the door and hesitated. "Oh, and keep the kid away from Mac. There's something about him that sets my neck hairs on end."

"Mac's all right."

Slim held firm to the door. "You asked me for a favor and I'll do it. Now I'm asking for this from you. Keep him away from Mac or no deal."

Mouse nodded his agreement and Slim left without another word. Once Slim left, Mouse went into his bedroom, shutting the door behind him. A moment passed and the door clicked open once again. Franky closed his eyes as Mouse came toward him. A second later, he felt the pallet he was lying on being pulled across the floor.

Franky waited long after Mouse released the blankets before opening his eyes. He looked around the room and realized he was now sleeping on the floor beside Mouse's bed. He could tell by his breathing that Mouse was asleep.

Lying in the dark, Franky thought about the things he'd heard. *Could it be true? Could Miss Anna really be my mother? What did that even mean? Is that why she was nice to me? Was that what mothers did? Slim said Mouse is my uncle. What does that mean? Tobias – Mouse must be his street name. What kind of name is Mouse? He said he would guard me. Does that mean he is going to be my guardian?* Franky swallowed. *Judge was my guardian until Garret and JT killed him. Is that why Judge told them to go? To protect me? That must have been why Mouse killed them. He did it to protect me. Then it's true, Mouse really is my guardian.* As the night wore on, Franky thought of Mouse and how the man had shot both men who'd hurt him without uttering a word. Lying there in the dark with Mouse sleeping nearby, he'd never felt safer. Though Mistress Anna had given him food, she'd never sworn to protect him. She'd only told him secrets and made him promise not to tell. If that was what mothers did, he didn't need one. In that instant, Franky knew he'd never return to the asylum. He was staying with his guardian, the man who'd sworn to protect him.

***

Cindy placed the journal pages in her lap as she digested all she'd just read. All the lies and misunderstandings that shaped her uncle's life. She looked and saw Linda had also finished her stack of papers. "So I guess Frank did find out about his mother. It's a shame Anastasia and Tobias didn't tell each other the truth. Things could have been so much different for all of them. Still, I'm surprised Uncle Frank didn't want to go to her."

"Why would he?" Linda asked.

"Because she was his mother. He's just a boy. Boys need their mothers."

Linda sat her pile of papers on top of the ones she'd already read. "You're thinking about this all wrong."

Cindy handed her mother her stack of papers. "I am?"

"You're thinking about the kids in your classroom. Those children know what it's like to have parents. But you have to remember Franky was raised in the asylum around mistresses whose job it was to care for large amounts of children. With the exception of his mother – before she was banned from the nursery – I doubt that boy ever got held, much less cuddled. You read it yourself; the only thing he remembers of Anastasia is she was nice to him. You're nice to the children in your classroom; do you see any of them choosing you over their parents?"

Cindy thought about that. "No, I don't think so."

"Tobias just earned hero status. He'd have to do something pretty bad to push that boy away now," Linda said.

"Mouse-Tobias killed the men right in front of him. You don't think that's going to sink in at some point?"

"No, at least not in the way you think," Linda reasoned. "That didn't bother Frank. Look at what he said to Joey. He wanted them all dead."

"I daresay you're right." *Not that I blame him.* Cindy felt herself blush. It wasn't like her to wish harm on a person. She quickly changed the subject. "No wonder Uncle Frank never spoke about the judge."

"Or the abuse he endured," Linda agreed. "Why, I thought it was the war that had gotten inside his head."

"Can you imagine how different his life would've been if he'd gotten to stay with the judge? Just that short time engrained his love for reading. I don't think I ever saw Uncle Frank without a book until he got sick."

"Never," Linda agreed. "That man loved to read."

Cindy looked over at the journals. "I'm glad those monsters didn't take that from him."

"Too bad he couldn't have inherited Judge's library," her mother ventured.

"You know, I always wondered why Uncle Frank didn't hold on to his books after he read them. Him being a voracious reader and all. Maybe that's why. Maybe holding on to a collection would have been too painful a memory."

"Could be. I always thought of him as a minimalist. It never occurred to me to ask the reason for it."

Cindy thought of the boxes they'd found in the back of

Frank's closet when they'd boxed up her uncle's belongings after placing him into the facility. They'd donated his furniture and few items of clothing, but had kept the two medium-size boxes that were labeled *private, do not throw away*. Already feeling guilty about placing him in a facility and clearing out his belongings, she opted not to further breach his privacy by going through boxes he thought worthy of hiding from prying eyes. She'd placed them in the attic and not given them another thought, until now. She glanced toward the attic and made a mental note to check them out once the weather cooled.

"Earth to Cindy," Linda said, bringing her out of her musings.

"What, I didn't hear you."

"I asked if you want to get something to eat or read some more of Frank's journal."

Cindy looked at the remaining stack of papers, eager to discover what other secrets they held. "It's still early; let's read a bit more."

"Works for me," her mother agreed. Linda had long proclaimed herself to be the keeper of the journals. She pulled the next group of papers from her pile and retrieved Cindy's for her, handing her the stack. "These should be interesting."

"Why's that?" Cindy asked, removing the paperclip.

"Because," Linda said, returning to her seat, "he gets to meet your grandmother."

"Spoiler," Cindy teased, though she'd just been thinking the same thing. Not for the first time, she was eager to learn about the woman who'd kept her distance while alive. She'd learned so much about her since discovering the journals. She started reading Franky's words, silently praying they wouldn't disappoint her.

Chapter Twenty-Five

Franky followed as Mouse led the way down the stairs. Dressed in new trousers, black socks, and a pristine white button-up shirt, he looked much like the man walking in front of him. Even the black slouched hat he had on matched the one Mouse wore.

Mouse stopped in front of a burgundy convertible and Franky's breath caught. The sight of the car sitting there with the top down instantly conjured images of Judge and all the times they'd ridden in the Cadillac, Judge pointing out things they'd read about and telling the history of the buildings as they passed. Franky had loved that car nearly as much as Judge did. Instantly filled with heartache, he pushed the memories away. Not letting his feelings show, he remained stoic as he slid across the seat of Mouse's car. He wanted to ask where they were going but was afraid of the answer. What if Mouse had changed his mind about sending him back to the asylum? *I won't go!*

"I have some work to do today," Mouse said as he started the engine. "You're to do as I say without any backtalk. When I'm talking, you're to remain quiet. There are some conversations you are not to hear. If I ask you to step out of the room, you're to do so without hesitation. Is that clear?" Mouse said without taking his eyes from the road.

Franky nodded his head.

Mouse looked in his direction. "You don't say much, do you, kid?"

Franky shook his head.

"You hear well enough, though, don't you?"

Franky nodded.

Mouse looked at Franky once more. "You heard everything last night too. Am I right?"

Franky's eyes grew wide. He'd been so careful not to get caught eavesdropping. *How did he know I was awake?*

"You're a lot like me, Little Man. I can tell. I don't miss much either. You do something wrong and I'll know about it, understand?"

Franky nodded once again.

"Good. Now, about what you heard. You know you have a mom and she lives at the asylum, right? Use your words. It's hard to see when I'm driving."

"Yes, I know," Franky said softly.

"I guess it's no secret how I feel about the situation. But Slim – that's the guy I was talking to. He's an all right guy – you get into trouble and I'm not around, you go to him. Anyway, Slim thinks I should give you a choice. You want to go back, I'll send you." Mouse sighed. "No, I'll take you myself. But you want to stay, then that's all right too. I have a job for you, but don't you worry about that, don't think you have to stay because you owe me anything. You don't. What I did I would have done for anyone, understand?"

Franky nodded, then remembering what Mouse said, answered out loud. "I understand."

"Good. Don't tell me yet. I want you to take your time and think about it for a while. If you decide to stay, I'll tell you about the job. How's that sound?"

Franky wanted to tell him there was nothing to think about, that he'd already made his decision last night. But since Mouse told him to think about it, he didn't want the man to think he was acting out of haste. "Sounds good, sir."

Mouse laughed. "My name's not sir."

"No, it's Tobias." Franky started to add Uncle to the

name but didn't know what that meant, so he refrained.

Mouse frowned, and for a moment, Franky thought he'd said something wrong.

"My name is Tobias. Most people call me Mouse. It's my street name."

"It's not much of one," Franky replied.

Mouse brushed the hat from Franky's head. "I think I liked you better when you weren't talking."

Franky blushed, retrieved his hat from the floor, and placed it back on his head.

"The name suits me just fine. You can call me by either name, but if you're on the street, Mouse will be the one you want to use. People know me by that, and you'll get respect if people hear the name and know you are under my protection."

"Are you really my uncle?"

Mouse hesitated. "I am."

"What's an uncle?"

Mouse's expression turned serious. "It means we are related by blood. We're family. No one messes with my family and lives to tell about it."

"Then why'd you tell Slim not to tell anyone?"

"Because while it is good to have family, there are some that would hurt you to get to me. For that reason, it's best that no one knows. Not ever. If anyone asks, you're under my protection. That will be enough. Understand?"

"I think so. Judge told me he was my guardian. He said it was his job to protect me. That's why he's dead. He told the others to leave and they killed him." Franky's mouth went dry. Mouse had told him not to talk about what happened. Since he'd already started, he decided to proceed. "Does that mean you'll die too? If you have to protect me?"

Mouse held his arm in front of Franky. "Pinch me."

"What?"

"Go ahead. Take your fingers and pinch my arm," Mouse prompted.

Franky reached up and pinched the skin on Mouse's arm. When Mouse kept it there, he pinched harder. When at last Mouse pulled his arm away, it was covered in red splotches.

"See that?" Mouse asked, holding the arm for Franky to see.

"Yes," Franky said softly.

"Dead people don't bruise. I already protected you, and yet, here I am, still alive."

Franky smiled and Mouse pulled his arm away.

"I wish Judge didn't die."

"Judge was the guy in the room, right?" Mouse didn't have to say which room. Franky knew. He remembered the last time he saw the man and blinked away tears that threatened.

Franky nodded his answer.

"He was good to you, then?"

"Judge was the best. He even taught me to read."

"No kidding? You can read?" Mouse sounded impressed.

"Judge said I was the fastest learner he'd ever seen," Franky said proudly.

"I had a book once," Tobias mused. "Some man gave it to me on the train when I went to meet my mom."

Franky wasn't sure which surprised him most, that Mouse had a mom or that he'd ridden the train. He decided to go with the latter. "You rode the train?"

"I've ridden a few."

"And you found a mom? Where is she?"

"It didn't work out."

"Why not?" Franky pressed.

"Some boys are not meant to have moms. I guess I'm one of them," Mouse replied tersely.

"I think I'm one of them boys too. I had a mom and she didn't even want me."

"What makes you think she didn't want you? Because of what I said last night?"

Franky shrugged.

"Now don't go letting what I said cloud your judgment."

"I'm not. I knew my mom. Course I didn't know she was my mom until now. But I knew her. We talked some, but she never told me she was my mom. She didn't want me."

"You said that before. What makes you so sure?"

"She used to talk to me about the trains. She said I would maybe ride on one someday and find a family. She made it sound like a good thing. If she'd have told me she was my mom and asked me to stay, maybe I would have. But she didn't. She just talked to me and told me how it would be if I went. I'm not going back, Mouse. Even if you wanted me to, I wouldn't go. I'd run away," Franky said firmly.

"You've made your decision, then?"

"Yes. I'm staying here with you."

Mouse smiled.

"You're not mad?" Franky asked.

"No, Little Man, I'm not mad. You can stay with me for as long as you want. But I'll not hold you here. If you ever decide to leave, just let me know and I'll do right by you. All I ask is that you promise you'll say goodbye before you go."

Since Franky didn't have any plans of going anywhere, he didn't have a problem agreeing. "Sure thing, Mouse."

Mouse weaved the car around a horse and wagon. A short time later, he pulled into a parking lot and parked amongst several other motorcars.

Franky looked up at the building, counting the floors to what had to be the tallest building he'd ever seen. While he'd only glimpsed New York City briefly en route to the train station, he was reasonably sure the building in front of him was taller than any in the city where he was born. He'd daresay it was taller than any in Chicago as well. He looked up, reading the name on the front of the building – Book Cadillac Hotel – and instantly thought of Judge. *Judge liked books and his beloved Cadillac.* Oh, how he missed the man. Franky sighed. How was he ever to get over the pain of losing Judge if there were always going to be reminders? He was still pondering that when they went into the building and he followed Mouse into the elevator. Franky wondered where the attendant was as Mouse pushed the button and the door began to close.

The door slid shut and something inside of him snapped. Instantly, he was back inside the small shed. The air went stale and he couldn't breathe. Franky ran to the door and started pounding on the heavy steel, demanding to be let out. He felt a hand on his shoulder and turned his anger on his attacker. A bell sounded, the door opened once more, and Franky bolted, racing down the long hallway with only one thought. He had to get out of the building. He needed to breathe without his lungs feeling like they were too full to suck in air. He saw a door at the end of the hallway and pulled it open, relieved to see he'd found the stairs. He raced downward, oblivious to anything but the need for escape. He opened the door, racing outside as it slammed shut behind him. Once outside, the air began to seep into his lungs. He took a breath, thankful he was finally able to take in the air he so desperately needed.

The door opened. Mouse stood in the doorway, frantically looking from side to side. He was breathing hard and Franky wondered if he too felt the fear within the room. As Mouse approached, Franky noticed several red marks on his face and arms.

"What happened, Mouse? You look like you've been in a fight," Franky said as the man grew near.

Mouse tilted his head as if he didn't hear him right. He started to speak, then hesitated before beginning again. "What happened in the elevator?"

At the mention of the elevator, everything came flooding back. Though he didn't understand what had happened, he knew it was he who inflicted the marks on Mouse's body. Instantly he was afraid Mouse would change his mind about letting him stay. It was all Franky could do to keep from crying. Instead, he looked his new guardian in the eye as Judge had instructed and said the only thing he knew to say. "I'm sorry."

"What happened?" Mouse repeated. There was no emotion in his voice as he spoke.

"You told me not to speak of it." His voice trembled as he spoke.

"Have you never been inside an elevator before?" Mouse asked.

"I have. Many times with Judge." His voice broke at the mention of the name. "Only this time, it was different. When the doors closed, I thought…I thought I was inside the shed and I couldn't breathe. I'm sorry I hit you. I thought you were…I'm sorry."

Mouse's brow rose slightly. "Is that why you opened the door to the bedroom last night?"

"I couldn't breathe," Franky repeated.

Mouse cast a glance toward the building. "How are you with stairs?"

Franky took a long breath and let it out slowly. When he spoke, his voice was strong. "I like stairs."

Chapter Twenty-Six

Franky stood in the hallway of the Book Cadillac Hotel staring in the window of the barbershop. It had been over three weeks since his rescue, and in that time, he'd rarely left Mouse's side. On occasion, Mouse would nod his head ever so slightly, a gesture Franky knew meant disappear. Without speaking, Franky would do just that, slipping out of the room unnoticed. He was always dismissed when Mouse was with the man called Big Mike and today was no exception.

He was still standing there, nose pressed against the window, when he felt a hand on his shoulder. He was about to brush the hand away when he turned and saw Mac. Mac was Mouse's friend and shared the apartment where Franky now called home. Mac smiled and looked down his long nose at Franky. While Mac had never done anything to him, Franky always managed to keep his distance from the guy, until now. He wasn't sure what it was about Mac he didn't like; maybe it was just the fact that Slim had warned Mouse to keep the man away from him.

Franky glanced through the window, hoping Mouse was watching. No such luck. Mouse was standing next to Big Mike's chair with his back to them.

Mac leaned in close. "Must be a bummer having to stand outside like a baby."

Franky answered with a shrug.

"Mouse is going to be tied up for a while. Come with me and I'll show you around the place." Mac said, clasping Franky's shoulder once more.

"Mouse told me to stay here." Franky attempted to shrug free, but Mac held firm.

"He won't mind if you're with me," Mac said, increasing the pressure. "I'm just going to the cigar shop. We'll be back before Mouse even knows you're gone."

Franky thought about banging on the window to get Mouse's attention but decided against it. Mouse made it clear he was never to be disturbed when he was conducting business, especially when that business had to do with Big Mike. Reluctantly, he nodded his concession.

Mac released his grip and smiled as he led Franky away from the barbershop. As Franky's guilt lessened, he started to relax. Upon doing so, he noted the subtle and not so subtle differences of walking with Mac instead of Mouse.

Mac seemed to be in no hurry as he walked through the halls of the hotel greeting people they met along the way, often laughing at comments Franky didn't understand. At first, he couldn't put his finger on just what bugged him about walking with the man and then he realized the man was just loud. Always talking and drawing attention to himself. It was as if he demanded the attention of everyone he came in contact with.

Mouse was different. Mouse always seemed to walk as if on a mission. He didn't speak unless spoken to, and at times, it was as if the man seemed to disappear. Not in the physical sense, but Franky had followed him enough to see he could walk through a crowded room winding in and around people and do it all without being noticed.

"Get up here, kid; you're creeping me out. I swear if I didn't know better, I'd think I was walking with Mouse," Mac said, motioning him closer.

The hotel was busy as always, with people mingling in the vast hallways and sitting in chairs along the way. Two ladies in lace-lined dresses that stopped at the knee sat next to the window, smoking cigarettes attached to long, thin tubes. A couple of young men in suits said something he couldn't hear. The women's eyebrows shot up in surprise, and they each shook their heads furiously. The men tipped their hats and continued down the hall. As Franky passed the women, he noticed their faces tinged with pink. He looked over his shoulder at the men, wondering what they had said to make the women blush. The men had looked okay, dressed in their finery. He wrinkled his forehead, puzzled by what he just saw. Judge had often pointed out boys and men dressed in rags and told him to be cautious of degenerates. Riding through the streets of Chicago with Judge guiding the way, the type of men Judge had warned him of were easy to pick out. But here in the hotel, everyone was always dressed like what Judge had referred to as good, upstanding citizens with good moral values. Franky thought about the men he'd just seen.

Is it possible for a person to be dressed nicely and still be up to no good?

He cast a sideways glance at Mac. The man was dressed like someone Judge would have said to be upstanding, and yet there was something about him that made Franky's skin crawl. Judge had taken him to a play once, and after the performance, Judge had taken him backstage to meet the performers. Franky had been surprised that Judge would introduce him to people dressed in rags. Later that night, Judge had told him the people they'd met were actors, dressing a certain way to play a part. Franky looked at Mac with a new understanding.

He's just an actor dressing for the part. Judge would not wish for me to trust this guy. He wasn't sure how he knew that, but he was certain it was true. *I need to go back to the barbershop and wait for Mouse.*

"I need to get some smokes," Mac said, and ducked into the store before Franky could voice his objection. Mac nodded to the sales clerk as they entered then went to the far side of the room where mirrored walls held glass shelves loaded with cigar boxes. The top boxes were open, showing dark cylinder-shaped cigars. Mac picked one up, slid it under his nose, moaning his approval as he inhaled. Much to Franky's surprise, Mac used his free hand to slip three cigars into his pocket. He glanced at Franky and gave a nod to the counter.

"I don't have any money," Franky balked.

"Keep your voice down," Mac hissed. "You trying to get me nabbed."

Franky shook his head in reply.

"You don't have to have money." Mac's voice was calmer now. "Just watch me. I'll show you how it's done."

Franky chanced a glance at the clerk, who was busy helping a hefty gentleman wearing a Fedora hat, then turned his attention back to Mac.

"It's all sleight of the hand. You gain their attention with this hand." Mac picked up another cigar and repeated his inspection. "Then, keeping your movements slow, you make the grab with the other. The key is to keep the other hand moving. It keeps them distracted. Think you can do that?"

It sounded so easy. Franky swallowed his fear. "I guess so."

Mac looked over at the clerk then gave Franky the go-ahead.

Franky held his breath as he picked up a cigar and brought it to his nose. He inhaled as he grabbed another with his free hand. The stench from the cigar reached his nostrils just as Franky lowered the cigar toward his pocket. He sneezed, drawing everyone's attention.

The clerk raised his hand and pointed at Franky. "Stop, thief."

"Get out of here, kid. Run before they throw you in

prison!" Mac urged.

Franky dropped the cigars and turned on his heels. As he raced to the door, he was surprised to hear Mac and the others laughing. He pushed through the doorway, blindly running into the legs of a man who was entering. He tried to push his way through, but the man stood his ground. Franky looked up, his mouth falling open when he saw Mouse blocking the door. Mouse's eyes narrowed, his nostrils flaring as he looked about the room and took in the situation. His expression darkened as he focused his attention on Mac, who'd stopped laughing and looked as if he too was ready to run. Mouse pointed to a chair near the door and Franky hurried to the seat without argument. The store grew quiet as Mouse curled his fingers into fists and focused his anger on Mac.

"Now, Mouse, there's no need to get sore. We were only having a bit of fun with the kid," Mac said, backing away.

Mouse unclenched his fists and pushed Mac against the glass shelves. It was not lost on Franky that Mouse was nearly a foot shorter than Mac and yet it was obvious Mac was afraid of him.

"You so much as look in the kid's direction again and they'll never find your body. Is that understood?" Mouse's voice was cold.

"Jeeze, Mouse, I thought we were friends. I was only having a little fun. He's just a kid you found on the streets. Why take it personally?"

In a whirl of movement, Mouse pushed his fist into the mirrored wall just to the left of Mac's head. Though the glass remained in place, it now looked like an intricate spider web. "Not even a glimpse, Mac. Understand?"

"Got it, Mouse," Mac said, bobbing his head.

Mouse walked to the counter. "Tell Big Mike I'm sorry about the mirror," he said, handing the clerk several bills. As he turned from the counter, Franky saw blood on Mouse's hand. Mouse saw him looking and pulled a handkerchief from his pocket, using it to wrap around his knuckles. Mouse jerked his chin toward the door. Franky scrambled from the chair and followed him from the room.

Many times on the way to the Ford, Franky opened his mouth to apologize, but the words wouldn't come. He'd let the man down and now knew he must pay the consequences. He remained quiet as they walked to the Ford, expecting Mouse to lay into him once they were there. Instead, Mouse opened the door and waited for Franky to slide across the seat before settling behind the wheel.

Mouse drove out of the lot and headed out of the city. At first, Franky thought them to be headed home, but it soon became apparent they were not. Franky recognized the street; Mouse had driven there daily without saying why. This time, he eased the Ford to the curb and stared off in the distance. After some time, he turned to Franky and spoke.

"I have a job for you." His voice was eerily calm.

Franky was taken aback at his tone. *What? Isn't he going to yell at me?*

"Take a look at the white house," Mouse said, tilting his chin slightly.

There was only one white house on the side where Mouse gestured, so Franky had no issue finding it.

Though no one was around, Mouse kept his voice low. "You'll be keeping an eye on the girl in the house, following her, watching over her, and reporting back to me each night. I want her kept safe. If anyone bothers her, I'm to know."

Instantly, Franky's mind was racing with questions. *Keep her safe? But I'm just a kid. How am I going to keep anyone safe?*

"I'll teach you what you need to know and how to get

in touch with me if there's a problem," Mouse said, reading his mind.

"You want me to be a babysitter? I thought you said you had a job for me." It was the first time he'd spoken since the incident in the cigar shop. "Is this my punishment?"

Mouse looked taken aback. "Guarding my girl is no punishment."

His girl? Since when did Mouse have a girl? Wait, did he say I would be guarding her? "You want me to be her guardian?"

Mouse nodded. "Yes, I'm asking you to be her guardian. It's a big responsibility, but then you know that, don't you, Little Man?"

Little Man? Mouse had used that term before and Franky had thought nothing of it. However, this time, it sounded like a name. *Is that my new street name? Does he really think I'm a man?* The last thing he wanted was to let Mouse down again. He pulled himself higher and smiled.

"Does that mean you'll take the job?" Mouse asked once more.

"I'll take the job," Franky said, bobbing his head up and down. "And don't you worry, Mouse, I'll be the best guardian anyone ever had."

A slow smile spread across Mouse's face. "Good. Now let's talk about what happened back at the cigar shop."

***

Never having worked before, Franky had no idea what to expect except that he was to guard the girl. While he was grateful to have earned Mouse's trust, he was still unsure why the girl needed watching. She never did anything alone. Anytime she left the house, she was with her parents. If they went in the motorcar, Franky was to return to the apartment. If she and her mother rode the trolley car, Franky was to follow.

After the incident in the cigar shop, Mouse had started training Franky. As with book learning, Franky discovered he was a quick study. After a few near misses when he'd tried to strike out on his own, he'd settled down, and before long, he could pick pockets nearly as well as Mouse. He could slip into a store unnoticed and take anything he wanted without being seen. Some of the guys Mouse associated with often called him Little Mouse, saying it was uncanny how much Franky acted like his mentor, some even going so far as to say he looked like the man. Franky didn't mind, and if Mouse minded, he didn't say. The only one who seemed to dislike him was Mac, although he never let his feelings show when Mouse was near. Franky learned to steer clear of the man when Mouse wasn't around.

Franky sat leaning against the base of a large tree when Mileta and her mother stepped out of the house and started in his direction. They walked arm in arm, smiling and chatting merrily. Mileta always wore a smile, and her eyes twinkled when she was excited. Even at his age, he could see why Mouse liked her. He scurried to the other side of the tree and waited for them to pass. He held back then fell into step behind the duo as he'd done hundreds of times before, silently stalking as if he were a shadow. Neither turned to see who followed, as neither were aware he was there.

Chapter Twenty-Seven

July 3, 1929

Franky sat at the counter with his back to the tables, listening to everything the girls said. From his vantage point on the high stool, he could not only hear everything, but he could watch them through the mirror on the far wall as well. Oblivious to being eavesdropped on, the three were giggling, sipping on sodas, and discussing their holiday plans.

Millie – the name Mouse's girl went by – although her mother referred to her as Mildred, and Mouse still insisted on calling her Mileta – sat at the table with her two friends: Jane, a pretty blonde who was more developed than either of her friends, and Edna, a curly-haired girl with a slight overbite. They'd been sitting in the soda shop for nearly thirty minutes with Millie droning on about a boy of which her father was overly fond. Franky was listening intently as Millie had never mentioned any guys before. He had little doubt Mouse would be most interested in this new development.

"Father has invited Robert and his parents over for Sunday supper," Millie whined.

"Oh, then it is serious," Jane replied. "You don't sound very pleased. Tell me, Millie, is there someone else?"

"She's blushing!" Edna exclaimed. "Oh, Millie, do tell."

"Yes, Millie, do tell," Jane urged.

Millie looked from side to side to make sure no one was listening. Franky dipped his head to avoid making eye contact through the mirror. "There once was a boy I thought about a lot. Oh, but my parents would never have approved."

"Why not?" both girls asked at once.

"Because he stole a kiss." Millie's face turned a brilliant red and the girls gasped.

Edna's eyes went wide. "What kind of boy would steal a kiss without asking?"

"Why, the kind of boy my parents wouldn't approve of," Millie said, and the three burst out laughing.

"Who was it?" Jane asked. "Anyone we know?"

"Oh, please, don't keep it from us, Millie. I'll just die from suspense if you don't tell us who it was," Edna promised.

"I bet it was Joel. He's been making goo-goo eyes at Millie all summer," Jane said, eyeing Millie.

Millie wrinkled her nose. "Joel with the thick glasses? I'd say not. If he kissed me, I'd kick him in the shin."

Jane smiled. "So you mean to tell us you enjoyed this kiss."

The blush crept higher. "I didn't hate it."

"Why, Mildred Daniels, you're a tease. You simply must tell us who this boy is that has you so smitten," Edna demanded.

"I'm not smitten," Millie argued, though her eyes said differently. "It was only one kiss and it happened several years ago. Why, I haven't even seen Tobias since."

Franky choked on the soda he was drinking and quickly ducked out of view of the mirror.

Jane frowned. "I don't recall any boys by that name at our school."

"He doesn't go to our school. He doesn't go to any school that I am aware of," Millie replied.

"Did he…did you do anything else?" Jane's voice sounded hopeful.

"Why, Jane, what kind of girl do you think Millie to be," Edna said, coming to her defense. "Millie is as pure as silk. Isn't that right, Millie?"

"We didn't do anything else. I didn't even kiss him back," Millie said with a pout. "That's probably why I never saw him again."

"There there, Mildred," Edna said, patting her arm. "Don't you go fretting about that boy. My mother says a boy who takes advantage of a girl's good reputation would make a lousy husband."

Jane leaned in close. "My guess is a boy like that would expect other things as well."

Millie's eyes opened wide. "What other things?"

"First, they steal a kiss and the next thing you know, the boy has his hand up your dress," Jane whispered.

"Why would a boy want to put his hand up your dress?" Edna asked.

Franky tilted his head, straining to hear. He too was curious about the hand thing.

"This is not a conversation a lady should have in public," Millie said firmly. "My mother would never allow me to leave the house again if she found out we were discussing such things. And in a soda shop no less."

Edna scrunched up her nose and sighed her disappointment.

From his place at the counter, Franky did the same.

"Are you coming to the fireworks show tomorrow tonight?" Jane asked, changing the subject.

Millie finished the last of her soda before answering. "Perhaps. I'm not sure what time we're getting back from Point Pelee. If we get back early, then maybe, but I was hoping to work on the quilt I'm piecing. I've only got a few weeks to finish it so that I can sell it in time to buy my parents a proper anniversary present."

"We'll save you a spot just in case," Edna promised.

"My father will be here to pick me up any moment," Millie said, rising from her chair. "I promised to go to the store with him so we can purchase the supplies for our picnic tomorrow."

"Do try to make it to the fireworks," Edna urged.

As the girls said their goodbyes, Franky laid a coin on the counter and slipped away unnoticed. Once outside, he walked to the corner of the building and stood near a large freestanding billboard, blending into the scenery as Mouse had taught him.

Millie exited the store and waited. It wasn't long before her father pulled their Ford to the curb. She rounded the machine and her father stepped out, waited for her to slide across the seat before returning to his place and motoring away.

Franky waited for the trolley, then hopped onto the back step and headed to Mouse's apartment without paying.

***

"Are you sure she was talking about me?" Mouse asked after Franky told him of the conversation he'd overheard.

"She said Tobias," Franky repeated. "She said you stole a kiss. It was you, wasn't it, Mouse?"

Mouse paced the floor without answering the allegation. "Are you sure she said she was going to Point Pelee tomorrow?"

"I'm sure, Mouse. She and her parents are going to spend the whole day there."

Mouse pulled the keys from his trousers and tossed them to Franky. "Gas up the Ford. We're going to have a bit of fun tomorrow."

"Sure thing, Mouse," Franky said, clutching the keys in his hand. Excitement surged through his veins. While Mouse had allowed him to drive the motorcar before, he'd never allowed him to drive it without him coming along. Nor had he ever uttered the words "we're going to have a bit of fun." An idea occurred to him and he hesitated. "Mouse, can we have a picnic?"

Mouse pulled a wad of bills from his pocket, peeled off a few, and handed them to Franky. "Get the gas first then use the rest to get what we need. Get plenty. I'm going to have Mac and a couple of the boys come along."

Franky's enthusiasm waned. He should have expected it; Mac was Mouse's right hand man. "Sure thing, Mouse," he said, pocketing the bills.

***

July 4, 1929

Franky waited near the entrance to Point Pelee Park, watching for Millie and her family to arrive. From his vantage point, he could watch both the entrance gate and the parking lot where Mouse and the others were sitting on the hoods of their cars. As it turned out, he and Mouse ended up riding with Mac. Thumbs and Mule, both members of the Purple Gang, met them at the park a short time later. Mouse seemed more relaxed than Franky had ever seen him, smiling and gesturing with his hands as he spoke while the others laughed at what he said.

Mac had a bottle covered by a paper sack in his hand, as did Thumbs and Mule, the two men that had followed them over earlier that morning. He wasn't sure how Thumbs had come by his moniker, but for the other guy, it was obvious. His face was long and oddly shaped, his front teeth protruding from his mouth, making it difficult to bring his lips together – the combination much resembled that of a mule.

Franky heard the rumble of a motorcar and turned toward the sound. Peering closer, he saw John and Helen Daniels – Millie's parents – sitting in the front seat.

Franky ducked behind the sign then hurried to hide behind a nearby line of motorcars. Using them as cover, he rushed to where Mouse and the others were parked.

"That's them," Franky said when the Daniels' Ford pulled to a stop a few rows over.

"She's not with them," Mouse said when the couple exited their Ford alone. He turned to Franky. "I thought you said she'd be here."

Franky's mouth went dry. "She was supposed to. I heard her talking about it to her friends."

Mouse nodded to the automobile. "Go make sure she's not sleeping in the backseat."

Franky ran the short distance to the Daniels' Ford and chanced a peek inside. Mouse was right; Millie was not inside. Where is she? S*he said she'd be here.* Pushing aside the panic of letting Mouse down, he approached Millie's parents. Helen was giggling at something her husband said when Franky tugged on John's shirt.

Her father turned and cocked an eyebrow. "Can I help you?"

Franky smiled a half-smile. "Do you have any kids I can play with?"

"Not today, kid," John said, brushing him off.

"Are you sure? I'd like someone to play with," Franky insisted.

"We have a daughter, but she decided to stay home today." A frown tugged at Helen's mouth.

"She'll be fine, love," John said, placing a hand on his wife's shoulder. He winked at Franky. "My wife is struggling with the fact that our little girl is growing up. You remember that when you decide you are too old to be spending time with your parents."

"Yes, sir," Franky said before returning to where Mouse and the guys were waiting.

"What was that about? They could have recognized you," Mouse fumed when he returned.

"Don't worry; they were too busy making goo-goo eyes at each other," Franky said, rolling his eyes.

"Well, what did you say?" Mouse pressed.

"I told them I was lonely and asked if they had any kids I could play with." Franky beamed. "The mom looked sad and said she had a daughter, but she wanted to stay at home today."

Thumbs dropped to the sand, laughing. "All this trouble and your girl is home alone. You could've had the broad all to yourself."

Without warning, Mouse kicked the guy in the gut. "You talk about my girl like that again, and I'll do more than kick you."

Mac wrapped an arm around Mouse's shoulders and guided him away. A moment later, Mouse jumped into Mac's Ford and left without saying goodbye.

"Check out the kid," Mac said, smacking Franky's hat from his head. "Looks like the baby's going to cry."

"Knock it off, Mac," Franky said, scooping up his hat and shaking out the sand.

Mac laughed once again. "Watch it, tough guy; Daddy's not here to defend you."

"Mouse is not my dad," Franky said, narrowing his eyes.

A slow, sly smile slid across Mac's face as he pushed his white straw hat back on his head. "That's right, kid, he's not your dad. Mouse is one of us and you're not. One of these days, he's going to get tired of you hanging around. You better remember that."

"Yo, Mac, take a look over there," Mule said with a nod to the Daniels. "The kid may have been right about the dame being upset. It looks like they're getting ready to leave."

Mac appraised the situation then turned to Thumbs. "Get me the bottle."

Thumbs grimaced. "Are you sure? We didn't ask. Mouse might not be too happy if we do it without his permission. Does he even know what you had planned?"

Mac glanced at Franky, then puffed his chest. "Do you want to be the one to tell Mouse why the parents showed up when he was entertaining his girl?"

Thumbs must not have wanted to tell him as he walked to the trunk and pulled out a bottle, handing it to Mac, who wrapped it in a beach towel before strolling casually to where the Daniels were parked.

Franky and the others watched as Mac engaged the couple in conversation. Mac turned and pointed toward where Franky was standing and the couple smiled. Mac handed him the towel. John pulled the fabric back, then quickly covered it once more.

"Smart man," Thumbs said, nodding his approval.

Franky agreed. The last thing any of them needed was to get caught, especially at a public venue such as this. He watched as Mac clasped John on the shoulder and nodded in their direction once more, before raising his hand in farewell.

Thumbs and Mule crowded close as Mac approached. Mac lit a cigarette and took a long drag then blew out the smoke in a slow, steady stream.

"Come on, Mac, don't leave us in suspense," Thumbs said at last. "How'd you get him to take the bottle?"

Mac took another drag before answering. "I told him it was on account of him being nice to my kid brother. Told him little Franky here was missing his parents something awful, them being killed in a boating accident and all."

"That's a lie," Franky blurted.

"Of course it is, but they don't know it. It worked. They took the booze, didn't they?" Mac replied.

"Do you think they'll know it's laced?" Mule had no

sooner said the words when Mac elbowed him in the gut.

"Not in front of the kid," Mac growled. Regaining his composure, he sat on the hood of the Ford, staring in the direction of the Daniels' motorcar. It wasn't long before Mule and Thumbs joined, all watching the goings on. Franky thought it odd that none of the men spoke. Not wanting to raise their ire, Franky leaned against the side of the Ford, waiting to see what happened next.

Moments later, Millie's parents emerged from their automobile. Mrs. Daniels giggled and leaned heavily against her husband for support. Wrapping his arms around her waist, they staggered toward the water's edge and sat on the bank, looking out at the lake.

"It's time," Mac said, pushing off the hood.

Franky followed the three men, anxious to see what they had planned, though something inside told him he wasn't going to like it. *I wish Mouse was here*.

Mac stood a short distance from where the Daniels sat and motioned the others in closer. They were close enough to see the couple without fear of being overheard, not that it appeared the couple was interested in anything but kissing each other. Franky wrinkled his nose and turned, focusing on the sign a few feet away. *DANGER STRONG CURRENT. NO SWIMMING BEYOND THIS POINT!*

"I think they're pretty looped." Mac kept his voice low. "If we can get them in the water without anyone seeing them, the rest will be easy."

"The sign says it is too dangerous to swim here. Why do you want to get them in the water?" Franky asked.

"How ya plannin' on getting them in?" Mule said, ignoring Franky's comment.

"I'll push 'em," Thumbs offered.

"No, they have to go in on their own," Mac said. "It's

got to look like an accident."

"So how do we get them in?" Mule repeated.

Mac lowered his voice once more. "Here's what we're going to do. Franky here will go into the water. We'll send him in over there away from the crowd. Then we'll make a scene saying as how he can't swim and the old man will jump in to try to save him."

Franky looked in the direction Mac pointed and realized it was the area the sign warned of. Fear invaded his senses and he started backing away from the guys. "I'm not going in there. I'll drown!"

The words had no sooner escaped his mouth than Thumbs grabbed him and tossed him into the lake. The water engulfed him. He reached out, frantically clawing at the watery tomb. He bobbed to the top and gulped air before descending once more. Just when he thought to give up the struggle, he felt something brush his arm. A second later, that something gripped him tight. Franky fought for release.

"Quit fighting me, kid, or you're going to kill us both." Though the voice was muffled, Franky knew it to belong to Mac. *He sounds scared.* He felt himself being pulled through the water, lifted into the air, and placed onto a hard surface. Someone covered him with a blanket. It was hot, but there was no water, so he didn't complain. As he lay there trying to catch his breath, he heard a woman scream and wondered at the reason.

***

Franky sat on the hood of the motorcar with nothing to show from his ordeal but a lingering cough. People milled around the shore, several cops standing among them. Mac saw him watching and walked in his direction.

"The girl's parents are dead and there's nothing to be done about it. Cops said they were zozzled. Not sure where they heard that bit of news." Mac trained his gaze on Franky and the boy shivered despite the heat. "They don't know about you. Best keep it that way."

"I told you I'd drown. You shouldn't have told them to throw me in," Franky said in return.

"You didn't drown. You just swallowed a bit of water. Besides, you fell."

Franky narrowed his eyes. "I didn't fall."

"My story, kid. Thumbs and Mule will back me up."

"Mouse won't believe you." Franky coughed. "And I know you did something to that bottle. Just you wait until I tell Mouse."

Mac placed his hand on Franky's knee, slowly applying pressure as he spoke. "Listen, kid, the only reason I pulled you out of that water is because Mouse likes you. But he likes me more. Mouse and I are chums. You got it? You're not going to say anything to Mouse or anyone else. Ever."

Franky tried to pull away, but the pain was too intense.

"Hurts, doesn't it, kid? You see, it's like this. Because Mouse and I are Purples, that makes us chums. He'll take my word over yours. Besides, you go spreading lies about me and he'll send you packing real fast. And when you go, Mouse won't be there to protect you." Mac laughed a wicked laugh. "Trust me. I've been biding my time since you got here. I've been itching to cut you into little pieces and use you as fish bait."

Franky let out a breath as Mac released the pressure on his knee. He wanted to laugh and tell Mac that Mouse wouldn't believe him, but he wasn't sure. *I'm not a Purple*. Instead, he looked at Mac and said the only thing he knew to be true. "I hate you."

Mac lit a cigarette and blew the smoke in Franky's face, provoking another coughing fit. "Right back at ya, kid."

Franky crossed his arms and avoided looking at Mac. A whistle pierced the air. Mac pushed away from the motorcar and flicked his cigarette away.

The man angered him so much, Franky stuck out his tongue. Mac must have expected as much as he turned in time to see the deed and Franky instantly regretted the childish decision.

Mac lifted his arm and maneuvered his fingers into the shape of a gun. "I should've let you drown with the others. Next time, you won't be so lucky."

A chill raced down Franky's spine. He'd learned, when it came to threats, Mac was a man of his word.

Chapter Twenty-Eight

February 14, 1931

Franky woke to the sound of a door slamming. He stretched then kicked the boy next to him with the toe of his worn shoe. "Yo, Rabbit, get up. Mouse will be up soon and I have to go get some flowers for Mrs. Millie."

The boy next to him groaned then sat up, his hair sticking out in all directions. Stretching his thin arms wide, he yawned and wiped his eyes with dirty fists. "Mouse asked you to get flowers?"

Franky laughed. "No, he probably doesn't know what day it is."

"What day is it?" Rabbit asked, stifling another yawn.

"Why, it's Valentine's Day," Franky answered, not bothering to add that he only knew because he'd read it on a sign the day before. "A day dames like to get flowers."

"Want me to go with you?" Rabbit asked, running a hand through his frizzed hair. The apartment building on Hastings Street was the heart of Paradise Valley. Once a thriving Jewish community, it was now home to mostly black families. Rabbit had family in the area and was well-known in the neighborhood. Franky had quickly made friends with the boy and recruited him and some of the other boys to help him watch over Millie. Rabbit's family had balked at first since Franky was an outsider, but reconsidered upon finding out the boys would be paid twenty-five cents a week. In a time when most grown men in the city were out of work and begging for meals at soup kitchens, twenty-five cents was enough to keep

Mouse's family – Franky included – in the good graces of the community.

"No, stay here in case Mouse leaves. The bums will be up by now looking for their daily handout and I don't want to leave Millie alone."

Rabbit rolled up the tattered blanket they shared, climbed onto the window ledge, and shoved it behind a loose ceiling tile. His stomach grumbled as he jumped to the floor. "See if you can scrounge up something to eat. I'm starving."

Franky pulled on his coat and settled his hat on his head. "I'll see what I can do. Now go downstairs and stay in the hallway near the door and don't worry about Mrs. Millie. She has the baby to tend to now and won't be leaving the apartment much. If Mouse asks, tell him you haven't seen me yet."

Rabbit frowned. "Why don't you just tell him you're living here? He's gonna find out one of these days. He likes you. Probably he'd find you a place to live."

"Ain't nobody's business where I live, got it?" Franky said heatedly.

Though the boy was a few years older and at least a foot taller, he took a step back. "I didn't mean to rile you any."

"Not a word, Rabbit. Where I live is my business. Watch the door, and if there's any sign of trouble, you find Mouse." Franky sighed and hurried down the stairs. He hadn't meant to take his anger out on his friend. It was just that the boy had touched on a sore spot. The events at Point Pelee had drastically changed his life – all of their lives, really. Mouse moved out of the apartment that night and married Millie the next day. As of five days ago, they had become parents to a baby girl. Prohibition had taken its toll on the city and the streets of Detroit were getting tough with rival gangs trying to oust the Purples. Between his duties with the Purple Gang and his new wife, Mouse had little time for Franky, whose life mostly consisted of shadowing Millie and running the occasional errand for Mouse. While Mouse thought Franky still lived in the apartment with Mac, he'd slept on the floor in the upstairs hallway on Hastings Street from the day Mouse and Millie had moved in, sneaking down the stairs each morning to report for work. He'd done this every day for two years and Mouse was none the wiser.

As he expected, the line at the church was wrapped around the corner as men stood waiting for something to fill their stomachs before heading off in search of work. Though some were dressed in rags, it always amazed Franky that most of the men wore suits, overcoats, and bowler hats. Though they were dressed in their Sunday best, it was the shoes that gave away their desperation, as shoe polish was a luxury most could not afford.

Mouse had told him it was because of the Depression, so many men were without jobs. Franky wasn't sure what a depression was, but it didn't seem to affect Mouse, who always had money in his pocket. He did, on occasion, find himself thinking of Judge, wondering if the man were alive today, if he too would be standing in line begging for food. Most of the lines in his neighborhood were formed by men, though there were some areas where women stood waiting often with a child or children accompanying them.

Franky kept his eyes lowered as he hurried past the long line of men. It was one of Mouse's rules; keep your eyes averted, but be wary of your surroundings. He knew how to pick pockets and knew the tricks dippers used to distract their marks. Mouse had also told him the shame of picking the pocket of a working man, not that it mattered these days, as hardly anyone was working. He heard music and looked up. A broad smile spread across his lips as he saw Duke and Leopold, two elderly men leaning against the corner drugstore on Russell Street playing the harmonica. The men used to play on Hastings Street but had moved to Russell Street after the bread lines started. Both men acknowledged him with a nod before he stepped into the drugstore. The front room was empty as Franky moved up to the counter and slipped two meat pies into his pocket. He started for the door, heard someone cough, and looked over his shoulder to see Sidney, the young man who worked the counter, coming in from the back room.

"Morning, Little Man," Sidney said when he saw him. "What brings you in today?"

He'd hoped to leave without having to make a purchase. Fearing getting caught, he picked up two additional meat pies and placed two coins onto the counter. "I came for meat pies."

Sidney looked at the counter then raised an eyebrow at Franky. "You going to pay for the other two?"

Franky sighed; it had been a while since he'd gotten caught. "I was real careful. How'd you know?"

"I didn't see you, but I know I put twelve meat pies on the tray ten minutes ago and you're the only one that's come in." Though no one else was in the store, Sidney leaned over the counter and whispered low, "I won't say anything if you promise me something."

"What?" Franky whispered in return.

"After I buy this store, you're only to come in if you have money in your pocket."

That was an easy promise as Franky always had money in his pocket. He just chose not to spend it. He shook his head in agreement. "You going to buy this store?"

Sidney stood and ran a finger across his pencil-thin mustache. "The store's not doing well and I aim to fix that. Going to change the name and everything. Barthwell Pharmacy has a nice ring to it, don't you think?"

Franky frowned. "Why do you want to change the

name?"

"Because Barthwell is my name. I want people to know this is my store. Someday I'm going to have a whole slew of drug stores and they'll all have my name. You just wait and see." Sidney said willfully.

"You seem pretty sure," Franky replied.

Sidney stood and straightened his tie. "Boy, I've known what I wanted to be since I was around your age."

"You did?" Franky had once thought to join the Army, but since moving to Detroit, he never gave his future much thought.

"Yes, sir, I was sick and my momma had to go to the drug store to get me some medicine. She came home and told me how that pharmacist had mixed up the medicine special just for me. When that medicine worked, I knew I wanted to be the man that mixed up the medicine. I earned my money and went to college."

Franky remembered Judge talking about college. "Wow, you must have made a lot of money."

"No, sir, I did not. Why, the day I graduated, I was so poor, I couldn't even pay twenty-five dollars for my diploma. The dean of the college loaned me the money so I could get that piece of paper in my hand."

Franky blew out a whistle. "Why, I thought you said you were smart. I ain't never heard anyone paying twenty-five dollars for a piece paper, and not even a whole newspaper at that."

"A diploma is not an ordinary paper," Sidney replied. "It's a paper that says you are qualified to do something. Qualified means…"

Franky cut him off mid-sentence. "I know what qualified means."

"Well, aren't you the smart one. Most street kids don't

know the meaning of big words. How'd you come to be so smart?"

"I just know is all." Franky wanted to tell him about Judge, but Mouse had told him not to talk about the man. Afraid he'd say something he shouldn't, Franky started for the door. He put the meat pies in his pocket with the others, placed a hand on the handle, and hesitated, turning back toward Sidney. "I know a lot of big words. And I didn't have to pay anyone twenty-five dollars for no piece of paper to prove it neither."

Duke and Leopold were just finishing a song when Franky approached. "It's a cold one out here today, Little Man. We have to keep playing just so our lips don't stick to the mouthpiece," Duke said and broke into another tune.

Franky stood listening for a moment then tossed a penny into the hat that sat near Leopold's feet. As he crossed to the opposite side of the road he took one of the meat pies from his pocket and made a show of taking a bite as he approached the flower girl's cart. A good head taller and dressed in rags with a thin scarf covering her head, the girl eyed the meat pie in his hand and licked her chapped lips as he approached. She saw him watching and lowered her eyes.

Franky came to a stop a few feet away and stood on the snow-covered walk eating the rest of his meat pie, turning every so often so she could see. When he got to the final bite, he turned once more, resisting a smile when she licked her lips yet again. He finished his breakfast, folded the wrapper, and placed it in his pocket. Only then did he purposely make eye contact.

"What are you looking at?" The words flew from her mouth in a smoky stream against the cold air. She trembled and pulled her tattered coat tighter.

"I was looking at those fine roses you're selling. I sure wish I had some for my ma."

Her face softened. "You can have all you want if you're

willing to pay."

"I ain't got no money," he said and thought of Judge and how the man would not approve of him speaking in such a way. *"If you want to go far in this world, you'll do well to speak like an educated man."* Franky brushed the memory aside and continued the charade. "My ma would sure like some of those fine roses, it being Valentine's Day and all."

"You want charity; you go get in the bread line," the girl said tersely.

"I don't need bread. I just had myself a fine meat pie." Franky burped to hide his amusement.

"Yes, well, too bad you went and ate it all. I might have traded you a few of my roses for a bite or two."

This time, Franky did allow himself to smile. "Are you hungry, then?"

Anger flashed in the girl's eyes. "I am and I don't see what you find so amusing about it."

Franky held up his hands the way he'd seen Mouse do to appease someone. "I'm not laughing at ya; I just thought maybe we could make a trade. Being you're hungry and all."

"What kind of trade?"

Franky reached into his pocket and pulled out one of the meat pies, watching as understanding washed over the girl's face. She plucked four red roses from the basket. He shook his head and she added two more. Franky smiled his approval and reached for the roses. She pulled them back, holding them at a distance, not trusting him to keep up his end of the bargain. He smiled and handed her the meat pie. Only then did she relinquish the flowers.

She didn't wait for him to leave before opening the wrapping and attacking the meat pie in greedy gulps. Franky wondered how long it had been since she'd eaten. With so many people out of work, he further wondered how many flowers she was actually able to sell. *You got what you came for. Why do you care?*

He started to leave, heaved a sigh, and turned to her once more. Reaching into his pocket, he took out several coins, placing them in her trembling hand.

She shoved the coins into her pocket. "Do you want more roses?"

"Not today," he answered. "Someday I'll ask for more, but not today."

Her eyes brimmed with tears of gratitude. Franky turned, walking away before she could answer.

Chapter Twenty-Nine

Franky heard voices coming from the stairwell. He prodded Rabbit and both boys moved to the opposite end of the hall, each pressed into a doorway, watching. The stairwell door opened and two men strolled out, shouting and talking as if they belonged. Franky knew better, as he knew everyone who lived on the floor. Something about the men made his neck hairs stand on end. Maybe it was because their skin color matched his, a rarity in the neighborhood. Perhaps it was because they were dressed much nicer than most of the men living in the apartment. Even their shoes were shined to a high polish. Uncommon, when most men in the neighborhood couldn't afford food, much less a tin of polish for the shoes on their feet.

They're connected.

The men stopped on the far side of Mouse and Millie's apartment and continued with their bawdy jokes.

"They look like trouble," Rabbit whispered.

Franky nodded his agreement. Though they hadn't tried to enter, the fact that they'd stopped near Millie's door concerned him.

"Want me to get the others?" Rabbit looked ready to bolt.

Franky's mind whirled with the possibilities, one of which the men simply walked away without causing trouble. Unlikely, but plausible all the same. "Only if there's trouble. Until then, we wait."

Rabbit nodded his agreement.

The men grew louder and it wasn't long before Millie

opened the door to investigate the noise. As she stepped out into the hallway, the door closed behind her. She threw her hands into the air and began screaming at the men to be quiet, that she had a baby sleeping inside. She was so angry, she didn't realize she'd forgotten to button her blouse. Unfortunately, the men who were now lusting after her didn't know she'd probably been in the process of feeding her baby when she heard them. He'd seen that look before many times. That set of the jaw right before trouble broke out. *Millie's in danger.*

"Go, Rabbit, run and find the others and don't stop for anything." The words were no sooner out of his mouth than both boys raced down the hall. Franky stopped, placing himself between Millie and the men as Rabbit darted in between them and made a beeline for the stairs.

"Beat it, squirt!" the larger of the two men yelled.

"Yeah, you know what's good for you, you'll follow your little chicken friend down the stairs."

Franky squared his shoulders. "I ain't going nowhere. I'm staying right here to protect the lady."

The first man laughed. "You hear that? This little stain is going to take us on. The lady don't need no protecting. She's got us to look out for her. Isn't that right, Lyle?"

"Oh yes, James and I, we're going to look after her real nice now." James smiled.

Instantly, he was back in Judge's house and with Garret and JT. He knew what they were going to do to Millie. He froze, struggling with the sudden return of the memories.

"Oh look, Lyle, the nice lady is inviting us inside," James said and the men moved closer.

I'm her guardian. The thought jolted Franky into action. He doubled his fists and they burst out laughing.

"Just what do you think you are going to do with those two little rocks?" James asked, pushing him out of the way.

Something inside of Franky snapped. He got up, leaned forward, and rammed into James' leg. As he did, he opened his mouth and bit through the man's pants, tasting blood as he chomped down. For a moment, he was back in Chicago facing his attackers. James swore and kicked him in the stomach. Franky gulped for air as he slid across the floor. As he hit the wall, everything went dark.

***

Franky opened his eyes and moaned. He felt hands under his arms and looked into Millie's concerned eyes.

"Are you all right?" she asked, helping him up.

Franky rubbed his head. "I'm okay."

"Thank you for standing up for me like you did. That was very brave of you."

Franky wasn't sure what had happened after he blacked out, but he was glad to see Millie was okay. What he wasn't happy about was that his cover had been blown. How would he ever be able to protect her now? Not that he'd done a very good job this time. Some guardian he was. Franky rubbed the bump on his head and worried what Mouse would say when he found out he'd let him down. "It's my job."

"Franky will be fine. He has a hard head," Rabbit said.

Franky blinked, wondering when the boy had returned. He looked closer and realized that his friends Ducky and Roach were standing behind the boy looking unnaturally pale, Ducky's usually dark skin so light, his freckles looked as if someone had painted them on.

Millie turned toward him. "Good, and what's your name?"

"Hugh. Sometimes they call me Rabbit, 'cause I run really fast."

"Indeed you do. Thank you for bringing help," she said, glancing at the other boys. "You are all so brave." The boys beamed under her compliment. Millie glanced at her door. "Hugh, you wouldn't know anything about locks, would you?"

Rabbit looked to Franky.

Franky nodded the go-ahead to Ducky, who raced forward and opened the door with ease. Millie rushed inside and Franky motioned for Ducky to close the door. Franky motioned Rabbit closer and the boy cast a glance toward the stairs. Franky sighed, knowing Rabbit had used the only thing he knew that would save Millie. "She knows, then?"

Rabbit looked to the others before answering. "I had to tell them Mouse was a Purple. It was the only way."

"Is Mouse going to be mad at Rabbit?" Ducky asked.

Mouse is going to be mad at everyone. Franky rubbed at his head once again. "Did anyone call him?"

All the boys shook their head at once, eyes wide, hoping the task of sharing what had happened wouldn't fall to them.

"Mrs. Millie is my responsibility, I'll see to it." Franky said and watched as each boy released the breath they'd been holding. Franky walked several steps, hesitating when the room around him began to spin. Rabbit was at his side in an instant, helping him to the floor. Rabbit motioned for Ducky to follow and left without a word. Franky didn't have to tell them how or where to find Mouse; everyone tasked at protecting Millie already knew. Franky lowered his eyelids to thwart the pain from his pounding head. He'd let down Millie the same way Judge had failed to protect him. It didn't occur to him that he was put in an impossible situation; all he knew was he'd let both her and Mouse down. A part of him wished he'd suffered the same fate as Judge. At least then he wouldn't have the shame of facing Mouse. Wrapping his arms around his knees, he awaited his fate.

***

Franky slept curled in front of Millie's door, determined

to protect her and the child with his life if need be. It was the next morning when Mouse finally approached him, wanting to hear his side of the story. Dark circles tugged at Mouse's eyes and he looked as if he hadn't slept in days. Franky looked at the blood on Mouse's shoes and blew out a sigh of relief. "Is it done, then?"

"It is." Mouse's voice held no sign of regret.

"Is it my turn?" Franky asked, meeting his tone.

Mouse's brows lifted. "For what?"

Franky looked him in the eye and spoke the words he'd rehearsed well into the night. "Listen, Mouse, I've been around long enough to know how things work. A person doesn't do their job and they're dealt with. Don't you worry none; I'll not hold it against you."

Mouse lowered into a crouch. "Not until I hear your side of the story, Little Man."

Franky narrowed his eyes. "What's there to tell? You gave me a job and I failed. If it wasn't for Rabbit and the boys, Mrs. Millie would be dead."

"Tell me about those boys. Who are they? How did they come to be there? And how did they know about the Purples?"

Franky laughed. "Gosh, Mouse, everyone in the neighborhood knows you're with the Purples. You must know that. Why, until now, no one dared to even look at Mrs. Millie for fear of what would happen. Who were those guys anyway?"

"No one you have to worry about anymore," Mouse said, pushing away his question. "Now about those kids, I get the impression they thought they were working for me."

Franky swallowed. "They were, in a way. I hired them to help me keep an eye on Mrs. Millie. She's smart and I think she's seen me a time or two. I thought if I had guys to help me, we could do a better job of watching her. It was working too, until yesterday."

Mouse rubbed at the stubble on his chin. "Didn't you tell them she didn't know of my connection with the Purples?"

"Of course I did, I'm not daft. I trained them like you trained me. They're real good at shadowing. Only these guys were real tough, I wasn't awake at the time, on account I hit my head and all, but they were going to do really bad things to Mrs. Millie. They even threatened to take Fannie. So he did the only thing he could think of and told them you were a Purple. Don't be mad at them, Mouse. It's all my fault. I hired them and told them what to do if there was trouble. They knew what to say and how to find you if anything happened. If I'd done a better job guarding Mrs. Millie, none of this would've happened."

"The way I see it, Mileta is alive because of you," Mouse said, using the name he preferred calling her.

"I didn't do nothing!" Franky argued.

"But you did. You didn't run away, you tried to protect her, but the men were too much for you." Mouse lifted a hand to silence Franky, who started to object. "I shudder to think what would have happened to Mileta had you not hired the boys to help. Sure the boys protected her, but had it not been for you, there would've been no one there."

"Rabbit didn't run away. He ran to get help," Franky said.

"I know that now. I also know you've been paying those boys out of money I gave you. How much do you pay them?"

"Twenty-five cents per week."

"Twenty-five cents? That doesn't leave you with much."

Franky shrugged. "I've got ways of getting what I need."

"All the same, you'll not pay them."

Franky wanted to object, but he was too tired and his head hurt. "Want I should sit in the hallway?"

"No, I'll have one of the other boys watch over Mileta," Mouse said.

"They'll not work for free," Franky said.

"Who said anything about them working for free?"

Franky rubbed at his temple. "You did."

"No, I said you are not to pay them. If they're working for me, I'll do the paying," Mouse corrected. "A dollar a week and they answer to you."

Franky's eyes bugged. "For each of them?"

"For the ones that protect Mileta. If they are going to do a man's work, they should receive a man's pay."

"Just because you pay them a man's wages don't mean they can fight like men," Franky said sourly.

Mouse's brows knitted momentarily, then he smiled. "Tell the boys I'll pay them a man's wages, but they'll have to learn to fight like men."

"How do you suppose they do that?" Franky asked.

Mouse's smile broadened, giving the man a youthful appearance Franky rarely saw. "My pal Slim will teach you all how to fight. When he's finished with the lot of you, you'll know how to take down guys much bigger than you."

"You're joshing, Mouse. If you want us to fight, then why can't you teach us?" Franky asked.

"Trust me, Slim's the best."

Franky would've preferred Mouse to teach them. Sure, he liked Slim well enough, but he doubted the man could stand still long enough to teach anyone how to fight. "Is this some kind of joke? Slim's not even a Purple."

Mouse reeled on him. "Yeah, and neither are you. I plan on keeping it that way too. When you work, you work for me, not the Purples, get it?"

It wasn't like Mouse to turn his anger on him. Franky took a step backward. "Whatever you say, Mouse."

"I say it and I mean it. If anything ever happens to me, you beat it. You don't go working for the Purples and you don't go looking for Mac. You go to Slim and Slim alone."

"Sure, Mouse. Mouse?" Franky's voice cracked when he spoke, "If the Purples are so bad, why do you work for them?"

"Because I don't have a choice. I've been on the streets all my life. Being a Purple is all I know." Mouse sighed. "You look like you've been through a battle, Little Man. Appoint someone to stay here and go home. If Mac says anything, tell him I told you to take the rest of the day off."

Franky fought the urge to tell Mouse that he too was living on the streets. Or, rather, the hallway on the upper floor, but he was afraid Mouse would insist he move back to the apartment with Mac. Instead, he merely nodded and waited for Mouse to go inside 307 before starting toward the stairs. When he closed the door to the stairwell, he stuck two fingers in his mouth and whistled. "Mouse wants you to watch the door," he said when Rabbit, Ducky, and Roach came bounding up the stairs.

"He's not mad at us, then?" Rabbit sounded relieved.

"No, you'll be staying." Franky wanted to tell them all he and Mouse had discussed, but he was too tired and his head hurt.

"Where are you going?" Ducky asked when he started up the stairs.

"Home." Franky answered. As his weary legs moved him along, he was glad he didn't have far to go.

Chapter Thirty

June 30, 1931

Franky stood in the shadows watching Millie and Mouse. On an ordinary day, Mouse would have sensed he was nearby. But not tonight, as he was focused solely on burying their infant daughter. Franky had ridden to the cemetery with Mac and a couple of guys who were stationed at the front gate to make certain no one interrupted them. Not wishing to stay with Mac, he'd pushed aside his fear of the dead and crept close enough to observe the burial. A chill ran through him when Millie removed the blanket, kissed the baby, and placed her in the small wooden box as if laying the infant in a cradle to sleep. Though he didn't know the baby, he wept as they closed the lid, lowered her into the ground, and began covering it with dirt. Franky didn't know what happened to the child, only that she'd died. He listened as Millie spoke to the ground, watched as Mouse patted the dirt with the shovel, then followed unnoticed as they walked to where Mac and the others waited. Mouse gave a nod to the men, then ushered Millie into the Ford and drove away. Franky waited until they were gone and followed on foot. The sadness in Millie's words echoed in his heart. For the first time in a great while, he thought of Judge and wondered if he too were sleeping in a box in the ground. Somehow he preferred thinking the man sleeping than to picture the man dead.

***

Franky woke, instantly aware he was not alone in the hallway. He looked to his right, expecting to see Rabbit sleeping nearby. The boy was gone. The overhead light didn't do much to illuminate the hallway; he was up in an instant, searching to see what had the hairs on the back of his neck on end. He heard breathing, turned, and saw a shadowy figure pressed against the far wall. He tucked his fingers into fists, running though his mind everything he'd learned from his lessons with Slim.

"Not bad, Little Man, but if I'd wanted to hurt you, I would have done so while you were sleeping."

Mouse. Franky lowered his hands and started rolling his sleeping blanket. He climbed onto the windowsill and stuffed the blanket behind the ceiling tile, then jumped to the floor and faced Mouse once more.

"I went to Mac's to get you and you weren't there. Mac told me you haven't slept there since I moved into this building. Have you been sleeping here all along?"

Though he couldn't see Mouse's face, there was something about his tone that worried Franky. "I have."

"Why?"

"I'm closer if there's trouble." Franky wanted to tell him he was afraid of Mac but didn't.

"And what if there was trouble? How am I to keep you safe if I don't know where you are? If I tell you to be somewhere, I expect to find you there. Now get your stuff."

"No." The word was out of his mouth before he could stop it. Mouse moved a step closer and Franky looked to the stairs, wondering if he could make it.

Mouse placed a hand on his shoulder. "What did you say?"

"I…I said no. I'm not going back to the apartment and you can't make me." He couldn't believe he was really speaking to Mouse this way. "You told me to tell you if I ever wanted to leave and I guess I do, 'cause I'm not going back."

"You're telling me you'd rather live on the streets than

to live in an apartment with heat?" Mouse's voice was incredulous.

"No, I'm telling you I'd rather live on the streets than live with Mac."

"Is there something I should know?"

There's a bunch you should know. He was just about to say as much when he remembered Mac's threat. "No."

"Where are your belongings?" Mouse asked.

Franky looked to the ceiling.

"Get them. Now," Mouse said when Franky hesitated.

Franky did as told, leaving the blanket for Rabbit to use. He wouldn't be back. He'd pulled one over on Mouse this time; it wouldn't happen again. As soon as he got the chance, he'd leave. He had no idea where he was going, but he would not stay with Mac. Mouse didn't want him to have dealings with the Purple Gang; couldn't he see making him live with Mac was far worse? He was still planning his escape when Mouse stopped at the third-floor landing, opened the door to the stairwell, and walked to number 307.

Franky stood against the wall waiting for Mouse to go inside so he could make his escape, blinking his confusion when Mouse opened the door and motioned him inside. In all the years Franky had followed Millie, Mouse had never officially introduced them.

"Are you coming or not?" Mouse asked.

Franky pushed off the wall and stepped inside. Mouse followed, closing the door behind them. Having been with Mac and the others when they picked up her parents' belongings years earlier, he recognized the furniture with its shades of orange and browns. Thinking of her parents brought back memories of the day they died and affirmed his decision to leave the first opportunity he got. He would not go live with Mac and that was that.

Mouse walked to a door on the other side of the room, peeked inside, pulled the door closed, then tried the next. He took a step inside the room and Franky held his breath, waiting for him to shut the door.

"Wait there," Mouse said as if reading his mind.

Franky sighed and sat on the arm of the sofa.

Mouse returned a few moments later, and to Franky's surprise, Millie followed behind looking as if she'd just gotten out of bed. Franky was shocked by her appearance. Her dress clung to her in heavy wrinkles and her usually perfectly coiffed hair was now in desperate need of a comb. In all the years of following her, he'd never seen her look like this. He remembered how he'd felt after Judge died and instantly understood her sorrow. She stared as if she were looking through him. He ached to run to her to tell her he understood. His lips trembled and tears trickled down his cheek. He wiped the tears in angry swipes. A sob escaped his lips and he turned to go, fearing Mouse would label him a cry baby.

"He can stay," Millie said just as he reached for the doorknob.

Franky stopped in his tracks. *Stay? Here?* He pivoted on his heels just as Millie disappeared into the bedroom and closed the door. For a moment, he thought he'd heard wrong.

"I'll not be sending you back to Mac's. You'll stay here from now on. As far as Mileta is concerned, you are just a boy doing your job. She's in a lot of pain." Mouse touched his hand to his chest. "In here. Something tells me you know how she feels and maybe you'll be able to help her. I can't stay; things are heating up on the streets. I'll be back when I can. Mileta is my wife and that makes her your family. And a man must take care of his family. If she needs anything, I trust you to see that she gets it. I want someone near her at all times. Can you do that for me, Franky?"

Franky's mouth went dry. It was the first time since he arrived Mouse had referred to him as anything other than Little Man. Unable to speak, Franky merely nodded.

Mouse went to the window and looked out. "The boys know how to get ahold of Slim if they can't find me, right?"

"They do," Franky said, finding his voice once more. He wanted to add that Mouse was scaring him, but he'd already shed tears in front of the man; he didn't want him to rethink his decision.

"You'll sleep there," Mouse said, pointing to the sofa. He walked to the counter, held up a few bills for Franky to see, and placed them under the candle. "Check the cabinets and the icebox. If you need to go to the store, post one of the boys outside the door. Oh, and if you can, please try to get Mileta to eat something. She hasn't eaten since…she needs to eat."

Franky looked toward the bedroom door, unsure what to say.

"If you need to go to the store, do it soon. I doubt Mileta will be up for a while, but I'd prefer you to be here when she wakes. And, Franky, there's no need to run away. This is your home now. You'll not have your own room, but you'll be safe." Mouse left without waiting for a response.

Franky stood staring at the door waiting for Mouse to come back in and tell him it had all been some kind of hoax. When after some time he didn't return, Franky brushed away tears once again. Only this time, they were tears of relief.

***

August, 1931

Franky entered the apartment to find Millie sitting on the sofa. Her presence startled him as she rarely came out of her bedroom except to eat and go to the bathroom. He closed the door behind him and walked the short distance to the kitchen, placed the sack on the table, and then went to work emptying his pockets of the things he'd pilfered.

"I see Tobias taught you well," Millie said, watching him. "Does he not give you money for such things?"

"To be sure," Franky replied. "But it helps when you know how to make the money last longer."

"I'd like to make a quilt, but I have no fabric," she said, worrying the ratted quilt in her hands.

"I can get you what you need if you give me a list," Franky offered.

"Have you ever purchased fabric before?"

"No, ma'am." The formality felt awkward.

"You can call me Millie."

"No, Mrs. Millie," he said and smiled.

She gave a brief smile of approval before answering, "There is much more to making a quilt than gathering supplies. The fabric has to be the proper weight and I must make sure the colors blend so that the quilt is pleasing to the eye."

Franky thought about that for a moment. "Okay, you can come with me, but you'll have to leave the store before I get the fabric."

"Why is that?" Uncertainty filled her voice.

"Well, I can't steal a whole hunk of fabric with you standing there now, can I?"

"Franky, we are not going to steal the fabric."

"That's what I said. There's no way we can do it together without getting caught," Franky agreed.

"No, Franky. What I meant was neither of us is going to steal the fabric. We shall go to the store and purchase it. You do still have the money Tobias gave you, do you not?"

"Sure I do. I didn't steal it or nothing."

"I didn't say you did. I just wanted to make sure you have enough to buy fabric."

He wasn't sure how much it cost to make a quilt, but

Mouse had left him with enough money to get Millie anything she wanted. And if she wanted fabric, he'd see she got it. He took a glass from the cabinet and filled it with water from the faucet. "There's enough."

"Good. I'd also like to visit the cemetery while we're out."

Franky choked on the water. "Why do ya want to go there?"

"I wish to visit my parents and my daughter. If that makes you uncomfortable, I can ask one of the other boys to go with me. Rabbit or one of the others, perhaps," she said, meeting his eye.

Franky hadn't realized she knew any of their names. Not that he would send them. He needed to go so she could explain to him how to pick the fabric. That way, he'd be able to get her what she needed in the future. "I'll go."

"Are you sure you don't mind?"

Of course he minded; cemeteries made his skin crawl. Not that he'd ever tell her so. It wasn't his job to argue; it was his job to be her guardian. He'd let her down once. It wouldn't happen again.

***

Cindy hugged the journals to her chest and thought about all that she'd read.

"You're smiling," Linda observed.

"I hate that Mouse didn't deem it necessary to tell Grandma who Franky was, but I'm glad he saw fit to get him off the street," Cindy replied.

Linda stood, arching her back in a deep stretch. "I'm glad she didn't have to go through the trauma alone. Tobias was right in bringing him in. I think maybe somehow they healed each other."

"I agree. Between losing the Judge and nearly

drowning, he had to be messed up. These days, they would label it PTSD," Cindy said.

"These days, they have a label for everything. It's probably good he didn't get labeled. Made him tougher. Kids these days are too soft."

"And you want me to bring another one into the world?" Cindy regretted the comment the moment she said it.

Linda gave her the eye. "Darn toot'n. The sooner the better."

"I'm hungry," Cindy replied, hoping to distract her mother. "What do you want to eat?"

"Ice cream. Let's drive to Marlette and go to Luv More Ice Cream," Linda said, wagging her eyebrows.

"Mom, we haven't even had dinner yet. We need protein," Cindy reminded her.

"So we'll have them add some peanuts," Linda countered.

Instantly, a chocolate-dipped waffle cone came to mind. Cindy stood and headed to the bedroom.

"Where are you going?" Linda called after her.

"To get my purse before we both come to our senses."

Chapter Thirty-One

Cindy finished stirring the coffees and carried them to the living room, handing a cup to her mother, who was anxiously waiting to begin the next pages of Franky's journals.

"Thanks." Linda took a sip from the cup and handed Cindy her stack.

Cindy settled onto the couch, tucked her legs under her, and began to read.

The months before Mouse died proved to be most difficult. The rivalry on the streets was taking its toll on everyone, Mouse included. The bulls – that's what we called the detectives – were relentless in trying to bring down the Purple Gang and anyone associated with them. They'd hassled me and the boys, trying to get us to roll over on Mouse. Even the threat of jail wouldn't have made us snitch on Mouse. For me, it was because he was family. The others just knew better than to rat out a Purple. When Mouse died, it was like the world ended. I guess in some ways it did, at least the world as I'd come to know it.

***

December 5, 1933

Franky blew into his hands and rubbed them together to warm them. It had been two days since the landlord had shut off the heat for failure to pay. Franky coughed and pulled his coat tighter against the chill.

"Want some of my quilt?" Millie asked when he coughed once more.

Franky shook his head, not trusting himself to speak

without arguing.

"I know you're upset, but Tobias will be back any day. He'll take care of things."

"Mouse would want me to take care of this!" Franky yelled and started into a deep coughing fit. He hadn't meant to snap, but he was growing increasingly worried about Mouse, who'd gone out of town for a few days and was supposed to be back by now. In the past, when delayed, the man had sent word not to worry. He was late and they hadn't heard a word.

Millie set her chin. "Tobias made me promise to keep you out of trouble. You know the police are looking for a reason to pick you up. Do you think that landlord will agree to turn on the heat just because you ask him nicely? We both know it'll take money or force to get the heat back on, and we don't have any money left."

"Then let me do it my way." Franky sniffed.

Millie shook her head. "No. It's bad enough I have to ask you to steal food to keep us fed. I will not have you putting yourself in any more danger than necessary."

"And how am I to feel if I allow you to freeze to death?"

Millie sighed. When she spoke, her words came out in a frosty cloud. "I'm not there just yet. I am hungry, though."

Franky jumped from the couch and headed for the door, happy to at least be able to do something to help."

Millie called his name as he reached for the doorknob. "See if you can find an elixir for your cough and give me your word you'll not visit the landlord."

Franky hesitated.

"I'll give you a compromise. Go to the store and come straight home. If Tobias does not make it home tonight, you may visit the landlord in the morning."

He sighed and nodded his agreement before leaving.

Ducky was waiting for him in the hallway, his frizzy

hair stuffed under a cap a size too small. The boy jumped to his feet, gave him a once-over, and frowned. "You don't look so good, Franky."

"I'm fine," Franky grumbled. He wasn't about to be a crybaby about being sick. Nor would he confess to taking orders from a dame, even if the dame in question was Millie. That was the worst of it. He was supposed to be her guardian; it smarted that she wouldn't allow him to do his job. He could handle the bulls. He'd been doing it for years and hadn't got caught yet.

Ducky shrugged. "If you say so."

"I say so," Franky said gruffly.

"Sheesh, you don't have to bite my head off," Ducky said, matching his tone. "It's not like I have to be here, ya know."

Ducky was right. Things had been so tight, the boys hadn't gotten paid in over a month, and yet Ducky, Rabbit, and Roach had stayed loyal. Franky cupped the boy on the shoulder. "You'll come with me. The guys can look out for Mrs. Millie."

Ducky beamed his gratitude.

Roach and Rabbit sat just inside the entrance of the apartment building, huddled together for warmth. They looked up as Franky and Ducky approached.

"It's freezing out," Rabbit said as they neared. "Came inside to get warm."

"Not much warmer, but there's no wind in here," Roach said, scratching at his head.

Franky couldn't fault the boys for coming inside. He coughed and looked toward the door. "Just keep your ears alert. Mouse should be back any time and I don't want there to be anyone inside waiting for him."

"I thought Mouse was coming back yesterday," Rabbit replied.

"He got delayed," Franky said. At least he hoped that to

be the case. "You know he's not going to come back if he doesn't think it safe."

"Yeah, he must be delayed," Ducky said, parroting Franky.

"I have to go out for a bit and I'm taking Ducky with me. We won't be long. Make sure to keep your eyes peeled." Franky wanted to add that he'd had an uneasy feeling for the past couple of days, but then again, it could be the fever making him feel that way.

"You got it, Franky," Rabbit replied.

The wind cut through them the instant Ducky pushed open the door. Franky shivered and pulled his hat lower as he trudged through the freshly fallen snow.

***

Franky stomped his feet and canvassed the store as they entered, his eyes sweeping from side to side. Not seeing anyone looking, he went to work filling the cotton sack hidden under his coat. Ducky moved further into the store, constantly picking stuff up and putting it down again to draw attention away from Franky.

In the past, Franky would visit several stores, not wishing to dip too much from one place in these troubled times. Now he frequented this store, taking what he wanted as payback for the way the man had treated Millie and the unfair price he'd paid for the quilts she'd worked so hard to make. Millie would not allow him to interfere at the time, preferring instead to shield him as a mother would a child. Unbeknownst to her, he'd avenged her many times in the last few months. Franky eased a jar of peaches into the sack, scarfed up a jar of elixir, and gave a nod to Ducky, letting the boy know he'd finished. He took a step and remembered the journal he'd promised to pick up for Millie. Just as he was tucking it into his sack, Ducky approached, unaware the owner of the store was hot on his heels. The man looked over Ducky's shoulder and saw Franky placing the journal into his bag.

The man turned a brilliant shade of crimson and pointed a crooked finger in Franky's direction. "Why, you little thief! I'll see you..."

Before the man could finish his sentence, Ducky lowered his head and plowed into him headfirst, sending his spectacles flying as he scooted across the floor on his backside. The boy was still bent over laughing when Franky grabbed him by the collar and led him from the store.

"We'll not be going back to that store," Ducky said once they were clear.

"He'll be on the lookout for us, that's for certain," Franky agreed. "Pity too. I wasn't quite done with the fellow."

"You never did say what he did to rile you," Ducky said with a glance over his shoulder.

"He was mean to my mom," Franky replied.

Ducky's mouth dropped open. "You've got a mom?"

Actually, he did, but that was not the woman Franky spoke of. "Not really, but if I did, I think she'd be a lot like Mrs. Millie."

"I wouldn't mind having a mom like Mrs. Millie."

Franky laughed. "Cept when she told you what to do. Sometimes she treats me like a child."

Ducky sniffed and wiped his nose on the sleeve of his coat. "She's just worried about you getting nabbed by the coppers."

Franky patted his coat, feeling the bag hidden inside. "She needn't worry. I ain't been caught yet."

A few steps later, Ducky stopped, his mouth open wide.

"What's the matter now?" Franky asked.

"I was just thinking. If Mrs. Millie was your mom, that would make Mouse your pop."

"It wouldn't be all that bad," Franky said and began walking once more. "In fact, I wouldn't mind it at all."

***

December 6, 1933

Franky woke to find himself lying in bed snuggled next to Millie. He scrambled from the bed, wondering how he'd gotten there. His mind was still foggy from sleep, but he remembered taking the elixir before lying on the couch. No, there'd been a ruckus in the hallway. Someone had shouted that Prohibition was over and he'd knocked on Millie's door to tell her. She was awake and felt his head before insisting he bring his blanket into her room. He'd done what she said, but he firmly remembered bedding down on the floor beside her bed. *Then how did I get into the bed?* He tried to remember but couldn't recall. One thing was for sure: he wouldn't be there when she woke up.

He left the room and closed the door, careful to turn the handle so as not to disturb her. The first thing he noticed upon entering the living area was the heater was on. Though it had a long way to go to be warm, he couldn't see his breath when he coughed, so that was a start. He went to the kitchen expecting to heat up yesterday's beans, when he saw a small stack of bills lying on the counter. *Tobias has returned.* A knowing smile spread across Franky's face. *That explains why the heat is on. Good ole Mouse, I bet he really gave it to the landlord. That'll teach the man to mess with us.*

Feeling better after taking the elixir and sleeping through the night, Franky scooped up the bills. It had been a long time since they'd had a proper breakfast. *Best not go to the corner market. It's too soon. I haven't been to Delwood Market in a while.* He looked at the clock on the wall. *It's early. I can take the trolley car to Woodward Ave. I'll pick up a newspaper as well.* Mrs. Millie would like that. Thinking of Millie, he frowned. He'd still not managed to figure out how he'd gotten into her bed.

***

Franky was on the couch glancing at the morning paper when she entered the living room. Her eyes swept over the room and he knew she was looking for Mouse, who'd yet to return. Her gaze came to rest on the food lying on the counter and saw where he'd placed several eggs and a small bundle wrapped in brown paper. She looked to him then back to the wrapped bundle.

"Bacon," Franky said, watching her. "There is fresh bread in the breadbox as well."

"Thank you, Franky."

"Boy, if I could only find a way to slip this into my pocket." He turned the paper for her to see an advert for a used 1931 Buick Sedan.

"Those would have to be some mighty big pockets."

He pondered this for a moment. "Maybe I could ask Mouse to show me how to steal a car."

"Franklin, you will do no such thing. It is bad enough you steal what you do."

He hadn't been called that in ages. He thought to tell her she sounded like Judge, but he'd yet to tell her of his previous life, making up a fictitious family instead. He decided to keep up the deception. "Jeepers, you sounded just like my mother."

"Good. I'm sure she would not be pleased if you stole a car."

He folded the paper, placed it on the couch beside him, and decided to have a bit of fun with her. "The only thing that would make her mad is if I were not stealing it for her."

"Where are your parents, Franky?" she asked.

"Around," he said, avoiding the question for the hundredth time.

"Around where?" she pressed.

He shrugged.

"Don't you miss your family?"

The only family he'd ever known up until now had been Judge. *Maybe I should tell her about him.* Before he could utter a word, the door opened, and Tobias entered, carrying a small crate. The relief Franky felt at seeing him was short-lived as Mouse staggered a short distance and plopped the crate down on the counter. He turned in their direction and collapsed face-first onto the floor.

"He's zozzled," Franky said, shaking his head.

Millie rushed to his side, rolling him onto his back. "He's not drunk. He's burning with fever. Help me get him into the bathtub."

Franky raced to help.

As they removed his jacket, Mouse moaned, sending a chill the length of Franky's spine. Instantly, he was back in Indiana at the church with Mistress Childers. She'd been ill as well. The doctor had said if she didn't have surgery, she'd die. He looked at the man who'd rescued him and given him a purpose, silently pleading for him not to die.

"We need ice, Franky. Do you think you can get some?" Millie's eyes were brimmed with tears.

Franky was in the corner store, snatching chunks of ice from the icebox at the front of the store before he realized he'd even left the apartment. He grabbed a piece of burlap and placed the ice chunks inside, his only thought to save Mouse. A hand grabbed his elbow and he attempted to shake free.

"I've got you this time, you little varmint!" the store owner said, pulling him further inside the store.

Franky snapped out of his fog, realizing he'd finally been caught.

A flash of movement caught his attention. The store

owner made an *oof* sound and the next thing he knew, he was free. He picked up the burlap bundle and took off running, only slightly aware of Ducky laughing at his side.

Franky burst through the door of the apartment and ran straight toward the washroom. Millie was hovering over Mouse, her face nearly as pale as his. She took the ice and placed it into the water as Franky stared at the wound on Mouse's arm. He'd seen the same streaks before when he'd gone with Judge to visit a friend in the hospital. The man in the bed next to Judge's friend had them. When Franky asked what they were, Judge's face turned grim.

"We'll give him a few more moments, then we'll get him into bed," Millie said, wiping the back of her hand across her eyes.

"Those marks are death streaks," Franky whispered, repeating Judge's words.

"Mouse can't die." Ducky sounded incredulous.

"Don't be daft; everyone can die," Franky countered.

The boys remained silent as Millie dipped a washcloth into the cool water and placed it upon Mouse's forehead. She repeated the process several more times to no avail. Finally, she sighed and Franky knew the end was near.

"Help me get him out of the tub," Millie said.

The three of them went to work pulling Mouse from the tub, dragging him across the hall and lifting him into the bed. Millie tore off several strips from an old sheet and carefully rewrapped the infected arm. She packed the two quilts around him before climbing into bed next to him.

"Do you want me to go find a doctor?" Franky knew it was too late but felt the need to do something – anything – to help.

"We have no money with which to pay him," Millie replied softly.

Money?! Why, he'd find a doctor and make him come. Franky set his jaw. "I will try my best to persuade him."

"And I will help," Ducky said, copying Franky's stance.

Millie sighed. "Okay, boys."

Franky turned and ran from the room, and from what he knew he couldn't fix.

"There was a doctor in the store," Ducky said as they raced down the stairs. "I saw him with his bag."

Franky plowed through the snow, oblivious to the fact that he wasn't wearing his coat. He raced down the sidewalk and pushed his way into the corner market, searching the store for the doctor. He was so focused on finding the doctor, he didn't notice the bulls standing near the counter, speaking with the owner.

Franky started down the aisle and a man stepped in front of him. He recognized the man as Stim, a detective set on capturing Mouse. Franky pivoted, his heart sinking as Detective Green – Stim's partner – reached out and nabbed Ducky, who struggled unsuccessfully to get free. He started running, hoping to force his way past Stim. The man was ready for him, grabbing hold of his arm as he attempted to pass.

"Let me go. I came to find a doctor. A man is dying," Franky said, struggling to get free.

"Sure, sure." Stim chuckled. "Would that be the reason you stole ice from our friend here?"

"It's freezing outside. Why else would we need ice?" Franky said. The instant he said it, he realized all this could have been avoided if they'd have grabbed a pail of snow instead of going for ice. *Millie asked for ice.* He sighed his realization as he continued to break free.

"The boy's got a point. Besides, I've seen that kid hanging around Mouse's apartment building," Green replied. "Won't be any harm in checking it out."

"What's your name, boy?" Stim asked.

Franky just glared at the man.

"Listen, I can go check out your story or take you down to the station. Makes no never mind to me. But if someone is dying, they aren't going to get help until you tell me your name."

Franky remained silent, knowing Mouse wasn't going to live through the night.

"His name's Franky!"

"Shut up, Ducky!" Franky fumed.

"We have to help Mouse." Ducky's voice shook when he spoke.

A wide smile spread over both men's faces. Stim pushed him toward the entrance to the store. "Let's go, boys. We wouldn't want anything to happen to our friend Mouse now, would we?"

***

Franky sat in the back seat of the police car, his hand chained to the door. Ducky sat beside him, whimpering like a caged animal. He wasn't angry with his friend for ratting them out. Ducky was doing what he would have done if he hadn't known the truth.

Franky took his free hand and wiped the condensation from the window. As he sat staring up at the third-floor window, he knew his suspicions were founded.

"Mouse is dead," he said softly.

Ducky's eyes grew wide. "How do you know?"

"Millie just looked out the window. If Mouse were alive, she wouldn't have left his side." The window fogged over once more and Franky thought to clear it once again. As his hand neared the window, he reconsidered. Hiding behind the steamy curtain of glass, he gave in to his grief.

Chapter Thirty-Two

December 10, 1933

Franky sat on the sofa willing Millie to come out of her room. Four days had passed since Mouse died and she'd barely left her room except to go to the bathroom or trudge lifelessly to the neighbor's apartment to make phone calls, trying to learn where they'd taken Mouse's body. She'd not eaten, though he'd finally gotten her to drink small sips of water. Franky knew that was only to appease him so he would leave her alone. She'd grown more and more listless in the last few days. He'd postponed his own grief, feeling helpless as she sank deeper and deeper inside herself.

Making a decision, he rose and went to her door, knocked, and waited. When she failed to answer, he opened the door and went inside. Crossing to the bed, he took a breath then peeled back the covers. Grabbing hold of her arm, he pulled, dipping to the floor as he struggled to drag her from the bed.

"Leave me alone, Franky." Her voice was frail.

"No, you must get up," he said, tugging harder.

"Just leave me to die," she pleaded.

"No!" he answered more forcefully. "You must get up."

"I have nothing left. Just let me be."

"You have me." Franky was on the verge of tears. "If you die, I'll have no one."

"You'll still have your family."

"My family is dead." *At least the ones that wanted me.* "You're all I have left. If you die, I'll be all alone again. I'll have no choice but to join the Purples."

Much to his relief, Millie stopped fighting and allowed him to pull her from the bed. She toppled to the floor beside him, drawing him into her arms, rocking him as one would a child. Tears rolled down his face and he knew he wasn't alone in his sorrow.

He wasn't sure how much time passed before she released him. He only knew he felt comfort in her embrace. She pushed up to her knees, then stood, walked to the mirror, and heaved a heavy sigh. "I think I'll take a shower."

Franky nodded and went to the living room to wait.

She emerged sometime later, still pale and drawn, but her hair was combed, her clothes clean. "Franky, you know Mouse's friends, right?"

Franky stiffened. It wasn't like Millie to use Tobias' street name. "Most of them."

"I hate to ask this, but I don't know any other way. Can you go to them and ask them to find out where the police took him?" She stared at him, pleading for him to agree.

"I'll go," he replied. "I'll have the boys wait in the hallway. I don't have to tell you things have changed now that Mouse is…gone." He looked at her, willing her to understand. "Do not open the door until I return."

"Don't worry. I'll wait," she promised.

"There is cheese and crackers on the counter." He shrugged. "I haven't been out since…"

"It's okay, Franky. Cheese and crackers will be enough."

Franky posted Ducky at the door and took his time walking down the stairs. Millie hadn't known the position she'd put him in when asking him to get in touch with Mouse's friends. The Purples would be of no help. Mouse was dead. He had no more friends. Worse than that, they would wonder what loose ends he'd left behind. They say dead men tell no tales, but a vindictive wife was another story. It didn't matter that Millie didn't know anything. In the world Mouse once lived, people didn't like to take chances. It was only a matter of time before they made plans to have Millie join Mouse. He knew the invitation would likely be extended to him as well. It had been four days since Mouse was taken away; probably the only reason Millie hadn't joined him was because she hadn't left the apartment. Nor had the Bulls bothered to return to question her. As long as nothing changed, he could keep her safe. At least for now.

Roach was waiting when Franky got to the first floor. "It's hot out there, Franky."

It was December. Franky knew Roach wasn't speaking of the temperature. "Tell me."

"Two guys are sitting in a car three buildings down. They showed up after Mouse croaked. They leave, another pulls up, but they ain't gone for long." Roach gave a nod to the hallway. "Rabbit talked to them at the back apartment. They gave the okay for you to go out their window."

Franky looked behind him. "Rabbit's here?"

"Was. Had some things to take care of but promised to be back later."

Franky clapped Roach on the shoulder. "Ducky's upstairs. Anyone comes toward the building you don't know, get Mrs. Millie out of the apartment. Take her to the neighbors and tell them I'll take care of them later."

Roach's brows lifted. "You got dough?"

"I'm working on it," Franky said before turning and walking away.

***

Not knowing where else to turn, Franky headed to the gym. Mouse had stressed on more than one occasion if he was ever to find himself in trouble, he should contact Slim. He walked into the gym and stood looking for the man.

A gruff-looking man with a limp approached and pointed a gnarled finger at him. "You Franky?"

Franky blinked his surprise. "Yes."

"Come with me. Slim's been waiting for you." The man turned and walked away without further comment. For a man in his condition, he was considerably agile, walking quickly and taking the stairs with ease. When they reached the top, the man stopped and pointed to a door. "In there."

Franky hesitated.

"Go on, then."

Franky placed a hand on the doorknob and turned to thank the man, only to find him halfway down the stairs. Franky turned the knob and stuck his head inside.

"I expected you sooner," Slim said the moment he saw him.

"How'd you know I was coming?" Franky asked.

"Mouse told me." Slim closed his eyes briefly. Opening them once again, he blew out a long breath. "Mouse knew things were heating up. Said he'd told you to come find me if anything happened to him. You did good getting past my guys. They were supposed to contact me if you left the building."

Franky's eyes flew open. "Your guys? You mean the men watching the apartment?"

Slim smiled. "Mouse wasn't the only one with connections. Don't worry, my guys are good. They're there in case any of the Purples show up. They will, you know. It's only a matter of time."

"I know. I've got Ducky and Roach keeping watch. They have orders to move Mrs. Millie if anyone comes."

Slim's smile grew wider. "Mouse trained you well."

Franky grimaced at the mention of Mouse's name.

"It hurts like the blazes, doesn't it? Mouse was my best friend."

Franky's mouth dropped open. "I thought Mac was Mouse's best friend."

Slim moved around the room as if he were afraid of staying in one place. "Mac is nothing but a parasite. Mouse knew him for what he was but couldn't let on because the guy's a Purple. Give the rat time and he'll be at your door. You've got to get Mileta out of town before that happens."

Franky gasped. "You know her true name?"

"I've known her many years. How's she holding up?"

"Not good. I had to make her get out of bed. She wants to know where the bulls have taken Mouse. I didn't know what to do, so I came here."

"Mouse has been taken care of. I saw to it myself. I expect she'll want to verify this. But you have to convince her to leave."

"Me?" Franky had his doubts. "I'm not sure she'll listen to me."

"I can help with that." He went to the desk and pressed a buzzer. "Send Jimmy up."

"Which one?" a voice on the box asked.

"Hoffa," Slim replied. He pushed off the desk on the move once again. "I'll introduce you to Jimmy. He'll take you back to the apartment, drop you off a block away, then drive up like he's been waiting for you. That way, if anyone's watching, the stories will be the same."

There was a knock on the door and a man entered. Full-faced, with dark slicked-back hair, he had a look about him that said he wasn't a man you wanted to cross.

"Franky, this is Jimmy. Jimmy, Franky. Slim motioned the guy to sit and turned to Franky. "I've got to fill him in. Have you eaten?"

Not much. "No."

"Go downstairs and find Bobby, that's the man with the gimpy leg. Tell him I said to feed ya. We won't be long, then Jimmy here will take you home."

"What am I supposed to tell Mrs. Millie?" Franky asked in return.

"He'll tell you when he shows up at the apartment. That way, it'll be fresh in your mind and won't look rehearsed. Oh, and Franky, forget Jimmy's name. It's not important."

***

Franky opened the door to the stairwell and stepped inside. Jimmy had told him not to look inside the envelope, but he couldn't help himself. He gasped at the stack of paper money then gulped at the message that accompanied it. If he hadn't known where the money originated, he'd have been terrified. Pushing the note back inside the envelope, he raced up the stairs as Jimmy had instructed.

Franky was out of breath by the time he reached the third floor. He nodded to Ducky to kill the light before going inside. Millie was standing at the counter going through the crate Mouse had carried inside the day he died. Franky glanced at the scattered contents before waving the envelope in front of her.

"What is it?" Millie asked.

"It's for you."

"Yes, but what is it?"

"The man told me I shouldn't look inside. He said to give it to…" He hesitated. "To the tomato in 307."

Millie took the envelope. Her eyes grew wide when she looked inside. She pulled out the note.

Though she didn't read it aloud, Franky knew precisely what it said. **We've taken care of things. Your husband is keeping your folks company. This dough will help you fade.**

Be out of the city by noon tomorrow. Unless you wish to join the rest of your family, keep that pretty little yap of yours shut. P.S. I hear Florida is nice.

Millie's hands trembled as she returned the note to the envelope without counting the money. "Franky, who gave this to you?"

He worked to sound convincing. "I was just returning, and a man stopped in front of the building and motioned me to his motorcar."

She narrowed her eyes at him. "Who was the man, Franky?"

"I don't know his name," he lied.

She increased her stare. Franky glanced at the contents on the table before answering.

"I've seen him with Mouse, but I don't know his name." Another lie. *It's for her own good.*

"Did you look inside?"

Yes. "He told me not to."

"That's not what I asked you."

"I hear Florida is nice too," Franky said and looked at his feet.

Millie walked to the window, peering out before turning her attention to the envelope once more. After a moment's hesitation, she slid the envelope into the pocket of her dress and retrieved her coat.

Franky smiled. The plan was working. "Does this mean we're going to Florida?"

"We're going to check on my husband."

Franky opened his mouth, but no words escaped.

"It's December, Franky. It hasn't been so cold that the ground should be completely frozen, but I need to see for myself that Tobias is where they say he is. Understand?"

He nodded and followed her out the door. He closed his

eyes to block out the darkness as he pushed the button to the elevator. Though years had passed, he was still uncomfortable in small, confined spaces. As the door opened, Franky opened his eyes and took hold of Millie's arm. He placed a finger to his mouth and motioned for her to wait and breathed a sigh of relief when she listened. So far, all was going as planned. He stepped out of the elevator and was back within seconds. He waved her forward and held out his hand. "Give me the envelope."

"Keep the dough; I just want the envelope," Franky said when Millie's eyebrows arched.

She pulled the envelope from her pocket, removed the cash along with the note, and handed him the envelope. "What do you have planned?"

"I'm going to go out first. If anyone's watching, I'll make sure they see me with the envelope. They'll follow me to see why I didn't give it to you. Wait until they're well down the street before you leave. And make sure to stay close to the building so they cannot see you."

"Don't worry," he said when Millie started to protest. "I've done this before with Mouse. There's a small alley two streets down, which is too small for a motorcar to follow. I'll ditch the tail and be waiting for you when you get to the graveyard." He didn't add that Jimmy was going to pick him up as soon as he was out of her sight to ensure he arrived at Elmwood Cemetery before her and that a second car would follow at enough of a distance so as not to be seen. Once they were at the cemetery, they'd be on their own until they returned home. From there, it was up to Millie where she chose to go. He didn't have a preference in destinations, just as long as she took him with her. He wasn't worried about her taking him along. He had a backup plan. If for any reason she balked, he would tell her the thing Mouse had told him never to tell. He would tell her that he was family.

Chapter Thirty-Three

Jimmy dropped Franky off a block away from the cemetery. He was within sight of the gates when a yellow cab dropped Millie off at the front. She exited the car without surveying her surroundings, making him glad he was there to watch over her. He followed unnoticed as she walked to where her parents and baby daughter lay sleeping, staying out of view while she kneeled to clean the headstone and stood talking to those who would not hear.

Even from a distance, he could tell the ground had been tampered with. The snow was significantly less and though someone had attempted to cover their tracks, one could tell if they were looking. The mud within the snow was a dead giveaway. He pictured Mouse lying under the dirty snow and wanted to run and never look back. The only thing preventing his flight was the woman he'd promised to protect. He inched closer, listening to her words, tears leaking from his eyes as she told the wind that she would be leaving this night and promising to take Franky with her. He took a step closer and heard the leaves under the snow crunch beneath his feet. Millie jumped and turned, her eyes round as a frightened cat's. Mouse would have been disappointed he'd let himself grow so careless, and for a moment, he was grateful the man didn't know. He stepped up beside her. "I didn't mean to disturb you."

Millie placed her arm around him and wiped her tears with her free hand. "I am glad you're here. Would you like to say anything?"

Franky stiffened. "You mean talk to the dead?"

"I mean talk to Mouse," she replied.

"How do you know he can hear me?"

"How do you know he can't?" she countered.

She had a point. "What should I say?"

"I cannot tell you that. Just tell him whatever is in your heart."

He stood there for some time trying to figure out what to say. Finally, he removed his cap and let the words flow. "I've never talked to the dead before, so don't you laugh." He was going to mention Judge but didn't want to have to answer questions, so he decided to use "mom" instead, figuring if Mouse really could hear him, he'd understand. "My mom always said one should not speak ill of the dead, but I can't help it. I'm pretty sore at you for dying. I know you weren't my dad or nothin', but I kind of thought you'd make a pretty good one. You treated me swell and taught me how to dip pockets real good. I never knew my dad, but if you see him where you are, and he tries to pick a fight, you just tell him that you're my real dad and I said he should leave you alone."

He sniffed and placed his cap back on his head. "Do you think he could hear me?"

Millie swiped at fresh tears. "I think he heard you just fine, Franky."

"Good. Can we go? I don't want anyone to see me talking to the dirt."

Millie released him and glanced at the grave once more. "Yes, it's time for us to go. Did you have any trouble getting here?"

Franky sniffed and wiped his nose on his coat sleeve. "Na, Mouse taught me real good."

She looked toward the entrance. "Just the same, I would feel better if we slip out the back way. Oh, and Franky, do you know where we can find ourselves a map?"

While a fence surrounded the cemetery, they both knew there to be a break in the fencing near the back, one that he'd used many times to avoid detection. After going to live with Millie and Mouse, he'd shown Millie the route which they'd used from time to time. He nodded and started toward the break. "So we can find our way to Florida?"

Millie shook her head. "No, we're not going to Florida."

But we must. Franky stopped. "But I thought the note said…"

She cut him off. "I know what the note said, but we're not going where they want us to go. If they know where to look for us, they could maybe find us."

Franky blew into his hands. "Yeah, well, I hear Florida is warm."

"I'm sure there are other warm places, which is precisely why we need a map."

"I miss Mouse," Franky said softly. He would've known how to convince Millie to go where the note said. He pulled the fence apart and slid through the opening.

"So do I," she said, following close behind.

***

It took some doing, but they finally found a gas station that carried more than a local map. To avoid questions, they'd purchased a map of Michigan along with one that showed the entire country. The latter was now splayed out in front of them on the counter.

"How about California?" Franky said, pointing to the far side of the map. It was his sixth suggestion and he was getting tired of the rejections.

"How about something a little closer?" Millie countered. She folded the map multiple times until they could only see Michigan and the close surrounding states. She trailed a finger around the image. "Franky, look at this and tell me what you see."

Franky peered at the map. "I see Michigan."

"Yes, but this shape; what does it look like?" She traced the lower part of Michigan once again.

He didn't see it at first, but when he looked again, the image jumped out at him. "A glove?"

Millie smiled. "A mitten, to be exact. Hand me the other map."

Franky handed over the map of the state and Mildred unfolded it and closed her eyes. Opening her eyes once again, she gasped.

"What is it?" Franky asked, peering at the spot where her finger now lay.

Franky stared in rapt attention as Millie lifted her finger, tucked her hand inside her blouse, and retrieved a newspaper clipping, holding it just beyond his view.

Closing the map, she turned to Franky. "Time to get packing. We'll leave when it is dark."

That was more like it. "Are we going to Florida?"

"No, we're going to visit my family."

He wanted to ask her more questions, but it was easy to see she'd already made up her mind. Besides, Jimmy hadn't said they had to go to Florida; he'd merely said to get her out of town and made a suggestion of where they might go as he'd visited the place a few times.

***

While Franky hadn't had a say in where they were going, he intended to make sure they got there without issue, meaning using proper transportation. He left the boys to stand guard over Millie, called Slim to fill him in, and was now headed to the parking lot where he'd stashed Mouse's Ford the day he died. At the time, his only thought was to hide it so that the bulls couldn't confiscate it. Now he prayed that it was still there. The lot was dark when he arrived. He looked to the spot where he'd left the Ford and his heart sank. *It's gone…replaced by a pile of snow. Snow!*

Making his way closer, he realized the snow was in front of where he'd parked the motorcar. He rounded the pile and, for a moment, thought he'd been mistaken. That is, until he saw a second pile. No, not a pile, but the Ford covered in a layer of snow. He laughed his relief then stopped smiling when the laughter turned into a racking cough. While he was feeling better overall, the cough still lingered. He waited for it to pass then began the job of clearing the snow.

***

Franky parked at the end of the block and stayed in the shadows to reach the apartment building. He crouched low and crept inside, breathing a sigh of relief when he saw Rabbit leaning against the wall near the window.

"How are things?" Franky asked as he eased the door closed.

Rabbit cast a glance out the window. "Mac and one of the goons showed up a few moments ago."

Franky's mouth went dry. He'd hoped they could make their escape before the Purples arrived. "Anyone else?"

"There's another car that's been parked outside most of the day. Roach said you know the guys."

"I do." Knowing Slim's guys were near eased his anxiety. "The others should be here any minute."

As if saying it made it so, a motorcar pulled in behind Slim's guys and blinked their headlamps twice. "It's time for you and the others to go. I'll send Roach and Ducky down."

"Are you sure you can trust those guys?" Rabbit's voice held uncertainty.

"Mouse trusted Slim and they are his guys." Franky assured him. They will come in when they see you and the boys leave. You sure you boys want to do this?"

"You don't need to worry about us, Franky," Rabbit assured him.

"Okay, then give us a few moments to get ready before you leave. Make a show of making it look as if you're trying to sneak away. Make sure to place the blanket over Roach's head like I said. I don't want there to be anything left to question. The Purples need to think Mrs. Millie is with you so they will follow. Ditch them as soon as possible and don't get caught or they'll toss you in the river," Franky said, going over the plan once more.

"I'm glad you're getting out of this place, Franky." Rabbit's voice shook when he spoke.

"I'll miss you too, Rabbit," Franky said then turned and raced up the stairs. He had a similar conversation with Ducky and Roach before sending them on their way. He walked to the door and placed a hand on the numbered lettering on the door. Number 307, the place he'd called home the longest since leaving the asylum. He removed his hand and twisted the doorknob. Things were in motion – there was no turning back now.

The room was dark when he entered. "Mrs. Millie?"

"I'm here, Franky."

He clicked the door shut. "Do not turn on the light. There are two men watching the building."

"So we cannot leave?" He heard the disappointment in her voice.

"Sure we can. I worked it out with a few of the boys. They are going to make trouble and get the men to follow."

"Those men do not play nice, Franky."

"The boys have dealt with their sort before. Do you have everything ready?"

"I do, but how are we going to get it to the train station?"

"We don't need to. We have Mouse's motorcar."

"How? I thought the police took it away. And who shall drive it?" Millie asked, bombarding him with questions.

Franky sighed. "That's the difference between guys and dames. Dames sure ask a lot of questions. If I told the boys what I just told you, they'd know things would work out. You need to trust me, okay?"

"Okay, Franky, I'll leave our getaway up to you."

"Good. It's time to go." He opened the door, walked across the hall, and pushed the button for the elevator. He'd rather take the stairs, but time was of the essence. The doors opened immediately. Franky stepped inside, fought a rush of panic, and pushed the button to stop the elevator while they placed the things they were taking inside. When they finished, he patiently waited for Mildred to say a silent goodbye. She stood looking into the darkness for several moments before pulling the door shut and hurrying to join him. The doors slid to a close and panic gripped him. Suddenly, Millie clutched his hand and began to sob. He wasn't sure if it was her touch or that he knew she needed him to be strong, but his panic ebbed and he remained stoic the rest of the ride.

Franky touched Millie's shoulder as the elevator slowed. "We must hurry."

Millie brushed her tears away with the sleeves of her coat and nodded her readiness. Franky stepped out into the dark hallway, made a low whistle, and two guys joined them, each hurrying into the elevator to help carry their belongings. They moved to the doorway. As they neared, Franky saw someone waiting by the door. Moving closer, he saw that someone was Jimmy. He stood staring out the window before finally pulling open the door. Franky shivered as an icy rush of air filled the space.

"The chumps bought it, but it won't be long before they

figure out the ruse. If you hurry, you should be good for a clean sneak," Jimmy said.

"We need to go," Franky replied. He led the way to the Ford, which had been moved to the front of the building. They put their belongings into the back and the guys left without saying goodbye. Franky wasn't worried about their abrupt departure, as he knew they would follow at a distance until they were sure he and Millie weren't being followed. He maneuvered himself behind the wheel and blinked his surprise when Millie started laughing.

"You can't even see over the wheel!" She snickered.

He narrowed his eyes. "I can see plenty fine."

"Can you even reach those?" she asked, pointing to the three pedals on the floor.

"How do you think I got the car home?" He maneuvered the pedals, pulled the gearshift down, and the car lurched forward, driving for several moments without turning on the headlamps. Finally, he checked the mirror before turning the switch to illuminate the road.

"Do you know where we are going?"

"You said you wanted to go to Sandusky," he answered without taking his eyes from the road.

"I mean, do you know how to get there?"

"I studied the map."

"It didn't look very far."

It was his turn to laugh. "It's a map; nothing ever looks very far. Go to sleep, Mrs. Millie. It's going to be a long night."

She yawned. "Who was that guy?"

"Which one?"

"The one who looked to be around my age."

"His name's Hoffa. He goes by Jimmy. He's nobody." Slim had told him to forget the guy's name, but they were leaving and would never see the guy again, so he didn't see the harm in telling her.

"He seemed like the quiet sort," she said sleepily. "Doesn't seem at all suited to this line of work."

Franky wanted to tell her she was wrong, that the guy had instantly reminded him of Mouse. Both men had a way of getting people to do what they wanted without raising their voice. *It's the quiet ones you need to look out for.* Franky was going to argue the point, but Millie's breathing showed she was close to sleep. It didn't matter anyway; they were on their way to a new life. As Franky aimed the Ford north, he had no idea how truly different that new life would be.

Chapter Thirty-Four

The further north he drove, the smaller the towns became, leading him to wonder if he'd been right to agree with Millie's decision. By the time they finally reached the city of Sandusky, Franky was too tired to care about anything but finding a place to sleep.

"Mrs. Millie, we're here," he said, angling the Ford to the curb in front of the smallest hotel he'd ever laid eyes on. He sat staring at the brick building until realizing he still had a death grip on the steering wheel. Prying his fingers loose, he turned the engine off and offered her a triumphant smile. He'd gotten her here safely.

"You did good, Franky. I'll go in and get us a room," she said.

While he wanted nothing more than to close his eyes and sleep, he wasn't about to let her out of his sight. He slipped inside behind her and took a position by the door.

Millie stood at the front desk. A thin man appraised them. "Be needing a room?"

"Yes, sir," Millie said, nodding.

The man pushed up his spectacles. "Just you and your son?"

Millie looked over her shoulder, obviously surprised to see him there.

Franky took an instant dislike to the clerk. Something in the man's tone irritated him. He moved up beside her and narrowed his eyes at the man. "The lady would have had to be mighty promiscuous at rather a young age to have a son my age, don't you think? I believe you owe my sister an apology."

The desk clerk's face turned crimson. "I…um...I assure you I meant no ill regard. I just assumed…" The clerk glanced at Millie's hand. "I mean, I knew he was too young to be your husband. Will he…your husband, be joining you later?"

At first, Franky wished Millie had stayed in the Ford while he took care of procuring the rooms. Now he wanted her to leave so he could take care of the man in front of him. He drummed a finger on the counter "My brother-in-law grew ill and died a few days ago."

The man's blush deepened. "My condolences, ma'am. Influenza has taken a great many folks ill."

Millie glanced at Franky then back to the clerk. "A room, if you please. Two beds."

"You don't sound like you're from these parts. What brings you to our town?" the man asked, reaching for a key.

Franky balled his hands into fists. Millie placed a hand on his shoulder. "I'm here to see a family friend. My brother and I have had such a long drive and would like to rest up a bit before we visit."

"Oh, yes. Yes indeed. A local, then? What's the name? I know most everyone in town."

"His name is Paddy." Millie's voice sounded hopeful.

The man's brow creased. "Don't recall anyone with that name. Sounds like one of those nicknames. What be his given name?"

She sighed her frustration. "We, my family and I, have always called him Paddy."

The man adjusted his spectacles once more. "What about the last name? You know that?"

Millie reached into her pocket and pulled out the newspaper clipping. "Jones, it says his name is Paddy Jones."

The man leaned forward to see the clipping, but she

folded it before he could get a good look.

"We have several Joneses in the area, but I don't recall any of them going by that. You two go on up to your room. I'll do some asking around and let you know when you come down."

"Thank you," she said, taking the key.

Franky went outside to grab their bags before joining her in their second-floor room. The room was small, but it was warm and there were two beds. He looked at one of the brightly covered beds and yawned. "Boy, that man gave me the heebie-jeebies. I know bulls that don't grill people like that."

"He did seem a bit hinky. Maybe that's just his way."

Franky yawned once more. "You said we were coming to see family. What was that paper?"

She pulled out the clipping and handed it to him.

Franky scanned the clipping. WE RODE THE TRAIN. I AM LOOKING FOR MY BROTHERS AND SISTERS. PLEASE CONTACT PADDY JONES BOX 132 SANDUSKY MICHIGAN 48471. "So this guy we're here to see, this Paddy, he's not family?"

"He is as much family as you are," she said, returning the clipping to her pocket.

Franky yawned. "What train?"

She nodded toward the beds. "Pick one."

Franky jumped onto the bed nearest the wall and bounced up and down.

Millie laughed. "They are for sleeping."

"I know, but I've always wanted to do this." Though he'd thought about it, he'd not dared to attempt it when living with Judge. Somehow he didn't think the man would have approved of such antics.

"I did it too, the first time I was alone in my new room after my parents picked me."

Franky wasn't sure what surprised him most, that she was talking about her parents for the first time or that she'd just admitted that she too had ridden the trains. He stretched his legs out and landed on his bottom with a thud. "The people in the graveyard picked you?"

"They did. Right after we came over on the trains."

Franky worked to hide his surprise. "Were they good to you?"

She smiled. "They were very good to me."

And Mac and the others killed them. Just like Garret and JT killed Judge. Suddenly, he was filled with rage. "I wish the people who picked me were kind. If Mouse hadn't come for me, I would have killed them with my bare hands." Of course he was speaking of the ones who killed Judge. If only he'd met Slim and learned how to protect himself before going to live with Judge.

Maybe I could have saved him. Saved us. Then what would have happened to Mrs. Millie? The thought sent a chill through him.

Dumbfounded, Mildred sank on the bed opposite him. "What are you saying, Franky?"

Too tired to tell her the truth, he searched his mind for an explanation. "I'm saying that I rode the trains too. Mouse came to find me to see if I was okay. When he saw how bad things were, he took me with him. He told me not to tell you about the trains. He said you wouldn't understand."

Her face paled. "Did you know Tobias before he came to see you?"

"No, he just showed up one day. Said someone had sent him to check on me. When I told him how bad things were, he made me leave with him. He said he had a job for me." It was only a partial lie.

"What was the job, Franky?"

Franky yawned. "Why, to take care of you, of course. In return, he promised to teach me a trade. He showed me how to fade when I followed you, just in case your parents or someone else would see me. Then he taught me how to dip the pockets. When I got good at that, he taught me other stuff."

Her brows knitted together. "Wait, how long have you been following me?"

He shrugged. "A long time."

She met his eye. "How long, Franky?"

Another shrug; he was too tired to think. He yawned. "Maybe two or three years before your parents died."

She gasped. "But why?"

"Because Mouse said I was family, and that's what family does. We look out after one another."

Millie stood and paced the small room.

He was so very tired. "You look mad. Mouse was right; I shouldn't have told you."

"I am not angry with you, Franky. I'm just so confused, and I wish Tobias were here to answer my questions."

So do I. Feeling the weight of the world on his shoulders, Franky lay down, resting his weary head on the small pillow, and closed his eyes. "I miss Mouse."

***

Franky's mind raced as he followed Millie down the stairs. How had she convinced him to stay in a town where people lacked manners? He sighed; it wasn't so much that the hotel clerk lacked manners – it was just that he was so nosey. People in Detroit were inquisitive, but they didn't come right out and ask you your business. No, if someone in Detroit wanted to know about you, they'd ask around and get the scoop without making you any the wiser. It was just the way things were done. You didn't let your hand be known by telling people you were checking up on them. And why'd the man have to go and tell Millie about this farm they were on their way to see? A farm? They'd done all right over the years while living in the apartment. Who needed all that land anyway?

Franky didn't bother to hide his sour mood, one made worse by the fact that once again she'd made the decision without his approval. One minute he was sleeping, the next she'd woke him, going on and on about staying in this small town. Now she was looking to buy a farm. He'd tried to resist, but Millie had been so enthusiastic and begged him to stay with her. He'd nearly said no, then she'd played her ace card. She'd called him family, saying that now that he'd told the man Millie was his sister, it should be so, even going as far as telling him to call her Millie instead of Mrs. Millie.

"What do you know about farms?" Franky asked as soon as they reached the Ford.

"I know as much as you do," Mildred replied.

"Just like a dame." Franky laughed. "You've done gone all soft from that story he told. How do you know that guy in there ain't trying to flimflam you?"

She blinked her innocence. "What do you mean?"

Franky backed out of the parking space, grinding the gears, and headed out of town. "Come on, think about it. That guy has done nothing but ask questions since we pulled into town. He knows you're a widow and you told him you have money. Now, out of the blue, he just happens to know a guy who will sell you his farm on the cheap. You're such a chump, you're walking straight into their trap. Why couldn't the house be in town? Naw, he's sending us down some back road. You heard him; the house is next to the woods. How hinky is that? Probably where they'll bury our bodies after they rob and bump us off."

"You've been living in the city too long. This is the country. People in the country don't kill people for their money.

Besides, the house has to be out of town; it's a farm. They don't have farms in town. Where would you keep your horse?"

Franky stole a glance at her. "You were serious about that?"

"I was…if you want one. Do you even like animals?"

He shrugged. "Guess I've never given them a thought. A horse might be all right. Or a dog, as long as we don't have to eat it." He thought to tell her about the time he'd passed up a family because the woman wouldn't kiss a pig, but it sounded too unbelievable. He wondered for a second what would've happened if he'd agreed to being placed there. He sighed and turned the car onto Henderson Road. "All the same, you'd better let me do the talking. And don't stand too close to me. Anything goes down, you run and hide in those woods. If I can get away, I'll come find you after I put a knife in the guy's gut."

She stared at him, eyes wide. "Franky, I know you've seen things that you don't want to talk about, but I'm pretty sure we're safe here."

Safe. Franky wasn't even sure he knew the meaning of the word. The snow was deeper on the less traveled backroad and he had to work to keep the motorcar moving forward – fighting the wheel until, at last, the house loomed on the right. It was bigger than he'd imagined, even bigger than the one he'd shared with Judge. *Big enough to have my own room.* Franky had to admit it looked rather inviting, surrounded by the blanket of fresh white snow. He looked to the second floor searching the windows, wondering which would be his, if he chose to stay.

Franky pulled the Ford to a halt and pushed the horn to announce their arrival. At the sound of the horn, two large black dogs raced out of the barn, furiously barking their arrival. A moment later, a man followed them out of the barn. He was dressed for the weather. Wearing a heavy brown coat, knit hat, and black rubber boots, he had a black scarf wrapped around his face, allowing only his eyes to show. Franky placed his hand on the door handle. "I'd feel much better if you stay inside the car."

"Only if you stay where I can see you and keep your knife inside your pocket."

"Dames," he muttered then opened the door. The man approached, head hunkered against the wind.

"Hello, what brings you out on such a miserable day?" he asked and stretched a gloved hand toward Franky.

At least the man has manners. Franky accepted the greeting but kept the other hand tucked into his coat pocket, his fingers around the knife he carried. "I'm interested in doing some business with you."

"Well, if it's business, we should talk in the house. Too cold to think out here, don't you agree?" he said, releasing Franky's hand and nodding toward the house.

Franky took a step, then looked at the Ford, wondering if he should ask Millie to join them. After all, it was her money they'd be discussing.

The dogs continued to bark their greeting and the man lowered his scarf, revealing a brilliant red beard. He pursed his lips and whistled for them to knock it off.

Franky shivered, though he knew it wasn't from the cold. It was the first time he'd been so close to a man with red hair since Chicago. Thinking of Garret and all the things he'd done, his mouth went dry. Instantly, he thought to return to the Ford and tell Millie the man was not interested in selling the farm.

Before he had a chance, Millie rounded the front of the motorcar and fell into the stranger's arms. At first, Franky thought she'd slipped. He started to reach for her to save her from Garret's touch. Then recognition registered in the man's eyes and he wrapped his arms around her, holding her as if he never intended to let her go. Franky's mind cleared and he saw it was not Garret standing there holding Millie, but a stranger – looking at her as he'd seen Mouse do time and time again. As they stood embracing each other, Franky stewed, his fear turning into a slow burning anger. When he could take it no more, he cleared his throat, and they finally parted.

He could see icy streams of frozen tears on Millie's cheeks and the man's eyes glistened as well, staring at her the way he'd seen Ducky stare at a plate of freshly baked cookies on a counter. Franky set his jaw, not at all happy he'd lost control of the situation once more.

Chapter Thirty-Five

It turned out the stranger was no stranger at all. At least not to Millie. His name was Paddy, the man she'd come here to find. At Paddy's insistence, Franky sheltered the Ford in the barn. The three of them now sat at the dining room table drinking sweetened coffee to break the chill. A small black and white cat climbed into his lap, rubbing against his chest as if asking for attention. Franky used his free hand to stroke her and smiled when she began to purr. She cuddled in his lap and he continued to pat her as Millie told of her life since leaving the train. She told of being adopted and of losing her parents. She tearfully spoke of losing Mouse and of finding the newspaper clipping in with his belongings. Much to Franky's chagrin, She told of the stack of money, how they'd managed to escape without being followed. She smiled at Franky as she told how he'd driven all the way to Sandusky under such terrible driving conditions.

Paddy reached across the table and placed his hand on top of Millie's. "I'm sorry you've had such a difficult life."

Franky thought about smacking his hand away but elected for a more subtle approach and cleared his throat as he'd done multiple times since their arrival.

Paddy removed his hand. He then leaned back in his chair and spoke directly to Franky. "Thank you for getting the both of you here safe."

"It was nothing." Franky shrugged and continued to stroke the cat.

Paddy turned his attention to Millie. "I understand how

you came to be in this town, but how did you find me?"

Millie took a sip of her coffee. "We didn't know we'd found you. Bill from the hotel told us some guy named Howard was about to lose his farm. He said if I would agree to pay the back taxes, that this Howard fellow would sell the farm to me."

Paddy's face turned crimson. "The taxes are not my fault. My parents were good people, but lousy at finances."

"Yes, Bill made that clear. He said they left you with a huge debt that no boy your age would be able to recover from."

"Boy, I've seen more crap than half the people in this town, and they still treat me like a kid. If they knew where I came from and what I did before I got here." He shook his head.

"They…the people of this town, don't know you rode the trains?" Millie whispered.

Paddy looked at Franky before answering. "They told us not to tell. That's why I didn't use my real name when I placed the advert. I put that in the paper five years ago."

Millie blinked her surprise. "Tobias had it all that time and yet never told me. Did you hear from any of the others?"

Paddy waved his hand. "Most of them. I've been corresponding with a few. I'll let you read the letters later. I'd go into town every Friday to check that box, hoping to hear from you. And each time, it felt as if a knife jabbed me right in the heart."

Franky's blood boiled as Paddy spoke, his red beard taunting him with each word. Not only was the man professing his love for Millie, he seemed to be upset with Mouse.

Paddy pointed at his chest then leaned forward in his chair. "It doesn't surprise me much that Mouse found you. He had his sights set on you for years. It didn't matter that he knew I was in love with you. He was going to have you, and that was that."

He called him Mouse, not Tobias. Franky blinked his

surprise.

Millie seemed just as surprised. “You came straight here from the trains, did you not?”

Paddy nodded. “I did.”

“Then how could you know about Tobias’ keeping an eye on me?” Millie asked.

Franky saw her glance in his direction but pretended not to notice.

“I knew because Mouse came from the same streets I did. Our paths had crossed even before I was locked up in that asylum. When me and the boys went out for instruction, he would stop us and drill us about how you were doing and make sure none of us kids were messing with you. One day, Slick made the mistake of telling Mouse I had my sights on you, and he about beat me to a pulp.”

So Mouse didn’t like this guy either. Maybe he hadn’t been wrong to doubt the man’s sincerity. Franky struggled to keep his emotions in check, worried they’d stop talking in front of him if they knew what he was thinking.

Millie, on the other hand, wore her emotions on her sleeve. “Tobias did that to you? But why?”

Paddy drained his cup before answering. “Because he wanted you for himself.”

“What was there to want? I was a kid,” Millie was close to shouting.

“None of us were kids, Mileta. We weren’t allowed to be. We were small adults living in an ugly city. If not for the trains, we would have all died in that city as well.”

Franky trembled when Paddy used the name that had been reserved for Mouse.

Millie stood and moved to the window. “You’ve heard my story and about everyone I’ve lost. Are you saying I’m better off than if I’d have been left behind?”

"On some accounts, yes. Think about it. Even as bad as things were, at least you have lived. You've known love. Isn't that better than being institutionalized and rushing to eat your mush before someone bigger stole it from you? They would've turned you out when you were eighteen. You've had to read a newspaper or two. What would've happened to someone as pretty as you on the streets of New York when the banks collapsed? How many quilts did you make before the trains? How many times could you simply sit and play the piano just for the sheer joy of doing so?"

Franky didn't know what surprised him more, that Millie knew how to play the piano, or that if not for the fact that he'd decided to dislike the guy, he would have agreed with the things he said.

"I haven't played the piano since I left New York," she said without turning around.

Why not? He was just about to ask her when Paddy leaned forward in his chair and asked for him.

"Why in heavens name not?"

"Just like you said. They told us to forget our past. I never even told my parents that I played."

"And your husband did not see to it that you played?" His voice was incredulous. "What kind of a man was he?"

That was the final straw. Mouse was family and it was up to him to defend the man's honor. Franky pushed from his chair, knife in hand.

Millie walked toward him, keeping her voice calm. "Franky, put the knife down."

"I'll not have this guy speaking ill of Mouse." Franky's voice was shaking.

Paddy held his hands out. "I didn't mean to put your friend down. It just surprised me he didn't do everything in his power to make Mileta happy."

"Quit calling her that! Her name is Millie or Mildred," Franky spat. *Only Mouse calls her Mileta.*

Millie moved to his side. "Franky, Paddy didn't mean to disrespect Tobias. Please give me the knife."

"I'm sorry," Paddy repeated. "I think we're all letting our emotions get the best of us."

"Franky, Paddy is family. Just like you, remember? We're all family," Millie soothed.

Family. Franky lowered the knife, but instead of handing it to Millie, he folded it and stuffed it into his pocket. He narrowed his eyes at Paddy. "Don't speak ill of the dead."

Paddy's shoulders relaxed. "Never again."

Millie sighed. "I guess Franky and I should be on our way."

That's more like it. I'd rather go back to Detroit than stay here.

The muscles in Paddy's jaw twitched. "I thought you were interested in buying a small farm."

"And throw you out on the street? Never," Millie replied.

"I could stay." His words were merely a whisper.

Not on your life. Franky waited for Millie's response, shocked when she actually seemed to consider his request.

Millie laughed. "And what would the town's people say about me living in sin with you?"

"It wouldn't be living in sin if we were married." His voice held a mixture of hope and fear.

Married?! Franky looked at Millie to judge her response.

"I am a widow but a handful of days. The people of the town would think me a harlot."

"The people of this town would think you a woman being taken advantage of, not the other way around. It is I who would yield the bad reputation, taking advantage of a young widow in the throes of her grief."

Millie lifted her chin. "And how do I know that is not the case? Obviously, you know me to have money, or I would not have come."

Franky smiled inside. *That's better. We'll be out of here in no time.*

"Yes, your money is a great consideration. We can think of it as a dowry. But I assure you money is not the reason I asked you to marry me."

"And just what is that reason?"

Franky stared at Paddy. *Yes, what is the reason?* Millie turned toward him, but he kept his expression blank.

"Mileta, Mildred," he corrected. "I've loved you for so long. My heart has ached for you from the moment we left the train. I have dreamed of finding you, yet had no idea where you'd gone or who had taken you. I thought you were in Detroit, but for all I knew, you could have been a million miles away. Still, I dreamed one day I would find you and promised myself I would do anything in my power to keep you safe and love away the hurts in your life. Marry me. I will transfer the farm into your name, and if I ever prove to be a bad husband, say the word, and I will leave. It's my promise to you in front of the boy."

Millie tilted her head toward Franky. "Ask my brother."

Franky was incredulous. *Me? Why would I agree to such a thing?*

"Excuse me?" Paddy replied.

"Bill at the hotel thinks Franky is my brother. Since I do not have a father, I must insist that you ask my brother for my hand in marriage."

Ha ha. Florida, here we come.

"Franky, will you walk with me for a moment?" Paddy

said before Franky could give his answer.

Franky wondered what the man was up to. Nothing he could say would make him agree to something so preposterous. Curiosity got the better of him, and he followed Paddy through the living area and waited while he opened the door to the room to the left of the stairs. As the door opened, Franky stared in stunned disbelief. There, sitting against the far wall, was the piano on which Miss Anna played for him when he was young. It looked brand new. He wasn't sure how he knew it was the same one, but he knew. He looked at Paddy, who gave a subtle nod.

"I brought it back from New York earlier this year. It was the one Millie played when she lived in the asylum. I've only just finished restoring it. I know it sounds silly, but I thought that maybe if I were ever to find her, it would show her how much I truly care for her. I promise to do right by her, and by you too. We could be a family. You've seen how ugly the world can be. A woman needs a husband to look out for her. I can see you've done a splendid job of it until now, but wouldn't it be nice if you didn't have to worry about her all the time?"

Yes, it would. Franky knew he could take care of Millie, but he hadn't thought about her needing a new husband. He stared at the piano so intently, he could almost see the woman said to be his mother sitting on the bench playing out a tune. He thought to ask Paddy if he'd known her too but decided it didn't matter. A man would have to really like a person to bring a piano all the way from New York. He thought of the woman in the picture over the mantel in Judge's living room and how Judge said he would've done anything for her. Franky didn't want to like Paddy; there was something about him that didn't add up. Then again, it could just be that the man's hair color brought back painful memories. It was apparent he cared for Millie, and it wouldn't hurt to have help watching over her.

Besides, if Millie married Paddy, then he really would be family and, he was right: that's what families do – take care of each other. He lifted his head and nodded his agreement. In some strange way, having the piano here gave him a feeling of home. He took another long look at the piano then pulled the door closed.

As they returned to the dining area, Millie's face was filled with mixed emotions as she awaited his decision. Praying he was doing the right thing, he spoke. "You have my permission to marry him."

She stared at him as if expecting him to change his mind. When he didn't, she turned her attention to Paddy. "Will you allow Franky to stay with us for as long as he sees fit?"

Paddy grinned. "Of course your brother can stay. He's family."

"And will you stay?" she asked, turning to Franky once again.

Franky looked at Paddy. "Will I have my own bed?"

"Yes, and a room all to yourself to put it in," Paddy replied.

Franky decided to push his luck. "Will you buy me a horse?"

Paddy chuckled. "Better ask your sister; she's the one with all the money."

Millie laughed and nodded her agreement. "So I guess that means no wedding present?"

"What did your last husband get you?" Paddy looked at Franky as if making sure he hadn't said anything that would change his mind.

Millie laughed once more. "I'm afraid Tobias set some pretty high standards. He gifted me with a spoon he'd stolen from me when I was thirteen."

A slight smile played at the corners of Paddy's mouth.

He crooked a finger and motioned her to follow. He walked to the same room he had just visited with Franky and turned the doorknob.

Franky closed his eyes, picturing the piano once again. He was back at the asylum talking to Miss Anna while sitting next to her on the piano bench. He was upset about not going on the train with his friends and she consoled him, telling him it wasn't time for him to go just yet. She'd told him that he'd get to go someday, and when he did, he'd have a mother and father who cared for him and maybe even a dog to run and play with. Franky thought about the two dogs in the yard and a smile creased his face. He saw the smile on Millie's face and sighed. It had been a long time since he'd seen her smile. The cat jumped into his lap, purring against him. As he ran his hand through her soft fur, he realized that for the first time since leaving the city, he wasn't afraid.

Chapter Thirty-Six

May, 1939

Franky sat on the edge of his bed holding the stack of letters he'd found in the top drawer of Howard's writing desk. Letters written by his birth mom, which he'd read multiple times, his anger growing with each pass. She'd written of her love for Mouse, who she called by his given name. Written about her health, which seemed to be declining, and had mentioned her son Paulie over and over. Franky knew he should be happy to learn he had a brother, but he was too focused on his mother's rejection. Not once in any of the letters had she mentioned him, shown any remorse of losing him, or even bothered to ask about his wellbeing. Mouse had always said family was everything. It was apparent to Franky that his mother did not hold to the same sentiment. He placed a hand on each side of the stack of envelopes, intending to rip them to shreds. Thinking better of it, he shoved the letters into his jacket pocket and headed down the stairs. He left the house without saying a word and stomped his way toward the barn.

Howard came out just before he entered.

Franky yanked the letters from his pocket and threw them at the man. "I've lived under your roof for six years. Everyone in town thinks that you are my brother- in-law. I've called you Howard so many times that I forget that it's not your given name. We are supposed to be a family and you never once showed me these letters."

Howard bent, taking his time retrieving the letters. Only

after collecting them all did he speak. “What was I to say, Franky?”

Franky glared at Howard. “Those letters are addressed to Mouse-Tobias,” he corrected. “How did you get them?”

“They were in the crate that belonged to your uncle,” Howard said, leaving no doubt he’d read the letters. “Millie threw them away years ago. I pulled them from the trash without her knowledge and put them in my desk for safekeeping.”

“Why?” Franky asked, wondering if he was asking why she threw them away or why he’d kept them.

“You never mentioned your mother, so I wasn’t sure you knew who she was. Millie and I, well, we had history with Anastasia, having lived in the asylum at the same time as she.” Howard hesitated as if considering how much to say.

“Just tell me,” Franky demanded. “I’m not a kid anymore. I deserve to know the truth.”

“Your mother was not a kind girl. She made the lives of the kids in the asylum – mine included – miserable. Mildred fought back.” He smiled as if remembering. “She took it for a day or two, then pulled herself up and stood up to her. Until then, none of the kids ever even considered it. One day we were all standing in the meeting room playing and Anastasia sat down and started banging on the piano. She did it all the time so, we didn’t think anything of it. Nor did any of us realize how poorly she played. Then Mildred walked right up to the monster; sorry, but that was how we all thought of her. Without saying a word, she sits on the bench beside her. Now, we all thought Mildred was going to get clobbered, and I’m ashamed to say that, at the time, I was so frightened of your mother that I probably would have watched it happen. But not Mildred. She looked up at your mom and asked if she could give it a go. Looking back, I think Anastasia was just as shocked as we were because she agreed to let Mildred play. And play she did. It was as if the heavens had opened up and sent an angel to play us a tune because when she stopped playing, there wasn't a dry eye in the room. Not the mistresses, not us kids, and certainly not Anastasia. Things changed that day as Anastasia asked Mildred if she would teach her how to play. Mildred agreed, but under one condition, she had to leave her friends alone. I won't go as far as to say Anastasia was nice to us, but she did what she promised and left us alone."

"If you hated her so much, why did you keep the letters? Why not just throw them away?"

"I thought you might want to read them someday."

Howard was lying. Franky wasn't sure how he knew, but he knew. Maybe it was the quickness of his answer. Perhaps it was the set of his shoulders that said *I'm holding something back*. "So you thought reading letters from the woman that gave birth to me but never acknowledged me as her son would bring me comfort?"

"She loved you," Howard said softly.

"She loved me?" Franky spat.

"Yes."

"So much that she let them take me away? She told me I'd be going to a home with a family and a dog. Instead, I went…" Franky almost told him the secret he'd kept all these years.

Howard jumped on the opening. "Franky, what happened to you in Chicago? I know what you've told Mildred, but it doesn't add up. You can trust me with the truth, son."

For a moment, he thought about doing just that, telling Howard about Judge and telling him about Garret and JT and the atrocities they'd done, wanting nothing more than to unburden his soul of the evils left unspoken for so many years. Before he could open his mouth, the sun moved out of the shadows, its rays illuminating the red in Howard's beard. He swallowed his words, leaving the evils unspoken, instead lashing out at the only one he knew to blame. "Just because she birthed me does not make her my mother. You're never to call her that again. Furthermore, I wish her dead."

"You'll get your wish soon enough," Howard said softly.

Franky wasn't sure what he expected the man to say, but this was not it. "Those letters are old. How would you possibly know?"

Howard leveled his gaze. "Because I've kept in touch with her over the years."

"You've kept in touch with a woman you profess to hate!"

"I've kept in touch with many from the asylum," Howard corrected. "Your … Anastasia included. That's how I know she's dying."

Franky remembered him saying that he'd kept in touch with the others before. "So she's dying. You think that bothers me?"

"Does it?"

Maybe. "No, I'd spit on her grave if I saw it."

"I thought you weren't supposed to speak ill of the dead." Howard threw his words back at him.

"She's not dead yet. You said it yourself."

"What about your brother? Do you wish the boy to die as well?"

Franky hadn't considered that. "He's just a kid. Why would I want him to die?"

"Something's going to happen to him. Your mother might not have been there for you, but she's watched over your brother. After she dies, he'll be on his own. They'll send him to an asylum. Maybe they'll put him on a train as they did you.

He'd be about the same age as you were when they sent you out, and you know how well that went."

Franky's heart began to pound as he thought of all that could happen to the boy. It didn't matter that he didn't know the kid; he was family. "I'll go get him."

"And do what with him, Franky? It's not like bringing in a stray puppy or kitten. Do you think Mildred is going to let you bring home a kid?"

Franky thought about that. Millie had become more reserved over the years. "I don't know, but we can't let anything happen to him. Boys, they don't recover from stuff like that. Maybe I can move out and take him with me."

Howard frowned. "And give up all your plans of joining the Army? It's all you've ever talked about."

Howard was right, he'd dreamed about joining the Army for years, but Millie kept coming up with excuses. He'd even postponed joining after Howard cut off his thumb when Millie begged him to stay for a while longer to help out on the farm. He'd spent his days milking cows when he should have been protecting his country. Still, what kind of brother would he be if he let the same thing happen to the kid that happened to him? As he stood there debating, an image of George and Alfred came to mind. He hadn't thought of the brothers he'd met on the train from New York in years. But now he could visualize them as if they were standing right in front of him. George, the older of the two, had promised Alfred they would never be separated. He'd gone so far as to jump from a moving train to keep his promise. At the time, Franky didn't understand why, but now the reason was perfectly clear. They were family. He pulled himself taller, reaffirming his decision. "I will stay home if I must, but we can't let them send my brother to the asylum."

Howard's face brightened. "I think I can find a way to figure things out. But I'll need your help."

***

Franky wasn't sure exactly how Howard had persuaded Millie to agree to take Paulie in, but once agreed upon, things moved quickly. Though reserved, Millie seemed agreeable to having the boy come stay with them. Franky had helped to paint the unused third bedroom and Millie made a quilt for his bed with the help of Paddy, who sat next to her cutting the fabric into squares. So, on the night before Paddy was due to leave on the train to New York to get Paulie, Franky was surprised to be woken by raised voices, followed by the shattering of glass. He sprang from the bed, snatched the knife from his dresser, and raced down the stairs, which creaked his descent.

Millie was sitting at the table, her eyes brimming with tears as Howard stood a few feet away using a broom to sweep a broken plate into the metal dustpan.

"What happened?" Franky asked, lowering his knife.

"I dropped one of Mildred's good plates," Howard said as he stooped to clean the mess.

"Is that why you're crying, Millie?" Franky asked, not buying the ruse.

Howard stood and answered for her. "Mildred just has a case of the jitters. She's never had a child this young around the house before and she's afraid she won't be able to manage." Millie opened her mouth to speak and Howard cut her off once more. "She's also afraid you won't hold to your promise."

"My promise," Franky said, stifling a yawn.

"To hang around for a few years to help with the kid," Howard said, looking at Millie.

So that was it. While he loved Millie, she'd done everything in her power to keep him from joining the military. He walked to where she was sitting and kissed her on top of her head. "Don't worry, sis, I made you a promise and I intend on keeping it. If the kid comes to stay, I'll stick around for a couple more years."

Howard smiled. "See there, Mildred, what did I tell you?"

Franky stopped and kissed the top of her head once more for good measure. "But if you change your mind, I'll be on the first train south."

Howard's smile broadened and Millie looked as if she were going to cry once more.

"Wow, a man can't get a break around here," Franky teased. "That's the trouble with dames; they cry when they're sad and they cry when they're happy. You two try and keep it down. I'm going back to bed."

***

Wednesday, July 12, 1939

It had been nearly two weeks since Franky had dropped Howard off at the train station. He'd telegraphed to say he would be returning this day. Franky had driven Howard's Plymouth to town and parked it at the station before hitching a ride to the end of Henderson Road, where he'd walked the rest of the way home. Millie had been on edge since Howard left and today she'd turned to a total basket case, cleaning as if Eleanor Roosevelt herself were coming for a visit. She wrung her hands as she looked out the living room window for what had to have been the hundredth time.

"Mildred, you're going to wear a hole in the floor if you don't stop all that pacing," Franky said as if scolding a child.

"I don't know how you can remain so calm," Mildred said, retracing her path. "Howard called from the gas station; he and Paulie should be here any minute."

"It's just some orphan, Mildred. Don't let a six-year-old get you all worked up. He'll be scared, but he'll also be grateful to have a home. You must remember how that felt. Besides, this kid has had it good. He's never had to live on the streets," Franky said, sticking with the ruse Howard had concocted, saying it would be best if Millie didn't know that he was aware of the kid's background. When Franky had asked Howard why, he told him that Mildred wouldn't trust Franky to stay. Franky had argued the point, saying that he didn't like lying to Millie, but Howard had been quite convincing.

"Franky, I hope you'll refrain from making those types of comments once the boy gets here. You've had your share of trouble in your life. You best remember that and make sure Paulie feels welcome in our house."

Franky shrugged. "Don't worry; I'll go easy on the kid. I'll show him the ropes."

Mildred cast a glance over her shoulder. "So long as you don't show him any of the tricks Tobias taught you."

Franky narrowed his eyes. "If it wasn't for the tricks Mouse taught me, we both would have died of hunger when the Depression hit."

Mildred sighed. "You know I'm grateful to both you and Tobias, but that part of our life is over. I know we don't lead the most exciting life, but we have a good life, Franky. Better than most, and whether you wish to admit it or not, Sandusky is a great place for a boy to grow up. You're a man now; look how well you turned out."

Franky smiled. "Yes, and one day soon, I'll join the army and see the world."

A scowl crossed Millie's face, causing him to regret his words. Before he could assure her he would keep his promise to stay for a while, the dogs alerted them, barking their warnings.

"They are coming!" Millie said, hurrying to the small vestibule and slipping on her shoes. Franky waited in the foyer as she stepped out onto the side porch and waved as the car turned into the driveway. Howard blared the horn and stuck his arm out the window in greeting.

"How was the trip?" Mildred asked as soon as Howard opened the door.

Howard stood, stretching his arms in the air. "Long, but good. It sure was different riding the train as a paying customer. They had a separate train car to take a meal in, called it a dining car. It had tablecloths and real linens. And did you know they have bunk cars? It cost a few dollars extra, but I slept halfway across Canada."

"Well, what will they think of next?" Millie replied.

Howard laughed. "They probably had those same things when we came across, but us being kids and poor and all, we didn't rate that kind of service."

Howard rounded the automobile and opened the side door and disappeared from sight. A few seconds later, he stood and hoisted up a little strawberry blonde-haired boy high enough for them to see. The boy giggled and pointed at the dogs jumping and sniffing at his feet.

Watching from the small hallway, Franky smiled and remembered his first time seeing the dogs.

"Look there, son, that's your pretty new mama I've been telling you about the whole way home. You run over and give her a big hug."

Millie's shoulders stiffened and Franky wondered at her reaction. Was she not happy about becoming a mother? Though they pretended to be brother and sister, Millie was the closest thing to a mother he'd ever had and she'd done well by him. A little overprotective maybe, but all in all, he had no complaints.

Howard set Paulie down, and he ran up the small set of stairs and greeted Millie with outstretched arms. Franky resisted interfering as she reached down and rubbed the boy's mop of hair. “You’re a fine-looking fellow. Are you hungry?”

Franky swallowed as Paulie lowered his arms and nodded his head solemnly. So much for making the boy feel welcome. *She just needs some time to adjust.* At least he hoped that to be true.

“Good. Mother made some cookies. Come inside, and we’ll get you one.” As she turned to follow Paulie inside, Franky saw the frown of disappointment pulling at Howard's face.

Franky gave a nod to Howard and reached for the kid, who eagerly jumped into his arms.

“Hey, kid, I’m your uncle, Frank. Come with me, and I’ll give you the grand tour. We’ll start our tour in the kitchen, of course. Your mother Mildred makes some fine-tasting oatmeal cookies,” he said, then winked at Millie. He found it ironic that he hadn’t had a mother and yet for all intents and purposes, Millie had become his mother figure. The kid had been raised by their mother and now Millie was holding him at a distance. He wondered if he had to choose between the two, which he would pick. A small part of him was glad he’d be sticking around for a bit. Feeling the tension in the air, it was apparent it was not only his country that needed him but his brother as well. He thought of George and Alfred once more and decided he wouldn’t mind guarding over his brother for a while.

Chapter Thirty-Seven

December 24, 1941

Franky felt practically giddy when he exited the post office, draft notice in hand. He'd driven to town every day for months just to check the P.O. box, returning empty handed each day, until now. Others in the town received their notices over a month ago, and to Franky's surprise, most had been unhappy about the inconvenience of being called to serve their country – until the attack on Pearl Harbor. Now the local boys were strutting around town like roosters – each convinced their bullet would be the one to end the war.

The day after hearing of the attack on Pearl Harbor, he'd walked into the kitchen and announced he would be driving to Detroit that very day to enlist. It wasn't the first time he'd made that declaration. He'd been dreaming of joining the war since the day he and Judge had run into Joshua, who'd told him about how he'd lost his leg in the war. Each time he brought it up, Millie found a way of shutting him down then convincing him to delay his departure. Millie must have known he was serious this time, for the look of fear in her eyes nearly made him change his mind. He'd stood fast and they'd had a terrible row, him reminding her he was twenty-one and her wringing her hands saying she'd already lost nearly everyone she'd ever loved. In the end, she'd used her tears to her advantage, persuading him to stay until spring. He'd agreed but had been so upset with her that he'd slept in the stone outbuilding next to the barn. He'd nearly frozen that night, but pride wouldn't allow him to go back into the house. The next day, he'd collected wood for the woodstove and moved the rest of his belongings to the building. By then, he'd calmed down and was no longer trying to punish her, instead deciding to start distancing himself so it would be easier on her when he finally left.

He hadn't told her about the boys in town getting the notices, figuring he'd act just as surprised as she when word finally came. As the days turned into weeks without him receiving a draft notice, he'd grown certain that they'd somehow managed to overlook him, meaning he truly would have to wait until spring. He reread the notice before placing it into his pocket. Grinding the gearshift into reverse, he decided to find an extra special present for Millie as he was about to ruin her Christmas.

***

Franky moved about his room, going through his belongings. He'd moved back into the house after receiving his draft notice and was now going through his things deciding what to keep and what to part with. He heard a knock on the door and sighed. He wasn't in the mood for more of Millie's tears. She'd been crying on and off since he'd shown her the notice on Thursday. Even the new boiled wool gloves he'd given her for Christmas hadn't lifted her mood. It wasn't that he was angry with her; he just didn't know what to say to ease her fears.

"Come in," he said when the knock sounded once again. To his surprise, it was Paulie who came into the room carrying the small wooden biplane Howard made for him the previous Christmas. It had been his favorite present, one he still played with from time to time. Paulie tossed the plane onto the bed and sat next to it, watching as Franky moved around the room.

Franky cast a glance over his shoulder. Paulie sat on the bed with a somber look on his face, his shaggy bangs draped low on his forehead. Funny he hadn't noticed how red the boy's hair had gotten over the years. "You're not going to cry, are you, squirt?"

Paulie shook his head. "No, my mother said crying is just for girls."

Franky laughed. "Mother Mildred told you that?"

"No," Paulie said, shaking his head once again. "My real mother. The one I had before Mother Mildred. She used to cry too, but she told me I had to be strong, as men don't cry."

Franky felt his mouth grow dry. Paulie never spoke of their mother and Franky had never asked about her. Part of him didn't want to upset the boy; the other part preferred not to know. Now that he was going to war and all the talk of him maybe dying, he suddenly wanted to know about the woman. He had so many questions. *What kind of person lets go of one child only to keep another? What had he done to make her hate him so?* Franky walked to the other side of the room, pushed his door closed, then sat on the bed next to Paulie. "Do you remember much about her, your real mom?"

"A little," Paulie said, staring at his feet. "Papa said I'm not supposed to talk about her. He said it would make Mother Mildred cry."

"Well, she's already crying, so I think it would be okay. Especially if you talk about her just to me," Franky coaxed. "You said she was crying. Do you remember what she was crying about?"

"Sometimes she cried because she was sick. She told me it made her sad she wouldn't be able to see me grow up to be a man," Paulie said.

"Yes, I guess that would make a mother sad." *Unless she didn't care about the kid. Then she would send him off so that he could be raised by others.* Franky worked to keep the emotion from his voice. "And other times? What else made her cry?"

"I don't know."

"Sure you do, she was your mother," Franky pressed. "What made her sad?"

Paulie stuffed his fingers into his mouth, chewing on the ends of his nails.

The kid was getting nervous. Franky knew he had to be careful or risk him clamming up. "Paulie, did your mom ever talk about your brother?"

Paulie's head jerked up. "You know about him?"

I am him. "I do. Your papa told me about him. I'm not supposed to talk about him either. So now we both have a secret we can share."

Paulie wrinkled his nose and a frown tugged at the sides of his mouth. "He's not very nice."

"What makes you say that?" Franky asked, keeping the emotion from his voice.

"He went away and left my mother all alone."

"She told you that? And just where did your mother say your brother went?"

Paulie stared at him and Franky realized he'd raised his voice. "Sorry, kid, it just made me mad that your brother left like he did."

Paulie nodded. "Yes, she said he went to Chicago. Said the bad ladies sent him away without her knowing. She told me when she found out she thought to go get him one day, but that a lady sent her a letter that said he'd found a new family and was happy. Momma kept the letter. She'd read it to me when I asked. Sometimes, after she read the part that said he had a dog, she would smile and tell me I'd have a dog one day. We couldn't have dogs at the almshouse. Momma said there were too many mouths to feed without adding more. When Papa brought me here and I saw the dogs, I was happy, because Momma was right."

Franky felt as if someone had stabbed him in the heart. He knew the letter of which Paulie spoke as he'd asked Miss Adams to write it. At the time, he'd only wished to make Mistress Anna happy and had no way of knowing the repercussions doing so would bring.

"Momma said I showed up and healed her heart. She's dead now. I wish she'd written me a letter before she died." Paulie twisted his head and looked at Franky, tears brimming in his eyes. "Mother Mildred said you might die in the war. Will you write me a letter before you do so I can read it when I'm sad?"

The shield Franky kept around himself was in grave danger of breaking. He placed his hand on Paulie's head and ruffed the boy's hair. "Don't you worry about me, kid. I'm too tough to die."

"All the same, I'd like you to write me a letter," Paulie said, sliding from the bed. He reached for the bi-plane and handed it to Franky.

Franky hesitated. "What's this for?"

Paulie smiled, showing several missing teeth. "I want you to have it, so you'll remember me."

Franky swallowed the lump in his throat. Knowing how much it meant to the boy really tugged at his heart. Still, he'd been told he was not to bring any personal items with him to his indoctrination. "I'm afraid the Army won't let me take it with me."

The smile retreated.

"I'll tell you what, you keep it for me. That way, I'll have a reason to come back," Franky suggested.

That seemed to appease the boy. "Will you still write me a letter?"

"Of course I will. Paulie?" Franky said as the boy neared the door. "Did your momma ever tell you your brother's name?"

Paulie's face brightened. "Sure she did. His name was Franky, just like yours. Sometimes I pretend you are he, only you're nicer."

Before Franky could respond, Paulie left the room, closing the door behind him.

Left to his own thoughts, Franky thought of the woman who used to allow him to sit next to her while she played the piano. Who'd sneak him food and make him promise not to tell. He remembered the time when he was almost sent away on the trains and how happy she'd been that he hadn't gone. He'd been angry that all his friends had gone and yet he was made to stay. She'd consoled him by telling him that maybe he'd get to go someday and described the life that she'd wanted for him. His mother had not wanted him to go away. She'd told a lonely little boy what he'd needed to hear to get past the sorrow of losing his friends. As he lay across his bed remembering tidbits from so many years ago, he let go of the anger he felt for his mother. For the first time since hearing of her death, he mourned his loss. He might be a man on the verge of leaving for war, but tonight, he was a boy grieving for things that would never be.

***

So he did find out about his mother," Cindy said, wiping away tears. "Too bad he didn't find out earlier. Maybe he could've made amends with her before she died."

"And if he hadn't told Miss Adams to write the letter as she did, Anastasia could have gone to him. Then he would've been in a real pickle," Linda mused.

Cindy looked up. "How do you mean?"

Linda twisted toward Cindy and pulled her legs up underneath her. "Let's say for the sake of argument that Anastasia found out that Franky had gone to live with Judge. Then, let's say she somehow found the money to travel to

Chicago to get him. Does she stay there and make a new life for them both? Probably not. She goes back to New York and takes him with her. She makes her living playing the piano, so she would probably continue doing so. There were no child care centers. Women weren't supposed to work; they were supposed to take care of their children. Franky is left to his own devices and grows up to run the streets of New York. He's then worse off than he is in Detroit with Tobias looking after him."

"Still, it would have been nice if Franky had been there to look after her when she was ill. But if he'd went back, then he wouldn't have known how to pick pockets without getting caught. He would have ended up in prison, or worse." Cindy sighed. "It's the butterfly effect. I was thinking about that when we first began reading Uncle Frank's journals. It was when he nearly fell off the roof. If he had, he wouldn't have been there for Grandma Mildred, and if he hadn't, she might not have survived."

"Exactly," Linda agreed. "One turn. A single decision. Something that does not matter one iota, and yet not doing it, or turning the opposite direction, bam, someone's life is changed forever."

"You're pretty smart, you know," Cindy noted.

"I saw the movie."

"What movie?"

"*The Butterfly Effect*. It's crazy to think that if Judge wouldn't have opened his door to the likes of Garret, he'd still be alive. Just by trying to help a child, his life was taken and Franky's life forever changed."

"I wonder if he had to do it all over again if he would still take in the child," Cindy mused.

Linda pointed her finger at her. "Don't let what happened to Judge stop you from whatever is floating around in that pretty little head of yours."

Cindy stiffened. Could her mother know that she'd been thinking about possibly fostering a child? "I don't have a clue what you're talking about."

"I read an article recently where a couple rescued a dog from the pound and that dog ended up saving the whole family from a fire."

Cindy chuckled. "A dog is a far cry from a child."

"Yes, but that dog could have very well attacked and killed one of the children. You never know how things will turn out until you take a chance."

She knows. "And if the dog bites?"

"That's what muzzles are for," Linda said with a wink.

"You know we're not really talking about dogs, don't you?"

"I know." Linda's smile grew wide. "I'm not that senile yet."

Chapter Thirty-Eight

Cindy opened her inbox and scrolled to the last email from Bruce, the man who she'd emailed prior asking for information on the Shivelys. Opening the file, she hit reply and began to type.

Bruce, I'm reaching out to you once more to see if you can help. I'm looking for a woman named Anastasia Castiglione who would have died in New York City – I think – sometime around the first week of July, 1939. Her birth name was Anastasia Charlotte Millett. Never married, she changed her last name on her own. I do not believe there was anything official about the name change. I don't know where she was buried but know she lived in an almshouse prior to her death. No rush; just wanted to see if you could locate her.

Thanks for the help,

Cindy

She hit send, then scrolled through her mail, reading and deleting items in her inbox. Just as she was about to sign out of her account, she received a reply from Bruce.

Cindy,

I just wanted to let you know I received your request. If your lady was in an almshouse for the poor, I'm afraid she was likely buried in a pauper's grave. If that's the case, I may not be able to locate her. Don't give up just yet. I may get lucky and find out which almshouse she lived in. A lot of the poorhouses kept very detailed ledgers. I'll do some snooping and see what I can find out.

Bruce

She reread the email before signing out of her account—a *pauper's grave.* Tobias had written that a pauper's burial was feared by every kid he knew. A chill ran through her as she closed her computer. *I've done all I can do.*

Her mother was in the kitchen cooking breakfast when she entered the room.

Linda turned and gave Cindy a once over. "What's turned you so sour this morning?"

Cindy had thought to fill her mother in on her idea after she had something to tell. Since that might not happen, she decided to go ahead. "I emailed Bruce to ask him to see what he could find on Anastasia."

Linda's brow knit together, "Bruce?"

"Becky from school's brother. The one who's into genealogy."

Linda smiled. "The gravedigger guy? I love his email name."

"That's the one. Anyway, I was kind of thinking that since Uncle Frank seemed to make peace with things... I don't know; I just hate the idea of her being all alone."

"So what, you want to bury Franky in New York when he dies?" Linda didn't sound pleased.

"No, he'll be in the family plot," Cindy assured her. "I guess I was wondering what it would take to get Anastasia's remains brought to Sandusky."

Linda's mouth dropped open. "Just because he uses the name 'gravedigger' doesn't mean he's going to actually dig up a body for you."

"I didn't think he would. I'm not even sure if it can be done or if I can even afford it. I shouldn't have said anything until I know if it's even doable. It came to me during the night and I really haven't taken time to think it through," Cindy said. "Besides, he's already emailed me back and said he might not be able to find her."

"He found those Shively people," Linda said, wrinkling her nose.

"Yes, but they had money and could be traced through the social pages. Anastasia didn't have anything. Worse than that, she lived in a poorhouse. Bruce said it's likely she was buried in a pauper's grave."

Linda's face paled. "Those graves are not even marked."

"Which is precisely why we may never find out where her remains are buried," Cindy said with a sigh.

"Too bad we can't ask Frank if he knows," Linda said, turning back to the stove.

Cindy looked toward the living room. "We haven't finished his journals yet. Maybe they'll shed some light on things."

"Breakfast first, then we'll see what old Frank has to say. I made a bacon, egg, and cheese frittata. That'll help you take your mind off things," her mother said, pulling the dish from the oven. She put a slice of frittata on a plate and handed it to Cindy to try.

Linda was right; one could always count on bacon. She felt better the instant the salt hit her system. She began to relax. They'd have breakfast, clean up the kitchen, then return to the journals. This she could control.

***

April, 1942

I was healthy and able-bodied, so I had no issue getting through indoctrination. To be truthful, it took longer to get through the line of people looking to sign up than it did to determine I was fit for the Army. The same was true for boot camp. They sent me to Camp Wolters, Texas and it was hotter than the belly of a cook stove that summer. Maybe it was just that I was used to Michigan summers, but I thought I'd died and gone to damnation the first day of training. Looking back, I guess they figure if you can survive the Texas heat, you won't drop dead the moment the enemy starts shooting.

Everything I'd ever read about boot camp proved to be true. If you didn't understand something, you only needed to wait, because chances were the stupid question guy would ask it.

Every unit had one of those guys. You know the type. The DI – that's drill instructor – tells you to do something and the stupid question guy raises his hand to ask what he's supposed to do. The DI said to wear the red shirt and stupid question guy raised his hand to ask which one was the red shirt. I'm not sure if the guy was really as dense as he pretended or if he just enjoyed getting yelled at. Either way, he always kept us entertained. That is, until the DI heard us snickering and decided we'd put him up to it. After that, we didn't find stupid question guy so funny.

Even in boot camp, you had the jocks. The guys that wanted to show how big or how bad they were. As soon as the DI's back was turned, the jocks would start in on the rest of us. I wasn't a jock, but I wasn't a pansy either. It didn't take the jocks long to learn I wasn't one to be messed with. Some of the other kids – I say kids, because at twenty-one, I was one of the oldest in my unit. Anyway, some of the kids learned to stay near me – because the jocks thought they were with me and left them alone. I didn't send them away, but I didn't encourage them either. The last thing I wanted was to make friends. I'd been reading about war long enough to know most of the men in my company weren't coming back.

The clothes didn't fit, the food was awful, and everyone got to have a turn in the kitchen. KP they called it. I did have something funny happen one day when I was doing my KP duty.

I was peeling potatoes, and when I got done, one of the cooks sent me to get the butter. Now there were a lot of potatoes, which called for a lot of butter. So I went to the walk-in refrigerator and pulled out this huge tray of butter. Real butter in long sticks like we used to make on the farm and take into town to sell. Well, I was standing there staring at that tray of butter thinking about this one time when I was still living in New York and I'd stole me a whole stick of butter. It was well before Mouse had trained me on the finer art of stealing.

***

Franky unbuttoned the first three buttons of his coat, waited until he was sure that no one was looking, pulled a loaf of bread from the counter, and stuffed it into his coat sleeve. He looked around once more, smiling at his success. *Now to make it to the door without getting caught.* As he walked toward the door, the warmth of the bread surrounded his arm and all he could think was how delicious a pat of butter would taste slathered onto the warm bread. He hadn't had warm bread and butter since the morning before Judge was killed. Thinking of Judge made him blush. Judge would not be happy with his current circumstances. *I'm not happy with them either.* Maybe it was thinking of Judge. Maybe it was the warmth pressing against his flesh. Whatever it was, he set out to satisfy his desire. He saw the butter sitting on a plate on the counter, the yellow logs protected by a round cut glass dome.

Mr. Cooper, the owner of the store, was standing with his back to the counter writing on a pad of paper. Franky waltzed to the counter like a boy on a mission and slapped a penny on the counter loud enough for the man to hear.

"What can I do for you, son?" Mr. Cooper asked, turning around.

"I'd like some gumballs, if you please," Franky answered, using his best manners.

Mr. Cooper lifted the lid. "Any particular color?"

"Two orange and a red." Franky said and waited for the man to dig them from the jar.

Mr. Cooper peered at the arm that harbored the bread. "What's the matter with your arm, son?"

The question caught Franky by surprise. Scrambling for an answer, he said the only thing that came to mind. "Got stung by a wasp just this morning."

"Is that right?" Cooper said, leaning closer.

It didn't dawn on Franky at the time that the man was not fooled by his ruse. Nor did it occur to him that wasps would not be out in the dead of winter. "Yes, sir. Hurt like the devil it did."

Mr. Cooper turned back toward the wall and resumed counting items, then writing in his notebook.

When Franky was certain he wasn't looking, he lifted the dome lid with the purported injured arm and snatched out a full stick of butter with the other. Not knowing what to do with the butter, he stuffed it under his cap and replaced the lid before the man was any wiser.

Mr. Cooper turned in his direction. "Was there anything else you needed, son?"

"No, sir. I was just trying to decide what flavor of gumball I wanted to chew first."

Franky beamed with pride as he strutted to the door with his stash. Just as he was getting ready to leave, Mr. Cooper's brother approached. Though Franky didn't know the man's name, he'd seen him in the store a time or two. He waited for the man to oust him, but instead, he merely motioned for Franky to follow. Curious, Franky trailed the man to the far corner of the store, where the potbelly stove stood heating the room.

"I heard what you said to my brother." The man rubbed at his jaw. "Nasty thing, those wasp stings. You got to watch out for those and make sure the stinger is not still inside. They can give a boy a might bad infection if they get stuck in the arm."

"Oh, it's not stuck inside," Franky said, eyeing the door.

"Yes, well you shouldn't go out in the cold without warming up a bit all the same, isn't that right, Chester?"

Franky looked over his shoulder to see Mr. Cooper standing behind him.

"That's right, Woodrow." Mr. Cooper's face wrinkled with concern. "Wouldn't want you to get too sick to come to my store to buy gumballs. That is what you came in for, isn't it, son?"

"Y…yes, s…sir," Franky answered.

"I think the boy's already sick. Why, just look at the way he's sweating," Woodrow replied.

Franky was sweating. But not because he was ill. No, he was standing next to the potbelly stove and could feel the butter oozing through his hair. It wouldn't be long before it made its way past the cap he was wearing. "I really must be going."

"I don't know. You're looking pretty peaked." Mr. Cooper said solemnly. "I think that bee must have stung you pretty bad. Take your coat off and let me have a look-see."

"I think it must have stung the boy in the head too." Woodrow chuckled. "Why, it's already starting to fester. Look at all that pus running down the kid's face."

It's not pus, it's butter. Franky bolted toward the door followed by the roar of laughter from the two brothers who'd obviously figured out what he'd done.

Franky smiled at the memory, knowing full well the men had known what he'd done and intentionally kept him by that stove to teach him a lesson. It worked. While it wasn't the last time he'd stolen butter, it was the last time of using his hat to stow his goods.

"Castiglione!"

Franky turned at the sound of his name, surprised that Sergeant Greer had been able to get so close without him hearing. He'd had trouble with the man from the day he'd arrived. The guy reminded him too much of someone else. Maybe it was the way he looked at him. Perhaps it was the color of his hair. Except for Howard, and later Paulie, he'd never trusted redheads. Even with Howard, he always felt the man was holding something back.

Sergeant Greer stepped closer. "I see you eyeballing that butter. Don't tell me I don't know what you intend to do with it. I've seen it all before. Casanovas get lonely and need something to pass the time."

It was all Franky could do not to punch the man. A single pop in the nose would suffice. He stood firm while the man moved in closer, keeping his face slack so as not to give away how he really felt.

"You take that butter and put it where it belongs and when you do, there'd better not be one stick missing. Understood?"

"Yes, Sergeant!" Franky yelled so he wouldn't have to repeat himself.

"I've got my eye on you, boy. I knew you were too quiet. Now I know how you've been spending your time. Gonna call you Butter Boy from now on."

"Whatever you say, Sergeant." Franky knew he could make the name go away if he only were to take a moment and tell the man the truth. They'd probably have themselves a good laugh. But one thing he'd learned over the years, better to be known as a Casanova than a thief. A person doesn't want that kind of reputation, especially if he is one. People start watching you and it doesn't matter how good you are, you're gonna get caught.

Chapter Thirty-Nine

Sergeant Greer reached behind his back, pulled the knife he had hidden, brought it to the recruit's throat, and made the kill. A dirty move, as the recruit had him dead to rights before he'd pulled the extra knife. The Sergeant always had one more move than everyone else. Sometimes, such as now, resorting to cheating to maintain his unbeaten status. He'd gotten the best of Franky once, but not by much. The guy knew it too as he'd refused to fight him from that point on, choosing instead to send in recruits that were little to no match for him. Franky watched the recruit peel himself off the mat, tightening his jaw as the Sergeant used the toe of his boot to help move the kid along. If he'd had a way to gauge such things, Franky was certain his blood would be near the boiling point. The Sergeant looked in his direction. *Come on tough guy. Pick me. I'm onto your games now.* As if reading his mind, the Sergeant averted his gaze and chose Chavez, the boy sitting next to him. Franky blew out a breath to calm himself. *Stay calm, Franky, two more days and you're out of here.*

Chavez was actually a good match for the Sergeant, giving as good as he got. For a moment, Franky thought the guy had him until Greer brought his right leg up and kneed him just inside the upper thigh, a hair south of the family jewels. A dirty move, one Chavez would have gotten dinked for, but one the Sergeant used when he knew he was in jeopardy of losing. Chavez went down and Franky coughed an obscenity. The men around him laughed and Sergeant's face turned as red as the spikes of hair on top his head. To Franky's surprise, Sergeant pointed directly at him.

"Butter Boy, get your sorry self up here," he sneered.

Franky wasted no time joining the man on the mat. Sergeant was ready for him and had him on the ground within seconds. As Greer stood over him laughing, Franky was instantly back on Judge's porch with Garret using him for a punching bag as his friends cheered him on. Only this time he wasn't a kid and knew how to avoid the Sergeant's blows. Franky rolled and was on his feet, his arms around Sergeant's neck. Sergeant knew he was about to go down and lifted his leg. *He's going for the groin.* Franky hopped backward just in time to avoid the illegal kick, swiped Greer's legs from under him, and followed the man to the mat – hovering over him, his knife pressing against Greer's throat. For a second, Franky considered finishing him off.

"What are you waiting for, Butter Boy?" Garret's voice was eerily calm. "I've seen the way you look at me. You're among friends. Not one of these guys will rat you out."

Franky blinked. Turning his head, he saw his fellow recruits' hatred on their face, encouraging him to finish the job. He focused on the man beneath his knife. *Greer not Garret.* Franky smiled, pulling the knife away. He heard the grumble of disappointment as he stood and offered his hand to the man.

"You had me worried there for a moment, Castiglione," Sergeant Greer said, gripping Franky's hand. "What happened? Did you think you were already fighting the enemy or something?"

"Something like that," Franky said, releasing his hand. "Guess that will happen soon enough."

"Not as soon as you think." Greer laughed.

Franky hesitated. "Don't tell me the war's over already."

"Just the opposite. Things are heating up. The Colonel

told me today they are ramping things up. Going to be doubling the amount of recruits coming in starting next week. I told him I needed help in bayonet training and he told me to pick someone. I'll give you one guess who that someone is."

"Chavez," Franky's voice was hopeful.

"Chavez is good, but he didn't beat me." Sergeant Greer smiled a broad smile. "Bet you're beginning to rethink not using that knife of yours now, aren't you?"

Franky narrowed his eyes at the man and channeled Mouse. "If I want you dead, I know where you sleep."

Sergeant Greer swallowed. "No hard feelings about being kept back?"

"Don't call me Butter Boy again or I'll show you how sharp my blade actually is," Franky said before turning and walking away.

***

July, 1942

Franky stood looking out over the new company of recruits, deciding who to pick next. A difficult decision, being they seemed to be getting younger and younger. By the time they saw fit to send him into battle, he'd be changing diapers instead of fighting Japanese. He looked at a kid named Murphy front row center. *If that kid's eighteen, I'll eat my hat.* It was no secret a lot of recruits falsified their documents in order to enlist. *The kids are going to war and I'm staying here pretend fighting.* He sighed. *All I'm doing is giving them enough confidence to ensure they get close enough that the enemy don't have to waste a bullet.*

Making his decision, he pointed to the kid who, for some reason, reminded him of Ducky, albeit the boy's skin was much lighter and he was devoid of Ducky's signature freckles. Still, there was something in the way the kid leaned forward, eager for a chance to show his worth. The likeness reinforced when the boy sprang to his feet and nearly floated to the mat. Franky resisted a smile as he recalled how Ducky had gotten his name. He'd been thrilled at being asked to go out with Franky and the boys on a recon mission for Mouse. Fearing the approach of a rival gang, his friend had been so scared, he'd quacked instead of doing the bird call they'd practiced.

The kid in front of him cleared his throat and Franky's smile faded. *This isn't the streets of Detroit. This is war. And this time, I won't be there to help him. He's not Ducky!* That realization jarred Franky out of his musings. He sized Murphy up, five foot five and all of a hundred pounds. The kid's baby face flushed with anticipation.

This is going to be quick.

Franky nodded to the boy. "What's your first name, Murphy?" The kid smiled and Franky half expected him to be missing baby teeth.

"Audie, sir," Murphy said, pulling himself as tall as his short legs would allow.

"You old enough to fight in my war?" *My war, what a joke. I haven't even fought in my war.*

"Yes, sir. I've got the documentation to prove it."

Franky felt the lie as sure as the boy had said it out loud. "I think you're lying to me, son. What if I were to ask your mother how old you are? What would she have to say?"

Murphy frowned then recovered. "I reckon she wouldn't have much to say being she's dead, sir. But my sister would tell you I'm eighteen."

You have to admire the boy's tenacity. Franky held his arms wide. "Show me what you got, Murphy."

He'd no sooner gotten the words out of his mouth than the boy lunged toward him. To Franky's surprise, the kid was astonishingly agile, outmaneuvering him multiple times. In the end, Franky got the better of him and sent him back to his group.

Still, the boy had impressed him. As he watched him return to his place, Franky decided the kid might be able to last a little longer than he'd initially thought. With a little training, he might even live long enough to reach his eighteenth birthday.

Expanding his gaze, Franky searched the group for his next opponent.

***

Linda had finished reading before Cindy, leaving the room without comment. This was unlike her mother, so she went to check on her. Not finding her in the kitchen, Cindy searched the rest of the house before finally opening the door to her office. Linda was sitting at Cindy's desk, peering at the computer screen. When Cindy entered, Linda leaned back in the chair and smiled.

"You look pleased with yourself," Cindy said, sitting in the chair normally reserved for her mother. "Should I be worried?"

"I know how to use a computer," Linda replied.

Cindy wanted to argue that the last time Linda messed with her computer, she'd had to spend hours cleaning up the virus Linda had mistakenly downloaded. Instead, she opted for the softer approach. "Anything I can help with?"

"Nope, I figured this one out all by my lonesome," Linda said, turning the screen to show a black and white photo of a young man with dark wavy hair in an ornately decorated uniform. His dark eyes were incredibly intense, but what struck Cindy most was how young the man looked.

"Cute, but a little too young for you." Cindy laughed.

"Oh, but when I was younger…he was absolutely dreamy. All my friends thought so too. We weren't apt to watch war movies, but if this guy was on the screen, we'd watch all day long."

"Why haven't you told me this before?" Cindy asked.

"He died long before you were born, so I guess I never thought of it."

"And now?"

Linda pulled the screen toward her, clicked the mouse, then pushed it toward Cindy once more. Now on the screen was a Wikipedia page for the same young man, Audie Murphy.

Cindy stared at the screen for several seconds before saying anything. "Mom, you can't possibly think this is the same kid."

"It has to be, look at the date," Linda urged.

Cindy looked to where her mother was pointing. Murphy joined the Army on June 30th and went to basic training at Camp Wolters. The article went on to say his sister falsified documents so he could enlist. Cindy's heart swelled. "Do you think Uncle Frank knows about this kid?"

Linda nodded. "I'm pretty sure that's why he mentioned him."

"This infuriates me to no end," Cindy replied.

"What, that your uncle helped train a guy who turned out to be a real war hero?"

"No, I'm happy the kid went on to do great things. I guess I'm just frustrated by all the secrets. Grandma Mildred not telling us about the trains. Uncle Frank keeping mum about training a war hero turned heartthrob," she said with a wink.

Linda touched her hand. "But you're wrong, Cindy. They did tell us. They just did it in their own way. I'm sure they had their reasons, but at least we have their journals."

Linda was right, of course. Cindy sighed. "I am grateful they left something behind."

"You say that as if Frank is already gone."

"He might as well be. He doesn't talk to anyone." Cindy regretted her words the moment she said them. "I'm going to drive over to the facility. Want to come?"

"No, I think I'll stay home today. It sounds like you and Frank need to have a chat."

"I'm afraid it's going to be pretty one-sided," Cindy said, retrieving her purse from the table.

"What if he can still hear you? Cindy," Linda said before she closed the door. "Just in case, tell him I send my love."

***

Frank was sitting in his rocking chair with one of Mildred's quilts wrapped around his legs when she arrived. His chin rested on his chest, his eyes closed. Cindy sat on the bed watching him for at least twenty minutes before he finally opened his eyes.

"Hello, Uncle Frank. Mom sends her love. She wanted to come, but she decided to stay home and watch old Audie Murphy movies." To her surprise, his lips curled upwards. *Mom was right.* "You must have been a good instructor. Not only did that boy stay alive, he earned a ton of medals. I'd like to think you had something to do with that."

Frank's lips moved but made no sound.

She debated for several moments on whether or not to tell him they were reading his journals. *If he's in there, he already knows. If not, it won't matter.* She took a breath and blew it out slowly. Once she began speaking, she couldn't seem to stop. "We're reading your journals, Mom and I. I hope that doesn't make you angry. We haven't finished yet. I wish you'd shared them with me before. I have so many questions. I'm so glad Dad told you about your mom. I wish you would have been able to reconcile with her before she died. I do want to thank you for being there for Dad. He and I never spoke about any of this either. I wish you all hadn't felt the need to keep things from me. I'm part of this family too."

A single tear trickled down Franky's cheek, letting her

know she'd breached the darkness in which he now lived. She wiped her eyes, pushed off the bed, and brushed his tear away with her thumb. "I'm sorry. I didn't mean to upset you. I know I wasn't supposed to find the journals until you all were gone. I just don't understand why the need for such secrecy. I guess I'll never know."

Frank opened his mouth and attempted to speak once more. She leaned down, straining to hear.

"How's Mr. Frank today?" Reba, Frank's nurse, said, coming into the room.

Cindy pushed away hope of having a conversation with her uncle. "He's quiet, as always. How's the baby?"

"Not quiet." Reba laughed. "He's teething. Had me up most of the night." She moved around the room, filling his water container. She stepped closer, checking Frank's catheter bag to see if it needed emptying. It did. She continued to talk as she disconnected it. "You're the quiet type, aren't you, Mr. Frank? But you don't miss much. I can see it in your eyes. Always watching. Always keeping an eye on everyone. I bet he's always done that." She looked at Cindy, then emptied the bag before returning to reconnect the tube. "I wish I'd have known him when he was younger. I'm sure he had some stories to tell."

Yes, but not to me. Cindy walked to the rocking chair, leaned forward, and kissed him on the cheek. "He had a fascinating life. Didn't you, Uncle Frank?"

Frank opened his mouth then closed it again, reminding her of a fish gasping for air.

"I'm going now. I'll check back with you soon." Cindy turned to Reba. "Let me know if he needs anything."

"I will," she promised then turned her attention back to Frank.

Cindy was halfway down the hall when Reba called for

her. "Cindy, come quick, it's your uncle."

Cindy rushed down the hall, expecting the worst. When she got to the door, Reba motioned her forward.

"He wanted to tell you something," she said, stepping out of the way.

Cindy bent down, putting her ear next to his mouth, and placed her hand on his. Seconds ticked away and she thought she'd missed her opportunity. She was about to stand when he whispered two simple words. "You're family."

He closed his eyes. When he opened them again, she could tell he'd drifted away once more.

She gave his hand a gentle squeeze and kissed him on the forehead. Turning to Reba, she mouthed her thanks before leaving once more. Though he hadn't said a lot, he'd said all she needed to hear.

Chapter Forty

Cindy and Linda sat enjoying an early dinner at Elk Street Brewery. A comfortable evening, they'd chosen to sit outside at one of the two-seat tables. The bugs were nonexistent as a steady breeze whipped in and around the green umbrella meant to protect patrons from the sun – totally unnecessary today as the sky was covered with white puffy clouds.

A horn honked and Cindy lifted her hand in response. The driver rolled down her window and threw her arm up, wiggling her fingers as she yelled something lost in the wind. Cindy peered at the driver and sighed.

"One of your parents?" Linda asked, craning her neck.

"Worse, one of my former students," Cindy groaned. "When did I get old?"

Linda took a sip from her water glass and raised her brows. "You're half my age and I'm not old."

"Not quite half, but I'm getting there," Cindy said, taking a bite of her elk burger.

"You don't change your attitude, you'll be way older than me by the time you get to my age."

In some odd way, her mother's words actually made sense. She'd often felt as if their roles were reversed. Sometimes she thought her mother's frequent childlike behavior was age-related, but deep down, she envied her mother's gift of living in the moment. She took a final bite of her potato salad, wishing she'd inherited more of her mother's zest for life. The thought had no sooner came to mind than Linda finished off the last of her potato salad, dropped her plastic fork on the table, and dipped her finger into the plastic cup, tracing it around the edges and licking off the evidence. She pushed aside her empty container, suddenly rethinking her wish. Picking up her pickle spear, Cindy took a bite, her face puckering as she chewed. As she watched her mother's eyes twinkle with childish delight, Cindy marveled at the change in the woman since discovering the journals. She leaned back in her chair, happy they'd chosen to sit outside where they could enjoy the fresh air. They would resume reading the journals when they got home. Right now, she was content just to watch the cars go by.

***

June, 1943

By the time they released me from special training, a year had passed. I'd been promoted to Private First Class, and told I was heading to Italy to fight the Germans. At first, I was disappointed that I wouldn't be fighting Japanese; funny how many of us had never heard of Pearl Harbor until the attack and now we were dead set on paying back those that had forever changed our world. After the initial disappointment, I was raring to go. War was war, after all. Having been selected to be an instructor, I'd spent more time in boot camp than most. Teaching hand to hand combat, bayonet training, and even pretending to be the enemy while sneaking up on the recruits at Hell's Bottom – the last hurdle a recruit had to endure before being assigned to an infantry unit. I'd read everything I could on the subject since Judge taught me to read, mastered everything they taught me in boot camp and must admit to feeling pretty invincible as I continued on my journey. They loaded us onto a fleet of busses; all tasked to take recruits to the train station. From there, we'd be sent to New York to catch our ship. For some reason, it surprised me that to get to Italy, I'd have to go to New York. I had mixed thoughts about that as

I hadn't been back to the city where I was born since leaving in nineteen twenty-six. I knew my mother to be buried there and wondered if I'd have time to visit her grave.

***

It was near three in the morning of the third day since boarding the train, and the inside of the train car reeked of unwashed bodies and flatulence. Not able to sleep, Franky stood, intending to make his way to the dining car, hoping to get there before the morning rush. The doors that separated the cars opened and he stepped through thinking to stand on the connector porch for a moment and breathe some fresh air into his lungs. The smoke from the train proved to be less palatable than the air inside, so he continued to the connecting car. Stepping inside, he discovered the air just as repulsive. Not surprising, since the only inhabitants aside from the train crew were young men and boys who hadn't changed their clothing or bathed their bodies in the three days since leaving Camp Wolters.

Most of the men were sleeping in their chairs. The ones that weren't paid him little mind. As Franky walked through the cabin, a guy he didn't recognize stuck his leg in the aisle, blocking his path. The guy looked to be slightly older than him. Franky wondered if he'd been drafted or volunteered. Not that it mattered; he'd seen the guy's type before – sometimes the bravado was to hide fear. Sometimes they'd come from a neighborhood where the only way you survived was to be king of the roost. Sometimes, as it appeared the case here, the guy was just acting like a jerk. As Franky took stock of the man, the guy lifted his eyes and glanced at Franky's nametag.

Here it comes.

"Hey, Castiglione, got a smoke?" The guy's voice was smooth with a bit of an accent that reminded Franky of his years in the asylum.

Each soldier was given two packs of cigarettes a day – the tobacco industry's contribution to the war effort. Franky didn't smoke but carried the packs with him obliging nearly anyone who asked. Franky glanced at the leg blocking his way, then read the man's nametag – Russo. He pulled a pack from his pocket, shook one free, and offered it to the man, purposely keeping his fingers loose.

"How about I take 'em all off your hands, Castiglione?" Russo said, ignoring the proffered cigarette and palming the entire pack.

Some people are so predictable. Franky rocked back on his heels, keeping his voice low so as not to wake the man's seatmates. "How about you take the one I offered and give me back the pack."

Russo laughed. "I think you're mistaken; this here's my pack, kid."

Kid? The man was maybe five years his senior. Franky's first thought was to stomp on the man's leg and snap it in two. But that would ensure the guy got sent to the hospital, where he'd probably pick up a medal for being injured during a time of war. Thinking better of it, he swept the guy's leg aside, leaned in, popping him in the chops with his elbow. The guy's eyes rolled a few times and he blinked his confusion. Franky retrieved the pack of cigarettes along with the guy's wallet, saw a letter sticking out of the man's pocket, and took that as well. He tugged on the guy's dog tags and read the information, committing the details to memory.

Just as he started walking again, he looked to see a soldier watching him. The guy closed his eyes as Franky pocketed the paraphernalia and continued on his way.

The dining car was empty except for several cooks working behind a long counter. One of the men glanced at the clock and grumbled something about Franky being early before slapping a scoop of runny eggs onto a divided metal tin. He added a biscuit and two slices of bacon before sliding the tray onto the counter. Franky gathered the tray and sat at the table, enjoying his meal in peace. When finished, he removed the letter he'd picked off the man and began to read.

Dear Michael,

I fear I must have made you angry with my last letter as I have not yet received a reply from you. I know you must think me an unfit mother to beg the neighbors for food as I've done. However, the baby needs to eat, and as he is past the weaning stage, I alone cannot furnish enough for him. I know you said the Army has yet to pay you, but maybe if you go to them and apprise them of our situation, they will see fit to give you a small advance. I do not ask for much, just enough so I can see that our child not starve.

Your wife,

Isabella

Post Script, I've enclosed a photo of Leon and myself.

Franky sat the letter on the table and pulled the photograph from the envelope. The woman looked to be around his age with dark wavy hair pulled away from her forehead and flipping into rounded circles at her shoulders. He traced his finger over her thinly arched eyebrows as he stared into her eyes. For a moment, she appeared to look into his very soul as if begging him for help. His gaze drifted to the boy, who looked to be well into his first year. The thing that stood out most was that the boy wasn't smiling. *He's hungry. What's he got to smile about?* He turned the photo and saw that she'd written their names on the back in a nice legible script. He sat the photo down and picked up the letter, reading it once more. *Russo's a liar. Every soldier is paid while in training and the money is automatically sent home to the family. Unless he neglected to list them as dependents.* Franky's blood began to boil. Opening

Russo's wallet, he pulled out the bills and counted. Sixty-three dollars. *He's not sent any home, so where's the rest of it? Probably drank it away in town or used it to pay for other needs.* He drummed a finger on the table. *You have a beautiful wife and healthy son. Why do you not take care of them? They're your family. It's what you do.* He folded the wallet shut once again, then, pulling his journal from his pack, tore out a page and began to write.

Dearest Isabella,

I hope this letter finds you and Leon in good health. My apologies for not writing sooner. I've done as you requested and asked for money to send you and our son. This should keep you until I can send more.

Your husband

Franky started to add "Michael" then decided to leave the man's name off. *He doesn't deserve the credit.* He pulled a stamped envelope from the inside cover of his journal, copied the address from Isabella's letter, adding the note along with the sixty-three dollars before sealing the envelope. He returned the photo and letter to the original envelope just as the door to the dining car opened. Franky looked up to see Fisher, the man who'd witnessed him relieving Russo of his wallet. Fisher was a good head taller than him but looked to be simply coming in for a meal. Just the same, Franky decided to keep an eye on the man, who went to the counter and collected his meal. To Franky's surprise, Fisher joined him at his table.

Fisher eyed Russo's wallet. "You going to return that?"

"Planned on it," Franky replied.

"Any money in it?" Fisher asked then took a bite of scrambled eggs.

Franky shook his head. "Not anymore."

"The guy's a jerk, but that's no reason for you to take his money," Fisher said evenly.

Fisher seemed concerned but didn't appear to pose a threat. Franky pulled out the letter from Isabella and handed it to him, waited for him to read it, then showed him the photo. "I'm not keeping it."

Fisher blew out a low whistle, and Franky returned both the letter and photo to the envelope.

"Can't imagine putting the hurt on a dame as fine as that," Fisher said between bites. "Cute kid too. Must not have listed them as dependents. So what are you going to do, strong-arm the guy into sending her some money?"

Franky slid the second envelope across the table. "I prefer to take the direct route."

The sides of Fisher's mouth turned up. "You're an all right guy, Castiglione."

"You want to see that gets to the mail car?"

Fisher cocked an eyebrow. "You trust me to send it?"

"If I didn't, I wouldn't have asked." Franky stood and handed Fisher the wallet. "Mind returning this as well? You can tell him you made me give it back."

"I'll tell him I found it on the floor," Fisher said, placing the wallet in his pocket. "Want me to return the letter as well?"

"No, I think I'll hang on to it," Franky replied, placing the envelope in his journal and returning the journal to his pack. He wasn't sure why he felt the need to keep it; maybe it was simply because he didn't feel the guy deserved it.

"Castiglione?"

Franky looked up, ready for an argument.

Fisher grinned. "Got a smoke?"

Franky pulled a pack from his pocket, tossing the entire pack to him. "Keep it."

Fisher pulled a stick from the pack and lit it. "You know, you could have saved the hassle if you'd let Russo keep the smokes in the first place."

Franky shrugged. "Sometimes, things have a way of working themselves out."

Chapter Forty-One

It took twenty days to reach North Africa. Those itching for battle, myself included, were soon disappointed, as Algiers turned out to be nothing more than a holding camp where we picked up tanks, heavy weapons, and conducted training – always training – before continuing on to Italy.

We set up camp just south of Naples. When we weren't training, we were cleaning our weapons. When not cleaning our weapons, we were training. Days droned on with a vicious circle of promises that soon we'd be putting our newly learned skills to use. At night, the Germans would bomb the harbor and our anti-aircraft cannons would retaliate. Soldiers would play cards, ducking for cover as the shrapnel fell like rain. I'm not sure which caused more injuries in Naples, shrapnel or Pinochle. The war was raging all around us, but there we were fighting our friends over a game of cards. It went on like that for weeks until one evening in late January, they told us we'd be shipping out the next afternoon. Over a year had passed since I left Michigan and I was finally going to war. On the one hand, I was pleased, on the other, I was suddenly terrified.

***

January 22, 1944

Franky and his unit stood in the rain watching the ships vie for a spot on the beach. LSTs, LSMs, and Troop Ships stocked full of tanks and equipment all rolled in, collecting more troops than they had space for before heading away out to sea once more. As he waited for his turn, the men around him chatted amongst themselves.

"Wow, there must be a hundred of those suckers," someone said.

"A hundred and one, I counted," someone else said, his words met with laughter.

"Jeepers, I can't even read the numbers. How are we going to know which is ours?"

"No need for a number; they're all going to the same place. Just climb on board and hold on, those Germans are going to be shooting at anything that moves. We're going to be so log-jammed heading into the beach; it's going to be like shooting ducks in a barrel. Only this time, we're going to be the ducks."

"Knock it off, man. I've already got the shakes. You're gonna give me the craps as well. I'd hate to go to my grave with my skivvies full."

"No need to worry about that. You get killed on the beach, you won't get a grave."

"Baloney! They gotta bring our bodies back. Otherwise, how will our mothers know we're dead?"

A chill raced through Franky.

"Yo, Castiglione, tell the guy I'm right. Our mothers got to know when we're dead, right?"

"I wouldn't know. I ain't never had a mother," Franky said without looking over his shoulder.

"Ain't never had a mother? Everyone's got to have a mother. Why, a guy can't get born without a mother."

Before anyone could answer, the Sergeant ordered Franky and the rest of his unit to board the closest LSM. Close being relative, as they had to wade into the ocean to get to the boat – a transport ship already fully loaded with tanks and trucks along with other necessities of war.

Franky and the others went into the belly of the ship, then continued topside, in search of a spot to wait out the trip to Anzio. The ship was so crammed full of troops and supplies, Franky wondered how she managed to stay afloat, but she did, gliding into the harbor just as the sun began to set. As the ship waited her turn to unload, Franky maneuvered his way to the outer edge in an attempt to get more air. He pulled his poncho tighter and tilted his helmet to help ward off the rain. From his new vantage point, he was able to look out over the bay, watching the boats idle in close, drop their cargo, and move out once again. His stomach churned, matching the angry seas. He kept telling himself it was simple seasickness, but in reality, for all his bravado, he was terrified. What had been said on the beach had gotten to him – wiggling its way under his skin like a worm. Most of these kids had mothers waiting for them that would mourn the loss of a son. His mother was already dead and he'd not even gotten to say goodbye.

Get it together, Franky. It's just nerves jabbing at your gut. You've been itching for this far too long to go getting all sentimental now. Franky closed his eyes, going through bayonet moves to calm his nerves. Opening his eyes moments later, he looked out, surprised to see hundreds of LSTs and LSMs idling against the waves, each waiting their turn to offload cargo. Franky couldn't help think of the time he and Howard had driven out to Lake Huron hoping to catch some fish for their evening meal. As they sat on the shore waiting, a gaggle of snow geese landed just off shore. Howard had traded his fishing pole for his rifle and shot three geese before the others had sense enough to fly away. *The kid's right; the Germans could have their pick.*

The thought had no sooner formed than men started shouting and the ship's guns blared in rapid-fire. Franky looked up, his heart pounding as a German plane came into view. A moment later, the sea exploded, spraying buckets of water over their already drenched bodies. A second bomb landed so close, Franky thought the impact had burst his eardrum. The forward guns continued their assault until the enemy plane sputtered, leaving a trail of smoke as it plummeted into the sea. The boat he was riding in moved in closer, opening her bow. Franky's ears continued to ring as he followed the long line of soldiers down to the lower deck. Once there, there was no patience for indecision. If anyone hesitated, they were pushed into the water by the man behind them. Franky jumped from the boat, sloshing his way through the salty water, saying a silent prayer he'd at least make it onto the beach. Once on shore, he kept running, deciding if he were going to die, at least he'd be running in the right direction. The last thing he wanted was for anyone to think him a coward. It turned out that except for the two bombs dropped by that lone German plane, he and the thousands that arrived with him were able to sneak onto the beach unnoticed.

"I wonder if they award medals for ringing in the ears?" one of the guys asked, pounding the side of his head with his open palm.

Another soldier looked at him and tilted his head. "What?"

"Exactly!" the first guy said in return.

"Just be glad your ear's still attached to your skull," Sergeant Lynch said, coming up behind them. "Get your gear and get ready to move out. We had good fortune today; tomorrow, we might not be so lucky."

Sergeant Lynch was all of six foot four. The guys joked that Lynch was a beacon and if there were ever any shooting, he'd get hit first. Franky hoped that wasn't true, as the guy was straight Army. Franky felt safe with him in charge.

***

April, 1944

While they hadn't seen any fighting that first day, they'd had their share since. Once the Germans knew they were there, they didn't waste any time sending out the welcome wagon. Bullets fell as frequently as the rain, both relentless in their deluge. Though Franky thought he was ready for war, he soon learned nothing could prepare someone for the constant fear of death. He'd fired his rifle so much, his hands ached, but in all honesty, he hadn't a clue if any of the bullets ever hit their target. He'd fire when told and duck when the bombs whistled through the air, only to pop up again and shoot the faceless enemy. The days blended together, men getting shot, new guys taking their place. That was how he'd come to be in a two-man fighting hole with Milton Fox, a barely nineteen-year-old kid from Arkansas. Franky couldn't say that he liked the kid, but in the short time they'd shared the hole, Fox hadn't given him any reason to hate him, so that was a plus. By day, they'd fight the enemy; at night, they'd fix their bayonet just in case any of the Krauts tried to sneak into the camp unannounced.

"Do you think I'll actually have to use this thing?" Fox asked as he fitted the blade on the end of his rifle.

"No." Franky thought to lie and give the kid a good scare but decided against it. It was hard to scare someone when they were already scared. "At least not tonight. The Krauts seem to be content to hammer us with mortars for now. You leave the hole, you crawl on your belly. Stick your head up and you won't have to worry about your bayonet."

Fox set his rifle aside and took a swig from his canteen. "Why would I have to leave the hole at night?"

"Because you ain't relieving yourself in this hole," Franky said, eyeing the canteen.

"It's okay. I've got a big bladder," Fox said, taking another drink.

"All the same, if you got to go, you go outside the hole. I find out you didn't, I'll shoot you myself."

Fox lowered the container, screwed on the lid, and tossed it to the side. "What happens if I have to do the other? I mean, how do I sit without getting my head blown off?"

Franky rolled his neck. "You mean to tell me you haven't taken a crap since you've been here?"

"Not at night." Fox shrugged. "I guess I can hold that too."

"You crawl," Franky said, repeating himself.

"I know that. But what do I do when I get there? How do I go?" Fox asked once more.

Franky sighed. "You dig a little hole, then roll over."

"And then what?"

"You stare at the blasted stars." Franky blew out another sigh. "For Pete's sake, kid, do I have to spell it out for ya? You dig a little hole, dip your backside in, and push," Franky said. "Listen, if you're going to go, then go now. If not, I'll take the first watch while you get some shut-eye."

"I think I'll just wait and go in the morning," Fox said, settling in.

Franky didn't mind taking the first watch. He'd stay up all night if he had the chance. The fighting hole was just that. A narrow hole barely big enough for two people. Being crouched in that thing at night was sometimes more than he could stomach.

***

It was close to two in the morning and Franky's stomach was churning. All that talk about going had been building up over the last couple hours and he knew he wouldn't be able to sleep unless he took care of business. Thankfully, all the shooting thus far had been further north.

Franky elbowed the kid. "It's time to trade off. Wake up."

Fox was up in an instant, wiping the sleep from his eyes. "Where you going?" he asked when Franky leaned his rifle forward.

"Some of us don't have the option to hold it. Keep your eyes open and signal if you see anything."

"You're not taking your rifle?"

"I don't need a rifle to do what I'm going to do," Franky said as he slithered out the back of the hole. He belly crawled about thirty feet, dug a small trench, and took care of business before heading back. He was about twenty feet from the fighting hole when he heard the unmistakable whoomph of mortars being fired – at least five in quick succession. He knew if he didn't make it back to the fighting hole before they landed, he was as good as dead. Gathering his feet under him, he took off in a dead run, diving into the hole just as a mortar landed, lighting up the sky. He was in mid-air when he saw his bayonet glistening in the light of the enemy fire. *Fox must have moved my rifle.* Fire shot through his body as he landed on the blade. Mortars exploded, squelching his screams. Fox's face wore the mask of terror as he gripped the front of Franky's coat, screaming for a medic as he pulled him further into the hole. The night sky lit up once again, then everything went dark.

Chapter Forty-Two

Franky woke to the sound of steady rain. Nothing out of the ordinary about that – it had been raining steadily since they arrived in Italy. The problem was he couldn't feel it. He stared at the off-white sky for several moments, wondering why he wasn't getting wet before realizing he was in fact staring at the inside of a tent. He started to get up, felt a stab of pain, and lowered once more. A pole beside him held a bottle of clear liquid connected to a thick yellow hose that was bandaged to his arm. He looked to the side and saw row after row of cots, each harboring an injured man. *I'm at the field hospital.* He heard the blast of a bomb, and the bed beneath him shook. He attempted to get up once more and a woman in a not-so-white dress hurried to his bed. Worry tugged at her thin face and she looked as if she hadn't slept in weeks. A cream and blue scarf covered her head to keep her dark hair from flying into her face. Some of the strands had escaped and flitted around her face as she dipped to the side of his bed.

"You're in the hospital. Don't worry; you're safe," she said, speaking with a thick Italian accent. She placed her hands against his shoulders and pressed him back into the mattress.

"You're a terrible liar." Franky grimaced against the pain. "You're Italian?"

"I'm an American. My grandparents are from Italy. A small town not so far from here. I'm not even sure the town still stands." She pursed her lips together and checked under his bandage. "Are you in pain?"

"No," he said, gritting his teeth as she pressed the area

just below his collarbone.

"Now who's the liar?" A smile transformed her face, and for a second, he could see the beauty hidden behind the drawn face and dark circles. She caught him looking and quickly removed the smile.

"Got to be strong in the presence of a lady," he said, hoping for another smile.

She laughed. "I'm not a lady; I'm a nurse."

It had been a long time since he'd seen a woman's face, much less one so close, and thought to keep her talking. "Can't you be both?"

"Not out here." She pushed the strand of hair from her face with dirty hands. "Do you remember what happened?"

He remembered seeing the bayonet and hearing an explosion. Then he remembered hearing Fox screaming for the medic. He thought he remembered hearing Fox saying he was sorry. "I think the new guy tried to kill me."

She raised an eyebrow. "The medic said you stabbed yourself with your bayonet. Had enough of the war, did you?"

Franky was incredulous. He might not remember exactly what happened, but he knew this wasn't of his own doing. "You think I did this to myself?"

"No, he told us the real story. Apparently, after you left the hole, there was an attack. The guy moved your rifle out of his way to get a clearer view. That's when you came back, jumped into the hole, landing on your bayonet. I was just having a bit of fun with you. I told you, I'm not a lady. You're lucky the blade was clean and didn't hit anything vital. Maybe not so lucky that we'll have you back to your unit in a few weeks."

The sound of a plane had them both looking toward the ceiling of the tent. A panicked voice somewhere outside yelled for everyone to take cover. A brief look of terror crossed the woman's face. Franky acted without thinking, pulling her on top of him, shielding her with his one good arm. The bomb hit nearby, shaking the ground and spraying the top of the tent with debris. The cannons fired in retaliation and he continued holding her as shrapnel blended with the rain, some bouncing off the tent, others ripping through and bouncing off the ground. For a moment, he worried the tent would collapse and he found himself grateful he wasn't going to die alone. She trembled in his arms and he wondered if her thoughts matched his.

The air grew quiet except for the sound of rain. She pushed away, standing with her back to him, and he knew she was working to compose herself. She turned, her face flushed, then went to work checking to make sure he hadn't pulled his IV free.

He took hold of her hand. "You're a very brave woman…can I ask your name?"

She frowned, as if debating, then pulled her hand free. "My husband wouldn't be pleased."

She's married. He hid his disappointment. "I'm only asking for your name."

"Isabella." The name floated from her mouth in a whisper. She saw the shock on his face and nodded. "Just like your wife, yes?"

"My wife?"

"Your wallet fell open when I was moving your clothes. I saw the photo and thought to take a look. She's a very beautiful woman, your wife. It must be hard being away from her and your son."

"I would love nothing more than to be with them." He thought to tell her the truth but decided it didn't matter. At least the words he spoke were not a lie. He'd taken to pulling out the photo from time to time, staring at the woman he now thought of as his forbidden wife. The only woman who'd ever touched his heart, until now.

"She'll be happy that your injuries were not more severe," Isabella said, pulling him from his thoughts. She looked up, excused herself, hurrying to the tent opening.

Franky craned his neck to see what had taken her away from him. She was standing talking to a grimy-faced Chaplain. Though Franky couldn't hear the conversation, he could tell it wasn't good news. Perhaps one of her patients hadn't made it, a thought reinforced when Isabella ran from the tent in tears. Catching the Chaplain's attention, he waved the man over.

Though he was young, his face showed the empathy of a man who'd tended to many a dying man and his shoulders sagged as if the weight of the world rested upon them. Still he managed a smile when he approached. "What can I do for you lad?"

"I saw you speaking with the nurse and I was worried it wasn't good news."

The smile faded. "I'm afraid much of my news is not good these days."

"Yes, but she was crying. I'd like to know what it was you said," Franky pressed.

"Nothing that concerns you, lad. Do you need something? I could gather another nurse if you're in any discomfort."

"No, I'm fine. I'm just concerned about my friend," Franky said.

"You mean your nurse," the man corrected.

"She's my nurse, but also my friend. We've known each other for many years. Our grandparents lived in the same town just a few miles from here," Franky said, hoping the man wouldn't ask him for the name of the town.

"Oh, yes. I've heard her make mention of that before. You'll know of her husband, then. I'm afraid poor chap did not make it through our war. That is the news you saw me deliver," the man said, lowering his eyes.

Franky couldn't tell if he was more shocked or relieved at receiving the news. He didn't have a chance to debate his feelings, as a moment later, two Privates came in and loaded him onto a temporary stretcher. Carrying him from the tent, he was transferred to a hospital ship without ever having a chance to tell her goodbye, offer his condolences, or confess his deception.

***

Three weeks had passed since he'd arrived on the hospital ship. Though his wounds were mostly healed, his heart continued to ache. Not wishing to stay within the belly of the ship, he spent most of his time walking along the deck, watching the smoke bellow up into the clouds. The war was continuing without him, though he no longer seemed to care. Somewhere along the line, he'd lost his lust for battle. Now his mind seemed to be in a constant tug-o-war for a love that never was and one that could have been. He pulled the photo of Isabella and her son from his wallet, staring at it until he could nearly see both women. He'd done this so many times since arriving on the ship that he'd started referring to them as Duo Isabellas. *Two Isabellas.*

"Castiglione?"

Franky turned at the sound of his name, smiling at the familiar face. "Fisher, what are you doing here?"

"Took a bullet in the groin north of Anzio," Fisher said, hobbling to greet him. Leaning on a crutch, he extended his other hand. "How about you?"

"Bayonet to the shoulder," Franky said, shaking Fisher's hand and leaving out the particular details of his injury.

"I hope you got a piece of the guy that got you," Fisher replied.

"I think I scared him pretty bad," Franky said, returning

the photograph to his wallet.

"You still carrying that thing around?" Fisher asked with a nod to the wallet.

Franky shrugged without answering.

"Russo took a bullet in Anzio," Fisher said, shifting his weight.

"Kill him?"

Fisher laughed. "You don't think you're going to get that lucky, do you?"

"Doesn't sound like it," Franky replied. "Does the guy still wish me dead?"

"Nah, it was just a flesh wound. But between that and what he told me you said to him, it really shook the guy up. He's been sending money home several times a month. Even his card winnings. I know because he has me post them for him. He sees you again and he'll probably give you a great big kiss for saving his marriage."

"Lucky me," Franky said, sounding as insincere as he felt.

"Want to go get some chow?" Fisher asked when Franky's stomach rumbled.

"No, I'm not hungry," Franky lied. In truth he was famished, but lacked the desire to do anything about it. "Besides I'll be shipping out in a couple hours."

"You might not be hungry, but if you don't quiet that belly of yours, it's going to lead the enemy right to you. Come on, let's get some hot grub into you while we still can. After today, you'll go back to cold cans of crap left over from the Great War."

"I happen to enjoy the fruit cocktail," Franky replied.

"That's because it's the only thing fit to eat," Fisher retorted.

I wonder what they'll call this war? Franky thought as

he pushed off the rail.

***

Well-fed and feeling somewhat better mentally, Franky sat huddled with a group of soldiers on the transport boat trying to avoid the water spray as the craft bounced along the ocean waves toward Anzio beach. Much like when he first arrived in Italy, his stomach was in knots during the approach, only this time, he was not thinking of the impending battle. He'd shared his dilemma with Fisher, who'd convinced him to find Isabella and set the record straight. She'd probably be lost in her mourning and brush him off, but at least he'd know he tried.

The small boat dropped him and the other men off close enough to the beach they barely got their feet wet going ashore. While the others stayed on the beach waiting to be transported back to their units, Franky hurried off in search of the nurse that had captured his heart. He saw her the second he entered the tent, her back to him, speaking with another soldier. She was laughing but something about her tone made him hesitant to interrupt. As he drew closer, she laughed once more. He cleared his throat to get her attention. She turned and his heart sank.

It's not her.

His face must have shown his disappointment because the smile instantly disappeared. "Can I help you, soldier?"

"I'm looking for Isabella," he blurted, hoping she'd know where to find her.

The nurse frowned. "She's not here."

I can see that. "Can you tell me where I can find her? I need to speak with her." Even he could hear the desperation in his voice.

"No, I mean, she isn't here. They sent her stateside after her husband..." She stopped, unable to finish her sentence.

Franky felt the sting of her words. "Stateside?! Where?"

"I don't know. She was gone before I arrived. I only

know because I heard someone talking about it. I wish I could tell you who that someone was, but I really don't know."

Franky mumbled his thanks and turned on his heels. He wasn't sure what he'd expected, but he had at least hoped for a chance to speak with her. Maybe get her address so that they could correspond. He'd spent the days of his recovery thinking about Mildred and how she'd agreed to marry Howard so quickly after Mouse died and thought maybe fate would smile on him the same way. Only in his mind, Isabella would welcome his attention and smile more than he'd seen Mildred do. He'd thought little of Mildred since he'd left home. Partly, because Howard had taken over roll of guardian after they were married, and partly because every letter she wrote was exactly the same. Fretting over his leaving for war.

His dreams dashed, he walked the short distance to the beach to wait to be returned to his unit. Walking with his head down, he paid no attention to his surroundings until he heard a young soldier inquire about a meal.

"The mess tent is behind the field hospital," Franky said without looking up. He took two steps then froze. He pivoted back toward the man, his heart pounding. The man's eyes were round with disbelief, as were those of the men standing next to him. The soldiers standing near the men were talking amongst themselves, oblivious to what had just transpired. Suddenly afraid, Franky turned, racing toward the beach to where he'd left the others.

"What's the matter, Castiglione? You look as though you've seen a ghost," one of the guys said when Franky nearly plowed into the group.

"I tripped and thought I was going to fall on my bad shoulder," Franky lied.

"Too bad you didn't, then you wouldn't have to go back to the lines," the first guy replied.

Franky wiped the sweat from his brow, fighting the urge to look at the group of men he'd just left. When at last he gathered his courage, the men were no longer standing where he'd left them. "Where'd they go?"

"Where'd who go?" one of the guys asked.

"That group of men."

"You mean the German prisoners? They're on the boat," he said, pointing to the ocean. "They'll put them on ships and take them to POW camps."

"Yeah, and good riddance too; they've been jabbering in German ever since they got here. Probably planning their escape."

No, they were trying to tell someone they were hungry. Fear kept him from saying as much. He'd left the asylum at such a young age, he'd forgotten he knew how to speak German. Even when he'd answered the man, he hadn't realized he'd answered in the language most of the mistresses at the asylum spoke. He'd have to be more careful in the future. The last thing he wanted was for anyone to think him a traitor.

Chapter Forty-Three

It pained Franky to discover his unit had barely advanced in the month he'd been away. The only thing that had changed was a dozen new faces. He'd always been a loner, so it was no surprise that his return went mostly unnoticed. A few of the guys asked if he'd heard any news of the state of the war, only to drift away after he told them he hadn't any news to share. He preferred that to them making a big deal about his injury. He looked for Fox, but the boy was nowhere to be found. He thought about asking about him but didn't want anyone to think he cared. He'd just about given Fox up for dead when he showed up.

"Where's our hole?" Franky asked, grabbing his gear.

Fox's eyes bugged and his Adam's apple bobbed a few times. "You mean you still want to share a fighting hole after what I did?"

"I figure I'm safer in that hole with you than anyone else," Franky retorted.

Fox's eyes grew even wider. "How do you figure that?"

"You nearly killed me. So I suppose in the future, you'll think real hard before doing anything that stupid."

"Yes, sir, I sure will. Why, I feel real bad about what happened to you," Fox said, shaking his head up and down.

"Good, now show me where our hole is and quit calling me 'sir.' Last thing I want is for the Krauts to hear you and think I'm an officer."

"Yes, sir…er, I mean, okay, right this way. It's been quiet today. Been that way for the last couple of days with the

Krauts doing more shelling at night. I sure thought we'd be halfway to Rome by now."

"So did I," Franky said. He picked up his gear and followed as Fox led the way to the small two-man trench that would act as his home for the foreseeable future.

***

Franky sat on a half charred tree shaving the stubble from his face with the blade of his knife. He saw the mail orderly walking through camp and paid him no mind. He hadn't gotten anything in the weeks since returning. His mail had been redirected when he got injured and he figured the Army was too busy to chase him around. It would catch up to him eventually and Mildred would remind him to be safe. He dipped the blade into his helmet sloshing off the soap, then lifted it to his cheek sliding it along the taunt skin.

"Castiglione, mail call." The guy stopped in front of him, handing him several letters and a small stack of newspapers.

"Well, what do you know, the Army finally figured out I ain't dead," Franky said, placing the mail at his feet.

"What's with you, Castiglione? You're the only guy I deliver to that don't feel the need to look at the mail as soon as I hand it to him."

"Nothing that can't wait until I have time to give it a proper reading," Franky said, dipping the knife once more. The real reason he didn't open his mail was because the guy standing in front of him had been known to tell everyone of Dear John letters well before the guys involved were ready to share. Or spread other juicy gossip that he overheard along the way. Some of the guys didn't seem to mind. Franky, on the other hand, refused to give in to the man's need for drama.

"The Germans catch sight of that blade and you'll be too dead to read," the guy said then continued on.

Franky wasn't worried about being shot. Something had changed in him that day on the beach. He'd drawn into himself even more than before, speaking only when spoken to. He'd started having nightmares the night of his return. In his dreams, he was always a little boy playing war. But, in his dreams, he was using real bullets and the Germans he was fighting looked and sounded like the mistresses that had cared for him in the asylum. The face of his enemy had become friendly and the war had become a nightmare.

Once, he'd woken after a pretty vivid dream, grabbed his weapon, and fired into the night. That had triggered others to follow suit and an otherwise peaceful night had turned deadly. Later, when asked what he'd seen, he merely said he saw the face of the enemy. Fox knew the truth, but to his credit, he never told a soul. Since Franky never talked to him about his dreams, maybe the kid thought himself to be the reason for Franky's pain. After all, for all intents and purposes, Franky was normal before being sent away. Now the darkness had arrived and there was no cure. Judge had been right.

Franky finished shaving, dumped the water from his helmet, and placed it on his head without rinsing it out. As the soapy water dribbled down his face, he opened one of the newspapers, reading it from cover to cover. He always read the newspapers, mostly *Stars and Stripes*, first as men were always asking to read them when he finished. He'd gotten through half of the second paper when he blew out a low whistle. There on the page staring out at him was Murphy, the short kid that had impressed him on the sparring mat. The story touted Murphy's heroics on the battlefield and talked about all the medals he'd won thus far in his short career. Franky glanced at the picture once more. *You still look too young to be in my Army, but I'm glad you're still alive.*

Franky finished the papers and set them aside. Picking

up the small stack of envelopes, he thumbed through. Mildred, Mildred, Mildred, Howard, Paulie, Ducky. Franky pulled that one out of the pile and left the rest for later.

Franky,

I'm not much for letter writing, but thought I'd give it a try. I'm going to open a pastry shop when I'm done with the Navy. Since I only know about baking and you're pretty smart with all your reading, I thought maybe you'd like to be my partner. I'll cook and you can do the rest. I know you're probably thinking you don't know nothing about being a partner, but I'm sure the two of us could figure it out together. I'm not good at names, so if you agree to help me, I'll let you name it anything you want.

Your friend,

Cornelius "Ducky" Watson

Franky folded the paper, stuffed it into the envelope, then pulled it out once more. Taking out his pen, he scribbled the name *Duo Isabellas*. Frowning, he scratched a line through the name, tapped the pencil against his head, then lowered it once more. Touching the tip to the paper, he wrote,

Mia Bellas.

***

Cindy clutched the journal to her chest and sighed. She hated having finished her uncle's journals but was pleased they ended on a good note. She knew Frank had never married and now she knew how he'd come to be business partners with the man she'd always referred to as Uncle Cornelius.

"I guess we know how the bakery got its name," Linda said, placing her stack of papers on the table. "Who would've known Frank to be such a hopeless romantic?"

"I'm glad he wrote the journals. I feel as if some of the puzzle is complete. I wonder if he remembers what he wrote."

"I don't understand."

Cindy caressed the stack of journals. "I don't know. I know he enjoyed books. I wonder how he'd react if I were to take them to the facility and read them to him. Not all at once, of course. I could read them a little at a time, kind of like we just did."

"You going to start tonight?"

Cindy glanced toward the window. "I guess not. It's almost suppertime. I was thinking of going through Uncle Frank's boxes after we eat. You know, the ones that were hidden in the back of his closet."

Linda glanced toward the ceiling. "You put those up there years ago. You mean you never went through them?"

"No, it didn't seem right at the time. He still had lucid days and I was still in denial thinking maybe he'd get better. To be honest, I'd kind of forgotten they were there. I didn't really remember them until we started reading the journals. I guess it's safe to say Uncle Frank isn't going to get better." Cindy sighed. "We can wait if you want."

"No, I'm not tired. How are we going to get the boxes down?"

"They're not that heavy. I took them up there, I should be able to get them down again." Cindy winked at her mother. "That is, unless you want to climb up in the attic with me and save me the trouble."

Linda gasped and placed her hand to her mouth in mock surprise. "You'd make your dear old mother climb into the attic?"

"I thought you said you weren't old."

"I'm selectively old." Linda smiled. "And hungry. I'll find us a little something to eat while you get the boxes."

***

Cindy sat on the floor of the living room, pulled the first box closer, and used a knife to cut through the tape. Taking hold of the edges of the box, she glanced at her mom. "Ready?"

"Ready as rain." Linda's eyes were gleaming.

Cindy opened the box, peering inside. She dipped her hands inside and pulled out what looked to be an old briefcase.

Linda leaned forward. "Tell me we don't have to go on another scavenger hunt for the keys."

Cindy flicked the buttons with both thumbs and the levers sprang open. "Nope, it's unlocked." She opened the lid and sat there for a moment staring at the contents.

Linda tried unsuccessfully to see into the case. "You know, at my age, you shouldn't keep me waiting. How would you feel if I croaked and went to my deathbed never knowing what was inside the box."

Cindy peered at her mother over the case. "Being a little melodramatic, don't you think?"

"Is it working?" Linda quipped.

Cindy shook her head. *Just like dealing with a child.* Still, she'd seen her mother sad for so long, she'd never begrudge her a moment's happiness. "Mom, check this out."

Linda's eyes went wide as Cindy lifted a tattered bible from the case. When she spoke, her voice trembled. "Is that it?"

Cindy opened the cover as gently as possible, her hands shaking as she read the inscription. "*A lad who is willing to accept that he needs help will grow into a man who can achieve greatness. I give you this book so that you too may someday find your way.* And it's signed *Charles Loring Brace.*"

Linda took the book, treating it as gingerly as Cindy had. She turned it in her hands several times then opened it, rereading what Cindy had just read before flipping through the pages. She placed the bible in her lap and removed something from between the pages. "It's not uncommon to find things hidden within the pages of old bibles."

"What did you find?" Cindy's words came out on a

whisper as if they were doing something they shouldn't be doing.

After studying it for a moment, Linda handed her a well-worn photograph. Even without looking at the back, Cindy knew the photo to be of Isabella and her son Leon. "I can see why Uncle Frank was so smitten with her."

Linda had already turned her attention to a piece of paper she held in her hands. "She was a looker, that's for sure."

"What's that?"

Linda handed the paper over and placed the photo back into the bible. "The Western Union telegram notice sent out when Frank was injured."

"*Regret to inform you your brother PFC Benjamin Franklin Castiglione was on seventeen April slightly wounded in Italy. Period You will be advises as reports of condition are received. =UL10 The Adjutant General.*" Cindy sighed. "The teacher in me wants to correct it."

"Quit being a teacher and enjoy the history," Linda chided.

"You're right. Why send it to Paulie and not Mildred or Howard?"

"Franky must have listed your dad as his next of kin," Linda said. "Probably so his brother would have received the ten thousand dollars if Franky died."

"It makes sense. Dad was family and Uncle Frank promised to take care of him." Cindy handed the telegram back to Linda. "How do you know so much about this?"

"Your father was a military history buff. He must have gotten that from Franky. The better question is how do you not know about this? You're the teacher."

"It's not in the curriculum," Cindy said, handing Linda the telegram. "Anything else in there?"

"A couple newspaper clippings about the opening of the

bakery. Look, here's a photo of Frank and Cornelius."

Cindy took the paper, tracing her hand over the photo. "For all Uncle Frank went through, he seemed to have a decent life. The second half anyway. He always seemed happy. Though I always wondered why he never married. I thought once that maybe he and Uncle Cornelius…"

"I don't think so. Neither of them seemed the sort."

Cindy raised her eyes. "And what sort would that be?"

"I didn't mean that and you know it. I just mean I was around your uncle enough to know he liked women. You read his journals."

"Calm down. I was teasing you, Mom. Maybe Uncle Frank was the type that could only have one love. Mia Bella." *Or maybe what happened in Chicago messed him up for life.* She kept that bit to herself.

"Anything else in the briefcase?" Linda asked, closing the bible and handing it to her.

Cindy opened a small wooden box and gasped. She held up a small cream-colored book. "How about a signed copy of *Tom Sawyer*?"

Linda took the book and read the inscription. "*To Joe, the only man who never believed my lies. Sam.* Can you imagine how much this is worth?"

"We're not selling it."

"Pity. Something like that would have to be worth a fortune," Linda said under her breath.

Cindy placed the book back in the box and lowered the lid then picked up another, smaller box and lifted the lid. "Look, Mom, Uncle Frank's Purple Heart and dog tags." She handed her mother the case with the Purple Heart and read the dog tag out loud. "Benjamin F. Castilo. There wasn't room for his full name. 1607818 T42 O. The next line says Paulie Moore, P.O. Box 132, Sandusky, Michigan. Any idea what the number means?"

Linda looked at the tag. "I believe the first numbers are a way to identify him. The T42 would be when he had his typhoid shot. And the zero isn't a zero. It's an O. That would be his blood type."

Cindy was impressed. "Maybe you can come help me teach."

"Only if you throw out that curriculum you're always touting," Linda said, handing back the tag. "Anything else in the box?"

"No, I think that's it." She pushed that one aside and pulled the tape from the next.

"Anything good?"

"Uncle Frank's uniform. It still has his name tag. He's always been thin, but look how small he was," she said, holding up the green shirt and pants. As she held up the pants, something fell into her lap. A cold chill ran through her as she picked it up and held it for her mother to see. "Oh, Mom, look!"

Linda's eye's sparkled. "The little bi-plane Howard made for your dad."

"He kept it all these years," Cindy said, tracing her finger over the wings.

The telephone rang before Linda could respond.

"It's the facility," Cindy said, answering the call. Tears sprang to her eyes as she received the news that Frank had passed.

Seeing her face, Linda was already crying by the time Cindy switched off the phone.

"It was Reba. Uncle Frank passed about ten minutes ago. She said she was with him when he went." Cindy sobbed. "She thought he fell asleep, then she noticed he wasn't breathing."

"I can't think of a better way to go," Linda said and

handed her a tissue.

"The facility placed a call to the American Legion. Since he's a veteran, they'll be there when they pick up Uncle Frank's body. Reba said she'd call when they get there. I'd like to be with him when he leaves. Want to come?"

"I wouldn't miss it," Linda said, wiping her eyes.

***

Cindy stood next to her mother as two men from the American Legion somberly draped a flag over Frank's body, going to great lengths to make sure the flag lay even on all sides. Once finished, the older man looked at them and gave a subtle nod. Cindy gathered her mother's elbow and returned his nod. Both women followed as the men slowly wheeled Frank's body from his room, silently escorting him through the halls of the facility. Residents lined the hallway. Some held their hands to their heart, some held small American flags. Those that could stand did. More than one touched their hands to their lips and blew a silent kiss as they passed. A few snapped to attention and saluted their brother. Once out of the facility, the men loaded him in the back of the hearse and closed the door, then walked to the front, got in, and drove away without a word.

"I should have gone to see him instead of going through his stuff." Cindy sniffed. "I can't believe he's gone,"

"We lost him long ago; he was just biding his time until he told you his story," Linda said, folding her arms around Cindy. "Besides, I think I felt him with us at the end."

Cindy remembered the chill that ran through her when she discovered the little bi-plane. "You know, Mom. I think you're right."

Linda eased her grip. "Want to go to the funeral home?"

"No, they said they have the paperwork from when we met with them last week. Thank you for insisting we take care of it when we did, I can't imagine having to do it right now."

***

Cindy lay in bed thinking of the events of the day. They'd had a simple ceremony with a handful of people showing up before laying her uncle to rest. Members from the local American Legion and VFW honored him with a twenty-one-gun salute and played "Taps." She'd been presented the flag that had covered his body when he was wheeled from the facility and draped his coffin during the service. It had been folded and tucked into a triangle before being handed to her. She'd held it close to her chest as they lowered his coffin, and in her mind he was sleeping. He was right; it was easier that way.

She'd sent Bruce an e-mail, telling of her uncle's passing, asking if he'd found Franky's mother, telling of her plan to bring her remains to Michigan if the cost wasn't too high. So far, he hadn't replied.

Unable to sleep, she donned her robe, checked in on Linda to make sure her mother was sleeping before proceeding to the living room. With the exception of placing the flag near the rest of her uncle's belongings, she hadn't been in the room in the three days since his passing. Guilt had kept her away. Sinking to the floor, she opened the box and looked at the final item. A faded quilt that she knew to be the one her grandmother had made for him when they'd gone to live with Howard. She pulled it to her chest, buried her face in the fabric, and wept. The tears were not just for her uncle, though her heart ached for the man she once knew. She was afraid of being alone. Her mother was getting up in age and it was only a matter of time before she too were gone. *I just don't know how I'll get through that.*

Cindy's cell phone chimed. Lowering the quilt, she reached for it and saw an e-mail alert. It was from Bruce. Wiping her eyes, she clicked on the e-mail, waited for it to show, then read.

Cindy,

Sorry it has taken me so long to get back to you. This one has me stumped. Don't worry, I'm not giving up. As I said, I love a good challenge. Oh, and I'm sorry to be the bearer of bad news when you've had such a bad day, but I'm afraid even if I do find the woman, bringing her remains here would be next to impossible. With the grave being so old, there wouldn't be anything left to dig up.

Cindy scrolled down looking for more, but that was the end of the e-mail. A ding from her cell phone showed another e-mail from Bruce.

Me again, sorry, I fat-fingered the key and hit send before finishing. I was going to let you know another possibility would be to add a plaque to your uncle's grave. A memory plaque for his mother might be nice. I know you're having a tough time of it, but whenever I'm down, I always remember the words of my grandfather. How do you eat an elephant? One bite at a time.

Cindy sat staring at the screen. *Weird coincidence*.

She pulled to her feet, shook out the quilt, folded it, and draped it over the couch. She stepped back and kicked something hard against her big toe. Reaching to pick it up, she found it to be a small tin elephant. Turning it over, she saw writing underneath. She ran to the kitchen and pulled a magnifying glass from the drawer and held them both to the light. In the tiniest of script, she read, *How do you eat an elephant?*

"Okay, okay. I get the message," she said, casting a glance to the sky.

A Brief Note from the Author

I got the idea of having Franky go and live with the Judge after reading the story of John Green Brady. After running away from home, professing himself an orphan, and being sent out on an orphan train, John found himself in the care of Judge John Green. Judge Green was quoted as saying, "I decided to take John Brady home with me because I considered him the homeliest, toughest, most unpromising boy in the whole lot. I had the curious desire to see what could be made of such a specimen of humanity." Unlike Franky, Brady remained with Judge, was well educated, and served as Governor of the District of Alaska from 1897 to 1906.

Additionally, a note about the historical content in regard to the address used for the advert and for Franky's dog tags. I am aware that neither PO boxes nor zip codes would have been in use during the time the story takes place. I took creative liberty of placing my own author address within the book as an Easter egg of sorts, to see if I will actually get any mail delivered to that address.

Continue the journey with Slim's story, coming in 2021

A special thanks to:

My editor, Beth, for allowing me to keep my voice.

My cover artist and media design guru, Laura Prevost, thanks for keeping me current.

My proofreader, Latisha Rich, for that extra set of eyes.

My daughter- Brandy for helping with all the extras.

To my amazing team of beta readers, thank you for helping take a final look.

To my husband, thank you for your endless hours of researching, your help with all things genealogy, and for allowing me to bounce story ideas off of you. Your help with these and countless other things that help keep me in the writing chair is priceless.

Please find it in your heart to take a moment and go to Amazon to leave a review. Reviews are also welcomed at Barnes & Noble, Bookbub, and Goodreads as well. If you purchased the book at a signing or from my website, please begin your review by including that information. If not, Amazon may not allow the review.

Most importantly, if you enjoy this series, please tell EVERYONE and share in the reading groups! As an indie author, word of mouth is the best publicity I can get.
Thank you for taking this journey with me.

Sherry A. Burton

Please remember to follow me on social media and sign up for my newsletter on my website to be kept up to date with all new releases.

For more information on the author and her works, please see *www.SherryABurton.com*
Follow Sherry on social media:
https://www.facebook.com/SherryABurtonauthor/
https://www.amazon.com/Sherry-A.-Burton/e/B005PM6QFG?ref=dbs_m_mng_rwt_auth
https://www.bookbub.com/profile/sherry-a-burton

About the Author

Born in Kentucky, Sherry married a Navy man at the age of eighteen. She and her now-retired Navy husband have three children and nine grandchildren.

After moving around the country and living in nine different states, Sherry and her husband now live in Michigan's thumb, with their three rescue cats and a standard poodle named Murdoc.

Sherry writes full time and is currently hard at work on the next novel in her Orphan Train Saga, an eighteen-book historical fiction series that revolves around the orphan trains.

When Sherry is not writing, she enjoys traveling to lectures and signing events, where she shares her books and speaks about the history of the Orphan Trains.

CPSIA information can be obtained
at www.ICGtesting.com
Printed in the USA
FSHW020810281020
75259FS